The Tontine Trap

Paul Purnell

Grosvenor House
Publishing Limited

This book is published by
Grosvenor House Publishing Ltd
Link House
140 The Broadway, Tolworth, Surrey, KT6 7HT.
www.grosvenorhousepublishing.co.uk

A CIP record for this book
is available from the British Library

ISBN 978-1-78623-242-7

Also by the same author

“The Hireling”

“Scaramouche”

“The Storm”

“Dangerous Cargo”

And

“The Kazak Contract”
(First of the James Ballantyne Series.)

PROLOGUE

'Get me his file!' Melford sent the filing clerk scuttling across the office to the bank of computers in search of Ballantyne's records. The whole office could read his mood from the scowl on his face and the bark in his voice. He was the Head of Agent Control at the FCO, and had lost track of one of his 'disposable agents', James Ballantyne.

When the pages appeared on his screen, he sat scratching his chin while he read the CV and the HR Report.

REVIEW REPORT CV

GOV.UK

Foreign & Commonwealth Office (https://www.gov.uk/government/organisations/foreign-commonwealth-office)

REVIEW: 2306/17/BALLANTYNEJ

INTERNAL COPY
NON DISTRIBUTION

JAMES BALLANTYNE (d.o.b. 12/04/1986) has been employed in F.O. section 4 since June 2016.

Formerly Captain J Ballantyne. Royal Marines – resigned commission May 2016.

Service record indicates deployment in Iraq (2008) and Afghanistan (2013)

General Court Martial April 2016-charged manslaughter-acquitted- insubordination charges left on file.

Physical assessment. Med. Examination 12/06/16. A1

Aptitude Assessment.15/06/16. B 2. (see attached note)

Languages. Russian(fluent.) Farsi (fluent.) French (adequate.) Arabic (Saudi) (adequate.)

Weapon Training. A1.

Assignment. Kazakahstan Desk (Section 4) junior officer (grade 3)

Supervising Officer: Cavendale .E.

HR REPORT

BALLANTYNE J. (d.o.b.. 12/4/1988)

APTITUDE ASSESSMENT 12/06/16.

"This officer has spent 5 years in active service including Iraq and Afghanistan. His service record shows consistent high levels of initiative and engagement in field operations. His experience in covert small scale operations is exceptional. However, incidents of insubordination are recorded. The most serious (in 2011) leading to a G.C.M. at Falluja arising from an unauthorized killing of three insurgents. He was acquitted of manslaughter. Charges of insubordination were left on the file not to be proceeded with.

FCO Assessment of B2 (unsuitable) was made but over ruled in Order 16-2077 by Section Leader Sir Edmund Cavendale on 23/06/16.

23 June 2016

"I have personally interviewed Ballantyne and examined his service record. He comes to us with robust approval from his late Commanding Officer and I find him wholly appropriate for the Kazakhstan Desk. I have no doubt the B2 assessment was wrong.

I have no objection in HR asking for PP reports if necessary."

E.C.

'Where is he now?'

'We don't know, Sir. The last time we heard from him was in southern Kazakhstan. But there has been an enquiry from Omsk consulate about a man using the name of Ballantyne.'

'What the hell would he be doing there? He was sent to Astana! Get me Sir Edmund on the phone.'

The conversation between Melford and the head of the Kazakhstan desk was 'lively', and it emerged that the last contact was some three weeks before. Most of the exchange between the two controllers was who was to blame for failing to keep contact with an agent. They had no way of knowing that Ballantyne had crossed over into Russia, and were even less aware of the links with Ocksana Petrova, his Russian girlfriend.

CHAPTER 1

The grey concrete walls were depressingly familiar. James smelt the mixture of disinfectant and urine common to most hard prisons. What was new was the fact that he had been banged up in a Russian one. He had crossed the border from Kazakhstan illegally, but had not expected to be locked up. As a minor diplomat of the British Foreign and Commonwealth Office, he believed the local consul had been informed. It should have been sorted out when stopped by the border police.

'I am entitled to contact my embassy,' he said, 'and they will approve my release.' He spoke in Russian.

The prison sergeant shrugged. 'Just your name.'

'My name is James Ballantyne and my ID shows my credentials.'

'Credentials?' His eyebrows lifted in disbelief. 'You talk of credentials? You have no documents.'

James, for once, lost his cool. 'I brought my ID to the police station when I got arrested. You must have it with my possessions!'

'No ID. Move along.'

A squat, bullet-headed officer pushed him on with a shove and he found himself in a large, bare room with bars on the windows where a collection of men squatted or stood against the walls. Some glanced up as he came in; others simply ignored him, slouched in a world of their own.

The day when he and Ocksana arrived in Omsk, they were separated, but they discussed how they would deal with the situation. She had important connections in the Russian Air Force and in the Foreign Service.

'Don't fret, my darling, things will work out as soon as I am free of this mess!' She meant the trouble involving her sudden departure from the Kazakhstan Service. 'We will alert the British Embassy and get you away from here.'

His confidence was never as strong as hers. After all, he was the one who crossed the border illegally and was wanted in Kazakhstan. Still, he had diplomatic status and had committed no crime in the Russian Federation. A few days in prison would do no harm. Now, with his essential ID missing, he realised that it was not so simple. A general knowledge of prison procedure in Eastern Europe told him it would be more than a few days before he was with Ocksana again.

Several hours passed before the clanking arrival of a food wagon. A rush for the door ended up with a few casualties on the floor. Ballantyne stayed where he was, aware of the hidden danger of struggling with the crowd. He sat against the wall and waited. No food was better than a shiv in the guts.

A man in rags came and sat beside him. He was lean and tall, so when he crouched down against the wall his bony knees peaked in front of him. He looked sideways at Ballantyne.

'So, you don't like the food?' he said.' Better in the Palace Hotel, I suppose?'

'Where's that?' James did not want to start a contest with this sad figure.

'Anywhere!' said the thin man. 'I see you are a foreigner. Maybe you need help?'

'What makes you say that? Do I look needy?'

James used the Russian word 'mannomyu' to express his indignation. He knew how important it was to speak confidently in such circumstances. The tall man raised his hands and said, 'Peace! Brother, I am a man of peace! Just to find out if you need some stuff!'

Every prison had its 'servicer' – a man who could provide supplies of contraband, if you could pay for it. If you had no cash, then you could still get help, but you paid one way or the other. Ballantyne shook his head and turned away.

'Okay, milord.' The servicer shrugged and pulled a cigarette out of a packet tucked into his sleeve, 'You want one?'

'No, if I need one I'll contact you.'

Instinct told him that it was dangerous to rebuff this man outright. He must have important connections within the prison. The man unfolded himself from the wall and drifted away to talk with others. Ballantyne watched to see who his associates were. One was a small, wiry figure wearing a denim jacket and grey tracksuit pants. His face looked lopsided; a scar ran down his cheek and one eye had been displaced, giving a grotesque contortion to his expression. He stared at Ballantyne and spoke to the tall man. The man returned and stood over James.

'Come milord, Vadik needs to speak with you.'

Ballantyne nodded at the ugly little man. He crossed the room casually and looked down into the one good eye of the short man.

'Yes?'

The man came close to Ballantyne and stared up at him. His mouth gaped and showed his teeth like a worried dog.

'You, an American spy? You need friends in Russia.' It sounded matter-of-fact but the subtext was protection.

'Forget it, Tovarich, I shall be out of here within a few days.'

It was a mistake.

Two other men, bulky, hard-faced men, moved alongside him. They stood close and looked at him with stony expressions.

'You need help every day of your life here, friend,' said the weaselly little man, 'otherwise accidents happen.'

Ballantyne shrugged and said, 'What's the deal?'

'Just come to me when you want a phone or some sniff, then you owe me, ponimayu (understand)?'

He had heard it in other prisons. In Afghanistan and in Iraq, where he had undergone detention. He nodded. He needed a phone to speak to Ocksana and ensure some rapid action by the British Embassy.

'I need a phone now!'

The little man's face cracked into a distorted smile, showing his fangs.

'Meet me at dinner time.'

He nodded to the two minders and they moved away.

Time past slowly, partly because Ballantyne half expected a visit from the embassy, or at least the consul, and partly because he was keen to discover how Ocksana got on with her high-ranking connections. It gnawed at him that perhaps Kazak Security had managed to influence the Russians against her. He chivvied himself for the thought, since he marvelled at her ingenuity and resources. She was a special person.

The dinner hour arrived. Hunger pushed him into the scramble for food and he fought as keenly as the next man for his plate of stew and lump of bread. He knew that he was protected against attack. He squatted down against the wall and waited, scooping up every last drop and crumb.

The man Vadik came to sit beside him, showing his left profile with the scar and drooping eye. He did not turn to face him but spoke out of the side of his mouth.

'You pay now or want credit?'

'How can I pay now? Look at me!'

'You have a watch.'

James surrendered his few items, including his watch, when he was arrested.

'Sure, but it's in the property bag.'

'What type?'

'Breitling Voyager.'

Vadik grunted, his hand to his mouth as if pondering the deal.

'Okay,' he said at last, 'I look at it and we do deal.'

'How come? It's in the police store?'

Vadik said nothing but raised his good eyebrow.

James cursed himself for keeping his favourite watch when he could have got by with a digital junk one, but it was too late now. He needed a phone.

'I see you tomorrow.'

There were no bunks in the holding room but a gate was opened to allow the men to access to a corridor of open cells. Most of the prisoners filed into cells, but Ballantyne felt safer in the big room. He bedded down in a corner and pretended to sleep. There was little movement among the men who stayed in the big room, and Ballantyne was not approached. Later, he saw Vadik creep across the space and tap at the iron gate. A policeman came close and talked to him in a whisper, then he passed something across and went away.

In the early morning, the tall man in rags beckoned to him from the corridor leading to the cells. He had James's watch in his hand.

'Okay, we can do a deal. I get the phone for you.'

Ballantyne gripped the hand holding the watch, using sufficient force to lock it inside the man's fist.

'Good! But I hold the watch till I see the phone works.'

The man grunted with pain and nodded. He released his hold and James removed it from his grasp. Within a minute he was back. In his hand, a black shiny object, no bigger than a disposable lighter.

'Here,' he said, 'try it!'

James could not believe that this little black object could work, but he dialled Ocksana's number using the tiny keyboard. It was a finicky operation but it worked.

The number rang but there was no answer. He rang off immediately; maybe her phone was tapped and the longer he rang, the greater the possibility of a trace being made.

'See?' The gaunt man grinned. 'Chinese tech is good, no?'

There were traces of cellophane still wrapped around the stem and it dawned on James how the object had been brought in; a normal body search would not reveal it, only a cavity search . He spat on it and wiped it on his sleeve.

'Okay, I want more than this for my watch. What else can you do? I want a single cell.'

The man frowned and turned away, then walked through to the open cell area. In a minute Vadik appeared and limped across the room, his face contorted, fist clenched.

'You think you can bargain with Vadik?

Ballantyne held up his hands as if to push him away.

'Listen, you know my watch is valuable and all I need is a space to use the phone. I can't do it here, can I?'

The little man was taken by surprise by his disarming reply. Maybe he expected a physical face-off, but instead had to respond to a sensible suggestion.

He paused for a moment then threw his head back and grinned.

'You are one wily bastard, English! Alright, if you are here for short time we find you some space.' Then he stabbed his finger at James. 'But no more crazy ideas, the watch is mine!'

One of the henchmen went ahead and cleared out a cell, pulling two of the unfortunate inmates into the corridor. Ballantyne handed over the watch and stepped in and closed the heavy door; it had no lock.

This time she answered. 'My darling! Are you all right? Listen, I have the consul set up and he will come today, sometime, with a discharge paper, so hang on! Is there a payphone in the prison?'

James grinned. 'Better than that, we have our own supplies. I'll explain when I see you. Are you all right? No problems?' He rang off promptly and stowed the phone away in his pocket.

Outside in the hall a guard peered through the gate. He beckoned to Ballantyne. 'Come out England, a visitor for you.'

In a bare room in the police station, a man in a sheepskin coat sat at a table. He removed a fur cap and ran a hand through his hair.

'Good morning. I am Sergei Bassilev, the British consul in Omsk. You need my help.'

'I expected embassy staff. I am a diplomat, even if low-ranking!'

James was conscious of his remark but could not resist the comment; after all, he was senior rank.

Bassilev shrugged his broad shoulders. His face reminded James of a turnip ready for the pot; his skin was pasty but coarse and his hair stood up like a vegetable stalk.

'I do what I'm told, *Mister* Ballantyne, and the embassy contacted my office to come here.'

'Of course, I'm sorry!' James shook his head and held out his hand. 'How do we get me out of here?'

'Well, I need to take your photo and send it to the embassy for verification. It should not take more than a few days.'

'I was told you would have a release paper with you.'

'I'm afraid you were misinformed. The British Consulate has agreed a specific protocol for alleged criminals.'

James could feel his temperature rising. 'Look! I'm not a criminal, but I do need my credentials verified to get out of here. Contact the embassy to send someone with my verification.'

Bassilev stared at him impassively. He had heard similar complaints before.

'Okay, I take your photo and speak to the embassy. You realise the embassy is in Moscow; there is no office in Omsk?'

At once, James could envisage the grindingly slow procedure this limp official would set in motion. He needed a different method of getting clear of this morass.

'Okay. Take the photo and please expedite your instructions.'

The man took two photos and Ballantyne noted he took a typical set of mugshots – full face and profile. It dawned on him that this was a huge mistake; perhaps within minutes, his mugshot would be broadcast on websites throughout Russia and beyond.

He grabbed the camera and wrenched it out of Bassilev's hands. The man struggled with him, but he punched him away.

'What you do?'

Ballantyne went through the menu of the camera, deleting the photos.

'Okay, you can go now!'

Bassilev's face took on a purple tinge and he began to curse, but James pushed him out of the door and turned away in case he tried to take another photo before he left. The last he heard was the noise of uplifted voices in the outer office, as he found refuge of a sort in the detention room.

CHAPTER 2

'But I spoke directly to the embassy in Moscow!' Ocksana's voice sounded strained in the tiny phone that James held to his ear. 'It was all arranged for the consul to clear it up.'

'Well, they must have thought again, or I am *persona non grata* at the moment.'

'What do you mean?'

'They are making a point at my expense for what happened in Astana. After the trouble with the Kazaks, they are punishing me for going off-limits!'

'Let me think.' Her practical mind began to whirl. It was one of the things James loved about her, her resourcefulness and her fighting spirit.

'Look, I am keeping out of sight at the Severnyj Air Force base outside Omsk. I'll get together with old friends and we'll figure out a way to get you out. Just wait it out, my love.' She switched off.

Ballantyne joined the queue to get his share of bread and tea, staying within sight of the gate which led back into the police station. Not much happened for the next two hours; no one paid special attention to him, even Vadik kept a distance from him as if sensing he was already outside his domain.

The sound of raised voices caught James's attention. Through the limited view of the iron gate he could see a group of blue uniforms crowding round the station officer. They were arguing and pushing the duty officer towards the gate.

'Don't tell me what I can or can't do!' A large, bull-faced Air Force officer was shouting. 'I tell you I have ministerial authority to detain this man.'

By the time he reached the gate, the police officer was fumbling for his keys, only to have them snatched from his hands by one of the Air Force officers.

'You,' said the big man. 'You Ballantyne, you go with us.'

James got the message, and allowed himself to be pulled out of the detention block as a reluctant prisoner. They rushed him outside into a large Zim truck and were away in a minute. Inside, as he expected, was the figure of the one woman in the whole world who he could rely on. She hugged him and kissed him in front of the men. They raised a scornful cheer and James felt the colour rising in his cheeks. She looked radiant with her dark hair and ivory skin glowing in the shade of the lorry cover.

'To hell with the English embassy,' she said, and the group cheered enthusiastically. From the cab of the lorry, the broad face of the senior officer grinned through.

'You see, Tovarich – how bullshit baffles brains?'

James had to agree; the rules were the same in every country.

They drove directly to the airbase and went into the officers' quarters, in a block nearest to the runways. Out on the airfield, two fighters taxied out to the runway. SU30's. Ballantyne tried to avoid attention as he examined their equipment, to identify if they were the latest designs. He noted their heat-seeking missiles and non-standard 50mm canons, and memorised it for future reference.

The big, bull-faced man was Grigor Vasilich, the station commander. He had put on his full parade uniform with medals and braid for the bluff at the police station. He beamed at James.

'You see how we love our little songbird Ocksana? She should never have left us for those Kazak peasants!'

He gave her a hug that crushed her shoulders and she winced and rolled her eyes.

'You never let me fly the MIGs,' she said, 'so I flew away!'

Shots of vodka did the rounds once or twice. No one seemed to care about the consequences of their 'kidnap'.

James managed to catch her amid the raucous celebrations and arrange a quiet spot to talk.

'Wait till after the midday meal and we can talk at last. I'll give you a sign when we can get away.'

She kissed him lightly on the lips and drifted back into the noisy crowd. He spent the next ten minutes chatting to a young officer on secondment from Chechenya attending a fighter course. His information was interesting about the state of relationships between Federal Russia and its satellites.

Then the meal began. Ballantyne had some experience of meals with various military units, but this was beyond anything he had ever tried. A long table covered in a white cloth at the side of the dining room was crammed with food. In the centre of the room sat several round tables laid with immaculate care. The whole crowd of guests and officers moved simultaneously to attack. No one had precedence; the rush for seats nearest to the food was alarming. The noise of the assembly made it almost impossible to hear conversation, so James joined in the bunfight and his thoughts went back to the prison where the morning scrabble for food was not very different from the wave of diners in this group, apart from the quality of the food.

The meal continued into the mid-afternoon. It seemed endless. Course followed course, each interspersed with a speech and a toast. Ocksana squeezed her way between two jolly, roaring young men and managed to pull James out of the room. The corridor seemed like a silent cave after the noise inside.

'Poor darling! Is this your first meal with our Russian military? I should have warned you.' Her eyes sparkled with amusement and she put her hand in his with a tender touch.

He looked into her eyes and felt an immense rush of pure affection for this wonderful woman. Words were worthless coins in this currency, only the instincts of the heart mattered. They stood together for a while, leaning forward without touching, eye to eye.

'You'll never leave me, will you?'

His question was direct, as if his life depended on her answer.

Tears formed in the corners of her eyes and she kissed him, holding his head with her hand gently.

By four o'clock the lunch was almost over, and individuals settled in a variety of chairs and alcoves. They slipped away to a quiet room in the barracks and spoke about the future.

'What will you do?' he asked.

She shrugged and said, 'The first thing is to straighten out my situation with the Kazaks.'

'How?'

She smiled and her eyes sparkled. 'My godfather will help me out, I think!'

James thought of godfathers who turned up at a christening, then maybe sent a ten-pound note once in a while.

'Do you know who my godfather is?' Her grin told him he was in for a surprise.

'Papa Grigor, my lovely general! How do you imagine we got you out of prison?'

James felt a fool; here he was, free, not from his diplomatic status but because this wonderful girl could call on her connections to help him out.

'But what can he do about the Kazaks?'

'Listen, I will go to Moscow and he will find me a job in the ministry. That will shut the Kazaks up; they will not dare to take on the government!'

She looked into his eyes and read the fear they expressed.

'Darling, we have to be apart for some little time, don't we? You must go back to London to explain yourself so we have to be separated for a while.'

James liked the expression 'go back to explain himself' – if only she knew the storm he faced in Whitehall when he got back! Still, she was right; they would have to sort themselves out if they were to be together.

He looked at her quizzically. 'Does everything in Russia depend on who you know?' He grinned and shook her before folding her in his arms.

Later that night they spent what they knew would be the last one together for some time. They slept deeply after their passionate love and woke happily in each other's arms.

'Think of me, my love,' she breathed, as they lay together in the dawn light.

'Always,' he whispered, and yet he could not stop his mind from flying away to London and the prospect of his meeting with Sir Edward Cavendale, his desk chief.

While they had breakfast in the officers' quarters, a young officer approached. He was dressed in a flight uniform and saluted.

'General Vasilich asks you to attend a flight meeting in half an hour.'

They took it as a command.

'Of course.'

'Please bring your effects with you.'

Ocksana furrowed her brows. 'Effects?'

'General says you should be ready to fly!'

James's effects amounted to a pair of trousers and an aircraft shirt he had begged from a friendly officer. Ocksana grabbed her overnight bag and they went to the briefing room.

It was a large, bare room with a wall screen for projecting maps. In front of a desk were two rows of folding chairs and eight crew were already sitting there. Vasilich bustled in and James noted the puffy, purple shade of his face as he got to the podium.

Not a happy general this morning, James reflected, and sat up to hear the plan.

'Gentlemen,' he nodded to Ocksana by way of apology, 'we have to move quickly. I do not intend to have the whole Omsk police force on my back as a result of our little enterprise yesterday. We all know it was necessary and I intend to resolve the situation in this way. A troop transport flight is scheduled for Moscow today, and you crew members will carry two extra passengers with you. As far as you are concerned, they are security personnel. Flight crew to the briefing room, ready for take-off in one hour. Dismissed.'

When the men had filed out, Ocksana gave him a hug and told him how much he meant to her. He patted her arm and looked at Ballantyne.

'This is my little bright star; you must look after her, English.' His eyes were moist and James wondered if he would start to cry, but instead he punched him on the shoulder and pointed his stubby finger at him.

'More like, she will look after me,' James said and he put his arm around her.

'Come on,' she said. 'We need to clear out of here before the shit hits the fan!'

Ballantyne made a mental note to try to unlearn her of the Americanisms she had picked up.

Out on the runway, the dark green Antonov warmed up. Forty minutes later, they were high on their way to Moscow. Ballantyne looked at his woman, happily chatting away with the navigator, and began to work out what he could do to avoid the avalanche of trouble waiting for him in London.

CHAPTER 3

A clear blue sky, a sunset glowing over the snow-tipped mountains – the descent was perfect. James and Ocksana stepped down to a smiling welcome from the duty officer at the Kubinka airbase, outside Moscow.

'Good evening.' The officer saluted and offered his hand to Ocksana. He turned to James, and nodded. 'General Vasilovic has briefed us concerning you, Mister Ballantyne. I understand there is some urgency about your return to London?'

James nodded. 'I need to contact the British Embassy at once and get a travel warrant to fly to London.'

He did not think it would help matters to explain further; the embassy would need to know, but no one else.

The base was very similar to Omsk but much bigger. There was little chance of observing the military planes since it was getting dark and the runways were clear. Ballantyne got on to the embassy right away. A recorded voice took him through the usual tedious set instructions, with the 'Press one for X' routine, and he waited till that was over. Then a woman's voice came on the line. She sounded slightly familiar.

'This is the emergency line for the British Embassy. What is the subject...'

At that point, it dawned on James.

'Carol? Is that you Carol? It's me James, James Ballantyne!'

There was a pause at the other end of the line. 'James? Good God! We've been looking for you everywhere! Where are you?'

Carol Stevens had shared a desk with him some months before he joined the Kazak Desk.

Within a minute, he explained his need to get back to London on the first available flight.

'Too right!' she said. 'The Kazaks are steaming and accusing us of spying in Astana. What have you been doing?'

'No time to explain. Can you get me a travel warrant, pronto?'

'Hold on a second.' He could tell she was reading something. 'There's a flight to London leaving at eleven-thirty tonight. I'll get a courier to meet you at the gate. Don't go to the check in – there may be a check there.'

'Yes, but I need my ID as well.'

'What?' She sighed. 'Okay, but get out of my hair, will you?' She managed to mix exasperation and amusement in the same breath.

Ocksana caught the gist of the conversation and slipped her arm round him.

'So soon? My love?'

He nodded, reminding her of their talk about separation.

'Yes, but so soon!'

They sat together for a while; there was nothing to be said. They both knew it was inevitable. Then she sighed and kissed him, pulling him to his feet.

'Come on. Let's get to the airport and get you started.'

A taxi drove them to Moscow Main Station and they took the shuttle bus to Domededovo, avoiding the Metro Train Express service, which was new.

'Best to be safe, the express will be monitored,' she said.

They left each other in the main gallery and checked their phones. He held her close and whispered his love to her, then they went their own ways, not looking back.

As he approached the embarkation gate, a young man, evidently English, wearing a sports jacket and corduroy trousers, stepped up to meet him. Ballantyne silently cursed when he set eyes on him; the fresh-faced youth stood out like a neon sign, advertising British Embassy. Did they want him to be detained?

'I've got your travel docs!' he said. His voice brayed across the hall. Ballantyne grabbed the envelope and muttered an abrupt thank you, rushing to the security area as fast as possible to get away from him.

'Ungrateful sod!' said the courier, and made his way back to the exit.

The flight took off on time, and four hours later he was looking out of Terminal Three at Heathrow, in the mist and the never-ending bustle of the airport. He booked in to the Hilton to get some shut-eye, knowing that the morning would bring a summons from the FCO. He needed all his rest to be fit for what was to come.

CHAPTER 4

Breakfast at the Heathrow Hilton was no gourmet meal. A dish of congealed scrambled eggs and a pile of soggy toast was on offer and Ballantyne turned it down. The coffee stewed quietly on the hot plate, and he decided a cup of tea was sensible; he brewed it himself. The double-glazed windows showed the airport like a panoramic screen, with traffic moving silently along the adjacent motorway and planes taking off in an unnatural silence. It was not the ideal homecoming.

The mobile lay next to his cup like a jack-in-the-box waiting to spring to life. The chief of the Kazakhstan desk was going to strip him of his diplomatic status for the incidents in Astana and elsewhere.

But hell! They can't hang me! At times like these, a bit of gallows humour is invaluable. He looked down at the miserable machine and it buzzed as if it read his mind.

'Good morning, James,' a breezy voice, 'Sir Edward is expecting you at twelve. Where are you staying?' The voice was recognizable but James could not place it; a young man's voice, with a clipped accent.

'I'm at the Heathrow Hilton.'

There was a slight pause. 'Oh! I see...' Plainly the Hilton was not on the Foreign Office's list of acceptable hotels. 'Well, see you at eleven forty-five.'

Ballantyne went into the foyer and found a small kiosk selling 'English-Made Shirts' at ridiculous prices. He bought one and a tie; he could not appear in front of Sir Edward without a tie. Doing his best, he smoothed his hair, shaved carefully and caught the shuttle bus into town. Despite the heavy traffic, it was a pleasant contrast to be back in the tidy world of London, with its pavements and trees. Ocksana would like it too, he reflected, and his thoughts flew back to Moscow, wondering how she was getting on.

The Foreign and Colonial Office forms the corner of Parliament Square. The grand stone building imposes itself on the visitor, demanding respect. As James ran up the front steps, he recalled days long past when he faced a beating for some schoolboy crime. Ruefully, the comparison seemed appropriate. The uniformed doorman narrowed his eyes.

'Yes Sir?'

Ballantyne held out his ID card and stared at the man.

'Room Eight, Block B.' The abrupt response added more than a jot of hostility to his return and he felt his temperature rising.

For God's sake, get a grip! You haven't seen Sir Edward yet!

He knew his way to Block B, and passed through the ornate hallway to a corridor in the building behind. The marble was replaced with brick as soon as he passed from the first building to the next. Long passageways painted in faded magnolia stretched in each direction. A comparison with the Russian detention building rose in his mind – the same seedy, worn look – but his spirits rose a little. At least he was among his own at last. Room Eight had a door which looked even more distressed than the others. Its paint was chipped and an area around the door handle was grey with use. He entered without knocking.

'Good morning, Mister Ballantyne.' The woman at the desk stood up and came round to meet him. She was a thin figure dressed in a brown cardigan and a grey skirt. Her eyes behind her spectacles regarded him with curiosity, as if she wanted to imprint on her mind the picture of his face, before and after Sir Edward had dealt with him. She smiled faintly and James's heart felt like lead. She showed him into the office.

Sir Edmund Cavendale had spent twenty years in the army before taking up his post at the Kazakhstan desk. He had overruled a negative assessment on Ballantyne, and personal endorsed James's application to join the Service. He would have to justify it now.

He had become accustomed to military life and it never occurred to him to change his ways. He did not rise to greet James. Instead, he stared at him silently. James stared back, determined not to fall for such an old trick.

At last he spoke. 'What the hell happened?'

'I got caught up in a trap with an American agent, but I did get the treaty initialled.'

'Fucked up, you mean! I've had the Kazak Embassy on my back and what's worse, the bloody Permanent Secretary, moaning about 'commercial disaster'.'

Despite the complaint, Ballantyne sensed there was an undertone of sympathy below the surface. Cavendale's brows were drawn together but the corners of his eyes betrayed a slight twinkle, as if he was playing a part.

James decided to explain a little further. His first plan had been to keep to the minimum, on the basis 'Never complain: Never explain', but he followed his instincts and outlined the escape through Kirghizstan, leaving out his links with Ocksana.

Cavendale leaned back in his chair, fingers entwined, and listened closely. When it was finished, he stood up and walked to the window. Outside, Horse Guards Parade was lit up by a sudden shaft of sunlight. The harsh sound of a Guards sergeant drilling a platoon echoed off the buildings.

'D'you see that?' He turned and motioned Ballantyne to the window, 'That's what soldiers do! They obey orders!'

Ballantyne looked down on the parade ground and the file of scarlet uniforms marching across the smooth gravel.

'Yes, Sir, but marines have to use their heads as well!'

'And you used your head, did you? Lying to the Kazak Ministry and abusing our diplomatic immunity?'

Keep shtum! a little voice inside him warned James.

'Nevertheless. I want to discuss something with you, to see if we can get out of this mess.'

Sir Edmund moved back to his desk and motioned James to the chair in front.

'Do you know what a tontine is?'

James shook his head. 'Isn't it some horse-racing betting ring?'

'Not far off. It is a special investment device: a group of investors put a fixed amount into a fund, and the fund is shared out after a set period. If it makes money, they all win; if it loses, they share the losses, obviously.' He leaned forward. 'But here is the nub of the scheme. Every time a member dies, the shares of the remainder increase. If all but one fall away, then that man gets the lot.'

Ballantyne frowned. 'What sort of figures are we talking about?'

Cavendale smiled thinly. 'A billion each!'

'How many investors?'

'Eight that we know of, maybe more. This one started in the States, but has taken a nasty turn.'

'What do you mean? It doesn't seem anything to do with us.'

'When I tell you that two of the eight have already died mysteriously, maybe you can see that this directly affects us here.'

James frowned, still mystified.

'Don't you see? Two Eastern European oligarchs have died in the UK, and our standing in the Eastern Europe Block is at risk. They believe we are supporting American investors by condoning the elimination of their members.'

'Where do we come in?' Ballantyne began to feel uneasy. Was he being set up for a hospital pass?

'We can restore our position commercially by helping them discover who is behind these killings.'

'Who says they were killed? Maybe they died and it's a coincidence?'

Cavendale reached over, pulled out a file and threw it across the desk. It contained two reports. The first was a forensic report on the death of Casimir Kubalov, Russian COE of Rastov Chemicals. He had died as a result of a fall from a fourth-floor window onto railings in the street below.

The second report listed the cause of death of Grigor Yassivich, a Rumanian oligarch. Cause of death was by fatal injection of an excessive dose of cocaine.

'The point is, they died in our country, and they were both members of the Urals Tontine.'

'It could still be coincidence.' James could feel the faint stirring of interest, and was determined to fight it. After all, he deserved a break from slumming it around the Russian Federation.

Cavendale pressed his lips together and leant forward. 'Of course, this investigation would be arranged on a wholly different basis. This is not a FCO job; the operation is a joint one with the USA, and we can arrange special agent remuneration for the contract.'

Ballantyne knew of the big difference in pay between the US operators and his own meagre salary, which reminded him of the fact that he had received no pay for the last three months. He sensed this was the moment to speak up. It was obvious the FCO needed someone to take on this sticky job, and he would not let them buy him off cheaply.

'I am owed three months as it is, Sir.'

Sod them, they owe me!

Cavendale raised his eyebrows. 'Do you think your performance so far deserves commendation or special status?'

'I did the job and helped a US agent, so would say yes, Sir.'

There was a pause, then James saw the slightest twitch of the moustache and he knew he'd won the point.

'Well, all considered, I can endorse your claim, but,' here the older man pulled rank, 'we expect full reports and discipline in the future!'

'Of course.' Ballantyne looked him straight in the eye. They both sensed it was a charade.

'Well, go and see Melford in Operations, and keep me posted.'

Ballantyne felt instinctively like saluting, but caught himself in time and turned to leave the room.

'Is that Russian girl still with you?' James paused, struck by the fact that FCO knew about Ocksana.

He faced about, and saw Cavendale was grinning at him. 'You see, James, we aren't so dim as you believe. We've checked her out and she seems straight!'

Not sure whether to be angry or glad, Ballantyne nodded and made his way out.

It was only afterwards, as he walked down the corridor, that he thought what he should have said – but it was too late.

As he walked away, he tried to sift through the various feelings running through his mind. The first was relief; he had escaped dismissal for the obvious breach of diplomatic conduct. Hard upon that came the urge to get involved in this mysterious new enquiry; it suited his instincts, since it would get him away from the routine diplomatic drudgery. Yet he was concerned about Ocksana, and how he could combine a role in this covert enquiry with his desire to be with her. What he was reluctant to admit was the excitement he felt at going undercover and the appeal of danger. This conflict engaged him as he searched for the Operations Bureau among the indistinguishable corridors of Whitehall.

He persuaded himself he could make up his mind after he had seen what Operations could offer him. In his heart, he knew this was just a deception he had set up to postpone a decision.

Operations was a large room, with an open-plan layout of several desks and assorted workstations, each location set up with computers and printers, plus one or two machines he did not recognise. Nobody paid him any attention.

Adrian Melford worked from an office at the end of the big room. One of the staff pointed James in that direction, and he could make out the figure of a man tapping furiously at a computer keyboard.

'Sit down; get a mug and help yourself.' The little man nodded towards a kettle on a filing cabinet. James made a cup of tea after examining what was on offer. Nescafe and Bournvita featured predominantly, but he found a few teabags among the scattered packets. He sipped the tea and examined the figure still working the keyboard.

Melford was about fifty years old, with a large head and thick, horn-rimmed glasses. His hands drew Ballantyne's attention; they were encased in thin black gloves with the fingertips cut off, so that the ends of his fingers poked out like pink stubs as he kept up the staccato on the keys. Suddenly, he stopped typing and turned to look at James. His eyes, magnified by the strong lenses, looked bigger than normal and the brown pupils almost filled the frames.

'Cavendale is a bit of a shit, isn't he?' The question was tossed Ballantyne's way as if they were old friends chatting together. James sensed an ambush.

'Well,' he said, 'he did me a favour some time ago, so he's not so bad.'

'A favour?' The mouth twisted into a smile. 'There's always a first, I suppose!'

Ballantyne could think of nothing to say in response, so he kept quiet.

Eventually, Melford stopped typing and got up.

'Look, we can't talk here. Let's find a quiet spot to have a chat.'

James wondered what 'the chat' would reveal.

CHAPTER 5

Summer in Moscow can be hot. Ocksana walked to work along the square, feeling the warm wind from the Urals breathing heat into the dry air. She wore a summer dress, and knew that by noon, her office in the Ministry building would be stifling. She longed for the air conditioning she'd enjoyed in New York. Promises of promotion inside the FSB, arising from her sponsor General Vasilovic, had not come true, and she found herself in a section dealing with Chechen suspects under supervision. It was mostly office work, keeping files up to date, and well below her official status in the service. She decided to remain in the tasks assigned for the moment; James had not yet reported the result of his London interview with the FCO.

Her sense of disorientation continued. Ever since she reunited with her lover, her perspective had changed. Excitement and danger became a secondary aspect of her life; she loved her active role, but felt more vulnerable once she fell for this like-minded Englishman. The urge to phone him to find out what had occurred when he'd confronted his boss at the Foreign Office became irresistible.

James's number rang a few times before he answered.

'Hello, my darling, what happened?'

'Well, I'm still alive! Cavendale is a bit of a bluffer…'

She broke in, 'What is that? A tyrant?'

James laughed, 'Sorry, my love, no – what the Americans call a 'bullshitter'.'

'In what way?'

He explained in more detail how the interview went.

Ocksana's voice took on a worried tone. 'Does this mean you have to undertake more danger to be accepted again? It sounds like dirty tricks, not bullshit to me!'

James realised he had made a rod for his own back. Now he would need to placate her, if he wanted to do the operation Cavendale offered.

'Don't worry! It's not tricky. I haven't got the details yet, but it's checking out European personnel – nothing interesting.'

He began to realise that bullshitting was a convenient tool sometimes; he had no idea what Melford would suggest when he saw him in the Operations Room. They exchanged notes and enjoyed this contact, while hoping to meet within the next two weeks.

'Just keep me posted, my darling!' she said.

Back in the office, thoughts of London and James still buzzed round her head as she opened a new file on her desk. It was an unusual colour. Most files on Chechen suspects were brown: this was red.

It contained instructions MOST CONFIDENTIAL. She read the brief with interest. It dealt with a recent source of information, about transfers of large sums to continental banks from the Chechen Treasury Funds. The enquiry sought to identify the nominees involved. It was far and away more significant than the routine tasks she had been given, and sparked her interest immediately. She checked her hair, straightened herself and went down to the director's office.

Max Rubin was a man who rose high in the service through the Akademi. A brilliant mind, from a family who served in Soviet organisations for the last fifty years. He had risen within the service of the Federal

Republic, just as his father and forefathers in the Soviet, and he knew his worth.

'This is not a surprise, my dear Miss Petrova. I expected you.'

Ocksana's graceful eyebrows furrowed.

'You see, I left that file on your desk! Like a bait for you!' He laughed and sat with his hands behind his head.

She smiled and pressed her lips together, frowning slightly. 'Am I a golden carp, or a minnow?'

'Oh certainly, a magical fish from the deep pool.' A reference to the *Tales of Gorodin*. 'This interesting file; would you care to comment?'

'Have we contacts with the continental banks? After all, Swiss banking is difficult.'

Rubin sat up and held out his hands across the desk, palms up; she kept her hands in her lap. His podgy face was set in a close-lipped smile, and she noticed a drop of spittle formed in the corner of his mouth. His eyes betrayed him; there was no warmth in their gaze but they burned with fire.

'Let me take you into my confidence,' he leant forward, and it was difficult to avoid his outstretched hands. She sat back. 'I have looked for a suitable junior officer to handle this complex case for some weeks. I believe you could deal with it.' His smile became more aggressive as if he demanded her agreement. He tried to make eye contact and his fingers touched her arm.

'I don't know what you mean. What is involved?' She left her arm under his touch for a second before moving away.

'Maybe we could discuss this in more congenial circumstances?'

His smile took on a different aspect; she thought he looked like Red Riding Hood's grandma, his teeth projecting from his crimson mouth.

'I never discuss my work outside the Bureau,' she was hard pressed to think of the best line of defence, 'it might arouse suspicion.' Even she realised this sounded pretty feeble. 'And,' she began to think harder, 'my fiancé is returning tomorrow from London.'

Rubin subsided into his chair and looked intently at his papers.

'Well, I may have to reconsider what to do; it is a difficult assignment.'

She got up and nodded and left the room.

Outside, she felt a mixture of emotions. Obvious repulsion at the cheap seduction technique, yet a feeling of regret at losing the chance of a task she knew promised travel and excitement. It made the humdrum office job almost unbearable, and she began to wonder how she could stay in Moscow when her heart was in London.

Within minutes, the eyes of the whole Bureau were upon her. As she returned to her desk she wished they still had the old-fashioned offices from Soviet times. She discovered what the women called 'The Rubin Call' was common practice in the office, and she was told to ignore him. One of the older women confided, 'He always tries it on, but don't worry, the jobs are allocated at a higher level so he has little say in it.'

Ocksana got back to work with just a spark of interest, hoping that a chance of transfer might still be open.

Later that day, her phone rang. 'Hello, Miss Petrova. Will you come to my office and bring the confidential file with you. This is Eva Brod.'

'Certainly, where is it?'

The voice took a sharp edge. 'Ask!'

Biting her lip, Ocksana tried to control her rising temper and made enquiries to find out.

The third floor was noticeably different from the rest. The corridors were lined with paintings and photographs; the floor was carpeted, and an air of calm soothed the spirits. At the end of the passage, a woman stood in the doorway and beckoned her sharply. Inside were two other people: an elderly colonel in uniform and another man, who sat in a corner. The woman, Brod, pointed to a chair. Ocksana took her time to be seated. She had taken an instant dislike to this woman with the rude manner, and was wary of this call, which seemed to be some sort of interview.

'I am Colonel Zhukov.' The man in uniform spoke softly and smiled. 'I am head of International Enquiries at the Moscow Bureau. You already know Madame Brod.'

Ocksana interrupted. 'No. I have never met Miss Brod.'

She deliberately did not use the courtesy title. She went on, 'I work in the Chechen Section, under Mr Rubin.'

A slight flicker passed over Zhukov's face at that name, but he went on.

'We know you have seen the red file. Is it correct that you have contacts in London?

She thought quickly. 'No contacts, but I know some people in London, yes.'

'And you spent some time at the Washington Embassy, did you not?'

'That was before I moved to Kazakhstan Security, at the request of Central.'

Madame Brod snorted, 'Kazaks are barbarians and pirates, with too much money swimming around their country.'

The colonel grinned and his eyes widened. 'You must be a brave girl to survive with those brutes!'

She began to warm to him, but watched the woman out of the corner of her eye, sitting stiffly in her chair and apparently making notes. It was time to take a little initiative.

'Who is this gentleman?' nodding towards the man in the corner.

Surprised by her direct approach, he stood up and bowed slightly. 'I am Dr Aflak. I work for the department.' Then he sat down without another word.

'You may have guessed, Miss Petrova, he is a psychologist, an indispensable addition to our staff.' Zhukov's dry remark left her in no doubt of his opinion.

'Is this a reassessment?' She wondered why this review was necessary.

'Do not be alarmed,' the older man smiled disarmingly. 'Modern personnel tests have to be applied, you know. It is nothing personal.'

To Ocksana it seemed very personal, but she bit her tongue and smiled. She noticed no sympathetic response from Madame Brod. There followed a quarter of an hour in which she was asked about her time in Kazakhstan and her return to Russia. She omitted her connection with Ballantyne and the interview ended without incident.

On her way back to the ground floor, she decided to take the elevator. As she stepped in, Dr Aflak got in beside her. There happened to be no other person in the cabin. For a moment, they stood side by side in awkward silence. As they reached the ground floor he spoke for the first time.

'I wonder if you can spare me a few minutes?'

His timid enquiry disarmed her and as she turned to look at him, he took her arm and directed her away from the general office. She pulled away from him.

'What do you want?'

'Please! I must speak with you.' His hunched shoulders and urgent whisper compelled her attention.

He walked ahead of her into the rest area where staff ate their meals, and sat down at one of the corner tables.

It was the first time she had looked at him closely. Aflak was a dark-skinned man about five feet six with cropped black hair. Pockmarks disfigured his face and he wore heavy-rimmed spectacles. He fidgeted, twisting a ring on his finger and looking down at the plastic surface. She waited for him to speak, aware that she was dealing with a doctor who would interpret anything she said.

He paused for a second, then burst out with a gush of words as if he had waited till now to unburden himself. 'I have to find somebody to help!'

Ocksana sat back and watched him intently. Was he setting her up for something? Was this some sort of test of loyalty? What could be the reason for this outburst?

She said nothing and waited.

CHAPTER 6

'How could I help?' Her question was a guarded response to his sudden outburst.

'I need someone to talk to...' again he hesitated. 'You are the only person I know outside the apparatchik of Government services.'

'But I am not that person.' Ocksana did not want to be drawn into some subterfuge, or worse, a trap to catch her.

'But you are newly returned from foreign service, and have been in touch with Western authorities. Are there connections which might help?'

He rubbed his eyes, and she noticed how he wrapped his arms around himself as he spoke.

'Please hear me out! If I can't find help, terrible things will happen, and it will be too late to stop them!'

She had no doubt in her mind that he was in fear; she felt obliged to listen.

'Go on,' she said, and made sure she sat back so that anyone watching would not see them in close conversation.

'I've been attached to the Russian medical service for three years, but I am Syrian by birth. Moscow has maintained close support to the government in Syria for a long time, but now things have changed.'

'In what way? Everyone knows of our support for the regime in Syria.'

'We are the White Helmets. Do you know what that means?'

'Some sort of relief team at work in Syria?'

'We are not government relief, we are independent people.'

Ocksana was puzzled. 'So why would you need help?'

'Russia has turned against us and intends to treat us as insurgents! I have to get a message to my brothers before it is too late.'

She made a quick calculation. Russian Foreign Service would monitor any communication from Moscow to any agency in Syria, so it was conceivable that Aflak could not warn them by normal means. The only way would be to physically pass the message.

'So?' She waited to find out what his next move would be.

'You would save many lives if you did this one thing.'

He looked away for a moment, then he made eye contact for the first time.

'I can report that you need a period of reassessment before reassignment in the Service,' and, before she could make a response, he went on, 'you might make a journey, say to Paris or London, and pass the message to safe hands.'

Ocksana needed no mentor to warn her of the risks involved in this scheme, but at the same time she jumped at the prospect of going to London and being with James. Her mind began to adapt the idea to her own ends.

'If I was on reassessment, maybe I could take a few days' leave within the procedure to visit abroad?'

Aflak's eyes widened, he caught her idea immediately. 'Yes! Yes! I can include it in my plan.'

Cool reflection told her this idea might work. With the reassessment agreed, the plan was viable, and allowed her to meet James as well. Was there a downside? She saw none, and the prospect of London filled her with excitement.

'If you can get this passed by my superiors, then I will consider it seriously, but I make no promises.'

He leant forward as if to take her hand, but she moved away and got up. 'Of course, any contact will have to be official, so I'll wait for your report.'

He nodded and she walked away, watching to see if they had been observed.

The following days were tense with expectation. She dared not phone James with any real information, and knew he would sense if she avoided any subject; it was better to wait before speaking to him.

On Monday, two days later, her workstation phone rang. It was Rubin.

'Come to my office at once.' His tone was very different to the one he had used before.

He sat at his desk, frowning at the paper in front of him.

'Personnel sent me this instruction, I don't understand. You have been assigned here for the last three weeks, and now they say you must be reassessed? This is absurd, you are dealing with several files and I will look into this. It would mean delays and disruption!'

She put on a puzzled expression.

'Go back to work and we will find out what happens.' Without a word, she walked back to the open-plan office. Rubin could not see that her fingers were crossed as she left.

That night, against her resolution, she couldn't resist calling James in London.

'How are you, darling? Are you still at the mercy of the old dragon?'

James laughed, 'I am meeting with another, smaller reptile tomorrow, and that should be interesting. But more important, when can I see you? Shall I come to Moscow, or can you get away for a few days?'

Her pulse raced as she longed to tell him what might happen. But mindful of security, she dared not speak the truth.

'No point in your coming here till you know what your situation is over there. But we will meet soon, my sweet!'

Her familiar voice, so exciting but so practical, charmed him in its usual way.

'I need your common sense, my darling, but your distance is torture for me.'

She laughed and it flew all the way to London, like a kiss. They chatted for some minutes and she felt sure that no phone tap would find anything suspicious.

The following day, Rubin called her back. He avoided her gaze.

'Some new protocol apparently requires your reassessment. Pass your files to other operatives and report to Medical Branch. If this takes too long, you will make up time when you get back. Good day.'

If he had given her a prize, she would not have been happier. It was difficult to wear the appropriate expression as she handed over the ugly brown files to other members of the team. She wanted to burst into laughter, but had to shake her head in bemusement as if the whole process was an absurd imposition.

At the Medical Centre, Aflak had prepared his report already. He explained how he had 'examined her' and found her under 'serious strain arising from traumatic experiences in Kazakhstan'.

'I will authorise a short period of leave before return to work. Now, I ask you to consider this simple job to save lives!'

'Tell me.' She maintained a certain reserve, even though she had determined to go to London.

'A colleague in Paris can pass direct messages to the headquarters in Aleppo. The message is simple: Russia has targeted us as partisan supporters and proscribed us. If he can pass that message through quickly, we can save many lives.'

'Why should Russia do this?' Ocksana was mystified; a sudden change in policy seemed strange.

Aflak shook his head. 'Don't you see? We work only in the areas held by ISIS and the al Qaeda. They believe we support them.'

'Do you?'

He looked wide-eyed at her. 'Merciful heavens! You must believe me! Of course not! We dedicate ourselves as Muslims to the preservation of life.'

She felt the need to reassure him, and took his hand. 'I will pass the message. What do I have to do?'

He explained the identity of the courier and how he could be contacted. The location was a Lebanese café in the 12th arrondissement. The man was a waiter called Latif. Nothing was written down.

He handed her the pass authorising leave, and she left a copy on her desk for official use.

Within an hour, she had booked herself onto a flight to Paris, and by seven p.m. Moscow time she was airborne. She texted James with her flight just as she landed; to do so in Russia was a serious risk.

Her sudden departure had consequences. Next morning, Rubin had an unwelcome visitor.

Madame Brod walked through the general office with a slow step, as if inspecting the personnel and finding them unsatisfactory. She appeared at Rubin's office without notice, and he gazed in amazement as she tapped on the partition which separated his section from the main room.

'What brings you here, Madame Brod?' He rose from his seat, brushing a file of papers to the floor.

'An incident, Mister Rubin, involving one of your staff. Tell me about Miss Petrova.'

Rubin settled back into his chair. Nothing would give him more pleasure than to investigate the privileged Miss Petrova.

While flight Aeroflot 2378 was on its way to France, wheels began to turn in the Special Branch in Moscow.

CHAPTER 7

Stephen Melford had survived a tour of duty in Northern Ireland with a little luck. His right arm had been blown off in an Ulster bombing, but he was a real survivor who had spent time in Lebanon as well as Northern Ireland. Ballantyne knew a little about his background before he knocked at the door of Operations Chief in Whitehall.

'Come in James,' The voice seemed friendly and warm and the man who sat at the desk got up to welcome him. His right sleeve was pinned neatly to his suit jacket and he held out his left hand in greeting. Ballantyne had never met him before and was a little taken aback by the familiar tone.

'I've heard a lot about you. Come and take a seat, we have much to talk about.'

James sat in one of the easy chairs set away from the formal desk area; Melford sat in the other. It was a good time to observe the man in charge of Covert Operations. The figure was stocky but well built; the shoulders were broad and his neck thick. His hair grew thickly and stood up on his head, reminding James of a brindled bulldog. A broken nose and bright brown eyes completed the picture of a man of action, albeit desk bound.

'I've had a bad press, I think,' began Ballantyne, 'Got tangled up with a US agent out in Kazakhstan..'

'Oh! I know all that,' Melforsd dismissed it with a wave of his hand. 'Sounds as if you had a bit too much excitement. What do you think of this idea of Cavendale's?'

'The idea seems a bit fanciful, I have to say. What evidence is there of a plot to eliminate Tontine members in the UK? Two deaths in strange circumstances is hardly a basis for a joint US/UK operation--sounds more like a police matter.'

Melford smiled to himself then he went over to the desk and brought back a piece of paper with a US State Department heading. He grinned as he handed over. 'Read this.'

It was a Report by a team of Special Agents dealing with surveillance on two suspects over a period if three weeks prior to the present date. The Report concluded that both suspects were known agents of a Rumanian magnate and were present in London when both deaths occurred. It listed their criminal records and the information about their activities in criminal violence.

When he finished reading, Melford took it back and looked keenly at Ballantyne.

'You may be right, but Our Cousins across the way think it's kosher and I have instructions to give support.'

'What you mean,' said Ballantyne, 'is you want to send the minimum staff to show willing on this wild goose chase!'

The other man raised one eyebrow. 'Oh come now! We must show solidarity!' But his eyes belied his expression. 'In any case, they might be right! And what fools we would be if we did nothing!'

He shifted in his seat and leant forward. 'Look James, all we want you to do is take little time and look into this. If you come back with nothing we can say we tried and pull out sharply.' He paused, 'Of course, the Office would be very grateful.'

There was no need to spell out what that meant.

James put on a show of reluctance. 'Let me have the Report overnight and I'll look at it and come back tomorrow, is that OK?'

Melford nodded , 'But I need to know then.'

Outside the office, Ballantyne's heart raced with excitement. A chance to work single handed in an international enquiry ! Exactly what he would have wished for, and it had just fallen into his lap!

The journey back to his flat in Earlsfield South London went like a breeze. He bought a take away from Carluccio's and settled down to read the Report more carefully. The US agents had done a good job; the surveillance was thorough and the background convictions were fully described. The principal subject was Emilio Kasurov, thirty eight y.o with convictions for murder and other violence; past employed in the Stasi but recently working for Gregor Bastin, a Rumanian oligarch in the Non ferrous metals industry who controlled 34% of the metal coming from Rumania. The second subject was another Rumanian thug with less history.

The file gave their addresses and associates while in the UK, so there was plenty of material to follow up. James took a nightcap of whisky and turned in.

Next morning, he was on the phone pronto.

'I think we can do something with this, when can I come in to see you?'

'Sooner the better, but don't let anyone in on this yet. OK?'

James biked in to Whitehall and was with Melford by 9.30. They arranged the details of pay and allowances. He was agreeably surprised at the rates the US

Government gave their Special Agents, and signed off his mandate there and then.

'Remember, I must be your only contact for reports.' Melford wagged a finger at him, 'Cavendale is not your Team Leader on this.' James gave a slight smile at the 'modern' techie name. Once, long ago, the word 'Boss' would have done.

His first thought was to tell Ocksana of the good news, but he waited till he had worked out his first move. Where would he start? The Report indicated an address in North London in Haringey where Kasurov had lived recently. It would do for a start.

That evening, he fired up his Yamaha XT600 and rode across London to Haringey. Using the Yamaha gave him two advantages; anonymity plus a speedy method of getting to and from his target. He had modified the bike with road tyres and exhaust but maintained its original drab colour. It had been registered in the last owner's name.

The address from the report was a flat above a barber shop. The night was fine and the road quiet. Street lamps had just come on and the shop was shut. He parked in a row of cars about a hundred yards away and walked bareheaded past the shop on the other side of the road. The only sign of life was a light from the first floor where an uncurtained window glowed. Ballantyne tucked himself into a side alley and watched.

Time passed like glue-each minute clung to the last as if to taunt him with frustration, but at last, a figure appeared at the street door and made its way to the Pub at the corner. He followed and entered the pub by a different door. The saloon bar was separated from the public by an old fashioned screen, a relic of old times when customers were divided into classes of drinkers.

From a corner of the saloon he caught a good look at the man from the flat. He was leaning on the bar and looking straight at Ballantyne though the gap between the screen! Ballantyne pulled out his cell phone and did his best to cover his face as if listening to a message. When he looked up again, the man had turned away and was paying the barman. Ballantyne moved to another location and lost sight of him for a while. He had not recognised the man from the photos in the report. This man was taller than Kasurov and bulky with a pronounced jaw; unshaven with the narrow eyes. His wild black hair pulled back behind his head.

Ballantyne had an immediate feeling of danger, an instinct formed in various encounters and he made a note to look at files of extradition targets as soon as possible. After a few minutes, the man gathered up some bottles in his arms and made his way out of the pub. He had not bought a drink at the bar for himself. It was easy to follow him back to the address as he ambled along the dark street. Just then, a car pulled up further down the street. Its lights cast a beam down the road shining on the man and outlining Ballantyne against the buildings behind him. He turned in at once as if to enter the nearest house and fiddled with the door lock. The car lights went off and two men got out, chatting to the man with the bottles. Ballantyne could hear them speaking in the quiet of the night but the language was familiar but strange. Then he realised it was probably Rumanian which sounded much like Italian. As the front door opened, he saw the face of one of the visitors; it was Kasurov.

'*Enough for one night.*' He was satisfied with his good luck; identifying the house and confirming its connection with Kasurov in a single observation was more than he expected. He rode back across London with a grin, enjoying the empty roads and a spurt of speed as he bombed along the Embankment towards Battersea bridge and home. The Report showed the photos of the other mercenary employed by Bastin, the suspected Oligarch, and it was the face of the man in the pub. His name was .... Tomorrow, he would put a plan to Melford.

He took a whisky to bed, feeling he'd earned it. He slept well until his phone rang three hours later. It was Ocksana.

CHAPTER 8

Flight 2378 landed at Charles de Gaulle on time and Ocksana stepped down into a world she had almost forgotten. The air was temperate in contrast to the fierce heat of summer Moscow; the shops and bars glowed with life even after midnight. It recalled her student days and memories. Feelings she had almost forgotten; the freedom of student life; the excitement of new romance. Her thoughts turned at once to James.

His phone rang three times before he answered. His voice was sleepy and at once, she felt the need to be with him again.

'Wake up my darling. I have a surprise for you!'

'You tell me now? What time is it?'

'It can't wait, you poor sleepyhead! I'm in Paris!

It took James a second to get a fix on this.

'In Paris? How did that happen?'

'Never mind that, can you get here?'

'Of course, are you there on....' he hesitated... 'on business?'

She wanted him so much, she longed to tell him, but instinct stepped in.

'I can't come over to London at the moment.' She said. They spoke for only a brief time; just enough for James to clear his mind and make arrangements to call later with flight information.

The first thing Ocksana did, as soon as she left the hotel, was to buy a cheap cell phone and text James to let him know. She kept her old one switched on to allay any suspicion in Moscow. A text came through early in the following morning telling her his time of arrival. She had three hours to fill and bought a city map to identify the location of the target café in the 12th arrondisement. It was a suburb in the south of the city.

The woman in the kiosk handed over the Map with a caution.

'Mes Excuses, Mademoiselle, you must not go to the 12th alone!'

Her eyes scanned Ocksana's face, 'Do you realise what you are doing?'

She put a sympathetic hand on her arm, 'Take a man with you.'

There was nothing she could say by way of explanation, so she smiled and waved at the old woman and sat in a café to study the map. The plan confirmed what the old woman had said; the district was obviously a focus of North African immigrants; mosques and shisha bars were numerous and, more significantly, the Brigade de Frappe had its Headquarters there. It meant that Police armed patrols were on the spot!

James arrived at 12.30. She saw his tall figure and light brown hair long before he could make her out among the welcoming crowd. He looked at her and her heart melted; he was her one true love and she ran to embrace him. He looked at her for a long moment.

'Is this my brave Cossack? I've waited so long!'

He crushed her in his arms and no words passed between them. After a while, they joined the crowd making their way out of the terminal and took a taxi to her hotel and chatted over a brief lunch as if they had never been parted.

'Where is this place?' She explained what she had promised to do and the location of the contact.

Ballantyne frowned. 'Does this sound straight to you?' His eyes narrowed as he considered the scheme.

'I have no doubt about Aflak's sincerity. His concern is beyond doubt.'

'Yes, but the organization: What do you know about the White Helmets?'

She shifted a little in her chair. 'Well, we see them on the news and in the papers don't we?'

He leaned back and looked at her. 'My darling! Do you trust sincerity in our game?'

'No! But I trust my instincts! I fell for a British agent didn't I?'

He had to smile and took her hands tenderly. 'You are wonderful! Let's just take a few precautions before you pass the message.'

'Come to my room and get settled and we will have time to do this later.'

She pulled him from his chair and they went back to her room. They didn't find time to talk about the White Helmets.

Five o'clock came and went before she shook him awake.

'Get up, Detka,' using an expression every Russian mother used. 'I want to be there before it's dark.'

He groaned and rolled out of bed, watching her slim white body as she towelled her hair. The blue scar on her thigh was still there and he stooped to kiss it. She smiled.

She knew which Metro line to use and within a half hour they emerged into the 12th arrondisement at Porte Doree. The Bar they were looking for was close to the Metro station. Fleur de Beirut was spelt out in white letters above the glass door. Outside, zinc topped tables were placed on the narrow pavement taking up most of the space. Two men sat at one of them sharing a hookah pipe which stood on the floor between them.

'Quick, walk on.' James took her arm and they strolled along the busy street on the further side of the road. A bar offered a view of the front of the café, so they took an inside table at the window. Ballantyne bought drinks and they settled down.

'What was his name, again?'

'Latif, he is one of two waiters, so Aflak told me.'

They watched the front of the café. The smokers remained outside and Ballantyne noticed they seldom talked; one of them used a cell phone from time to time.

A waiter came out and stood leaning against the wall smoking a cigarette.

'What do you reckon? Is he our man?'

'Let's wait and see if it's true there are two of them.'

Ocksana stood up and went to the bar to borrow a newspaper. The barman smiled, 'Le Tangier Journal--pour vous, Madame?'

She gave him her searchlight smile, shrugged 'Faute de mieux.' and took the paper to the table.

James smiled at her. 'While you were away I've solved our problem! The other waiter is a woman!'

Sure enough, a large woman in a kaftan was cleaning one of the tables and speaking to one of the men sitting outside. The male waiter stood further along the wall, smoking; some distance from the men, obviously taking a break.

'This is my chance!' said Ocksana, 'watch me!'

She strolled along the side of the road opposite the café, looking up at street numbers along the way. Then she crossed over and approached the waiter with the newspaper in her hand. Ballantyne could see her speak and the slight reaction of the man. Then she smiled and returned to the bar.

'Ok, he's the one! I have to meet him at the back gate in the street behind.'

They got up and left the bar, ambling down the street to the corner and turned out of sight into the adjacent street. The back of the Café led into a narrow alley lined with rubbish bins; refuse lay everywhere and they picked their way cautiously to the back gate. It was a steel door painted in dark green and it was impossible to see what was behind it. A sound of scraped metal warned them that someone was opening the door. Ballantyne stepped back, ready to deal with any sudden response, but the waiter they had seen slipped through the gap in the doorway and joined them.

Up close, he was a man of medium height, dark skinned and extremely thin. He wore European clothes--a white shirt and black trousers. He looked piercingly at the two. 'Tell me again who sent you?'

He spoke in French with a difficult accent.. Ocksana explained the message and mentioned Aflak's name. That was enough to calm the man and he nodded.

'Yes, I will pass the message at once. May Allah bless you for this!'

He looked furtively up the alley, bowed, then stepped back behind the door.

James looked at Ocksana. 'What do you think? Is he genuine?'

She shrugged, 'I've done what was asked. If The White Helmets are genuine, then lives will have been saved.'

'And if not?' She grinned and the corners of her mouth turned up into that delicious grin that James adored,

'Well, then we'd better get the hell out of here!'

They hurried back to the main street and emerged casually, walking away from the café.

'Don't look back,' Ballantyne held Ocksana's arm as they walked along, but they took a moment to look in a shop window. One of the men from the pavement table was following them. At the next corner, Ballantyne stepped quickly into a shop while Ocksana walked on. The man followed her. He stopped after a few yards and began to look for the missing target. James caught him by the arm and swung him against the wall.

'You like the lady? Or is it me you're looking for?'

Ballantyne spoke in French. He held the man by the folds of the jellaba and felt a knife hidden in the waistband beneath. The man kept still and did not attempt to reach the weapon.

He said, 'Let me go! I don't want to harm you! Maybe we're on the same side!'

James held him firmly and waited for Ocksana to reach them.

'What the hell are you talking about?' He shifted his grasp and wheeled the man into an alley. This time the arab smiled and held out his arms in a gesture of surrender.

'Let me show you!' He pointed to his right top pocket inside the jellaba and James cautiously pulled out a worn ID card. His name was Mansur Allibi.

'Contact Gendarmerie, my friend, and find out for yourself who I am.'

He smiled as if everything had been explained. James handed the ID card to Ocksana. She frowned and asked, 'How does this explain why you were doing following us?'

'You are Miss Petrova. We have been keeping a watch for you since you arrived yesterday! Your interest in Latif attracts attention.'

Then he turned to Ballantyne. 'If you would be so kind as to release my jacket, I can satisfy your curiosity and we can behave sensibly.'

It struck Ballantyne that the second man at the table would realise by now that something had happened to his colleague. He scanned the street for any activity. Too late. Blue lights flashing from police cars told him they were tagged and surrounded. He let the agent go and stood very still; Ocksana did the same.

'Get In!' A combat officer in balaclava and field uniform pushed him into a plain van and the agent inside put cable ties on his wrist and forced him down onto the floor of the vehicle. Ocksana was manhandled into a police car and the convoy moved off. It had taken less than half a minute to arrest them and remove the group from the scene.

Ballantyne was impressed. There was no siren used either before or afterwards which told him he was in the hands of a major unit of the French Security not the gendarmerie. No one spoke to James and his guards never took off their face masks even inside the van. The journey was short and he was brought out of the van under a canopy between the vehicle and the building. The police car with Ocksana inside drew up behind them and he caught sight of her as he was brought inside the building. She looked calm and he was confident she would manage herself well.

'Sit down and let me help you with these cuffs.' The man who spoke was short and square like a block of marble. His bullet head and short neck gave the impression he was carved out of one piece of stone and his shoulders formed the base of the statue. He took a knife to the plastic bands that bit into James's wrists, then attached a handcuff loosely to the right wrist and a table leg.

'You should be more comfortable now.' He smiled and his cobra eyes gave no warmth to the suggestion.

'Look! This can easily be cleared up. Just take a look at my passport; it's in the hotel on Rue St Etienne. My name is James Ballantyne and I work for the British government.'

Ballantyne had left his documents behind deliberately in case they met danger at the rendezvous with the waiter Latif. Now he wished he'd ignored his usual routine.

'All in good time Monsieur, first let us know why you attacked an officer of the French Security?'

Ballantyne suppressed the grin which was rising. He recognised the technique he had used himself in the past, where you put the suspect off guard by accusing him of crime he had not committed to place him at a disadvantage.

'Check my credentials first and I'll tell you exactly what you want to know.'

The man stood still and leant over him.

'I will do exactly what I want to do.' He looked down in to Ballantyne's eyes to stare him out. Ballantyne stared back using a trick he had been taught in Afghanistan when questioned. He stared at a point just above the eyes of the interrogator which avoided eye contact but appeared to confront the opponent eye to eye.

'Maybe you need to establish the facts before making allegations.'

James enjoyed the reaction in the man's face. The man pressed his lips together and sat back, his eyes squinting at James in a quizzical way. His hands caressed the top of his shaven head for a moment as he considered what to do next. A knock at the door broke the silence. A uniformed policeman told the interrogator that he was wanted.

The man left James with the officer. Within two minutes, he was back and attached James to his own wrist and took him down the corridor to a larger room where Ocksana sat attended by two figures in plain clothes.

Ocksana smiled at him but indicated she too was handcuffed. Ballantyne saw at once this was not an interrogation room. For a start, there were comfortable chairs and no high beam lights. Two individuals sat behind a desk and Ocksana sat in front of them. He was given a seat alongside her but out of touching distance. He looked keenly at the two officials. One was a man dressed in civilian clothes, a studious type with thick rimmed glasses and a severe look on his face. He studied some file in front of him and then glanced at Ballantyne.

The other was a woman of about fifty, smartly dressed and well groomed; no mere bureaucrat, he reckoned.

'Mister Ballantyne,' she began, 'it is sometimes amusing to confront companions with each other's explanations and to see what results.'

She did seem amused, but the man, fidgetted with his pen.

'If we are playing a game,' Ballantyne answered, 'maybe we could join in if we weren't handcuffed.'

She ignored the reply.

'Tell me who you say you are?'

'James Ballantyne, I work for the British Government.'

'Really?' Her brow furrowed. 'There is no record of your employment at The British Embassy. Have they lost your records?'

She shook her head in mock despair.

'No.' James sat upright,' You haven't asked the right people!'

Ocksana sensed the rising temperature and sent a signal to him across the room.

The studious man broke in. 'Don't waste our time with repartee--if you have another contact, then tell us.'

'Yes I have, contact the Foreign Office in London and deal with the Kazak desk, The Chief is Sir Edmund Cavendale.' James realised he must not mention his connection with Melford.

The woman turned to Ocksana, 'Why did you not mention this when we asked you about your companion?

Ocksana fixed her eyes on her. 'Because I didn't know the name of his chef de cabinet,' she went on, 'you questioned me about my credentials and connections with 'The White Helmets' not Mister Ballantyne.'

James took the hint from her reference to 'Mister Ballantyne' and logged it mentally. The man left the room, obviously to check the information.

Ocksana leant forward, 'By now you must have checked my credentials with Moscow or we would not be in this room!'

The woman smiled, an effort which barely moved her lips.

'You are right, but it does not explain your involvement with the white Helmets. You know they are a proscribed organization as far as Russia is concerned!'

Ocksana took up the challenge with a question of her own. 'Why is my involvement of interest to you? France has not proscribed them?'

Two vertical lines formed between the immaculate brows of interrogator. 'Any activity by a foreign agent on our soil is of interest to us, especially when she is associated with another foreign subject.'

Ballantyne could see that the situation was becoming difficult.

'Let me suggest a way of clearing this up. If I contact my superior and invite him to identify me, then you can ring the Foreign Office and confirm through the authenticated number, will that help sort this out?'

She was silent for a moment, then she pushed the phone across the desk towards him. He rang the number of the Kazak desk and was put through to Cavendale's desk.

'James, what in God's name is this all about?' The voice was audible throughout the room.

Ballantyne tried to explain how he had been detained but the voice burst through his explanation. 'Put me onto the damned fool screwing things up!' James passed the phone to the elegant woman.

'Est que vous etes un cretin?' The mangled French poured out of the handset which she held at a distance from her ear.

'Monsieur, mes excuses, mais...' she had no chance to break the flow and put the phone down.

She turned to James. 'Is this some kind of blague?' In her startled condition she had forgotten the word for 'joke.'

Ballantyne looked down and away for a moment, then he said 'Sir Edmund is a little ..er ..choleric but if you look up the official number of the Foreign Office you will be able to verify that you were speaking to my chief.'

Eventually, she confirmed his identity and put the phone down. The studious man had re-entered and passed her a note. She looked at it in silence, then she stood up.

'Your conduct has been irregular and caused considerable trouble to our Securite Nationale. I propose to make a report to your embassies about this matter and require you to leave France immediately.'

She got up and left the room, turning away from them; her heels tapped like a pair of castanets as she swept out of the door. Ocksana bit her lip. 'Let's go.' As they made their way to the front of the building, her furrowed brow drew James's attention.

'What's up my darling? Isn't this good news?'

'When they report this to Moscow, I'm in deep trouble. Contact with the White Helmets will need some explaining! 'Specially as I'm meant to be on leave!'

They discussed the turn of events for some time and James did his best to re-assure her.

'Look, best thing is to come straight out with it before they send for you don't you think?'

She rested her chin on her hands and shook her head. 'You don't know the Bureau! They already questioned my leave of absence and probably the contact with WH demonstrates my unreliability!'

James took her in his arms, perturbed by this unusual sign of fear in the woman he loved and admired.

'Maybe, you should stay with me and not go back?'

She pulled away and softly kissed his brow.

'No, my darling, there is nowhere I could go to be secure. I must face them and deal with it. You're probably right, to confront them may be the best option.'

They spent a very quiet afternoon in their hotel; made love tenderly in the evening and agreed to return to their bureaus on the next day. What would the immediate future bring?

CHAPTER 9

'What the hell have you been up to?'

If the other members of the Kazak desk didn't know that Ballantyne had returned, they knew it by now. Sir Edmund's voice carried down the corridor and through to the main office. Delighted glances passed between the staff, pretending to work as the tirade went on.

James stood mute. He knew he could never stop the flow. One waited till the typhoon blew itself out.

'Well? Explain yourself? Didn't I tell you to lie low? What in God's name am I to say to Melford? I told him you were just the man for his project!'

A moment's pause.

Ballantyne took a deep breath; 'Sir, I was trying to help my...'

'Trying to help! God's blood! When you help, all hell breaks loose and I have to shovel shit to get you home again.'

'I'm very sorry; I never expected trouble with The French Surete. If anything, I suspected the Syrians might be difficult.'

Cavendale subsided from boiling point to simmer.

'What have the Syrians got to do with it?' The purple spots in Cavendale's cheek grew less conspicuous. His curiosity was aroused; a good sign.

Ballantyne quickly explained the issue between the Russian policy and the activity of the White Helmets and Ocksana's meeting with the Parisian contact.

Sir Edmund sat back in his chair. Work recommenced in the nearest offices as disappointed staff realised the fun was over.

'Wait a minute, Melford better sit in on this.'

Cavendale punched a number into the phone and within a minute, Melford joined them. James groaned inwardly. He hoped to deal with each one individually; now re-inforcements had arrived.

Stephen Melford looked glumly at the pair as he tramped into the room and sat on a chair near the wall. He said nothing but his horn rimmed glasses seemed to send rays of suspicion at James. He repeated the gist of the story again.

Melford scratched his head with the frame of his spectacles.

'How come you were in Paris anyway? I told you to shadow a man in Finsbury Park not Bois de Boulogne.'

Something told James he was toast; any explanation would be rejected and the more he talked, the more he dug a pit for himself. He decided to try the old ' sad dog' routine to lessen the grief.

'I was stupid I know, but I couldn't let my girl get into trouble could I? She was trying to do good and didn't realise what she'd got into.'

Melford glanced at Cavendale and then up at the ceiling as if searching for guidance.

'Had it crossed your mind to tell me? Is discipline a word that means nothing to you?'

James said nothing; a silence like a blanket covered the room. He stayed mute, forcing one of the others to break the silence.

At last, Cavendale said, 'Can we expect you to keep us informed of every activity from now on? Do you realise that Special Operations needs to know what its agents are doing?'

Melford had to get his bite as well; 'I want your assurance that you will stick to the instructions I give you in the future.'

Ballantyne nodded and stood up. 'I understand. May I go?'

Melford looked at Cavendale who nodded and then at James.

'Report to me tomorrow morning and I will give you further instructions.'

In two strides Ballantyne got out of that door and away down the corridor.

That night, he phoned Ocksana to find out her situation.

'My poor boy!' her voice soothed but there was just a little edge of hilarity as he recounted his persecution. 'What brutes these English are! They have ice in their veins!

Did you tell them I was in trouble?'

'I told them you were in mortal danger and I rescued you, but they lashed me all the same! What about you?'

'I told them I followed a lead on the White Helmets and it's true!'

James made a mental note to get his excuses from her in future.

'Ok but I must keep out of sight for a while, till things settle.'

'Ok, all my love. My Detka!'

He put down the phone and felt very alone. Was it the first time he realised how his life had changed? Now he was part of a couple and bonded to this woman, so far away. He reflected how the feeling had been growing since they parted in Russia. It was not a wholly pleasant sensation; to be worrying about the other one while engaged in dangerous activity.

He arrived promptly on time at Melford's office the next morning. On the desk was a dossier with many photos laid out.

'See if you can recognise the man you saw in Haringey.'

Ballantyne picked out a photo at once. 'It's Kasurov.'

'What about this man?' Melford pointed to the head-shot of a squat bald man with a scar on his forehead.

'No, who is he?'

'That's Bogdan Sala the head of Ruma Enterprises. He is of interest to us,' he went on, it appears the Tontine has split into two factions and Sala is connected to the Russian section.'

'Is he anything to do with Kasurov?'

Melford gave a thin smile, 'You have firmed up that piece of information. We believed that was the case but your sighting confirms it.'

'How so?'

'Because the address is one of a number owned by Sala's Property company in the UK.'

Ballantyne felt he had been ill treated by 'The Firm.' They employed him 'off the record' to locate Kasurov at no risk to themselves, then bollocked him for a bit of independence. He made a mental note to log plenty of hours at the US rate.

'See if you can find out a line on the other occupants of the address and any further info on Sala.'

'Will do.' Ballantyne got up to leave.

'And I want a daily report.' Melford's voice followed him out into the corridor.

That evening, James rode once again to the street where he had seen Kasurov. He settled in the same bar and waited. The pub was the only one in this street, with no off licence nearby. He chatted to the barman and made sure his name stuck; he chose Jim as he usually did since it was easy to remember. It was a slow evening with few people in the bar. The barman was not really interested but thought it might be good for business to chat.

'You lookin' for work?'

'Could do with a bit of part time, y'know, nothing too serious.' James gave him a smile and a wink.

'Lots of fellers hereabouts in the same boat.'

'How so?'

'Well, the Benefit doesn't cover the good life does it?' He gave Ballantyne a meaningful look, 'we all like a bit of extra, isn't that so?'

Ballantyne nodded and sipped his pint.

'Here's a boy who knows the ropes.' The barman pointed to a figure just pushing through the street door. It was the same man James had seen on the previous occasion; the one he traced to Kasurov's door. He came to the counter and put three twenty pound notes on the bar.

'Gimme Budvar like usual.' His voice was low and he stared at James as he waited for the beer. His eyes were almost hidden by the thick eyebrows but they were black and suspicious.

Ryan, the barman, heaved the three crates onto the counter and pointed to Ballantyne.

'We was just talkin' about occasional work and earning a few bob.'

'What you mean?' The eyes turned on James as if he was a specimen on a slab,

'You look for work?'

'I'm out at the moment but not too keen!'

'What you do?' The black eyes studied him.

'A bit of labouring but I'm a delivery driver HGV.'

The big man sniffed and picked up two of the crates. Ballantyne gestured towards the third one; the man nodded and Ballantyne picked it up and followed him out of the pub.

The barman grinned and shouted after them, 'Watch your step, be lucky.'

Ballantyne knew he needed luck; he watched the man with the crates as they reached Kasurov's door. He put down the crate and made to leave.

There was an exchange between the man with the crates and a man from the house, in a language James did not understand, obviously about him. Then the man with the black brows beckoned him to come in.

From the noise inside, a party was in full swing, loud voices and singing poured into the street. Ballantyne smiled and gave a thumb's up, hefting the crate down the hallway to the room at the back of the house. There was such a crowd, he had difficulty in tracing Kasurov among the dancing, singing mob. He sat at the back of the room and away from the revellers. Beside him sat a dark haired girl. Ballantyne guessed she was Italian; slim but full breasted and with glossy hair which she enjoyed flicking from side to side. She eyed him as he came in and their gaze lasted just too long for safety. Kasurov followed her direction and frowned. He beckoned the man who brought Ballantyne in and they spoke for a minute.

Then he shrugged and dismissed the man with a wave of his hand. Ballantyne grabbed a beer and tried to speak to the nearest man who nodded and smiled by way of contact. It was enough to take Ballantyne out of sight for a few minutes and he took the opportunity to scan the crowd and assess what he had got into. Obviously, this was a celebration for Rumanians, but not everyone was stamped with the distinct mark of violence which Kasurov and his henchmen displayed. Ballantyne had seen enough examples to recognise the type at once. Old men and women mixed with the harder types and some young girls dressed in trashy gear and fake tans, completed the scene.

One of Kasurov's aides came over to where Ballantyne stood talking with signs to the older man.

'I see Ivan brought you in to celebrate, what's your name?'

'Jim, I met him in the pub and brought the beer across!'

'That's ok. This is Dacia Day! We celebrate our free nation!'

'What's it mean?' James showed interest. 'Is it your National day?'

The man grinned. 'No, my friend, any day is Dacia Day when ......says so!'

He indicated Kasurov, who in return raised his glass. Ballantyne smiled and nodded.

By three o'clock the next morning, the crowd had thinned out and Ballantyne got closer to the main group. Kasurov kept himself aloof, protected by three heavies who sat drinking at his feet. They sprawled on the floor and occasionally lifted the skirts of passing girls, who flounced away angrily. This produced raucous laughter and catcalls; it seemed to be a party game.

Kasurov leaned forward and prodded one of the men to fetch Ballantyne.

'You know Ivan?' He gave James a hard look; the man seemed part drunk or drugged.

'Seen him in the pub and he said 'Come along''

'Sure! Ivan, good man, big muscles!' A general laugh followed and it was obvious they regarded Ivan as a bone head.

Ballantyne smiled and nodded; 'Did me a favour anyway.'

'What you mean?'

'He said you might have work for me and I could come over.'

Kasurov turned a sleepy eye on James. 'Oh! What could you do for me, English Boy?'

'I can drive and keep my mouth shut.'

The Rumanian studied him again. Ballantyne saw that the man's expression changed; he was not the sleepy half cut foreigner he pretended to be. This man was dangerous and used deception as a weapon to defend himself. They exchanged looks and for a moment James felt the power of a sinister personality attempting to dominate him. He held out until Kasurov turned away to speak to one of his minders.

Then he spoke directly to Ballantyne. 'We have need of a driver for one job. My man is sick and the drive is today. You want?'

Ballantyne nodded and stood up. 'What's the pay?'

'I give you same as others --this is test, English, not job for life!'

James shrugged his shoulders by way of agreement and went outside to sit on the doorstep. The air was fresh and the light increasing as dawn approached. The last of the party stumbled past him on their way out. He felt the cell phone inside his jacket and realised he would have to hide it before he made any move in Kasurov's company. They were bound to check him over and the numbers in the phone were like a death warrant. He never expected to make contact directly with the Sala organization and had not prepared himself for undercover work. He pulled off the back and flipped out the simcard as quickly as he could.

A voice spoke over his shoulder; 'What you do? You have problem?' A man had come out of the house and was sitting on the step above him.

Ballantyne quickly looked down on the pavement as if searching for something.

'Dropped the facking thing. Lost the card!' He just had time to slip the simcard into his sock before the man bent down to help him.

He looked up into the face of the observer. Had his bluff succeeded?

With the grey dawn light Ballantyne could make out the shape of the van parked about fifty yards down the street.

'Come!' The man in the black anorak tapped him on the shoulder and set off ahead of him in that direction. It was Kasurov. He had not spoken to him since they met at the party inside. The fresh air as just the tonic Ballantyne needed to clear his head for the coming events. Without reporting to Melford and without adequate preparation, he had plunged into the mechanism of Sala's operation.

What was the 'driving job' Asurov needed?

CHAPTER 10

Flat number 4 ***** Street was on the second floor. Ocksana climbed the stairs past the concierge's door. Like most Moscow blocks, this one had a caretaker who acted as watchdog and spy for the police. Everybody understood this and took steps to keep their business confidential. The glass door opened as she passed the window. A wizened face wrapped in a kerchief peered out like an inquisitive mole. 'Ah! My Petrovina, you are back from Paris France?'

'Yes, and I didn't forget you!'

Ocksana searched in her luggage and brought out a box of soaps branded with 'Worth Paris' across the top. She handed over the pretty gift and the old woman's eyes assessed its value.

'Very nice, my niece will like this,' and with a nod she closed the door. Ocksana smiled. It was important to confirm where she had been. Now she felt confident the information would get to her superiors rapidly.

Two letters lay on the mat inside the door. One, an invitation to an anniversary dinner at the international college she attended in St Petersburg. The other was a curious scrawled note on lined paper. She examined it more closely. A dirty, unstamped envelope. The flap appeared to be intact but when she looked closer, she could see the surface was uneven. Somebody had opened and resealed it.

'Prends garde un piege avec les blanches.'

It was obviously cryptic for some good reason, and written in poor French. Two facts stood out. Someone wanted to warn her about a trap connected with the White Helmets, and the authorities knew by now.

Next morning, at the Bureau, she rang Rubin, her head of section to report in. He sent for her.

'The red file has been reserved for you on Madame Brod's instructions. I re-allocated the remainder of the files to other personnel. Please confine yourself to that one file.'

'Am I to refer queries to you or Madame Brod?'

He gave a tight-lipped smile. 'You will report to Madame Brod.' He turned away and drew a file of papers towards him.

She found it difficult to assess the significance of the assignment. On one hand, it seemed a positive sign of approval from the Bureau, but it also placed her directly under the surveillance of this powerful and hostile woman. She re-read the summary, tracing the funds from Chechenia to three Swiss bank accounts, and went up to the third floor as she had done before.

The office door stood open and she could see the outline of the woman hunched over some papers.

'Don't stand there, come in!' The voice brought back the last time she had been summoned to this office.

'I have been told to report to you, not Mr Rubin ...' she began.

'Of course. Why would you report to him if you are allocated to my section?'

Again, the curt response and the furrowed eyebrows.

Ocksana vowed she would do her utmost to escape from this hellcat.

'Sit down and tell me what you have learnt about the file.'

In a few minutes, she related what she recalled.

'Then you appreciate we must start by examining the Chechen root of the matter?'

Ocksana nodded, but mentally retorted, *Of course, you dimwit, anyone can see that!*

As if the thought had been spoken, Brod stared at her.

There was a pause and the woman lifted her head to look her in the eyes. They stared at each other for a moment.

'I am sending you to Grozny with an accountant to examine the books of the State Disbursements Office, which controls the Petro Chemical Industry.'

'But Chechenia is a republic? How can you implement that?'

Brod gave a thin smile. She leant forward, 'No need for you to concern yourself. I arranged everything. You will have authority from the Head of Principal Industries to conduct a 'survey' into efficiency. That is enough.'

Ocksana could think of nothing to say at that moment. The task was a dangerous one: everyone knew of the hostility between Moscow and the Chechens. Was it the 'trap' that the note had warned her about? It seemed unlikely, since there seemed no obvious link between Syria and the Chechens.

'When do I leave?'

'As soon as you have arranged things with Boris Bashlivi.'

Ocksana assumed this was the accountant.

'When do I meet him?'

Brod handed her a card with the details of his section.

'As soon as possible. Make the arrangement.' She turned back to her paperwork and never looked up again.

Ocksana clenched her fists and left the room clutching the red file. By the time she reached her desk, she had simmered long enough to realise her position. First of all, she was away from that hateful woman; secondly, investigating a major crime allegation was stimulating and maybe she would have a chance to meet James away from Moscow.

Looking up Grozny in Google, it was clear that the assignment was unattractive. The city was large and commercially important but without much attraction. If she was there for some time, she would feel very isolated.

A young man walked into the general office as she reflected on this. He approached her desk boldly.

'Miss Petrova?'

She nodded.

'I'm Bashlivi.' The name meant nothing to her. He added, 'From accounts – we are working together on the Disbursements Office job in Grozny.'

He stood near the desk and smiled at her. He was six feet tall and slim, with blond hair. He looked down at her with his hands clasped behind him. She wondered how he had learnt of the mission so quickly.

'I have just been told of the task myself,' she said. 'When were you assigned to it?'

He shrugged, 'I knew two days ago. I have been preparing the file with the necessary IT software to analyse the data.'

The suspicion that she was being manipulated began to surface in her mind. Why would she be assigned to an accountancy enquiry? She had no training in this field. Why send her to Chechenia, with its volatile relationship with Russia? An instinctive alarm rang like a bell in her ear.

'Let me take a day to prepare a plan and arrange accommodation,' she said.

He shrugged again. 'Transportation has already done that. All you will need is the briefing notes.' He handed her a bulky envelope. 'I'll be in touch tomorrow.'

As he left, he waved and sauntered out.

Ocksana clutched the desk and inwardly cursed Brod and the Ministry.

CHAPTER 11

They met at the airport. By the time Bashlivi arrived, the flight to Grozny was due to depart.

'Where have you been?' Ocksana stared at him as he sauntered into the departure area.

'I had business to deal with and some further instructions.'

He smiled and pursed his lips, as if her enquiry was tiresome. Then he brushed back his blond locks with a wave of his hand and joined the queue for boarding. She decided this was not the right occasion to raise a protest since he had arrived on time, but she marked it as a sign that he was trouble. They sat next to each other for the two-hour flight; he studied his documents and she mused on the problems that would face them when they arrived. A Russian audit team investigating major Chechen investments was as tricky a task as defusing a bomb. If it went wrong, then the explosion would send shock waves through Russia and beyond.

At Grozny, there was no one to meet them. As they waited in line for a taxi, a large black ZIM limousine drew up and the driver leaned out.

'Please accept a lift with the compliments of Mister Shouvaloff.'

Bashlivi was at the door of the car before she could stop him. She pulled him back.

'Wait! Who sent you? Who is Mister Shouvaloff?'

The driver got out and took off his cap respectfully.

'I have my instructions, Madame. Mister Shouvaloff is the manager of the Mitre Hotel where you are accommodated.'

At this, Bashlivi grinned at her and jumped into the car. 'This is what we need! Cooperation from our Chechen cousins!' He laughed and pulled his valise in beside him. Ocksana got in. Her face was flushed and she gave a thin-lipped smile.

'Do not act without my advice. This could have been embarrassing to our mission. You need to learn discretion in these circumstances.'

He looked across at her with a half-smile, his blue eyes narrowed.

'I am just your accountant, Madame Petrova, but we have to act as we see fit, do we not?' His eyes challenged her as he held her gaze. She matched his look and held eye contact.

'Then do your job and do not compromise mine.' She sat back and looked out of the window.

The journey into the centre took them through a wasteland of broken-down buildings, factories with no sign of activity and empty residential streets.

'How long has this been abandoned?' Ocksana leant forward to speak to the driver.

He shrugged and half turned towards her. 'A long time, Madame, we have suffered much in the war.' He meant the conflict between the Chechen rebels and the pro-Russian National Forces. 'But we are strong people and will survive!'

She reflected on her mission: if her enquiry revealed what Moscow suspected, then survival for the poor was not so likely. She made no reply.

The Mitre Hotel was near the Minutka Square in the centre of Grozny. The facade was typically cosmopolitan in style, but once inside it revealed itself as an old-style Soviet bloc institution. Concrete corridors led to the rooms and cheap furniture was standard. There was no such thing as a hall porter in this world.

I wonder when they took down the photos of Stalin? she thought as she dropped her bags on the bed. It was still late afternoon and she wondered what to do. To re-read her brief was too boring, and she had no wish to meet Bashlivi before dinner. Just as she settled down to read a magazine, the phone rang.

'Miss Petrova? Mister Shouvaloff would be delighted to offer you a welcome drink at six o'clock, can you meet him?'

Ocksana felt a keen interest in Mister Shouvaloff. There had been no reference to his name in the briefing and yet he was making an effort to make contact. How did he know she and Bashlivi were on that flight? What business of his was it to make this contact?

She agreed to meet him, and did not ring Bashlivi to tell him. It occurred to her to check Moscow for any information about the Chechen, but her pride stopped her from asking for help from Madame Brod or her secretariat. She took a shower and changed for the evening.

Just before six, she wandered down to the ground floor and took a short walk down the avenue. It was a cool evening but still light. She had put off phoning James until she'd arrived in Grozny, but she couldn't wait any longer. She reckoned it was about 2.30 p.m. in the UK. The number rang for a long time but he did not answer. She rang off before the answerphone responded. Feeling disappointed, she returned to the foyer of the hotel and found Bashlivi sitting there with a smile on his face. He wore a smart dark blue suit and a cream shirt open at the throat. His blond hair occasionally drifted down over his face and he brushed it back languidly. He got up as she approached and looked at her with one eyebrow raised.

'I was wondering if you would come.' He gave her a long look.

'I was invited and had nothing to do. Why do you ask?'

He tilted his head and stepped close to her. 'I thought he wanted to make separate contact with me. He sent me this message.' He passed a scrap of paper to her discretely. It was a piece of hotel note paper.

It read: *Meet me for a drink at 6 p.m. I have something to ask of you. MS.*

Ocksana crumpled the note and looked around the room. There were several groups of tourists and businessmen. No one appeared to pay any special attention to her.

'Okay. Go to meet him after we talk, and tell me later.' She stepped away and turned to look in one of the mirrors in order to scan the crowd for observers. She saw a large man in a blue suit approaching with a smile on his face. His arms were extended like a wrestler about to engage his opponent. He went directly to Bashlivi and embraced him like a bear mauling its prey.

'Welcome Tovarich! I have many things to show you. Come! I have a room specially for us.'

Boris Bashlivi stepped back for a moment, then smiled and went arm in arm with the big man, casting just one puzzled glance back at Ocksana who nodded and turned away.

She felt the unmistakeable instinct that she was on the fringe of some serious malpractice but found herself unable to identify what it was. Maybe political skulduggery, or fraud? The obscure remarks Madame Brod had made came back to her:

'You have no need to concern yourself, I have arranged everything.'

She went into the dining room and sat by herself. The room was crowded and she was unable to detect if someone had been detailed to watch her. The meal was uneventful and the food unappetising; this increased her longing to hear James's voice, as some comfort in a dreary world.

'Hello, my darling!' His voice came through loud and clear, lifting her spirits in an instant.

'Are you still in Moscow?'

Her heart beat wildly, and she listened eagerly to the familiar voice which thrilled her so much. They chatted excitedly for some minutes before he turned to serious matters, but from then on their conversation took an absurd formal tone as both realised that someone somewhere was recording every word.

'When will you be back in Moscow?'

'Probably in a week's time.'

'Be careful my love!'

They both felt shackled by the need for anodyne chat when under surveillance, so the conversation ended with a series of neutral remarks which belied their true feelings. Nonetheless, Ocksana felt a huge relief to hear his voice and knew very well that he felt the same.

Later that night, when she had decided to go to bed, a knock at the door announced Bashlivi.

His face was flushed and his sleek hair was disarranged carelessly.

'Can I come in?' He leant on the doorway and looked down at her in her nightdress.

She saw in a moment that he was half drunk and her instinct was to shut the door in his face, but the meeting with Shouvaloff was significant and she needed to know.

'Come in, and tell me what happened.'

He walked into the room and slumped into a chair uninvited. His long legs jutted out as he lay back with his head on the cushions.

He smiled, lips slightly parted as he took a long look at her.

'Give me a drink and I'll tell you.' His eyes wandered over her figure silhouetted by the bedside lamps.

'No, tell me now and then go to bed!' He grunted and held out his hand, but she ignored it.

'Ocksana! We can work together, but you know how much I'm attracted to you.'

She turned away and went to put on a dressing gown from the bathroom, but he followed her and put his arm round her shoulder as she moved away. She could feel his breath on her cheek as she twisted out of his grasp and held her palms up against his chest, holding him away.

'Let me go!' she pushed hard and with a twist of her foot tripped him; he fell back onto the floor. Sprawled on the carpet, he took a moment to realise what had happened. Then he scrambled to his feet, ran his fingers through his shiny blond hair and sat down.

'No need to be so upset,' he muttered, 'just being friendly.'

'I'm not upset. Do you think I pay attention to drunks? Now, tell me what happened.'

Her manner seemed to sober him up and he took a moment to collect himself.

'Shouvaloff invited me to visit the Finance Office at PetroMax, to look through their books with him.'

'What has he got to do with PetroMax? He's a hotel enterprise magnate.'

'He says he works for 'The Mogul'.'

'Mogul? This is not middle history! There is no Genghis Khan!'

He shrugged and rolled his eyes, 'Sister, this is the New World of Enterprise! Of course there are Moguls in Chechenia, and in Russia and Kazakhstan.'

She bridled at the patronising manner but kept her temper in check, appreciating that he had information which was useful.

'So, what have you arranged?'

'I am going with him tomorrow morning.'

She moved to the door and held it open.

'I will be coming with you. Do not leave without me.'

He held his hands up and swayed his way to the door. 'Okay. Okay.'

She pushed him out and locked the door. She heard him moving erratically along the corridor.

She got into bed and slept instantly.

CHAPTER 12

The van was a grey Mercedes Sprinter. Its number plate was foreign, and Ballantyne supposed it was Romanian. Kasurov tossed the keys to him and he got in behind the wheel. It was left-hand drive, and for a moment James needed to adjust himself to the controls.

'Is a problem?' The keen eyes of the Romanian watched as Ballantyne settled in and started up. James said nothing but pulled away into the silent main road. The route took them north out of Hackney and up towards the M1. As soon as he was settled behind the wheel, Ballantyne took a moment to see who was travelling with him. Apart from Kasurov, sitting beside him, he could see through the open hatch that there were two other men in the back. There was no load, so they were going to collect something. Ballantyne fumed to himself. He was already outside the network of the department and in open breach of his promise, given only days before, to report his progress. Worse still, he had no backup or equipment, not even a mobile or a weapon on any kind.

'Up the river without a paddle' came into his mind, but strangely he felt an exhilaration from being outside the limits of the FCO and back on his own. They travelled as far as the junction with the M1, then Kasurov indicated they needed to turn off into a lay-by where a roadside café in a trailer was set up. The sign read 'Fill up B4 M1' and a thin column of steam spiralled up into the air from the spout of a narrow chimney. There was a big twelve-wheeler parked a short distance from the café. Kasurov indicated they should park nearby. There was just one other car in the lay-by and it was at the far end of the space.

'Good boy! Now you go have tea, English! Enjoy!'

He slapped James on the shoulder and pushed him in the direction of the tea shack. There were two men leaning against the drop-down counter, and James nodded to them.

'What's it to be, my love?' The tea lady, wrapped in an old ski jacket, leant over a large aluminium teapot and grinned at him. He pointed to a mug and she poured the dark brown tea and pushed the milk bottle along the counter towards him. One of the men grinned and nodded in the direction of the twelve-wheeler.

'Collecting passengers?'

Ballantyne put on a blank face; he knew perfectly well what the man meant, but had no idea if Kasurov was collecting immigrants or not. He said nothing, but shrugged.

'Better not, my son, Immigration have this road sewn up and you'd never get a hundred yards down the road.'

Ballantyne blew into his tea and shrugged again. 'I'm just a driver, not my business.'

'Don't do it,' the café lady leant forward and hissed in his ear, 'they's round the corner by the old pub!'

Ballantyne looked towards the big truck and saw Kasurov talking to the driver. He left his tea and strolled down to join them. The driver looked at him and stopped speaking. His dark skin and black eyes scanned Ballantyne for a moment.

The Romanian spoke quietly to him and the man turned away, as if to hide his face from a stranger.

'You need to know, Immigration are down the road towards London, just about four hundred metres away.'

'So what? Is no problem for me!' Kasurov's lips curled in a dry smile.

'Okay, just thought I should tell you.'

'Good boy! Smart thinking! I like that.' He turned to the other driver and pointed to Ballantyne. As far as he could make out, he was explaining who James was and the other man looked back at him with a stare. Ballantyne nodded to him as a greeting. The man did not acknowledge it. The two men motioned Ballantyne towards the back of the giant lorry and the driver began to unseal the rear door, which was securely locked. By this time the two men from the van had joined them, and they stood apart looking along the road in each direction. Nothing could be plainer than that they were sentries, to protect and warn the team as they unloaded whatever was in the container.

At a signal, James brought the Sprinter van round to the back of the lorry. He could see inside as the men pulled heavy boxes out of the load and began to transfer them to the van. When he joined in he was unable to tell what the markings meant, but each box was heavy and covered in some waxy material which he recognised as typical military dampproof protection.

'Enough!' Kasurov held up his hand as they shifted a sixth box into the van. There were many more inside the lorry container and as far as Ballantyne could tell, they were all the same size.

'Now you go to depot,' he pronounced it *depott*, 'with GPS.' He handed an over an envelope and a Garmin route finder; Ballantyne placed them on the dashboard.

'Who comes with me?' His instincts signalled danger as he got into the cab.

'You good boy, no need for company, I trust you.'

It was obvious he was being set up as a patsy. Here, within a mile of the motorway and with the knowledge that Immigration officers were in range, and maybe Customs, he was being sent on a delivery with unknown merchandise. There was nothing he could do except go on or run for it. For a wild second, he contemplated driving away and jumping out as soon as possible, but he reckoned his chances were poor. What really nagged him was that he would be throwing away what chance had given him to penetrate Sala's operation.

He got in without a word and switched on the GPS.

The voice of the refined lady, 'Turn right and in two hundred yards, join the main road,' made him laugh out loud; the contrast between her calm manner and his hazardous position was too ridiculous. A glance in the rear mirror showed up the lights of the car which he had seen parked in the lay-by.

As predicted, just past the pub was a blue van with no markings. He drove on expecting to be flagged down any second, but nothing happened. This raised his temperature; why did the patrol ignore him? A long way behind him, he made out the sidelights of a car following him.

Was it the same car from the lay-by? It was too dark to be certain, but dawn was breaking and soon he would be able to identify it. He travelled on for several miles without incident until he reached a roundabout near the North Circular. The traffic had increased and, just as he left the junction, a white car flagged him down, pointing to the near side of the road.

This is it, he thought, *Muggins in the middle! When this gets back to Melford, I'll be in deep shit!*

The Customs officer took his time getting out of the car, in the traditional ponderous way. He came round to the driver's side and leant on the open windowsill.

'Morning! Had a nice drive?' His voice was pitched as if just repeating a useless formula. 'Will you step out of the van please.'

Ballantyne nodded and got out, leaving the door wide open. By this time a second Customs man had appeared and stood next to James as if to guard him.

'Mind if I examine your load?'

'Not much choice, I reckon.'

'Spot on, *sir*!' The title was not a sign of respect.

The three walked round to the back of the vehicle and Number One opened the doors. He pulled out a heavy box and dumped it on the ground. With a Stanley knife he slit through the waxy outer wrapping and tore open the sacking interior. Ballantyne was as curious as the others to look inside. With some difficulty, the first officer fished inside and pulled out a brown paper parcel. It was about ten inches long and six wide. The paper was a thick greaseproof type, and it took some time to tear it loose. Inside was a large book – a Russian/English dictionary.

'What the hell?' He fixed his gaze on the heavy book and threw it on the floor, his eyes narrowed. 'Where have you come from?'

Ballantyne kept a straight face with difficulty.

'I collected them near the M1 and was told to deliver them as per.'

The second man jumped inside the van and began to attack the other boxes with his knife. It was hard work. More heavy books – this time hardback Russian textbooks on mathematics.

The men avoided Ballantyne's eyes and threw the first one back into the van.

It was time to have some fun,

'Hey! What am I to tell the guv'nor about the mess you've made?'

'Tell 'im what you fackin'-well like.' The veins in Number One's throat stood out like thick cords, and he slammed the rear doors and walked stiffly back to the car.

'Can I tell 'im you're sorry?' A parting shot drew no reply as the car moved off smartly.

It was light by this time, and within a minute Kasurov drew up in an old Volvo; it was the car from the lay-by.

The man beamed. 'Good joke, Hein? We have big laugh at fackin' Customs!'

Ballantyne assumed an indignant pose.

'You set me up, you bastard! You knew they would pick on me.'

'Calm down English, what harm? You done good and earned your pay!'

'Too right! Gimme the cash and let me go.' He held out his hand as if expecting payment at once.

'Look, they chased you and we got away! What is better?'

Ballantyne frowned.

'We moved the stock after you gone with the Customs in chase of you!'

The role he had played was clear now, and at once Ballantyne realised he had earned enough trust to get inside the network if he played his hand skilfully. He turned away as if to reflect on his situation.

Kasurov spoke to him. 'Come back to our place and I'll see you looked after. You're a good boy!' and he patted James on the shoulder like an affectionate father.

Well I'm in, but this was not the plan! What do I tell Melford?

There was plenty of time to reflect as they drove back to North London, but no simple answer occurred to him. He was in deep but without back up; on his own again.

CHAPTER 13

The four men in the back of the van were celebrating as Ballantyne drove back to Hackney. The success of the trip sent them into a rowdy drinking mood. From time to time a hand passed through the partition to offer booze, but James pushed it aside.

'Good boy!' Kasurov, sitting beside him, nudged him and took the bottle himself. 'You should have been with us when we raided the Serbs in Kosovo! God! What a show!'

'Why, what was special?'

'We were paid in dollars and had as much choice of women and stuff as we wanted!'

He paused as if to taste the experience once again, then he turned to Ballantyne, his eyes red with tears.

'My friend, that was the great time! Now we are flunkies of the Moguls and what freedom do we have?'

Ballantyne said nothing. Kasurov paused again and took a long pull at the bottle; he looked ahead and said nothing more, but his red lips quivered, and Ballantyne made a mental note of his sudden changes of mood and merciless character.

At his house, the men were detailed to unload the heavy boxes, while he and James went inside. He took out a cash box from a wall safe and thumbed off six fifty-pound notes.

'Here you go! You want more work?'

Ballantyne grinned and nodded.

'Here!' Kasurov opened a drawer in the desk and handed him an old Nokia phone.

'Old ones – best, you have our contact number in it – if a problem you junk it, okay?'

'When will you want me?'

'Soon. You got passport?'

'No,' James lied.

'No problem, we go to Constanza, long drive, and I get you passport, next week.'

Ballantyne took the money and the phone, and left. His Yamaha was still parked in a motorcycle bay with others. He decided to motor north in case he was followed and gunned the bike through the streets till he was sure of clearance, then made his way down the North Circular back into town and to Whitehall, musing on how he could explain his lack of contact with Melford. It was three o'clock by the time he arrived and the gatekeeper took one look at him and waved him down. James's unshaven face and dirty jeans made him look like the greasiest courier in London.

'No bikes in here, mate, only authorised vehicles. Take your bike round to the front and deliver there.'

He realised that without ID he had no credibility, so he parked at a bay in Birdcage Walk and walked back to the main gate. Within a few minutes, a young girl had arrived and after a good look at his grubby appearance led him through to the corridor to Melford's office.

On the way, he rehearsed what he would say to alleviate the storm which could break over his head, but when he reached the office, the door stood open and Melford was speaking on the phone. He motioned for James to sit and finished his call. He put his head in his hands and James waited to see what would happen.

'Okay,' Melford sighed and looked up, 'where have you been?'

Ballantyne was taken aback by the mildness of the query. He recounted the events of the last few days and the prospect of the journey to Romania. Melford smiled – James had never seen this phenomenon before.

'Okay, then you will need a back story. Go down to Personnel and get one.'

James slipped out of the chair to make a quick getaway.

'But don't bloody well keep out of sight again. Understood?'

In the basement, they gave him an NI card in the name of James Kelly, a reference from an Irish haulier and a bogus HGV licence. He turned down a passport since he expected a false one from Kasurov, which would provide evidence against the gang.

It was an early spring day. As he walked out into Green Park he felt the warmth of the afternoon sun. The early blossoms on the chestnut trees and the magnolias in the park gave a boost to his sense of freedom. He did not expect a call from Kasurov for some days, and the FCO had okayed his mission. All he hankered for was a touch of Ocksana to make life feel good. He longed to speak to her, but knew the Nokia in his pocket was out of bounds. He had lost the SIM card of his old phone when he set off going north with the Romanian crew. He walked into Victoria and found a money exchange booth, they always had a payphone for international calls.

He dialled her number and, after a short pause, he heard a soft 'Hello?' Her voice, but spoken with much caution.

'My darling!' He couldn't restrain himself, even though he knew how important it was to be discreet on an open line.

'Is it you?' Such a silly response, but still it sounded wonderful.

'Are you still at home?' He hoped she would understand he meant Moscow.

'No, my love, I am away for a few weeks but ring me after six o'clock UK time.'

He realised at once that she was in an awkward situation, and closed down the conversation.

'Okay, later.'

It sounded brutal but he knew it to be necessary. Thankfully, any trace would be useless. He went back to his Yamaha and rode into Soho, Chinatown, to be among the crowds. It was better than being alone. He had given up his flat in Battersea before setting out for Kazakhstan. He needed a flop house to stay in without trace for a few days till he set out for Constanza. One of the seedy hotels near Victoria station fitted the bill.

'How many nights?' A thin woman with peroxide blond hair came to the door. She hardly glanced at him, but took the cash for a week and wrote a receipt on a piece of paper.

'Baths are free but we lock up at midnight.'

He said nothing, and was shown a room about twelve feet square with a television and a window looking out onto the back garden. It suited him. He could get out and back easily if needed.

Two days of boredom followed. He went out each day at eight in the morning, just as a working man would do, and came back about seven. He spent the day in the library nearby, reading up on Constanza, or in the research section of FCO but that meant a chance meeting with Melford, so he tended to restrict visits to late afternoon.

Then on the third day, Kasurov rang.

'Hey, English! I need you. Okay to meet?'

'Sure, where and when?'

'Come to Hackney like normal.'

'How long will the trip be?'

'Two weeks max – come tonight, okay?'

Ballantyne agreed and put together his things. He had no weapons and thought about going back to Personnel for a gun, but two things prevented it. Firstly, the documentation, forms and permissions in triplicate; and secondly, it would be more convincing if he was armed by the Kasurov gang themselves. But he walked into Victoria and bought a Scout sheath knife from a second-hand shop; it felt good.

By eight o'clock that evening he had parked his Yamaha at a different location near a police station and went to the house where the party had been. He did not believe that it was Kasurov's pad since he was a shrewd man, but it was obviously his meeting place.

Ivan the bearded minder opened the door and gave him a bear hug of welcome. He smelt of sweat and garlic, reminding James of days in Kazakhstan, where he had got used to the tang of unwashed bodies. The hall seemed full of equipment: rucksacks and cooking kit, plus some camouflaged sleeping bags. Kasurov was in the kitchen with three other men. Two of them were gang members he had seen before but the third man was a stranger.

Something about this man stirred a memory in Ballantyne's mind, but he could not place him. His dark, mid-European face with its distinctive curved nose gave him the air of a Janissary fighter from the Ottoman empire. With his piercing eyes and long black hair pulled back from the face he looked like an angry eagle. There were two gold rings in his ears and others on his fingers.

'This is English!' Kasurov waved his hand at Ballantyne, and then at the third man. 'He is Bilan – a bad man, a gypsy!' He laughed and the gypsy twisted his lips into a half-smile: he said nothing.

'So, what's the plan?' James ignored the gypsy's stare.

Kasurov called in Ivan and explained the trip. They would take it in turns to drive across Belgium and through Germany to Constanza, and get instructions from Sala when they got there. Pay was mentioned but he told them the usual arrangement would be made. Ballantyne decided to leave that till later, since the others did not raise a query about it.

'What are we taking across?' Ballantyne raised his eyebrows.

Kasurov grinned. 'No worries, we pick up our stuff in Hungary!' He laughed and placed an affectionate arm around the gypsy's shoulders. 'Let's load up and go!'

Boris and James picked up some gear and went out to the tall Mercedes Sprinter van outside. It was not the same vehicle they had used to offload the bulky crates from the lorry. To his surprise, the cargo space was empty except for some sling benches attached to the side panels; much like the interior of a personnel carrier in the army. There were no windows but some ventilation panels set in the roof. The other men followed, with Kasurov and the gypsy taking the front seats. James took a good look at the others in the back. Ivan he knew by now, but the other two were strangers. They had that scuffed, battered look of mercenary soldiers who have seen bloodshed many times. They dozed against the canvas straps which held the seats, accustomed to the swaying of the van as it moved. Neither spoke but Ivan chatted to Ballantyne over the noise of the motor.

'You bin to Dacia?' He meant Romania.

'No, but visited Kazakhstan once, not too far away!'

The big man scoffed, 'Listen, my friend, Dacia is paradise to compare with Kazak. The women!' He made a swirling gesture which needed no interpretation, 'You wait!'

He made no response except a nod and a smile. Despite his caution, he had a soft spot for the big man, whose simple mind was far below the cunning brutality of the others.

At Dover, Kasurov handed him his passport. It was Romanian. His name was Petr Vasilli.

The photograph was not him but a nondescript dark-faced man who stared defiantly at the camera.

A mugshot from some Roma police file, I expect.

The formalities took the usual hour before they could board the ferry, then the men bought crates of Budva and vodka and sat in the bar. Ballantyne took one bottle then found a spot to sleep nearby.

Once landed, they set off with Bilan the gypsy driving, and changed every three hours or when they stopped for fuel. Ballantyne's turn came as they drove through Austria and stopped outside Vienna for meals and a short rest.

By the evening of the second day, they turned off the motorway at a town called Gyor and parked outside a warehouse on the outskirts of the town. The crew from the back of the truck jumped out like boys on a school holiday. Ballantyne felt the same after the many hours of ceaseless movement. They swarmed into a café/brasserie and took over, grabbing bottles from the counter and shouting cheerfully at the old woman who stood petrified behind the counter. The night was a long one. To keep a clear mind, Ballantyne kept to vodka, largely watered down, while the crew drank on. Bilan, he noticed, watched the others as he drank round for round with them yet he showed no sign of the drunken antics of the others.

At one point, he stood up and began to dance, a slow foot-tapping dance, and soon the whole room began clapping and singing a strange ancient song in a language James did not recognise.

His manner was calm and arrogant and he performed as if he commanded the crowd; almost a demonstration of native pride. The men shouted for him to continue when he finished, but he sat down and took to his bottle once again.

By seven thirty the following morning, they were roused and pushed into the van for the crossing into Romania. No one apart from Ballantyne, Bilan and Kasurov was in any state to notice that they passed through the customs barrier with just a wave, although it was evident that Kasurov had oiled a few palms to get through.

The Romanians gave a rousing cheer as they woke and realised they were in their native country. Bilan showed no pleasure; James realised very well that gypsies were reviled here, probably for good reason.

'We bypass Bucharest,' said Kasurov, 'but it's still a long way to Constanza.'

'What's the plan?' Ballantyne looked at him with an innocent glance, although he was keenly interested in the events to come.

The big man shrugged, 'You'll find out when we get there.' He said no more and it was not James's idea to push for an answer.

Two hours later, they drove off the motorway into a quarry which Bilan knew, and set up zeroing their weapons. He spoke to James for the first time.

Pointing to the sniper rifles, he said, 'You had one of these before?'

'Not this model, the English version.'

His dark eyes lit up. 'You army?'

Ballantyne nodded, 'But a long time ago.'

The gypsy waved his hand, 'Still, good lessons will last, no?'

He set up a makeshift stand out of a log and some blocks of wood, then jammed his rifle into the blocks. As he began to zero in, James could see the process was primitive. For his own weapon, he found a sturdy tree where he jammed the stock firmly but with enough space to adjust the back and front sights easily. Then he placed a target at two hundred yards and began his adjustments. The sound of ranging shots and curses came from the area where Bilan worked; it was obvious he was having trouble trying to adjust the sights.

Nothing was said as Ballantyne continued his ranging shots, adjusting the sights as the shot struck the target. When satisfied, he put three bullets into the centre of the target. After a short while, the gypsy came over and watched him. He nodded with approval and shrugged.

'Maybe this is better system. You look at mine?'

James was surprised by the admission of failure from a man who prided himself on his expertise in this area. With a nod, he took the other sniper rifle and repeated the procedure.

Bilan took the rifle and offered a cigarette.

'No thanks, no trouble. Both okay now.'

'Come to tavern with me tonight when we stop in Krakow. I speak with you.'

It was plain that not everyone was following Kasurov's plan. He looked forward to the rendezvous with some curiosity.

CHAPTER 14

Kasurov called a meeting that afternoon and began by handing out bundles of Euros. Ballantyne looked at his share; it was 500 Euros.

'This is your starter. We need to finish the job to get your bonus.'

One of the Eastern Europeans was grumbling and looking at the others for support.

'Maybe we get in too much hot trouble for these wages.'

A look from the Romanian was enough to suppress the protest.

'You signed up to me, and you stay with me!'

He paused to look round the group; no one spoke. He brought out a map. It was an area of country with Constanza at the centre. He had ringed an area outside the city itself.

'This is the target, his name is Ashken.'

The gypsy snorted, 'A fracking Russian! What he do in Romania?'

Kasurov shrugged. 'Who cares? We get paid by results and ask no questions.'

While the briefing was going on, Ballantyne wrapped the stock of his rifle, the adjusters and the scope with gaffer tape. He was not going to be caught by fingerprints. When the hit was over he would strip off the tape. Bilan noticed this and raised an eyebrow, but said nothing.

Kasurov detailed three of the men to be backup and allocated Bilan and Ballantyne for the kill.

'Who will ID the target?'

'Trust me. I have the job of meeting him and choosing the spot.'

James felt sick at the prospect of a cold kill. He had killed before but never in cold blood. For him, there was a great difference between a shot in a firefight and this. He had to find a way to avoid the fatal shot.

He said, 'Why are we doing this? I like to know why I do things.'

The gang leader turned a puzzled face towards him and paused for a moment.

'You are a problem English, you ask too many questions...'

'No! I need to know what I'm doing. I kill for a reason, not just on orders.'

Kasurov took another moment to consider, then he said, 'Ashken is trying to bilk our boss and moving into Romania, so **** wants him removed.'

That was enough in Kasurov's mind to justify the assassination.

They made their final move to a location about five kilometres from the target, a stone farmhouse with a walled enclosure. It had a driveway about a kilometre long which snaked up through trees to the high walls. It made an effective fortification.

'I will meet Ashken to discuss drug supplies and other matters, and that will give you the ID. You must find the spot for the shot after I've gone.'

'We have to set up inside his property?' Ballantyne could not disguise his dismay at the suggestion.

'You get paid well for a hit, so earn your pay!'

James looked at the gypsy, who merely shrugged. There was little more to be said. He felt obliged to follow the other's lead on this. He went to the van and took off his scope, leaving the rifle behind, and joined Bilan behind the vehicle.

'What do you think of his plan?'

Bilan looked sideways at him. 'Why not go and blast him tonight? I know the man and can do it with infra-red, easy.'

This was a startling new piece of information for James. Normal precautions dictated that men recruited for this type of operation were unknown to the target. The risk of double-cross was reduced in that way.

'We have trouble with Kasurov if we do that.'

Bilan paused for a second, but just one second, 'What we do is the job he is paying. Why he complain?'

'Yes, but it's not his plan. I mean, he will want some explanation why we did it tonight.'

The gypsy gave James a stare which looked straight through him. 'To hell with Kasurov. I am not his servant, I am Bilan, and I work for many but no one tells me what to do. I do it right.'

Ballantyne thought quickly. They had to infiltrate after dark in any case. 'Well, if you reckon you can take the shot, that's up to you.'

Bilan's eyes creased into a thin smile. 'It's good.' He took his rifle and began to strip it carefully.

Just after twilight they set off on foot for the farm. Ballantyne took his scope with night sight and was pleased that he had managed to avoid the dilemma of taking the shot. If he had been obliged to take it, he would have fired to miss, which would arouse suspicion and possibly expose their position. It took half an hour to reach the perimeter of the farm. At the gate there was no guard but they could see the laser alarm was in operation. They skirted the fence for about a kilometre and found themselves above the farm, about a kilometre away. James snipped the barbed wire and waited for any alarm. Nothing happened, so they dropped down inside the wall and waited.

After a few minutes they moved forward, but froze as the sound of an engine cut the stillness of the air. A quad bike was roaring down the track running inside the wall. The man riding it used a searchlight, swinging it from side to side as he approached their spot. Then he cut the engine and the light. Ballantyne saw he was using a night scope to scan the area. After a few minutes, he used his intercom and then set off back the way he'd come.

They found a spot which suited them. It was above the house, but well outside the perimeter wall which surrounded the house. Anyone could see the observation posts and defensive positions; well set up to cover every arc of fire. Bilan made himself comfortable, resting his rifle on his backpack. Ballantyne crept forward and settled down to take a long look at the house and surrounding buildings. The level of the house was below the top of the curtain wall, and there was no chance of observation except from their position above, which was about fifteen hundred yards away.

He set aside his night scope; the front of the house was well lit. A veranda extended along the whole façade, with several chairs and a dining table in place. A manservant was laying the main table for a meal. Candles, silverware and white linen cloth demonstrated the style of living.

'What time is it?' Bilan opened one eye and looked at James.

'Nine-thirty; looks as if they will eat soon.'

Taking his rifle, the dark man slid up to the point where Ballantyne lay. Within a few minutes a group of three stepped out onto the veranda. One was a lean, tall man wearing a yellow silk shirt and light trousers; the second was a blonde in a slim blue dress, and the third was a little fat man wearing a scruffy white suit, creased and well-worn.

Bilan nudged Ballantyne and pointed to the fat little man. James was taken aback; there was nothing to indicate he was important. Even his manner was deferential to the tall man.

By gesture, James asked, 'Are you sure?'

The sniper tossed his head in irritation and pointed again at the little man, then he adjusted the rifle and looked through the scope. He tested the wind with a blade of grass; the night was still.

Down below, the party sat in the living room area for some minutes. By chance, the target man sat side on to the sniper, which spoilt any shot. Bilan waited, never moving a muscle, his finger stroking the trigger guard. Things changed. The target man moved to the table and was supervising the servant; he was facing them and the gypsy took up position again, wrapping the sling round his shoulder to steady his aim.

Ballantyne stared as the death scene was approaching. The figures were just tiny images in his viewfinder. He had some doubt that the shot would be effective at this range; it was at least a kilometre, or more. He found himself willing the shot to miss, but his stomach tightened as the seconds passed and Bilan took aim.

The elegant man and the girl were walking towards the table as Bilan fired. The crack of the high-velocity bullet was piercing and for a split second nothing happened. Then James could see a plume of blood jet out of the little man's chest. Ballantyne cursed under his breath. His wishful thoughts were dashed; now it was too late, the work was done.

They moved at once from the position to a location further along the hill. This was standard practice in case of observation or some technical surveillance. They continued to watch the scene below. Men rushed onto the veranda, others spread out into the grounds. Someone fired a burst of automatic wildly and arc lights came on around the curtain wall.

Two women bent over the fallen man. Ballantyne knew from the position of the wound and the inert body that the shot had been fatal.

One feature stood out from the frantic scene below: the tall man, who had been just a few feet from the target, stood up squarely and peered out into the night. He showed not the slightest fear and seemed to challenge them to shoot.

'Who is he?' Ballantyne asked.

'A stupid prick. Come, let's get out of here.'

James kept the image of the man in his mind. He felt he would see him again.

CHAPTER 15

Petrovax Corporation was more than a petrochemical conglomerate. The appointment at ten the following morning was scheduled by Shouvaloff, but Ocksana realised they would be dealing with some of the top enterprise executives in Chechnya. Her research had found the links between several major scientific and industrial enterprises amalgamated within that corporate name.

She met Bashlivi in the hotel lobby. He was smartly dressed, but she noticed that he seemed more subdued than usual, which she assumed was a relic of the episode the night before. A chauffeur was waiting for them and drove them to the main office across the centre of Grozny.

Bashlivi broke the silence.

'I have no idea who the 'Mogul' is. I tried to find out last night but everyone seems very cagey about it.'

'What do you mean, 'cagey'?'

He shrugged, 'I mean evasive. It is not a name to use in public. There is something mysterious about him.'

She made no comment; the whole enquiry into the accounts of Petrovax was fraught with political dangers, and more than once she had suspected they were being used for some indirect purpose, different from the overt goal.

As they crossed the city, the contrast between the older buildings and the few ultra-modern commercial blocks stood out starkly. The infrastructure, roads and transport services reminded her of Soviet times in Russia. Horse-drawn carts and battered vehicles filled the streets and clogged the traffic. The limousine blared its way through the crowds like a warlord through a mob of slaves, giving no quarter to anyone, old or young. The crowd parted as it passed and the two Russians flinched at every near miss. Within twenty minutes they had crossed the city and arrived at the gleaming tower of Petrovax Corp.

Shouvaloff was there to greet them. He smiled, and Ocksana noticed for the first time that he seemed nervous, as if anxious to make a good impression or aware of some obscure tension.

'Glad to see you!' He exchanged courtesies and led them to a suite of offices on the first floor.

Sitting at a large leather-topped desk was a man about fifty years old. His hair was a shade of intense black, obviously dyed, and he wore a beard to match. He looked down his nose at the two visitors without saying a word.

Shouvaloff introduced them and the big man nodded, but remained silent. He motioned for them to sit in front of his desk and continued to examine them silently. Ocksana returned his stare, but Bashlivi began to shuffle his papers and fidget.

Then the man spoke. 'I am told you have come to examine the accounts of the petrochemical industry.'

He measured his words as if they were valuable items to be received with care.

Ocksana nodded. 'We have been tasked to verify the asset value of the various companies within the petrochemical industry. Moscow has a substantial interest in the welfare of your economy and we mean only to confirm the fundamental figures.'

'And how do you intend to do so?'

Boris spoke up for the first time. The man behind the desk turned towards him slowly, like a cannon traversing towards a target.

'We have a prepared investigation to submit to the main accountancy departments...' he began.

'Who gave you such authority?' The man stood up and placed his hands on the desk. They reminded Ocksana of two lumps of wood. Bashlivi shrank into his seat.

'I believe Madame Brod of the Economic Audit Authority had arranged this...' his voice began to falter, 'or am I mistaken?'

He looked desperately at Ocksana. She held up a hand.

'We would not have set out from Moscow without the necessary authority. Please check with your Chef de Cabinet.'

'Shouvaloff, did you arrange this pantomime?'

Wondering how the manager of a hotel could be responsible for a protocol agreement, she looked to him for some explanation. The powerful man growled at his lieutenant and the man fumbled in his briefcase to find a document.

'It was minuted at the last finance meeting...'

'To hell with your meeting! Nobody examines our accounts without my permission!'

He pointed to the door. 'Get out, you spineless peasant!' Shouvaloff gathered his documents and made for the door. Bashlivi rose to follow him.

'Stay where you are!' The big man had resumed his seat and motioned them to sit still.

Once they were alone, his manner changed; he smiled and pulled a cigar humidor towards him. As he selected a cigar, examining it with care, he spoke.

'Do not pay attention to Shouvaloff. He is the major domo of the company. He is an apparatchik of no consequence. Tell me the real reason why you are here?'

Ocksana was the first to regain her nerves. 'We are employed by Moscow Bureau, as he said. What do you believe our role is here?'

'I don't know, but we work very well with our Russian colleagues and this visit is unexpected. Tell me who your director is.'

'Madame Brod, and indirectly Mischa Rubin.'

The name of Rubin struck a glimmer in his eye. He leant forward and spoke in a soft tone.

'Have you heard of the Mogul?'

They both nodded.

'Now you see him!' He threw back his head and shook with a rumble of laughter.

'My name is Argun Beria, I am the Mogul!' He spread out his arms in mock imitation of Jesus Christ, 'You see me in person! Rubin knows who I am.'

'What do you want of us?' Ocksana spoke bluntly, knowing they were in a perilous spot, trapped between Moscow and this Mogul. There was no room for pretence or bluff; they were in his hands.

'Suppose I told you I was your friend?' His eyes glistened with amusement. 'I could save you a great deal of time and provide you with recompense to your satisfaction. What would you say?'

She returned his gaze. 'I would say you were playing a stupid game with us.'

He roared with laughter. 'But I am enjoying this game! You see, I like you and will give you my protection.'

'What do you mean? Are we in danger here?' She realised they were enmeshed in some power game between Moscow and Chechnya, but had no idea of the rules.

'Listen,' the Mogul leant forward and fixed her with his eyes. 'Understand me, I want you to have access to everything you want, but you will be accompanied by my associate, not Shouvaloff.'

'So be it, when can we start?' She met his gaze and sat stiffly as she spoke.

'I will arrange a meeting for this afternoon, here at Petrovax.'

He sat back, slouching comfortably in his chair, and smiled. He reminded her of Tartar princes in the storybooks she had seen at school. The same expression of coldblooded malice was there.

All this while he had faced Ocksana, but now he turned to Bashlivi.

'I know who you are. You are Rubin's minion, are you not?'

Bashlivi sat up, pulling his files towards himself as if to form a barrier between them.

'I work in Mister Rubin's department, yes.'

'Tell him from me, 'The Tontine is safe'.'

Bashlivi looked blank. 'The Tontine?'

'Don't bother your mind; just tell him what I said.'

With that, the Mogul waved and they had no choice but to make an exit. He said nothing more.

Outside, there was a minute when neither of them said a word. Maybe it was relief or bewilderment at the nature of the encounter.

Bashlivi broke the silence. 'What does he mean, the Tontine?'

'I have no idea, but it means something to your boss!'

Boris shrugged. 'Well, I suppose I should tell him, but let's see what this meeting turns up. The sooner we can get back to Moscow, the better.'

For the first time, Ocksana felt a glimmer of sympathy with him. Plainly, he had no idea of the connection between the Mogul and Rubin in Moscow. He was as in the dark as she was, and there was this in common between them. She took a quick glance at him as they went back by taxi; his face was ashen and he still carried his files as if they were a shield.

Back at the hotel, she tried James's number but it was unobtainable. The dull, monotonous tone made her miserable. It was clear that he was on some covert exercise and had cut his phone contact. She realised she would have to wait till he called her.

The afternoon meeting began unexpectedly. Shouvaloff was at the office in Petrovax when they arrived.

'Have you been allocated a supervisor yet?' His question inferred he was aware of the discussion after he had been sent away from the earlier meeting.

'No, we were told to meet him or her this afternoon.'

The man pulled Bashlivi aside and spoke to him urgently. 'Make sure you record everything that happens. Moscow will want to know.'

He nodded and sat down with Ocksana to await the new arrival.

They did not wait long. A tall, slim woman approached them, smiling as if she recognised them.

'Welcome to Petrovax, I am going to help you with your survey. My name is Tamara Aliev.'

Ocksana took a long look at this lady. First impressions were not good. She wore a business suit of black with a white silk shirt and high heels. Her hair, arranged carefully in a chignon, revealed her long neck and bright earrings. There was not much about her to reveal that she was an accountancy worker. It raised suspicions in Ocksana's mind.

Bashlivi responded warmly to her greeting. He bent over her hand in an old-fashioned way, like a courtier at a reception. Ocksana pursed her lips; this was no way to behave among foreigners.

She spoke up. 'Thank you for meeting us. Please show us where we can set up our office to begin.'

The woman turned without another word and led them through a long corridor to a room with a desk and two chairs. A computer was set up at one of them.

'I hope this will be sufficient for your task.' There was a touch of frost in the air.

Bashlivi smiled. 'Of course, can we contact you when we are ready to start?'

She smiled sweetly at him. 'Just ring my number; it's on the speed dial.' She pointed to the telephone and swept out of the room.

Ocksana sniffed and set about rearranging the room.

Igor waited till she had arranged what little furniture there was to her satisfaction.

'If I set up our analysis programmes, perhaps you could have a word with Shouvaloff; he wants to chat privately with you.'

She had suspected some connection between the two men ever since they arrived, and was keen to discover what it was.

'Where will I find him?'

'He will be in the General Staff Hall, waiting for you.'

'How does he know I will be there?'

Bashlivi had trouble making eye contact. 'I promised him you would be there.'

She frowned, and paused before saying, 'Very well, I shall go immediately.'

She knew he expected a reproof but she felt it would mar the connection between them. A compatriot on her side was valuable.

The Staff Hall was a large room on the ground floor. It was a mixture of canteen and common room. Shouvaloff was standing near a window, looking out onto the main entrance hall as if expecting someone.

He caught sight of her and went to one of the seating areas, and settled down to smoke a cigar without looking in her direction. She went to a table and picked up a magazine then sat opposite him within speaking range. No one paid attention.

'Boris says you have something to tell me.'

Shouvaloff continued to light his cigar, taking time to catch the flame.

'Did you get a message in Moscow about the White Helmets?' He spoke clearly but his hands still covered his mouth as if adjusting the cigar.

Ocksana stiffened with surprise; the scrawled warning to beware of a trap with the White Helmets had slipped from her mind.

'Yes, but what does it mean?'

He leant forward so that his face was a short distance from hers; he pretended to tie his shoelace.

'You carried a message to them despite the warning. You are being monitored by the KGB.'

She sat back and looked blindly at the magazine. Her mind churned over the significance of this. Her mission to Chechnya, when she was not qualified for the job; the hostility of Madame Brod and Rubin; the strange mission to oversee the accounts of a subordinate country:

these things began to make sense. She was being set up for treachery. Moscow was moving in some cynical way to use her as a scapegoat in a propaganda exercise.

Her hands trembled slightly as they gripped the magazine.

'Why are you telling me this?'

'I have spent five years trying to save Syrian lives, and do it best from my position. And I do not want you to fall stupidly into this trap.' There was an authority which belied his usual timid manner, and she felt the weight of his words as he spoke.

He went on, 'Argun Beria is a member of the Tontine. He lives for profits and will eliminate every obstacle in his way.'

She was in the dark. 'Every oligarch lives for profit. What makes Beria different? And what is the Tontine?'

Shouvaloff sat slouched forward, as if burdened with a heavy load. The pretence of relaxation had disappeared. It was as if he was crushed by some knowledge too dangerous to conceal.

'The Tontine is a group which shares power among themselves and controls basic materials in world markets.'

'That is not exceptional. It is similar to OPEC with world oil. Many cartels control production.'

Shouvaloff engaged her eye to eye.

'This is unique,' he said, 'every time one of the group dies, the control passes to the remainders, don't you see what that means?' His eyes were bright with energy. 'There is an incentive to be the last survivor!'

Ocksana took a minute to absorb this. If Beria was with Moscow on this plan, it would mean that the elimination of Tontine members was in Russia's interest; a means of gaining control over core world industries.

'My interest in the work of the White Helmets; maybe that is against Russia's interests?'

He nodded in an exaggerated way, as if a slow student had at last grasped a simple equation.

'So you are vulnerable; you must get away!'

She stood up and turned away from him. She made no sign of farewell and went out of the room as casually as she could manage. From now on, her mood changed. She was a target.

CHAPTER 16

Kasurov looked at them for a long minute – it seemed endless.

'What the fuck you do that for?'

Bilan stared back at him. 'I took the shot. It was good. What you moan about?'

Ballantyne could say nothing. It was in direct conflict with the plan explained the night before. The simmering tension that he had expected was now near boiling point.

'Look,' he said, 'you don't need to change a thing. You go down there this morning just as you said and show your surprise. It gives you a let out.'

The Romanian squinted at him and growled. 'That may be, but now I am in danger if they think I done it.'

'Then let's go down with you and watch your back.'

There was a pause. Kasurov scratched his beard and shrugged.

'Well, you put me in this mess, you better get me out.' He pointed a finger at Bilan. 'But you, stupid gypsy, stay out of this. Understand?'

Bilan turned away and spat on the ground. Kasurov ignored the gesture.

The small group made up of Kasurov, Ballantyne and two of the mercenaries set off in the van, leaving the rest to pack up and prepare for escape. The journey took about twenty minutes. Kasurov gave no instructions, except to make sure the weapons were stowed in the undercarriage of the van. For the mercenaries, protecting their boss was routine and they needed no briefing. At the gate, this time, two armed men; they stopped and searched each of them. They made a call for instructions and after a pause, waved them through.

The long driveway followed the contours of the hill and Ballantyne drove to a point hidden from the gate. Each man collected a handgun from the container except Kasurov, who tapped his fingers on the dashboard and urged them to hurry up. James understood his feelings – going into this perilous situation unarmed – but there could be no alternative; he was bound to be searched again. The house came into sight on the crest of the hill and once again Ballantyne acknowledged the layout of the fortifications, which defied a direct attack. The only defect: it was overlooked from a distance of 1,500 yards. No one had predicted a long sniper shot.

They parked below the house and Ballantyne took the trouble to reverse into a space so that they could get away quickly if necessary. A plain-clothed sentry gave Kasurov a quick body search and led him up to the terrace above. Ballantyne and the others stayed below.

From their position in the yard, it was difficult to see what was going on. Obviously, some serious event had occurred; an ambulance and a police vehicle were parked nearby. Up above, he made out a group talking and the occasional flash of light as photographs were taken. The figure of the tall man he had seen the night before stood out among the group, and at one moment he came down the steps to speak to them. It was a chance to take a good look at him.

He was more than six feet tall and lean. His face, tanned and clean shaven. What attracted attention was his eyes. They were a clear, pale blue, almost translucent; they had a chilling effect, as if they pierced through your mind and exposed your thoughts. He studied each one of them closely. Ballantyne looked down to avoid their inspection.

'You can see a tragedy has happened here. No one need know the details. It will be in the papers that Grigor Ashken has died but nothing more. Do you understand?'

He stood in front of them and stared at each of them in turn. They nodded.

Then he smiled and his smile reminded James of the mouth of a cobra, white teeth and sharp fangs. He turned away and went back up the stairway. Even the two mercenaries showed signs of relief as he left, exchanging glances as if to seek assurance and support.

Kasurov came down the stairs after half an hour and motioned them to mount up.

As they drove away, Ballantyne glanced up at the terrace; the tall man stood watching them.

He spoke to one of the others, who fixed his binoculars on them as they went.

Kasurov sat in the cab and roared with laughter. 'Son of a bitch! That gypsy is a wizard! A clean kill from that distance! Wait till Sala hears about this!'

Ballantyne said nothing. He had put Sala out of his mind ever since this operation began. It was still unclear why Sala wanted this plutocrat killed, a man so far away at the other end of Europe. There must be some overarching scheme in place which was hidden from him at the moment; assassination was certainly part of it. The guilt he felt from last night left a sour taste that lingered on.

'Who was the tall man who spoke to us?'

'He is Emiliano Corvo, the head of Industria Ferrofabrica, a top man in Italy.'

'What's his connection with Ashken?'

Kasurov looked at him. 'Don't bother your mind about him, English, just drive.'

Ballantyne did as he was told and the journey continued in silence.

The campsite had been cleared and the crew were ready to load up. The Romanian found Bilan sitting smoking on a stump. He held out his arms to the gypsy and hugged him like a brother.

'Maestro! You are a genius! No one else could have pulled off that shot.' He kissed him.

Bilan shrugged and stepped away. 'You pay me for the job, I do it.'

Unfazed by this, Kasurov went to the van and pulled out a bottle, obviously vodka, and handed it round after taking a swig.

They left after a further check of the site and headed towards Constanza. The arrangement agreed upon was a payout at the rail station before they dispersed. On the road back, Bilan drove and kept looking in the rear mirror.

'What's the problem?' Ballantyne sensed some tension.

'Is a jeep following us.'

About four hundred yards behind, a Toyota truck had joined the road and was travelling in the same direction. Bilan slowed down and the truck slowed down too. He accelerated and the other vehicle caught up with them but stayed on station. In the back, Ballantyne was busy pulling the gaffer tape off his rifle and not paying attention to the road. His prints were not going to be found if the police ever got involved.

'Hey, English,' Kasurov called from the cab, 'keep a check on the Jeep and be ready to fire!'

The Toyota kept station with them until they reached the outskirts of Constanza, then pulled over and stopped. They saw the front passenger radioing some message.

'They are cautious guys,' said Kasurov, 'maybe they send message to others in Constanza.'

'So what we do?' Bilan quizzed him.

'Same as before, we pay up and split. They can't check on all of us.'

At the station he paid off each of them: two thousand Euros and instructions to ensure they travelled separately. The mercenaries disappeared at once, but Bilan and Ballantyne stayed with the van.

'Listen, I give you more if you burn the van and dump the weapons.'

The gypsy twisted his lips in a half smile. 'Trust you to give the shitty jobs to us. You better pay good!'

Kasurov shrugged and peeled off several fifty-euro notes. 'Keep the weapons if you want, but torch the van good.'

Ballantyne spoke up, 'What do I do when I get back?'

'What the fuck you like!'

'No, I mean, do you want me to make contact back in the UK?'

'Maybe Sala has job for you, keep the phone and ring when you get back.'

With that, he hailed a taxi and disappeared into the heavy traffic downtown.

The two sat for short while in a café by the station. They failed to see the two young men on a motorbike who trailed the taxi away from the station.

'Where shall we dump the van?' Ballantyne felt impatient with the untidy finish to the exercise. He had to report to Melford with the important information connecting Sala and his gang with the Ashken murder. A web of criminal contacts was emerging from the several incidents, and it was paramount to collate it all.

Bilan sipped his coffee. He tilted his head and half-smiled.

'You go and I take the van, no problem.'

'And the weapons?' Ballantyne sensed the truth. 'You run a big risk if they trace them.'

Bilan shrugged, 'We find a use for them, leave it to me.'

It was pointless to dispute the matter and Ballantyne let it pass. At any rate, his fingerprints would not be traced.

'Okay, I'll go and wish you luck.'

To his surprise, the gypsy stood up and hugged him, and said some words which James did not understand but which meant some blessing, then he walked away without another glance. Ballantyne put it out of his mind. Sentimentality among mercenaries was a factor he had seen in several different war zones, and seemed to apply here too.

On the train through Romania, he longed to speak to Ocksana, but he only had the mobile given to him by Kasurov. His impatience grew with every mile and by the time he reached London, the first thing he did was grab a payphone at the Eurostar Terminal and dial her number.

There was a long pause, then at last he heard her voice, faintly at first, then as the connection improved he heard her unmistakeable accent.

'My darling! How long it's been! How are you? Are you safe?'

Words poured out of her in a stream without interruption, and he laughed as he tried to reassure her that all was well. Eventually, she stopped and listened to him as he explained he was back in London and safe.

'And you, my sweet, is everything smooth?' They both knew what he meant: was she in danger or not?

'I have some problems, but can see my way to clear up within this week.'

He frowned at this. To him it meant she was engaged at a difficult moment and was unhappy.

He said, 'I'm on a payphone. Can you speak in clear?'

She gave a sigh. 'Thank God, I need to share this situation with you.'

She set out the dilemma: the conflict with the Mogul; the involvement of Rubin in Chechen affairs; and the covert purpose behind the Moscow vetting of Chechen business.

James's knuckles grew white as he gripped the handset; she was in danger and he could do nothing about it.

'Listen, can you get out of there quickly?'

She paused for a moment. 'No, if I was to run now my life would be changed forever.' Her tone took on a firmness he had heard before. 'I won't be put off; there is a mystery here and I mean to find the answer.'

He begged her to drop it and come to him in London, but her resolve never faltered.

'My darling, if I ran now I would never be happy, even though I love you with all my heart. Can you understand it?'

Her voice had a keening sincerity beyond the words themselves. He had to accept them.

He spoke of his longing and he heard the break in her voice as she swore they would be together soon. Then they broke off contact and he felt empty and alone once more.

He got a cab back to the B&B in Victoria, and paid in Euros. The driver made no protest. At the back of the B&B where he had stayed before, the Yamaha was still locked up. He felt played out, dropped onto his bed and fell into a deep, untroubled sleep.

CHAPTER 17

Morning came creeping through the small window, bringing with it the smell and noise of the busy street. For James, the familiar bustle brought him back to reality with a start. At first he dreamed he was sharing a bed with Ocksana, but footsteps along the uncarpeted corridor outside reminded him where he was.

A knock on the door brought him wide awake.

'Hello, you awake? I need some money from you.'

The skinny blonde was shouting outside and he stumbled to the door.

'You've had the room for three weeks an' you only paid for two. I kept it for you as I promised.' She looked up at him through her lashes like a girl of seventeen, posed with one hand on the doorframe and close to the door. He held it ajar and looked down at her.

'You are a doll, I had to do a rush job but was always coming back.' He smiled and kept the door between them. 'I'll be down in a minute with the cash.'

She looked disappointed, as if she had expected a different response, and went downstairs.

His clothes were grubby; he had left what he'd taken with him in Constanza. The prospect of a bath was irresistible and he wallowed in the water like a hippo. Getting back into the same clothes again was not so good, but all his kit had been left in the store room at FCO when he gave up his flat.

She was downstairs in the kitchen when he came down, and she was smoking her first cigarette of the day; the ash drooped from the fag like a grey dribble.

'Look, I got paid in Euros, so I'll have to get change.'

'Is that right?' she said, squinting at him through the smoke. 'Well, you can leave fifty with me and go up to the station, I don't mind.'

He peeled off a note from the wad he had and she eyed him with renewed interest.

'Come in for a drink when you get back.' She smiled and blew smoke out of the side of her mouth, 'I'll be waiting.'

One of the cafes in Lupus Street was open and he negotiated a hot breakfast from the Italian owner with some Euros, before visiting the money exchange inside the station. It gave him time to focus on what he could tell Melford. It was standard practice to file a written report, but he brushed that thought aside, knowing that what he had was highly important and should not wait.

Melford was in the office when he arrived. As he began to explain what he had found out, he interrupted him.

'I need to bring in Myers from the Russian desk to hear this, it affects him too.'

A few minutes later, a tall man in a shirt sleeves arrived and tapped on the open door. He saluted Melford and took a hard look at Ballantyne.

'So you're the renegade? I've been waiting to meet you.' He held out a hand and gripped James's hand tightly. 'I'm Raymond Myers.'

For the next hour they debriefed him, and Myers made copious notes as they spoke.

Ballantyne was puzzled by the introduction of someone from the Russian desk.

'I appreciate the man killed was Russian, but is that significant as far as you're concerned?'

Myers nodded, 'You see, we're getting indications of some sort of conspiracy organised by the KGB to gain control of heavy industries on a continental scale.'

'But the man was a Russian! How does that fit into the picture?'

Myers shook his head. 'I have to confess this is only a theory, but I believe there must be some other organisation competing to seize control, and they have set about eliminating Russian key players.'

'This man, Bala, he's not Russian, is he?' Melford asked. 'Maybe he is paid by another group to neutralise Russian influence?'

Ballantyne spoke up. 'I went to Romania at Bala's instructions with a team set on assassinating Ashken. It seems probable that Bala is a mercenary, paid by this other syndicate.'

Ballantyne shifted in his chair. It was becoming obvious they were lining him up for another undercover job. He thought of Ocksana and whether he could help her, but he realised there was nothing he could do if she was determined to stick with her assignment.

Melford turned to him. There was a hesitation in his voice.

'I suppose you need a bit of leave?'

'Well, I have to find another pad where I can come back to, and a rest would be good.'

'Suppose I have a word with HR and see what they can find for you? Will that help?'

James grinned. 'I had no idea Human Resources had any uses! Yes, great!'

'Take a day or two to find your feet and I'll be in touch.' Melford reached for the phone.

Within the day, James was set up in a one-room flat in Pimlico, furnished by IKEA in the uniform style beloved of civil servants. There were no personal touches and James realised this was a matter of policy. The Office kept such places clear of material which could be used to identify personnel.

He used the payphone in the station to ring Ocksana again. The connection was difficult and he tried three times before the call went though. It was the evening, and her voice was husky and sleepy.

'Hi! My darling, it's me!' He felt a fool for saying it. 'Are you asleep?'

'Yes, my sweet, I do sleep at night!' But there was a warmth to her voice which hit the spot as memories of other times flooded back.

Nothing they said had any real significance; it was the contact they wanted, not information.

After some minutes, she told him she hoped to be back in Moscow within a week and how she longed to be with him again. He knew he could not be there but made her promises which he knew he could not keep; it was better than dashing her expectations at once.

They rang off and he walked back to this new apartment, which was only ten minutes away. He found a good spot for his Yamaha and secured it.

Later that evening, he headed back to pay what he owed at the B&B near the station. He tried to persuade himself he was just paying a debt, but it didn't work. He felt the need of some female company, even if it was a skinny peroxide blonde. Somehow, in some unfathomable way, his chat with Ocksana had triggered a need which was only remotely linked to her.

He rang the bell; it was nine in the evening. She came to the door wearing a dressing gown which she held to her body. It outlined the shape of her breasts and revealed a little of her thighs.

'Hello you! Have you brought me something good?' She turned and walked back inside, glancing over her shoulder. He noticed how her hips moved as she ambled down the hall.

'Thought you might want to know, I've found a pad so won't be coming back.'

'Is that all you wanted to say?' She moved closer to him as he stood by the door of her room, looking up into his eyes. 'Tell me if there is anything else you want?'

His pulse was racing, and before he knew it he was pulling at the dressing gown, stripping her as she held her face up to be kissed. They moved in one surge to the bed against the wall and grappled in a hungry, stormy passion which was beyond control. For minutes they were locked together, immersed in a struggle which both could win. Then it subsided and they lay panting together like exhausted wrestlers. Ballantyne felt good, and all the tension of the last few weeks was lifted from his mind. Next morning, they had sex again in the dawning light; then he lay there as she slipped away and pulled on her robe.

Her image through the shower curtain brought him back to the real world. One look at the untidy squalid room and the stupidity of what he had done was enough to focus his thoughts.

What would she expect of him now? How could he extricate himself from the casual link he had made with this woman?

She came back into the room, rubbing her hair with a towel. In the morning light she looked wan and old, with grey roots showing through the damp hair. He moved to the shower and quickly washed himself as thoroughly as possible.

'I'll make some breakfast,' she said, and left him in the bedroom. He dressed quickly.

'No time,' he shouted, 'got to go – late already.'

She looked back into the room, giving him a long look; her eyes were dull with failed expectation. Her shoulders drooped and then she gave a faded smile.

'I suppose this job will take a few weeks.' She looked him in the eye; he looked away.

'I told you I got a new place.' He could think of nothing better.

She turned back into the kitchen and began to busy herself with the kettle.

'Yeah, right! You got a new place; you told me.'

He put on his shoes and went to the door leading into the hall. He put £50 on the mantelpiece and left. There was nothing more to be said.

That day he stayed in the new flat and tried to fathom a way to avoid another undercover role. He felt Ocksana needed his help. He had sufficient money, mostly in Euros, to last a few months on his own, but could not afford to break contact with the FCO completely. He still had hope of a permanent job and this stopped him from making a clean break.

Next morning brought an answer to the dilemma. His new phone rang.

'Ballantyne, Myers here. Can you come in today to see me?'

By ten o'clock he was in Myers' office, with the desk officer smiling at him like a favourite child.

'I have some good news for you! Personnel have approved your application to join permanent staff!' He held out his hand.

'Does this mean I can keep the flat?'

'Of course! And I'm happy to say they have designated you as Grade 3.'

'What does that mean?'

Myers went through the specifics of salary, pension rights and benefits in boring detail; James nodded as if he followed the rigmarole. Then he signed a document three times and sat back.

Now, the bad news, he said to himself, and he settled back in his chair to see what they meant to throw at him.

'Can I run this idea past you?' Myers was addicted to city-speak. 'Suppose we send someone to join one of the suspect groups and bring back hard facts about the conflict between the Russians and these other people? What do you say?'

Ballantyne studied his face; Myers looked as bland as a baby.

'Who exactly did you have in mind for this job?' Ballantyne narrowed his eyes and stared hard.

Myers said, 'Well, we have a few experienced operators who can do the job.'

'Experienced operators? Is that what you call men who put their lives on the line?'

The executive twitched and sat back in his seat. 'You know I didn't mean to disparage their risks, but we have to look at this in an operational way. What do you suggest?'

James leant forward and looked him in the eye.

'Why don't you try to recruit a mercenary to run the risks? Men like that will do anything if the pay is right.'

Myers raised an eyebrow. 'Do you know any such men?'

There was a hint of contempt in the question.

Ballantyne shrugged it aside. 'As a matter of fact, I know a few, but I have one particular man in mind who has no scruples about who employs him,' he paused and added, 'even the British Government.'

A frown crossed Myers' face and he adjusted his cuffs very deliberately.

'Are you suggesting we should pay a cold-blooded criminal to do our dirty work?'

The corner of Ballantyne's mouth twitched, 'Sounds dreadful doesn't it? Think of the money you might have to pay!'

Myers pressed his lips together as if he had to restrain an outburst, then he sat back and looked at Ballantyne.

'We shall have to consider this in committee. I'll let you know in due course. Meantime, see if you can make contact with this ... er ... mercenary and let me know discreetly what you can find out about him.'

Ballantyne got up and nodded. 'Leave it to me, but he is an elusive man and will need to have a hard commitment from you before he would act for us.'

Myers nodded and drummed his fingers on the desk. 'Yes, yes, I understand, but we make no move until the committee decides.'

James made a quick exit from the office. His plan to avoid another undercover job was working well, but the bonus was, he could drop out of sight for a while and help Ocksana get away from the difficulty she spoke about. That was the real task he had set himself.

Now all he had to do was find Bilan. He was the man for this job.

CHAPTER 18

The crowd inside Milan rail station swirled like a pool of disturbed water. Groups of passengers pushing their way through the crowd. Bilan sat at a café table overlooking the platforms, his dark eyes piercing the mob for his intended target.

Money had passed and his task was to bring down the young man who had violated the daughter of a Comorra boss. Nothing but elimination would do in the circumstances. He had waited for three days at the spot, following the instructions he'd been given: 10.30 train from Zurich; Carlo Zaborelli, student.

As his eye swept the concourse, he picked out the figure of the young man as he stepped from the train. His slim figure and expensive casual clothes marked him out as a 'preppi'. Bilan followed him as he left the platform and joined the pushing, clamouring mob on the general concourse. When the youth reached the densest part of the crowd, Bilan came up beside him and whispered his name in his ear, 'Don Carlo'. The boy turned and the knife slipped gently into his gut; Bilan turned away and pushed him against the wall. Nobody paid attention as the boy twisted, mouth gaping to call for help. No sound came from his lips and he slipped to the floor, head bowed like a drunken tramp.

Work done, the gypsy took a train north to Lake Garda and a room in a hotel by the side of the lake. It was a pleasant spot for a meeting, and he enjoyed the warm sunshine as it glittered off the lake.

'Is it done?' A thin-faced man in an elegant suit came and sat beside him. Bilan looked over the lake without glancing at the man.

'He felt nothing but the pain of remorse,' he said.

For the first time, Bilan looked at the man who had hired him. The order had been passed through the Comorra organisation and the money paid in advance, but he had never seen the contractor.

He knew at once who the man was; the thin man who had defied him when he took the shot that killed Ashken at the Romanian farm.

'Was she your daughter?'

The thin man looked off at the distant maintains around the lake.

'I ordered it, so make your own conclusions.'

The gypsy stared at him, fixing him with a look from his black eyes which was unmistakeably dangerous.

'I do draw my own conclusions – it's safer for me. I asked you a direct question. Why do you answer in that fashion?'

The man took a long look at him.

'Have you worked for me before? Your face seems familiar. Maybe you worked for the Comorra before?'

Bilan shrugged, 'I work for many people, I don't recall everybody I worked for.'

He turned away.

'Your face is familiar.'

'You are mistaken.'

The tall man stood up and left without a word. Bilan knew he had made an enemy, but he shrugged and lit a cheroot. Later that day he hired a car and drove overnight to Bucharest; he felt safer there. He was welcomed into the family and he disappeared into the caves around the capital, where the gypsies lived.

*

James had one lead in his efforts to trace Bilan. He recalled Ivan, the big man who kept the door at Kasurov's place in Hackney. Somehow, they had got on together, probably because he was treated like an oaf and Ballantyne was treated as an amateur: they had something in common.

He rode to the address at a time he hoped he would avoid contact with the gang, arriving at midday and watched the door from across the street. Nothing happened for more than an hour, and he wondered if the house had been abandoned. Then the door opened and the shambling figure of Ivan shuffled out into the street. James circled the block on the bike and came up beside him as he plodded down towards the self-service shop.

'Hi, man! How goes?'

The giant figure paused and beamed with recognition.

'You back in London? I got message, you finished job and gone to Ireland.'

Ballantyne shook his head and grabbed Ivan by the arm.

'Listen, I've been looking for you. Can you meet me at the café next to the off licence?'

It took a few seconds for him to register what James meant, then he nodded.

'It's okay, good. I need food!'

James rode on and parked the bike away from the café.

By the time they got there, the café was empty. As usual, their business closed when the morning rush of hungry workmen had gone. James ordered two full breakfasts to keep the cook-lady happy, and sat at a table facing the street.

They chatted while waiting for the meal. Ivan explained he was making a good living as a cage fighter and doing less for Kasurov. James told him a little about the Constanza trip.

'Do you know the gypsy, Bilan?'

Ivan roared with laughter. The table shook and the sour-faced cook glared from the kitchen.

'That bastard! Of course I know him! I fight him twice!' He went on to explain how he had been in the same circuit of bare-knuckle fighters as Bilan, before he joined Kasurov in England.

'We had good times in France and Italy before they threw us out.'

'What happened?'

Ivan shrugged his shoulders and sighed. 'Is bad trouble; a guy got killed and we were blamed.' James did not pursue the matter; he did not wish to disturb the delicate feelings of his companion.

'Can you make contact with him?'

He blew out his cheeks and rubbed his eyes. 'Maybe. I think he has girlfriend in club in London. Maybe she knows where he is. What's it for?'

James hedged, 'There's a job I can't do and I need a reliable guy.'

Ivan's eyes widened. 'You want Bilan to do a job? Listen, man, be careful, no one can trust that fackin' gypsy!'

'But if the pay is good, he'll take it, won't he?'

A shrug was all the reply he got.

'Tell me which club the girl works at, and I'll do the rest.'

'No good, I know you would never get in without me. It not open for Irish!'

Ballantyne knew at once what he meant; it was a meeting place for the members of the Balkan crime gangs, and his chance of getting in was zero.

'Okay! When can we go together?'

The big man fidgeted and scratched his chin. 'You get me rubbed out; you know, if things go wrong?'

James laid a hand on him. 'Listen, I won't go inside. You see the girl and bring her out for a rich punter, and I'll do the rest.'

Ivan threw back his head. 'Just like you, English! Poor Ivan does the donkey work and you sit on your arse! Okay, I meet you tonight at Piccadilly and I'll find the club. But you cover for me. Yes?' James nodded and they fixed a time.

'Bring plenty cash, okay?' Ballantyne nodded.

*

It was past midnight when they met. Ivan led the way to Old Compton Street, and then along a passage without a sign to some steps leading down to a green door. He signalled to James to stand away as he rapped his fat knuckles on the door panel. From the interior came the sound of gypsy music and a noisy crowd. The door remained shut. Ivan knocked again, this time with his fist; a voice shouted from the other side in some foreign language.

The big man heaved his bulk against the door and yelled. This had some effect; the door stayed shut but a slot opened in the upper section and a man peered through, into the dark outside. There was a short, loud conversation and then the door opened and Ivan pushed his way in. Ballantyne kept out of the way in the shadows.

He stayed there for about twenty minutes before anything happened. Then the door opened quietly and a slim figure slipped out. In the gloom of the basement area, all James could make out was the figure of girl with long, dark hair, about five feet five and wearing a low-cut dress.

She stood close to him and the smell of her perfume curled round him like a cloud. He could hardly make out her features in the gloom, but her eyes glittered unnaturally bright in the dim space.

'Ivan says you have a message from Bilan? How come you know Bilan?'

Ballantyne had no need to lie. 'We worked together in Romania last month. I have a job for him.'

She paused and looked back inside the club. 'Wait for me at the Roma Coffee shop after two o'clock. We can talk then.' She pulled at the door and was gone.

Ivan stayed inside, and after quarter of an hour Ballantyne left and wandered into Old Compton Street as the evening crowd thickened. That time of night was Soho time; every clubber and sightseer was on the street. Rubbing shoulders with Japanese camera geeks and tired-eyed *spielers* trying to pull unwary tourists into 'friendly' bars where they would max out their credit cards. He enjoyed the atmosphere and ate a sushi meal at a roadside stall, then as the time passed he moved to the Roma Café near the corner of the street.

The Roma Café was a landmark in Soho. Every Italian waiter and night owl within range took their last *ristretto* at the Roma. There was little space inside the cafe and the noise of shouting and laughter spilled out into the road. Late-night cars and Uber taxis had to pull round the crowd which filled the pavement and half of the road. Ballantyne waited at the edge of the mob and looked out for the girl. He was unsure if he could recognise her again.

What caught his eye was the way she stood: at the edge of the crowd, but commanding attention. She knew very well the impression she made, standing apart.

Her raven black hair was swept up onto the top of her head and she wore a bright red shawl round her shoulders. A white shirt far too large for her small frame was open at the neck and exposed the curves of her breasts. She had gold earrings and her long legs ended with high heels. She scanned the crowd and settled at last on Ballantyne.

'Get me coffee, I need pick you up,' she said, unaware of the accidental pun.

James waded through the crowd and brought back two espressos. She had found a seat outside by sheer buzzing attraction; at least four Italian men had offered her their chair. James was eyed with undisguised contempt.

'If you friend of Bilan, you tell me why he is not here with me now?' Her tone was pugnacious, and again he noticed the brightness of her black eyes. He reckoned she was still high on some upper, taken earlier in the night.

He lied, 'I left him in Romania, and he told me to say he would come back soon to the UK. But we need him now and he never leaves a contact.'

She tossed her head and turned away in anger. 'He is a stupid Balkan ape! He's with some Dacian tart and spending money like water! You want him? Pah!'

Ballantyne tried diplomacy, 'You're wrong, he talks about you all the time but he has to protect his family too.'

She turned back to face him. 'What he say about me?'

James did a quick check on suitable lies, and chose. 'He says he wants to settle here when it's quieter.'

She rolled her eyes, 'You must be the most stupid peasant in Britain! You believe that Roma?'

He looked down but said nothing.

Eventually he said, 'Well, we need him anyhow.' He looked up at her sideways as if he accepted her opinion and was apologetic.

She sipped her coffee and looked away for a minute, then she got up and told him to follow her; he obeyed. They walked down the road for some yards until they were well clear of the crowd. She stopped and lit a cigarette and looked him in the eye.

'Ivan says you pay me like a job.'

He nodded. 'How much?'

'Two hundred,' she said, without a blink of the eye.

'I've only got one-fifty.' He reckoned she was squeezing the lemon a bit too hard.

'Okay. Give it to me.' She looked down the road, as if bargaining was distasteful.

'What do I get for that?'

'I contact the family and will get you a number to ring.'

Ballantyne frowned. 'When do I get the information?'

She tossed her head and ran her fingers through her glossy black hair; her gold earrings danced wildly. She laughed and he felt the tang of her appeal.

She said softly, 'You'll never know, if you don't pay.'

Her eyes searched his to watch the effect she had upon him. He felt helpless; she was the only lead to reach Bilan, so he had no choice but to give in. He said nothing but handed over the roll of notes.

'Write your number here.' She indicated her wrist and he did so. She looked back as she disappeared into the night and waved to him. He felt a fool, and wondered what Melford or Myers would say.

CHAPTER 19

It was a chance Ocksana had to take. Her future security had been compromised by the bogus task she had been given in Chechnya. Now she faced to one woman who might help her or betray her.

Tamara Alieva confronted her with furrowed eyebrows and narrow eyes.

'Tell me what the problem is?'

In a few sentences, Ocksana outlined her suspicions about the task she and Bashlivi had to carry out and the fact that 'The Mogul' had made it clear he intended to neutralise the enquiry.

Alieva leaned back and scrutinised her.

'What you are implying is you believe most of us here are involved in the 'Tontine Scheme''

'Nothing is more obvious now that Beria has shown his hand.'

The tall woman got up and went to the window. For a few seconds she said nothing, then she turned and said;

'What you say is near the truth. When I heard of the audit enquiry from Moscow into our affairs, I began my own scrutiny of the books of Petrovax. It became obvious who pulled the strings and Russia still held power indirectly through its collaborators.'

'What can we do?' Ocksana felt a vibration of sympathy and wanted to exploit it.

'Maybe you should report your concerns to Moscow?'

'Impossible! Rubin is in league with Beria --he told me outright!'

Alieva shut the door to the control room where she had been working.

She looked through the glass panel to see how much attention was being paid to them; no one was watching.

'Look, I have no authority here but I do have inside knowledge of what goes on. You and Bashlivi are not going to find anything!'

She watched for the reaction.

A faint frown passed over Ocksana's face.

'I must tell you, I have helped the White Helmets and Moscow policy has turned against them, so I am under surveillance.'

The tall woman looked keenly at her.

'You realise that you will be subject to demotion and perhaps put on trial?'

Ocksana nodded; her bid for sympathy seemed misplaced.

Tamara bit her lip; 'I can see no other way but to send in a report whitewashing the enterprise. You have no chance of revealing the truth and a clean bill of health is what the Tontine will want.'

Wide eyed, Ocksana stared at the woman.

'But that will make me an accomplice and Bashlivi too!'

'You think you can expose Beria and his colleagues without reprisal?'

She shook her head as if speaking to an innocent child. 'Where do you think you are? In some American Netflix series? This is Chechnya and real life!'

Someone knocked at the door and Alieva went outside. As she left, she paused at the door and said, 'Do it now and get out !'

The door closed with a defining click.

It was not difficult to find Bashlivi. Boris had installed himself in the poky office they had been allocated and was deep into one of the files which had been sent up to them.

'I have some problems in loading the discs,' he explained 'and I need better copying facilities. This is not good enough.'

He looked like a peevish schoolboy deprived of his favourite toys.

'Never mind,' Ocksana had made up her mind 'We will manage.'

Bashlivi ran his hands through his hair. 'We'll never finish at this rate--look at the files!'

She put a hand on his shoulder and gently pushed him back into his seat. Then she sat beside him.

'Boris, you work for Rubin and you know his connection with 'The Mogul.' You have misunderstood your task here.'

Bashlivi fidgeted as he looked at her.

She went on, 'We both know The Tontine operates with Rubin in some way so we are pawns in their game. We must save ourselves.'

He slumped and seemed to shrink a little. 'Save ourselves?'

'Yes, we have to give Petrovax a clean bill of health!'

'But we have seen nothing yet! How can we do it?'

'Somehow, we have to find a way to close this down and get out of here!'

There was sufficient edge to her voice to penetrate the stupor affecting him. He sat rubbing the back of his neck for a minute; he said nothing but just stared at the ground. Then he looked up directly into her eyes.

'You knew all along it was a whitewash, didn't you?'

'You're wrong! But I do know if we don't sign of these accounts we are never going to get out of here!'

He nodded, he seemed older and defeated. 'What must we do?'

'Well, I look to you! Can you put together a Report based on leading files of company Accounts?'

'I can adopt the major Reports on file into a consolidated Summary but will that do?'

'It will have to do! If I am right, no one will question what we say. It's what they want to hear!'

Within a day, Boris had put together an impressive document based solely on published Accounts and Reports certified by Chechan Central Bank.

Ocksana brought it to Alieva's office.

The two women looked each other in the eye; Ocksana defiant. The Chechana took the Report with twisted smile and gave it a brief inspection. It took all of half a minute.

'This seems satisfactory; I will pass it on to Mister Beria at once.'

They parted without another word.

The handover had a cathartic effect on Ocksana. She felt liberated and relieved.

Even though she had just carried out a massive deception, her heart felt light and her conscience clear. She was surrounded by corruption and had been innocently co-erced to play a role in a massive lie.

What mattered to her was the knowledge that she had pulled away the mask of trickery that concealed the Tontine Scheme, at least as a far as the Russians were concerned.

She rang Tamara Alieva the next day to check that the two could return to Moscow.

'Of course! The Report has been approved and you can take a countersigned copy back to Moscow with you. We are most gratified.'

They boarded an Aeroflot that afternoon. Delivered to the airport was a sealed copy of the Report and a large bunch of flowers.

'With the Respect of the People of the Chechen Republic.'

CHAPTER 20

What do you mean, you got away?'

James's tone was a mixture of irritation and puzzlement as he took her call.

'We were set up – we were sent to Chechnya to whitewash a Russian deal!'

'Hang on, darling! I have to get up to speed on this. Who are we?'

Ocksana stopped in mid-sentence. She took a deep breath and began again, realising that James had been out of touch for more than two weeks.

By the time she had explained her account, the battery on her phone was tired out and they agreed to ring later on Moscow time, to decide what to do.

Ballantyne had heard enough to appreciate she had been set up by some Russian group with a clandestine purpose in mind. But which group, and what purpose?

At the same time, he was kicking his heels waiting for a possible call from the girl who could lead him to Bilan, the gypsy mercenary. It was obvious he must do something to get Ocksana out of this dangerous position, but he was torn between the two tasks.

By seven that evening, he had heard nothing from the gypsy and was beginning to lose hope of making contact. He rang Moscow and got the rest of the message about the Chechnya affair.

'Have you reported in to Brod or Rubin yet?'

'No. I have allowed Bashlivi to go ahead and sort out his boss. After all, he is the one directly involved.'

'But you have to take some steps to protect yourself, my sweet! They want to neutralise you for your other activity.' He did not specify the trouble about the White Helmets which had led to her problems. She paused, and he could feel her anxiety over the phone.

'Look, get out of there and meet me somewhere to give yourself some chance of clearing this up. Not London, they are always suspicious of our interference. How about Milan?' He had Milan in mind in case Bilan made contact.

'You're right, as usual, darling. I can get a flight tomorrow.'

'No! Do it now. You are just ahead of the game; this Bashlivi will have been debriefed today, and you can expect some action by tomorrow. Invent an aunt sick in Milan and just go!'

They rang off, and Ballantyne checked the flights from Moscow to Milan/Linate and from Gatwick to Linate. He could not make it that night, but a 9.30 a.m. flight was available.

Back in his dreary Pimlico flat, he made himself some scrambled eggs and sat waiting for the call. Television seemed more banal than usual, and he walked down to the local convenience store to buy a bottle of whisky to while away the time.

As he walked into the shop, he automatically checked who was there. Two men were wandering round the shelves in an aimless way. Each kept away from the other; when one moved to an aisle, the other moved on to another section of the shop, but neither appeared to be buying. Ballantyne had no weapon with him and glanced at the beer racks displayed in the fridge. He selected a long-necked bottle of stout with a thick base and brought it to the counter.

'Do you want it wrapped?' The young Asian guy behind the counter eyed him and gave him the change.

Ballantyne shook his head and held the beer bottle in his right hand, scooping up his change with the left. The whisky would have to wait.

Outside, he walked slowly along Lupus Street looking for a passageway between two buildings. What he wanted was a narrow gap where two men could not fight side-by-side. He found one next to a pub and stepped in, and walked a few yards down into the shadows. Two shapes walked past, and he recognised the men from the shop.

Within a minute they were back, staring down the alleyway. He kept still and gripped the bottle.

The first one stepped into the passageway silhouetted against the street lamps. Ballantyne smashed the bottle against the wall and held the neck in his hand; the smell of beer filled the air and the sound of the breaking glass echoed in the narrow space.

'Steady man!' The man held up his hands for Ballantyne to see; they were empty.

'What's your game? Stand still!' The dull light caught the shards of glass glinting from the end of the bottle.

'We're Special Branch! Come outside and I'll show you, we were sent to check on you!'

The man backed out into the street and the second man retreated a few steps. Ballantyne came to the entrance of the alley, but stayed just inside to prevent a double attack. He could see the two men clearly now; one was showing him a badge of some sort.

'Okay. Lay it on the ground.'

The figure stooped, and the badge glinted as it reached the pavement. Ballantyne picked it up. It read: 'Sgt Davis Wilson; Special Unit; Met Police.'

'What the fuck are you doing here? I'm not your unit!' James felt a burst of anger fuelled by adrenalin.

'Listen,' Wilson held up his hands, 'we were told to check on you by the FCO.'

'Who told you to? What business is it of yours? I'm not under surveillance.'

'It's standard stuff,' the second man butted in, 'every newbie is checked out by us when they join up.' He grinned at James and waved his badge.

Newbie! A wave of anger hit Ballantyne as he took in the fact he was watched by his own side. He had never been monitored by the army or by any other unit, and was beside himself with humiliation. He smashed the bottle neck against the wall and pushed past Wilson without another word.

By the time he got to the flat he remembered he still had no whisky, and he flung himself down on the sofa. The muscles in his neck throbbed and he sat for some minutes with thoughts of shoving the job, but as he slowed down he reflected on his responsibility to his lover and the prospect of life out on his own again. It had a cooling effect.

The phone rang at 3 a.m.

'Hey English! What's the problem?' The thick broken accent was unmistakeable.

'Bilan! You got my message! Listen I need to talk to you. I need a job done –understand?'

'Not good time, English. I feel tired, you know, want to sleep and fuck – tired man!'

'You do too much, gypsy! I need to talk with you – important.'

'Okay, but I need money – big money to work – you understand? Next week I go to Bratislava for festival trip – why you not come join me?'

Ballantyne made a quick calculation of the distance from Milan to Bratislava.

'Okay, I'll bring my girl and we'll have a party. What do you say?'

'Bravo! I make you a gypsy yet!'

Bilan gave a number where he could be contacted, and they made arrangements to meet in Bratislava on the Monday in three days' time. James reckoned that would give him time to get Myers on side and get the go ahead to recruit Bilan.

Now all he needed was the nod from Whitehall, and to protect Ocksana. Was that going to be difficult?

CHAPTER 21

Ballantyne 'Give me the Night Duty Officer' Ballantyne was in no mood for polite conversation.

'Who am I to say is calling?' The imperturbable voice of the switchboard operator came through.

'Dammit! It's Ballantyne, I need to speak to **** Myers.'

'One minute.' The phone went dead; James knew she was seeking help and simmered gently as he waited.

'James!' The sound of Myers' mild tone set Ballantyne's teeth on edge.

'I've just been rattled by two Special Branch – what the hell is going on?'

'Tell me what happened.' He had all the sympathy of a tender nanny with a grieving toddler.

'You know bloody well what happened!' He recounted the incident with a full descriptive vocabulary.

Eventually, there came a moment when blood had cooled and Ballantyne brought his mind back to the important topic. In a sentence, he explained the contact with Bilan and his intention to fly to Milan first thing in the morning. He never mentioned Ocksana.

'Have you money to cover the expenses? We shall need a schedule of expenses, you know.'

'Bloody Civil Service!' Ballantyne mused. 'Now I have to do their bleeding paperwork!'

He knew that he had plenty left from the Romanian contract, but he would need a refill from the FCO.

'I will make contact with him and sound him out. What do I say if he agrees?'

There was a short silence.

'Tell him we need information about Russian connections with the Tontine, and will pay well.'

Ballantyne grunted acknowledgement and shut his phone. He doubted whether Bilan would work for the miserable pay Myers could offer.

*

The flight to Linate was late taking off, and Ballantyne rang Ocksana from the airport.

'Oh! It's so miserable here, when will you arrive, darling?'

Her voice was like a tonic to him; a sweet exciting contrast to the cold perfunctory sound of FCO jargon. They spoke for a short while about where to meet, then James broke the news that they would have to go elsewhere. He did not say where.

'Oh! Where?' Her voice was a like an aria from a tragic opera. 'Can't we be together, just the two of us?'

'We will be, my love, but I have to do this road trip.'

'Oh! That sounds better!' Her voice brightened. 'Okay, I'll see you in the Arrivals.'

*

The British Airways plane landed with a thump at Linate, almost as if the plane had decided to dump its passengers as quickly as possible.

'Thank you for travelling with British Airways,' piped up the voice from the loudspeaker.

Not again if I can get another flight back, James thought as he queued for the exit.

It was no problem to find her at the barrier. Her figure, outlined in a fresh, bright linen dress, caught his eye immediately. She ran into his arms and for a moment the scent of her filled his mind with memories. His hands felt the warmth of her supple body and the contentment of holding her again.

'It's been so long.' They said nothing else for a while, then he walked with her out onto the concourse.

'I have to hire a car, but I want you to do the paperwork. Is that okay?'

She looked quickly at him then nodded, and she pulled out her licence and led him to a car hire booth. She never asked him to explain, and he remembered how resourceful she had been in Russia and Kazakhstan. He loved her for it.

They chose a Renault Megane with the larger engine and satnav, and were out of the airport within half an hour. The motorway was just a few kilometres away.

'Now, tell me what to set on the GPS?' Her eyes sparkled as if this was the first day of their honeymoon. James did not have the heart to explain at this moment.

'Just set the magic word 'Bratislava'.'

She looked quizzically at him.

Bratislava was a stretch away and not a destination a lover would choose. She didn't care too much, since they needed time together and she longed to be with him. It was an added buzz to be working together, even if it meant some danger. Her own dilemma seemed far away when she was with him.

She drove for the first three hours and they talked about the Russian versus Chechen struggle, and how she could make her peace with Rubin and the hateful Ms Brod. By the time they reached the Austrian border they had decided to defer any action till they had met Bilan.

'Would it be a sin to spend a few days in Austria?' Her eyes betrayed her excitement and she snuggled up to him as he took over the wheel.

'So, you came along to distract me, did you?' His right arm slipped round her waist and she didn't reply; she made no answer, he knew it already.

Graz is a city with an ancient history. It was on their route to Slovakia and made a convenient stopover. Finding their way into the old city was difficult, but the Schlossberger was just the type of hotel they wanted for a few days' respite.

'To hell with Myers and Co, they can take lump it or like it. We need some time together,' James reasoned. 'Anyhow, I doubt if Bilan will want to take the job.'

She smiled, and gave the keys of the car to a porter as they climbed the marble stairs into the famous entrance hall of the ancient hotel. Within a few minutes, they were enjoying the river view from their suite on the third floor.

*

Two days passed in an hour, and it was her query that brought the miserable real world back to life.

'Have we still got to go to Bratislava?' She looked down as she said it, knowing that she was bringing their dream time to an end.

He lay still and closed his eyes. The sunlight pierced the gap in the curtains and seemed to drill into his eyes. He turned over and hid under the pillow.

'Well, darling, you need him, don't you?'

He groaned; nothing was worse than to be told the truth. Eventually, he climbed out and staggered to the shower. It was only when she slipped in with him that he began to realise that the day was not so bad. When they left their room, the sun was glinting off the minarets and church towers, so numerous in this cosmopolitan city.

By midday they were back on the road leading to Slovakia. The drive seemed more enjoyable in the sunshine and the countryside was varied. Sometimes, they passed simple farms where life moved at the same pace as in centuries past; then through forest, where the road cut like a knife through the dense, dark trees. But as they approached the border, the mood was broken by the intrusion of factories and concrete buildings covered with graffiti, imprinting the tattoos of modern life on every surface.

The border was shut, even though the country had joined the EU. A wire fence had been erected on both sides of the road. Alongside the customs house was a shed, and the heads of several immigrants peered out at the passing traffic.

The border guards from the Slovene side walked round the car as if it was a museum piece, or a wonder from another world.

'Get out, please.' The uniform was grey and the eyes black.

James got out and opened the boot. The officer took a brief look inside and looked hard at him.

'Have you brought dollars into Slovakia?' The query was strange, and for a moment Ballantyne puzzled how to reply.

It was Ocksana, speaking from the passenger seat, who gave the right answer.

She held out her passport with a winning smile, and said, 'I am Russian, comrade, and I have come to see your glorious country for myself!'

She held out her passport, and Ballantyne could see there were dollar bills wedged in between the pages. The guard saluted her and smiled in response. He took her passport with a practised hand so that the dollar bills disappeared like a conjuring trick.

'Enjoy your visit.' He saluted again, and did not trouble to ask for Ballantyne's documents. With a wave he lifted the barrier and they passed through. Troubled, dark faces from the detention camp looked after them as they drove away.

She laughed at the expression on James's face, and he drove on hunched over the steering wheel for the next few miles.

'You proper Englishman! How much better to be Russian and know the rules of the game! You could have been there for hours!'

He had to agree, and looked across at the beautiful woman who knew more than he did. She was adorable and she pecked him on the cheek as a consolation.

Inside the old city, they found a hotel with a garage and decided it would be their base.

'It may take some time to make contact, so we need a spot to keep out of the way.'

She looked him in the eye. 'What more could we want? A hideaway from Mister Myers and my bosses in Moscow. We may stay here for years!'

They set out to explore the city, and to try to find Bilan. The number he had given Ballantyne was unobtainable and the only solution was to make direct enquiries themselves.

They began by listing the gypsy cafes in the city, and the task of visiting each one. It was a mission that James knew could lead to dangerous consequences. It did.

CHAPTER 22

Night falls early in Bratislava. By 6 p.m. the streets were dark, and only the dingy lamps on ancient poles gave some light. But in the centre, some shops and cafes shone brightly, pushing back the gloom of the long evenings.

Ballantyne studied the plan and prepared a list of potential locations to start the search. 'The gypsy quarter is some distance outside the town. Shall we try the gypsy cafes in town first?'

Ocksana looked away; she wanted to defer the task as long as possible. Taking his arm, they wandered through the brightest streets and sat for a while in a cafe bustling with a noisy crowd. He said nothing, but she felt it was useless to try to persuade him to put off what had to be done. The bars and cafes turned out to be just tourist dance halls with gypsy performers.

By ten o'clock, he fidgeted and finished his second drink.

'Come on, it's no good putting it off, we need to find him.'

Taxis were plentiful, and it only took a moment to find an old Lada waiting at a rank in the main street. James let her give the instructions; his Russian would have been a giveaway that he was not an Eastern European, and would probably attract attention. She asked the driver for a good gypsy restaurant and he looked at her with contempt.

'What you do with gypsies? Plenty of good Slovak eating in town!'

'But we want to hear their music!'

The man grunted and pulled away, muttering under his breath. As the journey went on, Ballantyne watched with care. They headed well out of the town and the road was dark.

'How far?' He forgot to keep quiet as his instincts warned him of danger.

The man pointed ahead, and they could make out some lights off to the side of the road. He drew up at a spot where there was no building, but a track led off towards the faint glow. They could just make out a line of makeshift houses, more shacks than buildings, in a meandering row stretching away into the dark.

'What's this?'

The driver shrugged, 'Is gypsy place,' and pointed to the meter for his fare.

'How do we get back?'

The answer was a shrug.

They got out. The old car did a quick turn and roared away in a haze of blue smoke. Now the night seemed as dark as a crypt, with only the road stretching faintly away into the distance. The light from the gypsy shacks was not enough to show the way. What drew them forward was the noise of voices and music blaring across the field. As they approached, they heard the jingling of heavy chains; two dogs like grey wolves sprang from the dark area outside the nearest shack. With a jerk, the chains pulled tight. A figure stooped out of the building, peering into the night.

Ocksana spoke. 'We come to look for a friend. We come alone.'

Ballantyne had no idea what she would say, and it was unexpected.

'Yes,' he said, 'we were told we could find him here.'

Another shape appeared at the doorway. 'Step forward.'

A flashlight caught them in its beam and both stood still. One of the shapes shouted at the dogs, and the animals backed off. The first man with the torch stepped out into the yard and motioned them to approach. He spoke in broken Russian. 'You want who?'

Ballantyne looked quickly for a weapon, and saw a pickaxe leaning against the wall of the hut. Keeping it in mind, he moved forward and stood in front of Ocksana. They could see clearly now, and the second shape held open the door.

'We are looking for a friend, Max Bilan.'

The gypsy scratched his beard and stepped aside. He wore an old tracksuit with 'Speed' written across the chest and, round his waist, a black band with golden chains hanging from it. His brown face was square and his hair cut short, like the fur of a brindle dog. James wondered if he wore gold earrings, but one look told him his assumption was wrong.

The second man, who stood at the door, was a thin, younger man with a pockmarked face. Long black hair reached to his shoulders, and when he opened his mouth gold teeth glistened. The older man nodded to his companion and they moved back into the room without a word. Inside the lean-to was a turbulent crowd. Some people sat round the edge leaning against the flimsy walls made of wood panels or corrugated iron. The bulk of them, a whirling mob of dancers, gyrated to the blare of rhythm from a loudspeaker; a guitarist and a drummer stood the end of the room. It was impossible to speak. Moving to the back of the long hall, the older man motioned for them to follow into a room beyond.

They found themselves in a lavishly carpeted space with a sofa and worn easy chairs. The smell of hashish hung in the air. Ocksana sat down but James stood at her side, ready to take action if things turned out badly.

'How you know Bilan?' The man's eyes were slits of suspicion. Ballantyne replied in Russian, explaining his connection in Rumania.

'He's a good friend and I have a job for him, but I lost his number.'

The big man laughed, and his belly shook under the gold-spangled belt.

'You expect Max to give a contact number?'

Ballantyne shrugged, 'We are friends and he had mine.'

'Different thing,' said the gypsy. 'Your number your fault, but Bilan, a wise man.'

'So you know where he is?' Ocksana broke in. 'This is urgent, not a game!'

He turned to stare at her and then he smiled. 'Lovely Russian lady, you must be patient! We are poor people and mistrust foreigners. If I give you information, I need to be paid!'

He took a swig from a bottle containing some cloudy liquid and watched them. Ballantyne sized up the situation. If they gave money, there was no basis for expecting anything but a rip-off; if the man had any real knowledge, he was more likely to contact Bilan to warn him, and that was a better bet.

'I don't pay to meet my friends. If Bilan finds out you made me pay, you know what will happen!'

The younger man smirked and looked at his partner. His hand moved to his waistband, and Ballantyne stiffened. From the back of the room a voice cut through the smoky air.

'Okay! Stop it! I know them!'

Out of the curtain poked the head of the man they were looking for. Bilan was grinning and holding out his arms to embrace them.

'No one comes to gypsies without an escort! You mad English! What did you expect?'

He looked at Ocksana, and before she could say a word, he grabbed her in a bear hug, crushing the breath out of her.

'You with this man? You crazy!'

The other gypsies looked on in surprise, and Bilan dismissed them with a wave.

James took a moment to look at him. Their joint exercise in Rumania taught him much about the skills and mentality of this wild man. Had he changed? Was he already engaged in some murderous scheme? Was it right for the British to engage with a man they knew to be a mercenary assassin? He studied the face intently, hoping to find some clues to the puzzle.

Bilan sat down in an easy chair and leant over to grab a bottle of arak on the table. His beard had been allowed to grow, so that it disguised his sharp features and distinctive jutting chin. Only his eyes, hooded as a vulture, were the same.

Ocksana noticed the tattoo stretching up his arm: a black dolphin, followed by a number. She recognised one of the emblems of a notorious Russian prison, Orenburg.

'You converted to Islam?' Ballantyne pointed to the beard.

Bilan smiled and held up the bottle. 'Would I give up my best friend? No. When Bilan is home, wine, women and rest, English.'

He sat up and leant forward. 'Now, tell me why you come here to see me?'

James set out the proposition as plainly as possible. He pointed out the division between the Russians and the other known Tontine members. Did Bilan want to act on behalf of the British Government, to prevent the takeover of essential resources?

Ocksana sat quietly; the gypsy knew very little about her, but she was conscious of his hostility towards Russian interests.

'Why should I help English politics with their own project, unless it pays well? You know I follow no one – I am Bilan.' He lifted his face and gave a hawk-like look at Ballantyne.

'Maybe you wish to pay back some of the harm they did you?'

Ocksana blurted out the remark before she could stop. James gaped at her; what did she think she was doing? She pointed to the tattoo, and Bilan looked down at it for a long moment. Then he stared at her and a slow grin spread over his face.

'Ha! So this little bird knows more than she tells! Yes! I have debts to pay in Russia.'

Ballantyne was confused. What did it mean? Evidently, Ocksana touched a nerve and his reaction was significant.

'Will I tell them that you are willing to help?'

'Not so. I not agree before I see what you pay. I go to Paris in a week's time, and you meet me there and say what they want and what they pay.'

Ballantyne agreed, and they arranged a rendezvous.

'Now, brother, you see how gypsies dance!'

He pulled back the curtain and they followed him back into the hall, where the whole room was drinking and the noise was intense. A cheer went up as he emerged and he raised his hand in salute. A voice called out some chant in Roma and the entire crowd took up the call.

Bilan stood in the middle of the floor and pulled off his braided jacket. For a moment he was still. The musicians began a soft melody with a pulsating beat. As the music swelled, he tapped once with his foot, and then the floor rang with the rap of his heels as he turned sharply in a spiral dance with his arms spread. Within a second, two of the young girls, skirts swirling, joined him and they moved in a sinuous pattern around each other.

The crowd broke into rhythmic clapping and others, young and old, began to join in. The beat and the excitement moved Ocksana to dance and she pulled James into the maelstrom of dancers. He did his best to avoid collisions, and made an attempt at the gyrations. He kept his eyes on her as she danced, moving her hips in time with the music and smiling at him. He ignored the amused glances, and felt once more the yearning for her which had been with him since he first met her in Astana in Kazakhstan.

Both James and Ocksana sensed they would never get away before the dawn. They realised it involved resisting every offer of drink or drugs that came their way. Excuses became more and more difficult as every man, woman and child thrust a glass or a reefer into their hands. Ocksana grabbed a bottle of arak and discreetly refilled with water. From then on, they held the bottle and shot glasses in their hands, as a protection against the mob hospitality.

Gradually, the stars disappeared and a sliver of sunlight rimmed the horizon. The crowd began to thin out and just a scatter of bodies remained on benches and sofas around the room. They found one of the young men washing at a tap outside one of the shacks. He worked in the city, and took them back to the centre. They spoke very little on the way; no one felt like talking. Once inside their room, they crashed out into deep sleep. Whitehall and Moscow slipped away into dreams.

When they awoke, the gloomy prospect of a confrontation with Moscow lay heavily on Ocksana's mind.

CHAPTER 23

Fourteen days had passed since Ocksana had left Moscow without permission. The tension between her and the Directive had been so powerful, she felt forced to stay out of the way for a time. James's trip to Bratislava had been the chance to distance herself from the clash between two bureaux of the state. Still, she had to face the scrutiny of Madame Brod on her return.

'Come in!' The voice, so familiar and unpleasant, brought back the old resentment from months ago. The task in Chechnya, designed to blame the Chechens, had brought her into danger when she had no idea of the covert purpose of the operation.

'Where have you been? The Bureau had not authorised leave.'

Ocksana looked her in the eye. 'You sent me and Bashlivi on a mission which was not explained to us, and I took leave afterwards to arrange matters which had to be done.'

The woman shrugged. 'It is not your decision to make or reject a mission.'

'Do you regard your staff as dispensable?'

The remark took Brod by surprise; she had not expected the response, and for a moment needed to find a way to deal with this impertinent agent.

'Perhaps you have been away too long in Kazakhstan to recall the disciplines of the Moscow Office. I will report this matter to the Chief of General Staff for his decision.'

She turned away and began to read the papers on her desk with a fierce concentration.

Ocksana blushed, and stood defiantly.

'Well, Madame, I will also wish to express my view to the chief about the protocol of agent employment.'

The air remained frosty for minutes after the meeting finished.

*

Clearing up the apartment was a surprisingly enjoyable occupation. For once, the task took her mind off the confrontation and was just what she needed. By the evening, she had settled on a response if she was called to account.

Later, she rang James. 'Hi, is everything okay in London? The Brod has been on my tail!' She recounted the episode, and he did his best to reassure her that she had done the right thing.

He asked, 'Can you make it to Paris? I will be over there in a few days to contact Bilan.'

She groaned. 'Impossible! I will have to stay till this dispute is over.'

'Do you think you can get away from the Bureau? It seems they have decided to treat you as expendable. Your life is going to be impossible.'

She agreed, but had decided to await the outcome of any decision by the General Staff.

'How will you contact Bilan?'

'He gave me an address in St Ouen, north Paris,' he went on, 'but I doubt he will accept what the FCO has to offer. But we'll see.'

*

The following day she received a call.

'The Secretariat has arranged a hearing for today. You are ordered to attend at 2.30 at the Tribunal Office in Potemkin Street.'

She dressed carefully. Hair pulled behind her ears in true Soviet style; a simple jacket and skirt of plain grey. First impressions had to be conventional, whatever her real feelings. The tribunal was part of the Ministry of Information, which brought a wry smile to her face. The one thing her department did not do was provide real information!

It was a large room, and the members sat round a mahogany table with their backs to the window. A bright shaft of sunlight illuminated the single chair set in front of it.

Ocksana felt she was Joan of Arc before the English Court in Rouen; condemned before trial. It brought out the stubborn Cossack instincts in her.

Against the light it was difficult to make out the features of the members arranged round the table.

Brod sat to one side, Rubin beside her.

The central figure cleared his throat. 'Madame Petrova, we have received the complaint of insubordination from your department, and you understand we have to make a decision based on what we hear today. Do you wish to say something to us?'

'Yes. I do wish to speak to the tribunal. I was sent to Chechnya with a view to whitewash the accounts of their principal industries.'

Brod jumped to her feet in an instant. 'General Brinkov, I must protest. We had no notice of this allegation and we need time to refute it.'

'Sit down!' His voice rang out and he stared her down. She sank back into her seat, jaw jutting in protest.

One of the panel turned to him and they held a whispered conversation. Then there was a general nodding among the members, and the general turned back to face Ocksana.

'We have to deal with several cases this afternoon and this matter will evidently take some time. Perhaps the department concerned will be able to reach some solution to the situation by the time it is to be resumed?'

The meaning was clear: a cover-up was required, and the department was being criticised for allowing this sensitive case to be aired in a tribunal. Madame Brod got the message at once. Her complexion turned chalk white and she turned to leave, brushing against a chair which fell to the floor. She strode out of the room, pushing the swing doors open with her elbow. Rubin followed quietly, bowing to the tribunal like a servant.

'You may go, Petrova.'

The general dismissed her with a wave of the hand. She had exposed an error of judgement in the Bureau and was not to be congratulated. If anything, she was a nuisance for taking an independent course.

She stepped into the corridor on dancing feet; she had exposed the Bureau, avoided severe discipline and delivered a serious blow to Brod and her underlings. She gave no heed to the consequences. In the thrill of the moment, all she could think of was to tell James that she had escaped the tribunal.

The telephone rang in his flat. He could hardly follow what she was saying, but her excitement was infectious.

'How did you do it?' Within a minute, she had told the story in one long breath.

'But my sweet, what about you from now on? They will get even, won't they?'

'Just let them try! The more they dish out trouble, the more I'll pull them screaming before the same tribunal they sent me to!'

James had serious doubts about her actions, but there was no advantage in saying so. He knew she would find a way out. Obviously, she had to stay in Moscow until this whirlwind blew itself out. There was no chance of her joining him on the trip to meet Bilan in Paris. Maybe it was a good thing. He had no idea who he would meet there, or what reaction the gypsy would make.

Back alone in her apartment, she felt very different to the upbeat girl enjoying her victory at the tribunal. Being far from James emphasised her vulnerability. Every time she left home she looked carefully along the street, and reminded herself to avoid the Metro and crowded shopping precincts. Walking in Gorky Park was safe enough, but her mind kept coming back to James's meeting in Paris. Was he risking himself in a trap?

CHAPTER 24

'What will you pay for a mercenary to do the job?'

Ballantyne sat in Melford's office, and watched the Director's face. Obviously, that question was unexpected. With eyes wide, he stared at James.

'Well, I am not sure. Why do you ask?'

'Because if you want to eliminate a leading Tontine member, you will have to pay, won't you?'

Melford frowned as if shocked by the blunt question.

'Her Majesty's Government cannot be a party to assassination, you must know that.'

James inwardly congratulated himself for putting the official off balance, at least for a moment.

'I'm not sure what you expect me to be doing.'

'You're now on permanent staff, so you must appreciate we must conform to normal standards.'

'Well, do you want me to contact someone outside the office, or to do the job myself?'

The Director sat back in his chair and put his glove hands together. If he had been a religious man, one might have thought he was praying.

'We want you to get information on the other members of the Tontine and leave the Russians alone.'

Ballantyne was puzzled. 'You already know the Russians have a hit list to eliminate the others, so who is going to monitor their activity?'

Melford smiled, as if he had the complete solution.

'That's where your gypsy mercenary comes in. We can use him to penetrate the Russian group and bring us the information we need.' He went on, 'Your expedition to Romania has established a good link with one of their men, Asurov, and you must stick with him.'

Ballantyne pondered the idea. It did seem to be practical sense, but how could Bilan be persuaded to undertake such a task?

'First, you will must persuade the gypsy to work for us, for a fee of course, and then we will have ears in both camps.'

James grinned. 'You are prepared to pay a mercenary? What do you expect? He won't do it for FCO rates!'

'Well, I might get the Financial Committee to upgrade the usual fees for "outworkers".'

'How much?'

'We could go to £1,000 sterling for good information, but we would need it quickly.'

'I doubt he would do it for that, but if you mean he should gather information for a limited time, then he might bite.'

That seemed to appeal to Melford. He nodded and leaned forward across the desk.

'Go and make contact. You say he is in France, well, go across and talk to him. Maybe he wants us on his side?'

James left the office with little hope of achieving the result wanted, but if it could be done, it was worth trying. But first, he went to the finance department and checked that his salary and expenses to date had been paid. He was learning fast.

The Eurostar to Paris left on time, and he arrived there at midday. The Gare du Nord was crowded and he made his way through the shoppers to the Metro, taking the line to the Porte de Clignacourt in the north of the capital.

He knew the rendezvous was in the St Ouen markets, but not the exact location. Bilan was too sharp for that. The gypsies infiltrated the flea markets and James had no doubt he would find him.

St Ouen market is a conglomeration of several braderie markets, popular with tourists and a mecca for shysters and pickpockets. It stretches over many streets and divides into different areas. Ballantyne chose the Malik, where gypsy children surround the tourist begging for cash or trying to sell trinkets. He ignored them. He watched for the older boys who weaved through the crowds, carrying objects from one area to another. These were the runners who transferred items from one stall to another as required. Following one who carried a paper-wrapped parcel, he saw him slip into a doorway and disappear.

Ballantyne went to follow, but a thick-set woman with folded arms blocked his path. She looked him in the face, her jaw jutting like the prow of a ship and her eyes challenging him.

'So, what do you want?'

'I'm looking for a friend, Max Bilan.'

'Never heard of him! Why you want him? This is not a stall. Go away!'

She turned as if to go back indoors, but Ballantyne held her arm.

'Look, I have a job for him. I'm not a "flic". I was told I would find him here.'

She paused and pulled away. After a hard look, she shrugged.

'You can wait outside and look at the crowd, maybe someone will turn up.'

That was all he could expect, so he sat opposite at a small bar and watched the doorway. Soon, a boy came out and ran off.

Ten minutes later, a tall figure strolled through the narrow alleyway between the stalls lining the streets. It was a different image from the man he had met in Bratislava. Gone was the untidy beard and wild hair; the gaudy waistcoat and shiny trousers; the lazy eyes and languid manner. This was Bilan ready for action: keen eyed and dressed in a grey hooded jacket and dark jeans. His jaw was clean-shaven and his hair bunched behind his ears. Hawk eyes scanned the street. When he saw Ballantyne, he gave no acknowledgement but sat at the next table, ordering a coffee.

'Have you got any interesting news, English?' As he spoke, he stirred his coffee; no one observing would realise he had begun to speak to the man at the next table.

Ballantyne replied as if he was merely acting for a client; he did not want to admit he was an agent for the British government.

'We want you to get information on the Russians who run the Tontine group. They will pay good money.'

'Too late! I have agreed a contract with Moscow already. I work with the Russians at their orders.'

'But you hate the Russians! You told me yourself how they treated you at the Black Dolphin Gulag!'

He turned for the first time and looked Ballantyne in the face.

'Yes, I remember! But Bilan works for pay and I choose the tasks! No one decides nothing for Bilan but Bilan.'

Then he smiled.

'You still good man, English, I give you a little advice.'

He looked straight into James's eyes. 'You recall the tall man on the terrace when I took the shot?' The memory was still vivid in James's mind – the sniper shot, the blood, the staring tall man who never moved after the shot.

'Watch him carefully,' said the gypsy. 'He is much too clever for the Russians and will destroy anyone in his way. His name is Corvo, you saw him after the shot.'

Ballantyne recalled the tall elegant man at the top of the steps after the killing at Constanza.

'Okay, I'll remember, but you are sure this offer is sound? The Russians will pay?'

Bilan laughed. 'What you think happen if they don't?'

His eyes glittered with real amusement at the prospect of what he would do if the Russians backed out.

There was nothing more Ballantyne could do. His trip had been a waste of time. But at least now he knew where the cards had fallen, and the extra risks he ran in this dangerous game.

CHAPTER 25

Tuesday morning turned grey and rainy. London never looked gloomier as James pulled back the curtain in the flat. Down in the street, binmen shouted as they banged and moved along the road.

Ocksana was still in Moscow; the visit to Paris had been a failure. Now he would have to do what his new masters wanted, and submit to drudgery.

It took a long time to get used to the discipline of Foreign Office life, with its combination of diplomatic finesse and underhand proceedings. He felt uneasy when he embarked on a mission, yet enjoyed the action when he was fully committed; a paradox he could not unravel. While his money lasted and he had the love of Ocksana, he was ready for most things, but the feeling he would be at the beck and call of Melford for any enterprise remained a bitter pill.

Checking through his kit before leaving, he was surprised to discover a cell phone in the kitbag he used for old equipment. At first, he had no idea where it came from, but he switched it on and the faint glow showed that it was still active. A few minutes on charge made it glow into life, showing a series of missed calls, dated six or seven weeks ago. The numbers meant nothing to him.

Cautiously, he pressed the number displayed on the screen. The first one was dead, but the second one rang; a UK number. By the third ring, a voice answered.

'Pronto?'

Ballantyne paused, then speaking in English said, 'What do you want?'

'Where are you?' The voice was heavily accented, but obviously understood him.

'In London. Do you need me?'

'Why you not answer before? We look for you. Sala has job for you.'

In a flash, James realised this was the mobile he got from Kasurov weeks before on the trip to Romania.

'I've been in Bratislava and just got back.'

'Well, get over here and speak with the boss!'

'Where? I never met him. Is Kasurov here?'

'No! Come to Manor Park tube station. Come at two o'clock. I pick you up. Is Miki here.'

Ballantyne did not recognise the name. Maybe one of the men who travelled to Constanza.

He rifled through the bag to find the Romanian passport crumpled at the bottom; it reminded him he was Petr Vasilli, or maybe Jim from Ireland?

Should he ring Melford and tell him contact had been made? Of course he should. Would he ring Melford? No! He was not going to report every single event to the office. Supposing the contact came to nothing? What good would it do to mention it? Anyhow, he wanted to make his own decisions rather than be the tail on the dog.

The underground from Pimlico took him north, and he arrived at Manor Park well before two in the afternoon. The stations led to an open hall where people went to shop and shelter from bad weather. At this time, a crowd of young people were filling the space, and he found it difficult to observe who came and went. He took a moment to check he had nothing identifiable on him, and when he looked up he saw a man standing near the barrier examining the passengers as they filed through. Short, squat and wearing a ski hat, his eyes shifted along the row of people as they passed. Ballantyne did not recognise him.

'You looking for me?' Ballantyne stepped forward and faced the man.

He said nothing but jerked his head in the direction of the street. Ballantyne followed him. Outside, parked on double yellow lines, sat a dark brown Jeep, the driver arguing with a traffic warden. As they arrived, the warden was writing a ticket and the man at the wheel cursed in a foreign language which Ballantyne did not recognise. They got in and the driver flung the paper ticket onto the road as he roared away.

'So you been working?' The man called Miki sat next to him in the back seat.

'Not much. I went to Bratislava for a job but got blown out, so I came home.'

The driver looked at him in the mirror and grunted as if in sympathy.

'Ja. If you stick with Sala you'll be alright for work.'

Miki laughed, and James surmised they were Sala's regular team.

The journey took about forty minutes and they drove back into the centre towards the Regent's Park area, parking outside a large house in a smart street. Ballantyne wondered why they had fixed a rendezvous so far away from the old location, but guessed it might be to deflect any surveillance.

A man in the drive motioned them to go round to the back of the property, and they entered what must have been the stable block in the old days. Another man in a dark suit frisked Ballantyne and led them through the house to a grand reception room near the front of the building.

James had never seen Sala before. He saw a man in a red velvet jacket, sitting back in a leather armchair smoking a cigar. A plume of blue smoke drifted above his head and he smiled and waved his hand in a gesture of welcome. It made a great change from the squalid locations where he had met other members of this team.

'Come in! I heard good things about you from Kasurov! Tell me what you've been doing?'

'Well, not much. I went abroad, looking for work, but no joy.'

The man took a sip from a glass on the table next to the chair and a long pull at the cigar. He eyed him attentively, and Ballantyne noted the narrow look in his eyes. He reminded James of a figure from his past, but he could not place him. Still, the gesture, the wave of the hand, struck a chord. Some time, some place, he had been in conflict with this man. A second later, he knew the answer.

It was Abramovic, the mogul he had met in Kazakhstan.

So this was Sala, the man who drove his own mistress to suicide. Memories of the brutality of Abramovic's henchmen stirred up bile in his stomach. Did the man recognise him? If so, the pretence of being an Irish hard man disintegrated and his life was in danger.

The long, elegant figure took a few more moments to examine him. Then he turned back to his drink and took a sip.

'I have important job to do in the next few weeks and can use a reliable operator like you. Are you fit to travel?'

'Yes, but what's the deal?'

'Not too difficult. Some merchandise needs moving from here to Madrid. It will only take a few days – less than a week at the most.'

'If I ask what it is, will I get an answer?'

Abramovic laughed. It was a sound with no humour.

'You can ask! It's all the same to me. It's part of a mechanism to disrupt the programmes controlling the Russian gas and oil lines into Europe. Very sophisticated, I believe, and I have paid a lot for it.'

'Can't you export it yourself?'

The man pressed his lips together and stared at Ballantyne.

'Do you think I would need someone like you if I could export it myself? This is high grade industrial software, owned by Shell and never been notified to the petroleum industry. No one else is supposed to have it.'

James tilted his head and narrowed his eyes. 'Do I have the okay to do it my way, or are you going to tell me how?'

Abramovic spread his hands out in a broad gesture. 'You know best! I pay you expenses now and five thousand when the item has reached its destination.'

'Pounds sterling?'

The mogul smiled. 'Why not? You operate here in the UK, so you get paid here in the UK.'

Ballantyne nodded and Abramovic waved to Miki. 'Show him the merchandise and give him expenses. See he gets the details from Elaine.'

Then he turned again to Ballantyne. 'I never leave things to chance. You will be watched, and I expect you back here within the week. Is that understood?'

James nodded quickly and followed the mercenary out of the room. He gave an inward sigh of relief. It seemed plain the Kazak had not recognised him.

Miki led him to an office at the back of the mansion, where a young woman sat at a computer.

'One moment,' she said, 'I need to verify what Mister Sala wants you to do exactly.'

She used the phone and nodded as she received instructions.

While she worked, Ballantyne watched her. She spoke perfect English but with an accent. Her eyes were brown and her hair very black, cut in a fringe which framed her face. He guessed she was Japanese or Korean. When she put the phone down she nodded to him to sit and he took a seat next to her desk.

'You will go with Miki and collect the merchandise from a warehouse near Heathrow. Is your passport in order?'

He nodded.

'Then here are your expenses, which I have calculated should be sufficient.'

He took the envelope she gave him and counted the money. It was 500 Euros. There was an address in Madrid on a piece of paper.

He smiled. 'Not much chance of a first-class return to Madrid with this, is there?'

She lifted her chin and stared severely at him. 'You don't look like a first-class passenger, do you?'

'Well, don't rub it in.' His attempt at humour had no effect.

She leant forward and pushed a piece of paper towards him. 'Sign please.'

He tried hard to keep a straight face as he signed for the money. It reminded him of the tedious procedure at the FCO accounts office. He could not suppress his grin as he collected the cash. *Even the Tontine have their own geeks!*

Outside, the Jeep waited, this time with Miki at the wheel, and they drove across the centre of London to collect his passport and kit.

'What's Sala's surname? Is he Russian?' Ballantyne already knew he was Kazak, but wanted to pry a little more from the henchman.

'He never said, he is Sala to me. He speaks good Russian, so maybe.'

Obviously, Miki had little status in the team.

When they got to Victoria, Ballantyne had to find a way to prevent his address being pinpointed, so he suggested they pull in to a McDonald's on the Victoria Road for something to eat; it was within a few hundred yards of his flat. As Miki queued for their meal, he left him and ran to get his things and passport. He got back by the time the man was wolfing down his Big Mac, and joined him.

The journey to Heathrow presented the usual struggle through traffic up the M4, but they turned off before Terminal Four and drove along a corridor of warehouses outside the perimeter fence.

'Stay in the car, will you?' Ballantyne nodded and watched the driver slip through a side door, into a big hangar with 'International Supplies' written in large letters over the main door. Within a minute, he came back with a parcel no bigger than a computer keyboard wrapped in plastic.

'There it is; no problem for you. Stick it in your bag and go through with hand luggage.'

There was not a lot to say. They drove to Terminal One and James approached the check-in desk.

'Just hand luggage?' The man at the desk paid little attention to the carry-on bag sitting on the counter.

Within a minute, Ballantyne he passed through security, the 'laptop' displayed for all to see, and was in the airside gallery which is Heathrow's answer to bedlam. Curiosity made him take the package into the men's lavatory cubicle to get a quick look. The Matrix was a plastic panel with a network of wires and anodes criss-crossing the board. It meant nothing to him, but a look told him it was important. Stowing it back into his bag, he caught sight of a small plastic button attached to the underside. Obviously not part of the original assembly; for sure it was a bug. Sala Abramovic checking on him? Or could it be some third party, intent on identifying where the item went? At least he was put on guard.

Flight BA 403 set off on time, and within two hours Ballantyne was queuing at immigration in Barajas Madrid. Would the handover go without incident? He felt the familiar pricking of danger at the back of his neck as he moved forward to the window, where the stone-faced police officer took his time to examine each passport.

The photo of 'Petr Vasili' looked implausible, and he wished he had not shaved that morning. Would the passport work?

CHAPTER 26

A week had passed with no sign of retribution from Brod or Rubin. Ocksana carried on her job at the bureau warily. It would do no good to raise her profile by complaining to the head of department, but a transfer was the sensible step in the present circumstances.

A call from Rubin caught her by surprise.

'Good morning! How are you?' His tone was light, and immediately Ocksana felt suspicious.

'I am about to go to work as usual. Is there a problem?'

'Certainly not! I have good news for you, and want you to come to my office this morning.'

Her voice must have betrayed her anxiety. His response was meant to be reassuring.

'It seems the Director has another section in mind for you. Come and see me as soon as you get in.' He put the phone down.

Since the week before, when she exposed Mme Brod, and indirectly, Rubin, to the discipline tribunal, she had no reason to expect a cordial call from either of them. This was curious and unsettling. She decided to put a confident face on, carefully dressing for an interview and taking care with her make-up. She was not going to be patronised by Rubin or some other apparatchik.

Outside his office, she sat under the gaze of his secretary, who gave no sign of what was about to be revealed. What section? What reason could there be to move her? She restlessly crossed and uncrossed her legs as she awaited his summons. After ten minutes – designed, she calculated, to unnerve her – he came to the door and ushered her in.

'Take a seat, Miss Petrova (even the formal title was unsettling), we are making some rearrangements in the department.'

He beamed at her across his desk; he'd never smiled at her before.

'There is a place for you on the Middle East station. How does that suit you?'

Her eyes must have betrayed her reaction, because he smiled broadly. 'Perhaps you have some doubts about it? I assure you we are perfectly content to let you go. There might be some friction if you stay here. Don't you agree?'

Ocksana was speechless for a moment. To have her wish granted from a man she despised was hard to comprehend. What could have been the cause of this event?

As if to answer her unspoken question, Rubin took up a letter and tapped the paper.

'I've just received a request from General Maklev, who is recruiting a team to rebuild our team in Syria. Now we have completed our mission and re-established the regime, we need to restore good relations with the various factions. He asks for volunteers to work over there.'

Still mystified, Ocksana tried to figure out who General Maklev was, and why Rubin should offer the posting to her. The answer soon became clear.

'Madame Brod has mentioned your connection with the White Helmets. A year ago, this was not appropriate (the word had much resonance), but things have changed and your contacts will be useful to us in this regard.'

She saw it now. They wanted to get rid of her as an irritant, and found a way to make it seem logical. One had to admire their astute tactics; a boost for her, and at the same time removing a possible source of disclosure to the senior controllers.

She smiled thinly. 'I did make contact with the rescue services in Syria, but I never treated with any dissident group.'

'Of course! Of course! No one suggests you did. However, you know well enough that state policy at that time forbade assistance to NGOs (non-government organisations). But that is all in the past,' he went on, 'we are going to rebuild Syria and you can be useful in that regard.'

She joined in the charade. Each knew perfectly well why this was being done, and yet their agreement never mentioned the truth. As far as Ocksana was concerned, it was like a release from prison, and for the other side, it removed a risk of enquiry which would damage their interests. God alone knew what those two were getting out of their connections with Chechnya.

She held his eyes in steady contact until he looked away. 'I would be happy to assist in any way I can.'

'Good, then I will report this to the Bureau and you can take it from there.'

He got up and offered his hand. She hesitated before taking his grasp, but eventually returned his gesture. His hand was cold and clammy; she made an effort to stop herself from wiping her hand on her skirt as she left.

She felt an enormous relief and could feel tears welling up as she stepped outside his office, but managed to control herself till she reached the street. As she sat at a bench in Lenin Square, tears formed in her eyes. It would be such a sudden adjustment to the world which seemed so bleak only hours before. At first, she felt ashamed that she accepted a corrupt arrangement to cover the activities of Brod and her underling. But a moment's reflection persuaded her she was entitled to some benefit from the treatment she received at their hands. The interview with the Chechen man called 'The Mogul' stayed fresh in her mind, and the risk of incidental harm from the arrangements between him and members of her department was very real.

Within a few minutes she dialled James's number in London, but got no answer, just his voice recording, but even that was a comfort; the sound of his voice, so reassuring and calm. She left her message and begged him to ring back. Then she went home to sort out her things and begin the process of winding up the outstanding files she had been working on.

'Why has she been chosen for this assignment?' This was the unspoken question on everyone's lips at the Bureau next morning. She felt the underlying hostility as she cleared her desk and passed documents to other workers. No easy explanation came to mind to explain the remarkable change in circumstances. She decided it was best to say nothing and let them think what they wanted. The only thing that rankled was the possibility they believed her to be Rubin's mistress, but repugnant as it was, she knew any denial would be taken as a confirmation.

That afternoon, she travelled to the department with the grand title of 'Diplomatic Reconciliation' and saw the Head of Bureau. The office was in a new building behind Rostov Square, one of the modern post-Federation blocks which heralded the new Russia. It had been designed to express the new regime of light and transparency which Gorbachov had promised; the only defect was the money ran out before the building had been finished. The façade was pure marble but the corridors remained undecorated. In the office on the first floor, she met a smiling officer who welcomed her with a warm handshake.

'I am Serge Prokovief, your team leader. Very pleased to meet you and impressed with your references. We have work to do and need enthusiastic young people with international experience. You spent some time in Kazakhstan?'

They discussed Kazak matters for a short while, and she noted he did not refer to her Chechen mission. Was this oversight? Or a deliberate omission? Maybe Rubin had left it out shrewdly to protect himself? Whatever the reason, she happily ignored it.

Eventually, Prokovief turned to business. 'We have an active role to play in Syria. For some time as you know, we supported the Assad regime against the terrorists. Now that the war is over, we must do our best to reconcile the population to the world of New Syria. We have to improve our standing among the factions who still resent us. How much do you know about the Syrian situation?'

They talked for some time about Syria, and Ocksana found herself warming to this genial man. He told her something about his service experience in Mosul and Raqqa, but made no attempt to embellish his account. She recognised in him something of the character which drew her to James Ballantyne; the quiet confidence and sense of humour which James had. Although Sergei Prokovief was dark and shorter than James, she felt sympathy with him that drew her to him.

'When shall I go?' She looked at him, he smiled, and she noticed how blue his eyes were.

'That's what I like to hear! If you can go I can get you on a flight in two days' time. You would fly to Istanbul and then on to Baghdad. Just leave an address in Istanbul in case of emergencies, and travel on to Baghdad as soon as you can.'

'What about training?'

'All training takes place there, it is impossible to appreciate the situation off-site. So you will spend some time in Baghdad with my development team. Does that suit you?' He smiled, and she noticed the creases which formed around his mouth as he spoke. It was attractive.

By the time she left, the sun shone and Moscow seemed brighter and more welcoming. Of all the locations she knew in her service, Moscow had been the least pleasant one until this day. Now the streets were lively, and even the rackety street cars had a charm she never felt before. In some strange way, her meeting with Prokovief increased her longing to be with James. Was it guilt? Had she somehow been distracted from her lover by this other attractive man? Nothing would be right till she could speak to him.

His mobile rang and again the voice message reproduced his voice in a mechanical fashion, frustrating her as if on purpose. Nothing unusual, she told herself, just the nature of their relationship, separated by place and time; it had to be accepted. Still, as she planned her departure, at the back of her mind it lay, like a sore which needed treatment.

The following morning, just after she woke, the same frustrating answer to her call. This time she left a message outlining the news and begging him to ring back. The morning was a busy one, and she collected her documents and packed, which kept her worries at bay. The flight was scheduled for noon, so she left early to keep herself occupied, getting to Sheremetevo well before time. The glitzy boutiques and fast food cafes held no attraction for her. She felt detached from this world and impatient to get away. The flight took off late, a frequent event, so she arrived in Turkey in the late afternoon and stayed at the airport hotel for the night. As instructed, she emailed the hotel address to the Moscow office. Excitement and anticipation meant she spent a fitful night's sleep. What would Syria be like?

CHAPTER 27

Bright sunlight greeted him as he queued for a taxi. James felt better as he breathed in the atmosphere of the busy airport. The activity was a reminder of other busy places, like Astana in Kazakhstan, where he had his first encounter with Ocksana. Those memories were still bright, and he used a public phone to see if he could contact her. He wished he'd brought his own cell phone with him, life would be so much easier, but the risk was too great.

Her voicemail responded, and he left a brief message to say he would be in touch in the next twenty-four hours. He was very unsure what would happen in Madrid. His task was simply to hand the Matrix over to someone who would find him by phone. He had no idea where or when.

The Puerta del Sol area appeared busy and central, so he booked into a small hotel in a back street and went in search of a decent cafeteria. He took the Matrix with him. One on the busy street attracted him with its glitzy gilded decoration; the Café de Luz. It smelt of strong tobacco and churros. A busy waiter took his order and he picked up a Spanish newspaper, doing his best to read with his elementary Spanish. The waiter put a black coffee in front of him.

'I see you are English?' The voice, husky and feminine. He looked up. She was smiling at him and stood close by his table.

'Yes, do I look so obvious?'

He couldn't help smiling, even though he was being propositioned at this time of the morning. This girl with shiny black hair stood hand on hip, as if she owned the place. No waiter intercepted her, and the other people simply ignored her.

'Can I sit with you for a moment?'

She sat down before he said anything and sat askew, her long legs crossed almost touching him under the table.

Ballantyne found it amusing. Here he was, just about an hour into his trip to Madrid, and already being propositioned by a beautiful woman. With nothing to do himself but wait for instructions, this was entertaining!

'It looks like you do whatever you want. By all means, sit and talk to me.'

He noticed her large blue eyes and the attractive dark eyelashes; her lips painted a bright crimson.

'I am learning English at the British Council, but we have no chance to speak with conversation, so I like to speak with English when I can.'

Nothing she said had the ring of truth to it. The British Council ran courses in conversation practice, and he doubted she would choose to speak to some tourist if he didn't look affluent.

'Well, what would you like to talk about? The weather? The Euro? Or how to make money in England?'

She laughed, throwing back her head and revealing the soft smooth surface of her throat.

'No! Of course I don't want to talk about the Euro! I want to talk about business!'

James was taken aback. What did she mean? He began to feel there was something more to this encounter than a simple pick-up. She moved closer and looked up at him through her lustrous eyelashes.

'What would you take to hand over the present you have in your briefcase?'

He stiffened, and his hand went instinctively to the bag on the seat beside him.

'Who sent you?'

For a moment James felt lost for an intelligent reply. The approach had been so direct and distracting, he had been totally taken by surprise.

'It's of no importance. Just tell me and I will see what we can do.' Her manner had changed in an instant. Gone was the winsome allure; her eyes scrutinised him and small lines of concentration furrowed her forehead.

He took a sip of his coffee to get a chance to work this out. Who did she act for? There had been no contact by mobile as agreed; yet she had traced him to this obscure café, in a busy part of the town? It made no sense. Then it fell into place; the small device on the base of the Matrix. His location had never been in doubt throughout his journey. They needed no cell phone to find him.

But that was not all. What did she mean by offering him a deal to hand it over? The answer could only be that some other person or group put it there, not Sala. They were monitoring Sala or had infiltrated his organisation.

From that moment on, Ballantyne was up to speed. He would need to identify this other organisation as a well as Sala's team, if he was to trace the outline of the network of the Tontine.

'Have you the clout to make me an offer?'

She frowned, 'What is this clout? Do you mean authority?'

He smiled bleakly.

'I'm sorry, but I need to know what I'm getting into. You must know I came here to deliver to a certain party,' he paused, 'and it wasn't you!' She said nothing, but the look she gave him was not alluring. She used her cell phone and spoke into it, covering her mouth.

'Okay. You can come with me and I will arrange a meeting for you.'

Ballantyne shook his head. 'I'm not leaving here to go anywhere with you. If you want a meeting, it will be on my terms. This place suits me fine!'

She spoke again into the phone, then nodded to the other party and turned to James.

'Have you the instrument with you here?'

He nodded. She confirmed it to the other party on the phone and switched off.

'I wait here with you and we will negotiate.' She signalled to a waiter and he brought her a cortado coffee and a churro. She nibbled it with her immaculate teeth, and James had to admit she was very attractive.

'I'm going to the *servicio*,' he said, and got up. She looked at him and pointed to a door at the back of the café.

'That's okay, there's no way out except through here.'

He took up the briefcase and followed her directions. There was no back door.

The cell phone was still active, and he dialled the number last connected.

The tone rang for a few seconds before a voice answered.

'Get me Sala or someone quick. I'm in Madrid, and there's trouble!'

A brief pause, then he recognised the smooth tone of Sala Abramovic. 'Yes?' In a few seconds, Ballantyne explained the offer.

'Stay where you are. We have your general location, what's the name of the café?'

He gave it and hurried back to his table. He had taken about five minutes, and she looked at him keenly as if she sensed he had been on the cell phone.

What concerned him now was the impending confrontation when the two factions met.

Scanning the layout of the café, he took in the position of the bar and the various booths and tables. There was no exit apart from the street door. Anyone would have to come in that way.

The table he had chosen was badly placed, directly in line with the door. The best he could do was move to a chair alongside the woman and facing the door.

'What do you want?' She was disturbed by his movement, and shifted away from him.

'Stay close!' His tone demanded obedience, and she reacted instinctively to his command.

Ballantyne kept his eyes on the door. It opened, and a man in a light suit walked in. The woman reacted by pulling herself away from James, and he grabbed her waist to keep her from getting away. He held her tightly and the man moved towards him, reaching inside his jacket for some weapon. James held her in front of him and jumped up, moving towards the bar. There were bottles and cutlery at hand, and he was unarmed.

The stranger pulled a knife from his pocket and crouched in a fighting position, shouting to the woman in Spanish. It was time to take the initiative; James threw the woman bodily away from him and reached the bar in two strides. The barman ducked below the counter as James grabbed a bottle and threw it at the man crouched on the other side of the bar. It struck him on the shoulder and bounced off, smashing on the marble floor. With a shrug, the stranger jumped for the bar, but before he could gain a foothold, Ballantyne gripped the knife hand supporting the man's body and pulled it away from the surface of the counter; the crash of the body landing among the glasses and bottles resonated through the area and they struggled along the bar till they reached the end. James wrenched the knife from his attacker and punched with his other hand.

They fell to the floor, and as Ballantyne held the knife to his throat, the other man stopped struggling and lay still. Most of the customers had disappeared, but the barman came forward to help pin the stranger down. Ballantyne looked for the sultry woman who set him up, but she was long gone.

'We get police, come quickly,' said the waiter, shouting to someone in the kitchen, but a voice countermanded the call and Ballantyne turned to see a tall man in a dark suit standing by the street door with an automatic in his hand.

'*Calma*! *Tranquil*!' He pointed the gun in the general direction of the man lying on the floor and moved closer. The waiter and the cook stayed still. Nobody moved except Ballantyne, who slowly raised his hands and stood up to face the stranger.

'You must be the messenger,' he said. His face was narrow and his eyes hooded; on each side of his nose two dark lines ran down to a mouth so thin it looked like a scar across his face.

Ballantyne noticed for the first time two men who had followed into the bar. They carried weapons, but, at a command from the thin man, stuffed them away and grabbed the prone attacker by the arms and pulled him upright.

Turning to James, the man spoke in English. 'Where is the Matrix?'

James looked across to the place where he had sat; the whole area was a wreck, tables and chairs, debris of spilt food and smashed glassware covered the floor. He went across and hunted through the mess. The Matrix had gone.

Nothing was said, the evidence was clear; Ballantyne spread his hands in a gesture of bewilderment.

The tall man paid little attention. 'Get him into the Jeep.' Then he pointed to James. 'Come with me, we have no time to lose.'

They bundled the prisoner into the car. As the faint but unmistakeable sound of a police siren could be heard in the distance, he crouched in the back. Within twenty minutes they reached a large mansion, and drove through the driveway to a courtyard at the back. Two men were waiting for them. One of them was Abramovic.

As the prisoner was pulled from the Jeep, Sala grabbed him by the hair and pulled him to the ground. His face was a mask of fury; gone was the suave cosmopolitan performance. His mouth was a slit and his eyes blazed with an evil glow. As he twisted the man's head he spoke to him in a low, sharp tone that everyone heard.

'You will tell me where the Matrix has gone, even though you will suffer an infinity of pain. To save yourself – do it now!'

The man reeled under the torture but could say nothing. It took the other man beside him to pull Abramovic away and persuade him to release the man into the hands of the bodyguards.

'Leave him, Sala, DRAGO! will make him talk.' Ballantyne did not speculate what that meant.

Abramovic stood up slowly and began to brush himself down. A different person was emerging from the contorted shape of the maniac. He smiled and smoothed his rumpled suit and brushed his glossy hair; the thin smile reappeared and he looked at James with calm eyes.

'Unfortunately, you must stay here until we discover what has happened, but I do not blame you in these circumstances. Have a word with DRAGO! he will look after you.'

It was a blow to Ballantyne; he had expected to report back to Melford in a few days, and he longed to get away to see Ocksana. Now he was a captive of circumstances beyond his control. Who had the Matrix? What would be the outcome of this conflict between the competing factions?

One thing seemed clear: the Tontine was breaking apart, and he was caught in the middle.

CHAPTER 28

'Madame, Madame!' The voice in the corridor woke Ocksana with a start.

'What is it?' In a split second she was awake and running for the door. The soft hotel carpet cushioned her feet as she crossed the bedroom. *It must be something serious*, she thought, as she pulled open the door. Outside, a maid in uniform held a message in her hand.

'The manager says it is urgent for you, Madame.'

Her mouth went dry, thinking of a hundred things which might have happened to James. But who knew she was here? More to the point, James had no idea where she was. It calmed her to rationalise her fears, and then she opened the envelope. It was written in Russian.

'Dear Miss Petrova. Events have forced me to return to Raqqa, and the training schedule is postponed. Will you be so kind as to report to the Russian Embassy in Irsten Street for interval arrangements? S. Prokovief.'

Despite her rational thoughts, it was a deep relief to know it was just a rearrangement rather than serious news. Black thoughts about the cumbersome Russian bureaucracy swirled round her head for a few moments, but soon vanished when she threw back the curtains to breathe in the noisy scene of a Turkish market in the street below her window. Swirling blue smoke from food stands curled upwards to disappear into an azure sky; cries from stallholders and porters pushing through the crowds made a noisy background; a police car edged its way through the bustle, occasionally blasting its siren to clear the way.

She showered and dressed quickly, activated by the energy of the scene below. As she went to leave the room, her cell phone rang and the voice she longed to hear was there.

'My darling! Where are you? I've been dying with worry – tell me how things are?'

The words rushed out in a tumbling stream, without a break, making it impossible to reply. James could hear the tears behind the words.

'I'm in Madrid and have to use a public phone – can't talk much, but I'm thinking of you my darling and we can meet very soon, but I can't say exactly.'

'What do you mean? I can't stand this uncertainty. What are you doing? When will you be free?' The frustration and anxiety in her voice hit him hard. How could he calm her concerns?

He spoke with a spurious confidence. 'Listen, my love, I will be out of here within a few days, and we can be together for as long as we like. Where shall we meet?'

She outlined the sudden and surprising change of direction her life had taken, and for a few minutes he enjoyed the relief they shared about her escape from Moscow bureaucracy.

'Brilliant!' His voice expressed some real enthusiasm. 'Stay there and we can enjoy Istanbul together!'

'At last!' Her voice filled with warmth and anticipation; he could feel the change in her mood at once and his own mood softened. He explained briefly his delayed timing, but left out what he had been doing. It made no sense to tell her of Abramovic and the reason he was detained. That could come later. He promised to ring again next day at a fixed time, and they rang off tenderly.

He put down the phone in the booth at the local metro station and faced the sour man who had been tapping on the glass for the last few minutes. With nothing to do, he wandered down the long avenues of shopping streets, wondering at the extravagance of the bright, fashionable women who filled the streets with their chauffeur-driven Range Rovers and BMWs. Eventually, he turned into a travel agency and checked out the flights to Istanbul. There were plenty, but the prices reminded him of the money Abramovic owed him and he took a taxi back to the mansion in Moncoa. He felt it was time to wrap up this trip with as much information as possible and bring it to Melford. But he wanted his money first.

The house was silent, and for a moment it looked deserted. No men guarding the front gate and no sign of servants or gardeners in the grounds. He did not try the front door, knowing Abramovic would be furious with any minion using it, but as he walked round to the back of the house he heard shouting and scuffling from one of the stables. He peered through a crack in the door. The man who attacked him in the café was suspended from a rope attached to a beam. His wrists were bound behind his back and the whole weight of his body was thrown onto the shoulder joints. His head hung low and he moaned in a soft, continuous way, like a whipped dog.

A squat, heavily built man sat on a chair in front of him. This man wore a dark suit and a white T-shirt with stains down the front. Ballantyne noticed the heavy army boots the man wore, which were smeared with some dark stains. It seemed likely this was Drago.

Other men stood at a distance, watching the prisoner as he swung slowly from side to side. One of them spoke to the seated man in a language Ballantyne did not understand, maybe Turkish, and the man smiled. Then he noticed the newcomer and turned to greet him.

'Ah! Jim, the Englisher. You come at good time, we have news!'

Ballantyne felt a correction to the assumed nationality was not the best response, so he nodded and stood near the door. The man got up; he held a long blade razor in his hand and whispered in the ear of the hanging man, then he slashed his cheek so quickly it was impossible to catch the movement. The tied man did not even know he had been slashed until blood began to stream from his cheek. Ballantyne turned away. This was barbarous. Bloodshed was something he knew, but not this torture.

'Be quick!' said the man with the razor. 'If you don't speak soon, you'll be dead!'

The man shook his head, but as the torturer approached again he burst out with a sound like a wounded animal; half cry, half shriek. No words, just a piercing high note which echoed through the building.

'Cut him down, let's hear what he says.' The stocky man wiped his razor on his sleeve and put it away. He sat down as the crumpled figure of the hung man collapsed on the floor, his arms still pulled behind his back as if he could not move them to help himself. One of the gang heaved him upright and words streamed from his mouth in a continuous babble of Spanish.

'*Calla te*!' With a swipe of his hand the squat man struck him, and for a moment the silence echoed off the walls. A smattering of blood spread bloodstains on the wall.

'Now, tell me slowly, where is the Matrix.'

Through swollen lips, the wounded man mumbled something Ballantyne could not catch, but it meant something to the interrogator.

'What's his name?' Again, a muttered sound.

That was enough. Drago nodded to one of the attendants and the victim, limp and helpless, was dragged out into the yard. He lay inert among the leaves and dust like a misshapen sack of old clothes. One shot to his head, at close quarters, disposed of him. Ballantyne stared without a twitch. He had seen such executions in the Balkans many years before. His first thought was that the shot was a blessing for the miserable creature who luck had deserted; his pain was over.

'Okay! This is what we do.' Drago marshalled the team. 'Get rid of this body and we go to Alcala, pronto. Get your kit quick – you too, Englisher!'

There were four men, plus the stocky man and Ballantyne. One of them reached inside a black truck parked in the yard and began to hand out firearms. A Makurov 9mm automatic was Ballantyne's weapon, and he secretly blessed the gods for the luck of the draw; a Makurov was his personal choice of close firearm.

He had no idea where they were going, but a sound idea of what they were going to do. As he climbed into the back of the truck, he picked up a box of 9mm ammunition and checked the magazine of his weapon.

Sitting close beside him in the cramped space of the truck was a dark-skinned young man wearing a balaclava pushed back over his forehead. He grinned at Ballantyne as if they were going on some holiday trip.

'Do you know where we're going?' Ballantyne asked.

'*Bien sur*!' The accent was French, and he was probably Algerian, Ballantyne guessed. 'This is where the Italian hides and we go to dig him out!' The grin on his face belied the clearly murderous mission he was engaged in.

'What Italian?'

'Signor Corvo, who thinks he's the Number One of the world. We show him!'

Two of the others grinned like schoolboys as they joined in the fun, giving high-fives to each other and waving their automatic weapons. Ballantyne noticed each one had chosen a Uzi machine pistol with a twenty-round magazine. Inwardly, he wondered what they would do when their magazine ran out in the first long burst of a firefight.

Their route took them out of Madrid and along the motorway towards Guadalajara. They travelled for about an hour then pulled off onto a dirt road leading into a forest. The truck was parked at an angle to the road so that it could be moved quickly to face either direction. Drago dispersed the team on both sides of the road, and left Ballantyne and the driver inside. The men hid among the trees which closed in around the track. In the silence that followed, the natural sounds of the woods returned, and a sort of peace settled on the place. Nobody spoke. Time passed, then the spell was broken by the sound of a motor approaching from the forest towards the main road. At once the mood changed: the driver sat up, his hands gripping the steering wheel; figures crouched lower in the bushes beside the road, and Drago held up his hand, pointing to the track emerging from the trees.

Out of a dust cloud, a convoy was speeding down the lane towards the highway. The first vehicle was a black

Mercedes saloon; the second, a pick-up with four men sitting in the open back; and finally, a closed van with some signing on the panels. As the Mercedes levelled with the first men of the ambush, a burst of automatic fire raked the windows and the car began to swerve erratically, accelerating down the road. The pick-up pulled up sharply and the men in the flat-top began to return fire as they dropped to the ground. Ballantyne saw at once that the ambush was going wrong, and ducked out of the cab and dived for the nearest cover. The windscreen of the truck he had travelled in shattered into a frost of broken glass as bullets sprayed into it. The driver fell sideways against the door before he had the chance to respond.

From his point of view, Ballantyne could see bodies sprawled on the road as the firefight continued. He paid attention to the closed van, which halted some distance behind the others. No one fired from it and nobody moved. Within a minute, he heard shouts from across the road and saw the pick-up skewed across the track, with two bodies draped over the side and other shapes inside. There was no sign of the Mercedes.

From the undergrowth, there were the groans of a wounded man. It was one of the men who had travelled with them from Mancoa. Drago kneeled and examined him. Ballantyne joined him, and he could see the wounds had left a large open gash in the man's abdomen; the red/bluish slime of intestines bulged out. He moaned and looked up as if pleading for mercy. The squat man put his hand across the man's eyes and put the barrel of his pistol to the man's temple. He turned away as he pulled the trigger and the body slumped lifeless.

One of the others ran to the van and held his gun up to the driver's window. Inside, the driver sat motionless with his hands in the air to show he was unarmed. Pulled from the cab, he lay motionless face-down in the dirt. It was clear, even from a distance, that there was some problem getting inside the body of the van. A second member of the gang tried the back doors and shouted. Ballantyne joined the others as they crowded round the back door.

'Come out now!' They could hear the faint sound of voices from inside, something in reply, but it was too muffled to understand. With a nod from Drago, one of the men aimed his Uzi at the door lock.

'No! Don't do it!' Ballantyne held the man's arm. 'You'll ricochet onto us!'

The man paused, startled by the sudden shout.

'Let me do it, with a single shot.' James signalled with his Masurov and the man stood back. Pointing directly at the lock, he took one shot and the door gave way.

Drago nodded to him and then pulled open the damaged door carefully. Inside was the woman who Ballantyne had met in the café offering to buy the Matrix. She looked different now. Her blue/black hair was pulled back into a severe bunch and her face was pale with fear. She stepped down with help and looked Ballantyne in the eye. Despite the circumstances, she faced her enemies with certain defiance. James was impressed; she still had that certain sexual allure which had attracted him from the first.

'Who is in charge here?' She looked about her as if she was inspecting troops on parade. The men were struck with her audacity. Then Drago stepped forward and grabbed her by the hair.

'Guess!' He pulled her down to her knees and leant down, putting his face within a few inches of hers. She stared at him eye to eye.

Then she spoke slowly and clearly. 'If you want the Matrix, you're wasting your time here. The thing was in the Mercedes. This truck was a decoy.'

Ballantyne was the first to get into the back, and he searched quickly.

'She's right. Nothing here!' Drago released her.

The Serb pulled out his pistol and held it to her head.

'So where did they go?' There was a click as he thumbed the safety off.

'Corvo is twice as smart as you! He wouldn't tell me, would he?'

The side of the pistol smashed into her temple and she fell, senseless.

Ballantyne could see that there was murder in the man's mind, and he felt almost powerless to prevent it. Still, he had to do something.

'Drago! She may know, and it would be stupid to waste her until we are sure she cannot help. Leave her to me for a while, and we can chase the Mercedes at once.'

The squat man hesitated with the gun in his hand. The pause was sufficient to make him think.

'You, Englisher! Come with me, and bring her with you.'

Then he turned to his driver and pushed him back into the four-track. Ballantyne followed quickly, dragging the woman with him into the open rear platform. They left in a grey burst of dust, with Ballantyne clinging on the side panel with one hand and gripping the unconscious woman with the other. The hunt was on.

CHAPTER 29

Rattling along the dirt track, Ballantyne could see nothing of the road ahead. Dust and the cab shape blocked his view. Suddenly, the truck took a swerve to the right and screeched to a halt. He was flung against the back window and he lost his grip on the woman. She pulled free, and was about to climb out when he grabbed her, and they tumbled over the side onto the ground.

Directly in front, the Mercedes had smashed into a tree, steam still rising from the engine. The driver lolled out of the door at a strange angle. He was dead. Another figure sat immobile in the passenger seat. Drago approached cautiously, gun in hand; the man sat with his head against the back of the seat with his eyes closed.

'Get out!' He remained still. 'Move it!' The figure began to stir, and he opened his eyes. Pulled from the car, he fell sideways onto the road and began to pick himself up. Drago kicked him in the crotch and put his pistol to his head.

'Where's Corvo?' The man seemed incapable of answering but Drago persisted, gripping the man by his collar and jabbing the pistol against his face.

'It's no good, chief.' Ballantyne pulled at the wild man's arm. 'He's well gone.'

Drago snarled and threw the man down like a sack of rags.

'Look in the car. See if the Matrix is still there.'

His driver obeyed, and brought out the briefcase with a smile. 'All okay.'

Opening the case was an event. Ballantyne had only seen it briefly, and Drago never. The plastic frame was black and an intricate web of silver electrodes zigzagged across the surface; it was covered in dust, and Drago brushed it tenderly as if handling a favourite toy that had fallen into rough hands.

He turned to the woman, who leaned against the side panel of the truck. 'Corvo. Where is he?' She turned her face away from him and said nothing.

Drago grinned. 'Will you be so haughty when my men deal with you?'

Her lips stayed shut; she wiped some dried blood from her cheek.

Drago pointed at her. 'What we do is this. All go back to ******.'

Again, James and the woman found their place in the back with the wounded Mercedes passenger, and the pick-up roared back to the main road. As they arrived at the mansion, ******* came down the steps with a smile on his face.

'Take them round to the stables,' he said, with a nod to Ballantyne. 'You see if you can persuade them to talk.'

Two of the security guards manhandled the wounded prisoner to the stables; James held the woman tightly and followed. With plastic ties, he secured the woman's wrists and glanced briefly at her injuries. Her smooth brown skin was dirty, and her face crusted with blood, yet she radiated sensual warmth from within that obliterated the obvious effects of grime and blood. She knew perfectly well the effect she had on him and looked away as if frightened; the turn of her head revealed her throat and drew the eye towards her torn shirt and breasts.

'Leave me alone,' she said in a low voice, and turned away quickly, facing the wall, her shoulder towards him. He bent to examine the wounded man. His eyes were glazed and unfocused; his hands doubled over his stomach and a trickle of blood dripped from his mouth. There was little he could do for him, but he held a plastic bottle of water to his mouth and the man sucked on it for a short time. Then the water dribbled from his mouth as his life drained away and the body stiffened.

'Poor sod! He never had a chance.' Ballantyne spoke out loud to see if he got a reaction from her. She gazed up at the ceiling but ignored him.

He persisted. 'Did you know his name?'

She turned at last, and looked at the stiffening body curled up on the dirt floor.

'I think he was called Tomas, he had a family in Naples.' She spoke with just a hint of feeling, which encouraged Ballantyne.

'Do you feel well enough to talk to me?'

She glanced down at the plastic ties around her wrists, and said, 'My wrists are bleeding.'

It was true; she had twisted her arms trying to ease the bonds, and he saw the red grazing where the plastic had bitten into the skin.

'I have no more ties, so if I cut them off, you will have to promise to remain still or I will call one of the others to help.'

She nodded, and he took his knife and snipped the ties.

Twisting, quick as snake, she flung herself across him and grabbed for the knife; her hands met his and for a moment they struggled hand to hand for possession of the weapon. He felt the soft, firm pressure of her breasts against his chest as she twisted and arched against him in a furious attempt to free herself. He rolled over her and pinned her down. She turned her face away, breathing heavily, and gradually relaxed as his weight clamped her to the ground.

James shook his head. 'Now I know what your promise is worth.' She said nothing, but looked up at him for the first time. There was a hint of amusement in her eyes. He held her down for a moment longer, enjoying the pleasure of the close contact with her body, then pulled her to her feet and pushed her into a stall and bolted it.

One of the men brought bandages and a bottle of water to the stables, and James explained briefly what had happened. The man shrugged and told him to report to Drago in the main house.

As he entered through the back door of the house, he heard raised voices coming from the main rooms. Curious to discover what was said, he walked softly along the corridor to a point outside the door. One of the voices was Drago, but he had difficulty in identifying the second voice because it was lower and softer.

'We can do a deal with Corvo: he gets back his girlfriend, and we get a share of the revenue.'

The other voice replied, but Ballantyne could not decipher what he said. He decided to find out who it was. He knocked at the door and went in. Drago stood next to the fireplace, and the other man was Abramovic, sitting in a large armchair with his back to the door. The Matrix sat on a side table next to the chair. They looked at him.

'I thought you should know that the girl is locked up; she tried to get away. The guy from the Mercedes is dead.'

Abramovic stared at him with narrowed eyes. It seemed as if he was trying to recollect something, but then he smiled and waved a hand at James.

'Good work, English. She is a precious object which we mustn't lose!'

'Why?'

'Because she is Corvo's mistress, and valuable! Nobody must harm her, you understand?'

Drago smiled. 'Do you know her nickname?' Ballantyne shook his head.

'She is La Diabla, and she would kill you if a chance occurred. You are a lucky man!'

James decided not to explain how he had let her free and the consequences, so he just shrugged.

'Can I have my money now? I want to make it back to London.'

'Sure, you earned it. Drago will fix it for you. I can use you again sometime, you did a good job.'

Ballantyne felt this was the moment to find out more.

He asked, 'This piece of kit; what's so special about it?'

Abramovic threw back his head and laughed. 'You no need to know, but I will tell you. We have the means to hack into the Russian oil supply lines and disrupt their contracts with the world. They try to stifle us, but now the game is different. We will control the supplies.'

He stood with his hands deep in his pockets and a broad smile on his face.

'But this Corvo, he is with the Russians?'

'No! Corvo tried to step into our shoes, but now we have La Diabla and the Matrix; he is insignificant.'

James did not dare to go further. He had enough information to help the FCO start their own enquiries, and it was time to get out.

Drago took him to an office and pulled banknotes from the safe. He counted 6,000 Euros and handed them over.

'Here, we got no sterling but you can change it back in the UK. Don't try to change it here or you'll be arrested!'

Ballantyne grabbed the bundle, and hitched a lift with one of the supply vans travelling back to Madrid.

As he left, Drago leant on the open window and said, 'Keep the cell phone charged, we may need you again.'

The journey back lifted James's spirits. It was like a three-day pass after a week's hard training in the Marines. The overwhelming sensation of relief and the adrenalin surge which came with the release of tension was just the same. The world seemed brighter, and the prospect of meeting Ocksana was now a reality free from the chance of interference from outside forces.

Back at the airport, he rang and she answered.

'I'm in Madrid, my darling, where are you?'

She explained briefly how she was delayed in Istanbul. 'But you can fly here easily from Madrid. Oh! Get on a plane at once!'

He laughed at her impulsive reply and promised to be there in a flash; there was a plane that left in an hour, and he would be in Istanbul in three hours' time. He joined the boarding queue and turned left at the plane door; this time, it was first-class travel all the way.

CHAPTER 30

'Do I look okay? Will he see a difference in me after so many weeks?'

Ocksana peered in the mirror and examined her face and hair. The reflection showed an oval face, dark green eyes and the light shining on her long black hair. For a second, she pulled her hair up on top of her head to see the effect, then scraped it into a bun. She frowned at herself and let it fall around her shoulders in a carefree way.

The initial excitement of the rendezvous in Istanbul wore off and she waited, a little anxiously, for James's arrival. She hadn't had the chance to explain fully what she was doing there or the mission to Syria which she had accepted. He said he was free now, with no timetable to keep to. Would he be upset to find her en route to some war zone where the remnants of ISIS were being mopped up? Then she told herself to be sensible; he already knew about her contact with the White Helmets, and he would understand why she went there.

The Atatürk Terminal surged with families arriving for a national holiday. There was no arrivals lounge but simply a convergence of passengers and public, pushing and shouting across the hall. She tried to ring James on the cell phone but got no reply. The flight had been logged on time, but there was no sight of him for the half hour after that. She began to worry – maybe he had missed the flight and been detained – but she forced herself to be calm.

At last, a tall figure emerged from the customs hall and her heart leapt. He looked haggard and unshaven, wearing fatigues like a soldier and carrying a rucksack. He gazed about and frowned for a few seconds when he could not find her in the crowd. She pushed her way through the chattering throng and rushed into his arms, as he dropped his bag and held out his arms to gather her in. They said nothing, just held each other for a minute before facing each other with a searching look.

'You look tired, my love.' She stroked his face and looked into his eyes. 'You need my care and attention, you poor boy!'

His wry smile meant more to her than a thousand tender words; she knew now he would always be hers and she longed to caress him after so much time apart. She took his hand and they made their way to the taxi rank. On the way to the hotel, she sat close with her head on his shoulder and said nothing. She knew instinctively how exhausted he was and how much he needed her.

She had changed from her room to a suite on the top floor, where they could be safe and enjoy privacy in this noisy, energetic city. The bed was wide, the wet room luxurious and the fridge well stocked. She wanted to bring him back to normal life, away from the traumas which seemed to follow him like shadows.

He showered and she slipped in to join him as he stood under the spray of warm water. As he held her, she could feel his returning strength and his passion for her. She melted under his urgent kisses and they met in an eager thrusting embrace. It was intense and brief, but within those moments they sealed their love without words. Afterwards, he carried her to the bed and wrapped her in a soft white robe and lay beside her as they drifted into a dreamless sleep. The sounds of the city melted away into a murmuring background and they lay together for hours, immersed in a cocoon of sleep, oblivious of the world below them.

When she awoke, it was dark outside. Slipping out of bed, she pulled back a corner of the curtain and watched the lights of the town. The dome of the Blue Mosque shone under the floodlights and appeared to be floating high above the streets. The noise of traffic penetrated the night as the urgent sound of horns clamoured for attention. James began to move, softly speaking her name as he turned to embrace the space where she had been. Quickly, she crept back into bed and wrapped him in her arms. His breath touched her cheek and she instinctively held him tighter. He opened his eyes for a moment, then closed them again; he wanted to reassure himself she was real and here with him.

He spoke. 'Let's stay here for a year and tell the rest of the world to get lost.'

She nodded and nestled closer. After a while, he moved and stretched, arching his back and arms; his strong frame filling the bed, overlapping her slim body. She loved the strength of his limbs and she wrapped a leg around his torso. He responded as she expected and he rolled onto her, keeping his weight on his arms as he entered her gently. They moved together in rhythm and enjoyed the mutual ecstasy which came to both simultaneously. Then he rolled to her side and they lay exhausted in each other's arms.

By late evening they felt hungry and stirred from the bed. James threw open the window and the noise from the street brought reality back with a bang.

'Are you hungry?'

She nodded and crossed the room, making for the shower. He watched her body as she moved: her slender waist and curving hips blending together in perfect symmetry, the long legs and the scar which ran down her thigh. It brought back memories of the wild chase across the border of Kazakhstan, where she had risked her life for him. For a moment he felt the sting of tears gathering in his eyes as the memory came back to him with such force, but he brushed it away. He made a promise to himself to keep her safe.

They dawdled through the area near the hotel and found a little restaurant with several locals eating there. A table on the terrace behind the dining room was available, and they installed themselves at a good distance from the bouzouki music in the main room.

'Tell me about your Syria trip.' The words she dreaded. It was hard to predict how James would respond to the facts that she would be entering another war zone. His own life had been cast in a dangerous mould. Would he object to her following a similar path?

'Well, I have agreed to try to rehabilitate the White Helmets. They have been sidetracked by Moscow for the last year, but the war is almost over and we want to mend our relationship with the Syrians.' She paused and added for emphasis, 'It means I can get away from Moscow and avoid the problems with Brod and co.' She hoped this would make the idea more acceptable.

He leaned back and crossed his arms.

'Do you have a real organisation to back you, or are they expecting you to work with the local authorities?' He raised his eyebrows, and she knew he was unhappy with her news. She took his hands and looked him in the eyes.

'I'm sure there is no real danger, I am not going to a war zone and I have the backing of the Syrian Bureau to protect me.'

He glanced quizzically at her and kissed her hands. 'I know you make up your own mind, Miss Moscow, but you have to think of me. I hate the idea of being out of touch and unable to protect you.'

She wrinkled her nose and smiled into his eyes. 'You never leave my mind; I live only for you and will watch my step every day, my darling.'

He tilted his head in acknowledgement and began to tackle the roasted lamb which flamed on the table in front of him., almost a half side of meat. They giggled as he struggled to carve off small segments. Beside the meat there were large portions of salad, spices and couscous to be dealt with, so they made a feast for themselves and Ocksana gladly avoided any more discussion.

Later, they strolled down towards the bazaar, where street musicians entertained the late-night crowds and snake charmers showed their doubtful skills with reptiles. The street life never stopped, and it was nearing three o'clock before they made their way back to the hotel. The excitement and latent weariness caught up with them and they fell asleep quickly in each other's arms.

The next day was busy with a round of tourist activity: the tourist bus, the mosque and the usual sights. It felt strange to join the tourists as one of them. There was no hidden agenda to their sightseeing and for a while Ocksana felt that normal life was possible.

'Maybe this is the way we can step back into normal life?' she asked. 'I mean travelling together without stress and enjoying ourselves?'

He hugged her. 'Yet you know, my sweet, this is not our real life. Let's forget it all while we can. Tell me, what should we do? Can we step down from the life we lead? I doubt it. Even now, I have to send a report to London about what happened in Madrid. I can't ignore it, can I?'

She looked down and avoided his gaze. It was hard to find something to contradict the truth of what he had said.

'Maybe you could file the report and drop out of the job. After all, they have other...' she looked for the word, 'operatives, don't they?'

He looked up into the distance as if to search for an answer, and ran his fingers through his hair. 'Yes, I could do that, but what could you do? Would you back out of the agency work? What would be your status?'

She looked up quickly. 'Do you think I care about status? In Moscow? What status!'

He stooped and held her hand. At that moment, they were standing on the riverside facing the big bridge which crossed the Bosphorus. She felt the significance of the moment. As if they were standing at a point between two worlds – the life before and a possible new life to come.

'Maybe I should make this trip the last one,' she said, 'and cut my connections with the Bureau. After all, they mean to keep me at a distance.' She reflected on the campaign by Brod to sideline her after she exposed the Chechen deception. She realised it was as much her pride as her career which had driven her to accept this Syrian mission.

James tilted his head back and glanced sideways at her in mock concern.

'Could you face a life with me in England?'

Ocksana looked wide-eyed at him for a moment, then she saw the half smile on his lips and punched him on the arm. She threw back her head and swore at him.

'You English are evil! You know the answer and just tease me for fun!'

They kissed in one long embrace and he muttered soft words to purge his joke. Then they made their way back into the old city and spent the rest of the early morning in bed.

It was nine o'clock before Ballantyne woke to face the new day. The urgency of reporting what had happened in Madrid was drumming on his brain. He acknowledged to himself he should have been in touch as soon as he left Spain, but Istanbul had pushed that aside. He got dressed and slipped out while Ocksana was still asleep. In the avenue, he found a phone booth and paid for a call to the UK number he had been given months before.

A voice answered. 'Business enquiries. How may I help?'

'I have a package for Mister Melford, when shall I deliver?'

'One moment, I'll try to connect you.' There was a pause and James looked at his watch – it was nine thirty UK time, maybe too early for Melford?

The familiar clipped voice came on the line. 'Who is this? Is this a package from Spain?'

'Yes Sir, I need to know when to deliver.'

'Get it sent by express to my office, immediately!' There was no mistaking the tone of voice.

'Yes Sir. It should be there tomorrow.' The phone went dead.

The day had somehow turned grey, and as he drifted back to the hotel James could feel a lethargy closing over him. It was exactly like returning to boarding school so many years ago, when separation from his family seemed inevitable but unnecessary.

This time, it was parting from Ocksana, when they had confirmed their love and decided to live in peace at last. The thought of leaving her to go on to a dangerous mission in Syria while he went back to England tormented him. How could he persuade her to leave it and come with him to safety?

He found her in the dining room, with a tray of food in front of her. Fruit, toast and scrambled eggs surrounded her and the grin on her face pierced his heart as he tried to force a smile on his face.

'What's happened?' She noticed at once. 'Has something happened?' She put down her glass and looked up into his face.

'No. I just have to go back to London pronto, and I hate leaving you here.'

She smiled faintly and sipped her juice; after a pause, she looked up at him.

'You expected this, and we both knew Istanbul was a dream. When will you go?'

Her face was pale and she made a big effort to seem normal, but it was impossible to hide the torment she felt at the frailty of her dream. They were caught in a web of circumstances which made escape almost impossible.

They finished the meal in a forced cheeriness, talking about their future after the Syrian mission was over. How James would look for a new flat in London. Which number they would use for their own conversations.

Anything which distracted them from the reality of separation which was about to happen.

Back upstairs in the suite, where everyday life seemed far away, she broke down in quiet tears as they held each other tightly. He found it difficult to say what he wanted. For a minute they stood clinging on to each other wordlessly.

Then he lifted her face and kissed her tears. 'Will you marry me when we return?'

She sobbed and nodded at the same time. Then she hid her face against his shoulder. 'You are my only love, and my family too. I could not go on without your love.'

She stood away from him and wiped her eyes, and they began to laugh. Some shadow of fear had been lifted and they both felt their future life would be different, more hopeful and fulfilling. A future where the pressure of their present tasks vanished, and they were free to do whatever they wanted. This feeling washed away the strain they felt on parting and they packed speedily and checked out cheerfully.

At the airport, in their usual way, they said goodbye without lingering. They knew with absolute confidence that their love was strong and would keep them together, however far apart.

James boarded the flight with new plans in mind, and the demands of the FCO were not among them. What would it cost to buy a flat in Pimlico? Could they live on his salary? Would she like living in London?

The plane droned on, and by four o'clock he was Whitehall bound on the fast link from Heathrow.

CHAPTER 31

The Mall looked bright with flags and lights as he dropped off the bus from Heathrow and walked up to the Foreign Office. Apparently, it was one of those days when London prepares itself for some celebration or state occasion. The trees were in leaf and the general mood seemed to be festive. It worked its charm on James as he reached the main gate. Even the doorman tipped his hat in salute, the first time he had been acknowledged, so his mood was buoyant.

He found his way to Block 13 and presented himself to the genteel lady at the desk.

'I believe Mr Melford wants to see me,' he said, and gave his name. She muttered something he didn't catch and hurried away, leaving him standing at her desk. For a short time he wondered if he had arrived too late to catch Melford – it was almost five o'clock – but the woman came back and led him silently to a room down the corridor.

Seated at an oval table sat Melford and another man James had never seen before. He was large and square, wearing a suit which barely contained his body. The jacket stretched across his chest as if it might burst if he coughed, and the sleeves stopped well above the wrists so that his large hands emerged like two sprouting bunches of bananas. His head was squared off with a military haircut and he stared at James with intensity.

James guessed he was American – it was not a difficult one. The figure stood up and held out his hand across the table. James prepared himself for crippled fingers, but the grasp was normal and not painful.

'Been looking forward to meeting you. Bob Harding, US State Department.'

Melford stood up and began to say something, but decided it was too late for introductions and sat down again. He cleared his throat and took a moment before he spoke.

'You perhaps realise that that the US State Department has had an interest in our mission for the last six months. Colonel Harding has flown over to meld the two branches of our enquiry and your arrival is timely. Perhaps you could give us a verbal report now?'

Ballantyne cleared his throat. Where was he to begin? What could he leave out? They did not need to know about Istanbul, did they? His mind went into overdrive, trying to process what he could tell them.

'I went to Madrid, following a lead from the Kasurov contact I made earlier.'

Melford sat up, his glasses slipped down his nose and he pushed them back impatiently. 'Is this in a report?'

'Well, no; I had to move quickly and there was no time,' James moved on rapidly.

The American ignored the reaction. 'Go on.' He leant forward, oblivious of the interruption. So James related the significant parts of the exercise, hoping that Melford would subside.

'So, you reckon there are two factions trying to stymie the Russian Tontine?'

Ballantyne nodded and the big American grinned. 'Suits us fine!' He beamed at Melford, who gave a half smile like a sick child.

'So what's our next move?'

Ballantyne shifted a little in his chair. It was not the right time to say what he wanted to do, knowing that Melford would be hopping mad if he pre-empted some scheme the FCO had hatched up. He looked at his director and shrugged.

'Of course, I've not had time to discuss the situation with the firm, so I couldn't possibly say, but it strikes me it would be good to choose which side to support.'

He looked at Melford, to register if he had said the right thing.

Melford paused and took off his glasses as if pondering a difficult question. James doubted he had a clue what to do, and was just gaining time to think of something.

'I believe it is important to distinguish between the sides—' he began.

'Yes, but what do we do?' the big American broke in. 'Do we blast one side or run with the Russians?' He looked at Ballantyne rather than Melford, as if he appreciated he would get the answer from that quarter.

'We know very little of the Russian setup, so we had better stick with the other side of this setup, don't you think?' Ballantyne looked to Melford for a response. Fidgeting with his glasses gave Melford a little time to come up with an idea.

'Yes, it seems the only thing to do, but we lack manpower for this game. What we need to do is get the Matrix away from them or destroy it.'

Harding shifted his bulk from one cheek to the other; he was plainly unhappy with this idea.

'Look, to destroy the Matrix will give the Russians an advantage. Their pipelines will be protected and they can knock out opposition with impunity.' Melford had to agree. He nodded and looked to Ballantyne for rescue.

The emphasis had shifted. It was plain to see that the senior staff were moving towards a decision which would involve direct action to neutralise one side or the other in the European segment of the Tontine. One thing was clear: Ballantyne was not going to get involved in any killing.

He measured his words with care. 'At the moment, the Matrix is in the hands of Sala Abramovic, and he has the mistress of the Italian, Corvo, as a hostage. So the advantage lies with him. We must expect a bloody war between them, even without any intervention by us or any third party. Why not stay out of it till it is resolved?'

Harding shook his head. 'No, we need to be in the loop. Waiting for the result is too passive. We might have to wait for months, or things may turn out in some unexpected way. No. we must be on the scene and be aware of the action.'

Plainly, they were ganging up on him. It was perfectly obvious that there was no operative who could take over the mission mid-term and successfully insert themselves into Abramovic's team or infiltrate Corvo's Italian group. Did they understand the pressure of undercover work? He doubted it. Bitterly he resented the cold-blooded way in which they discussed a task that could lead to assassination or torture. He was in a dilemma of his own making, and it worried him like a sore tooth.

Harding turned to James and put his hand on his arm; he leant forward and said, 'I know the problem;

I was in the DEA in Mexico for three years undercover. It was the hardest thing I ever did, but it was worth it. We brewed up the cartels and saved many lives. You could do the same, James.' The direct approach was forceful, but James knew well enough that it was a pitch to sell the idea to him.

They compare saving lives with stopping commercial piracy! Don't they see a difference? He tried to push the comment out of his mind and bring it back to the reality.

'Give me a day to think this through,' he said, 'I want to mull it over. It's pushing me back into the furnace and I have to consider it carefully.'

Melford stood up and smiled. 'Of course, take a few days, James, and we can organise backup for you as soon as we know your decision.'

Harding got up and made a gesture of agreement by attempting a high-five with one of his enormous hands, but James ignored it and nodded a goodbye as he left the room.

He decided to take a walk and ponder the dilemma in isolation. It was not just the risk of taking up the undercover role again; he had Ocksana to consider. Their commitment in Istanbul changed the scene forever. He had lived with danger for several years and enjoyed the excitement of the challenges he had faced, but now life had changed and he was no longer alone. Was it fair to her to plunge back into the false world of undercover work?

He made his way through St James's Park and found himself facing Apsley House at Hyde Park Gate. In front of him stood the memorial to the soldiers who gave their lives in the First World War – the granite shapes of the memorial stirred something in his heart. How important was he in the scheme of things? Unlike those men, he had the choice to serve or decline. What choice had they been given? If he could do something to prevent world disorder, should he stand aside and see it happen? It nagged at him and he walked on in frustration, undecided which way to turn. Eventually, he dropped into a pub in Knightsbridge to mull over his situation with a quiet pint, and sat in the quiet bar alone.

A party of young people were enjoying themselves in the other bar; the noise of their lively conversation filtered through to him. It brought to mind the pleasure of good company and the freedom young people enjoyed, and the contrast he had seen in several of the countries he had fought in. Kazakhstan, Russia, Kosova. Was it important to keep these carefree young people clear of the power of uncontrolled plutocracy? It seemed to him a huge question and too large a subject for his personal consideration, and yet he could not push the thought from his mind. Eventually, he compromised and decided he would talk to Ocksana and make up his mind after that.

Using his own cell phone, he dialled her number. There was the usual intermittent stream of interference and then she picked up the phone. 'Hello?'

It was as if all his worries were resolved in a flash. Her voice calmed his half-formed fears and he knew what he had to do. It would be wrong to abandon his task at this stage; no one else could carry on effectively without exposing themselves to incalculable danger. He knew the players in this dangerous game and could never brief another person in a way which would protect them from harm.

Her voice, so loved and so vital, brushed away the doubts. She was worth saving, let alone the millions of young people who knew nothing of the struggle between powerful factions to dominate the sources of energy and wealth.

'So, have you squared up to Melford?' Her tone was teasing and light. 'Tell me how you crushed him with a few remarks!'

Despite his solemn mood, James could feel his spirits rising, and he felt better already.

'Sure! I gave it to him both barrels, my sweet, and he collapsed!'

'What are these barrels you used? Is it good or bad?'

He laughed despite himself and explained.

'Now, tell me what is happening about Syria?'

She was going to Baghdad next day for training, and was already in touch with the White Helmet organisation to rejig their role.

'Now the war is almost over, there is no more function for the WH to perform, so I am briefed to find a way of bringing them into the recovery programme run by Russia in conjunction with the Syrians.'

The explanation confused him. 'But Assad's government is not accepted by all parties, the Americans for a start. How can Russia step into this situation without risk?'

She spoke with confidence. 'My love, don't trust the press. The position on the ground is different to what you have been told. ISIS and their supporters are driven into a small area around Raqqa in the north; the war is over, and the Americans know the Assad regime has recovered. The important thing is to help the Syrians build again, don't you agree?'

He had considerable doubts about this assessment, but he realised her access to hard information was a lot better than the news processed through the press.

'So, what will you be doing there in Baghdad?'

She sounded eager. 'We leave Baghdad in a few days' time and will be allocated to areas needing reconstruction. It is exciting work, James, I feel at last I am doing something worthwhile!'

He did not share her enthusiasm, but could not justify a protest without justification.

'Okay. But remember how you've been treated so far by Rubin and Brod. You must be cautious.'

She laughed, and he could picture her smile. 'I'm far away from those monsters! Don't worry please, darling. I can look after myself!'

There was nothing he wanted to say against this. He knew very well she was the most resourceful person he had ever met, and he adored her for it. What good would it do to raise doubts in her mind when she was capable and eager to work?

He told her nothing about his own dilemma. He had already made up his mind he would go on with the investigation; there was no point in mentioning it and creating a worry in her mind. They chatted about London and the future with the certainty of meeting in a few weeks either in Istanbul or in London.

Her last words touched a tender spot. 'You know, darling, I shall be with you just as soon as I can clear up this mission and then we will be together forever.'

He put down the phone determined to finally deal with the Tontine, so that he could finish the task he had begun and start a new life with Ocksana. The sooner, the better. He burrowed for the cell phone Assurov had given him and dialled the contact number. There was no turning back now.

CHAPTER 32

Two men pored over the workbench, adjusting a machine laid out in pieces. There were plastic parts and electric motors among the items.

'What radio frequencies can we use? How wide is the bandspread?' The speaker was staring at the second man, who seemed oblivious of his interruption. The silent man attached wires to a terminal before replying.

'I don't know yet. Give me a chance to assemble it without asking stupid questions. When I'm done, I'll let you know.'

A strong fluorescent light beamed down on the scene and highlighted the bench against a wall in a large warehouse building. Two guards stood at the door leading out into a yard, and they occasionally looked in to see what progress was being made.

'Give me some idea! Corvo is furious, and we must be ready soon or he will take drastic action. You must realise how dangerous our situation has become.'

The second man put down his tools and stared. 'I know what Corvo will do if it doesn't work. You think I'm stupid? This is the latest Israeli model and we have to learn its capabilities. Will it carry explosives? Can it operate silently at night? All of this I have to do and can't be done in two hours or so.'

This outburst stopped the tirade and the questioner turned and left the hangar, crossed the courtyard and entered the main house. Corvo sat in the salon, tapping his fingers in a rhythm on the polished surface of table.

'Well?' His face was furrowed with hard lines which creased his cheeks and emphasised the grim set of his chin. 'How is our expert managing the new toy?'

He listened to the explanation with keen attention and rapped the table with his knuckles. 'You tell Monsieur Pichon I want that machine airborne by tonight. No excuses. I need information and action. Do you understand?'

The messenger nodded and made a quick exit. Corvo rang a bell and called for his head of staff, Diego Garcia.

'Do we have a fix on the last position of the Mercedes?'

He recalled how the Mercedes had been intercepted in the forest road where the ambush had taken place.

'Si, Jefe! We have the location, of course, and we have traced their tracks as far as the *carretera*.'

'And which way did they turn? Towards Madrid or away?'

The man spread his hands in an expansive gesture. 'Away, Maestro, and we know Abramovic has a hideout outside Guadalajara.' He smiled as if he had good news to tell, 'I have gathered the men, they are ready to start at your signal!'

'Good! Send one man on a motorcycle up ahead to keep us posted, and we move at dusk. How long will it take us to get there?'

They discussed armaments and timing and he dismissed Garcia till later in the evening. An austere smile like a shadow passed across his lips as he rehearsed the attack in his mind. The loss of the Matrix was more than a strategic defeat; it was a loss of face which cut almost as deep. The kidnap of his mistress was bad, but nothing compared to the rest. He knew she would sell herself to the most convenient buyer as circumstances dictated.

By late evening, the drone was in operation. Pichon the engineer had tested it and was satisfied it could track a target.

'What about night camera?' Corvo interjected.

'Infrared images and telescopic sights,' Pichon announced with some pride.

'Good! Get in.'

The entourage set off: a four-track with the equipment and four guards, followed by Corvo and Garcia with an army personnel carrier behind. They turned on to the main road in the direction of Guadalajara and moved rapidly till they reached the outskirts of the town. They pulled off the road into a wood and disembarked.

By the time the drone was ready, the motorcyclist had returned and reported that the target had passed through the town.

'One man saw them pass his farm about two kilos further on, where the road divides. He says they are near the village of Alcelas.'

The black plastic spider-like machine crouched on the grass beside the truck, its gleaming body shining in the headlights. A whirr of electric motors made the sound of a malevolent insect and it skittered along the ground as if impatient to fly.

On a command from Corvo, it sprang into the air and lifted over the trees in a northerly direction. Pichon followed its progress on a small screen and the image panned over the forest as it followed instructions. Within a minute, it had cleared the trees and moved out of sight and sound. The screen showed a panorama of woods and roads in the grey images of the camera, then a large building set back from the road. Pausing, Pichon hovered it some distance away and then moved closer.

All the crew gathered round, watching as he guided the camera in a circuit around the house. Three vehicles were parked in the courtyard; they had found the hideout.

Corvo pulled at the engineer's sleeve. 'Can you get the GPS location?'

'Of course!' He passed the co-ordinates to the drivers and they raced for their trucks.

'Wait!' Corvo held up his hand. 'We go with the drone! Nobody goes ahead until I say so.'

There was confusion as the men switched off engines and put away their weapons, staring sullenly at their chief.

'We go quietly and slowly. We're not giving them notice of our arrival. Once we are in position, then we attack. Do you read me?' He glared at the crew and a few nodded sullenly in reply.

He took a few minutes' advice from Pichon and turned to Garcia.

'We travel in convoy with the drone in the lead. At my signal, we disembark, and I will give orders once we can see the layout clearly.'

The convoy moved off in an orderly line, not racing forwards but travelling at a normal pace. They passed a few vehicles on the way, but no significant traffic was on the road that night. When they reached a point where the GPS signal identified the manor house, they pulled onto the verge and killed the engines.

Again, the black whirring machine lifted off and passed above them in the direction of the house. It made the soft rustling sound of a spider scurrying across a leaf and then vanished from sight. They followed its flight as it circled the house and watched it identify the men who stood guard at various points around the house. Then it settled to a stationary position immediately above the building. The image showed two men at the gate from the road, and two men at the rear of the property. There were outhouses and a stable block where no movement could be detected. Vehicles parked in the yard had not changed position.

Garcia detailed two men to set up behind the buildings and signal when ready, and turned to Corvo for instructions.

'The APC will hit the gate and go straight for the house. At the same time, the backup will open fire and take out the guards.'

They waited for the radio signal to show the two men had reached position behind the house, then the armoured car moved off with men clinging to the sides. They dropped off as it approached the gate and crouched at the side of the road.

The engine screamed as the armoured truck accelerated towards the gate; the guards crouched and began to fire bursts of automatic fire; the gate split open, the noise echoing back from the building. Garcia jumped from the carrier and ran for the front door, with something in his hand. He jammed the package against the door and dived to one side. A flash of explosion lit the dark and a bloom of smoke burst from the doorway as the door blew inwards.

At once, the other men from the armoured personnel carrier dived inside the building and bursts of intermittent fire indicated where they were. Corvo stood outside the broken gate and waited for a signal to move in. Within seconds, he waved the rest of the team forwards and they made their way into the damaged building.

Corvo showed little elation or surprise; he put away his automatic and began to search the house for survivors.

'Where is the Matrix?' He ransacked the ground floor rooms and shouted to the men upstairs. It was not in the house.

From the stable block, the sound of gunfire brought the crew to attention. Two of Corvo's team lay dead next to the vehicles parked in the yard, their bodies crumpled on the cobbled floor. The courtyard was brightly lit with floodlights.

'Hold your fire!' shouted Corvo. A silence as sudden as a slammed door brought all sound to a halt. 'Come out and give up the machine, and we'll leave!'

There was a moment of silence, then a voice from the upper floor answered.

'Okay, we'll come out if you show yourselves and drop your weapons.'

'Agreed! Come out slowly and bring the Matrix with you.'

The first figure to appear was La Diabla, her black hair disarranged and dressed in some type of battledress with a belt accentuating her slim waist. An empty holster hung from the belt and she stared warily at the scene as she stepped from the safety of the doorway. Shielding her eyes from the glare, she picked out Corvo and ran to him across the yard and embraced him. He put his arm round her but kept his eyes on the doorway. In quick succession, three men emerged, one holding a leather case, holding it high in the air. Garcia took it from him, looked inside and nodded to his boss.

Striding back into the house, Corvo led his mistress away; just turning enough to look at Garcia for a second. It was a deadly signal. A burst of machine-pistol fire tore into the three prisoners, and within a second three more bodies fell lifeless onto the cobbles.

'Where is Abramovic?' The question was the first thing he said to her as they stepped inside the house.

'Jesu Christo! Give me time to catch my breath! I've been locked up in this piss-hole for two days and never saw him.'

Corvo avoided her eyes for a moment, then his tone softened.

'Well, you understand how important this matter has been to me. I wanted you back and the loss of the instrument was crucial.'

She narrowed her eyes and there was little warmth in them. 'Did you think what might happen to me? Or was the Matrix more important?'

He shrugged and looked down for a moment. 'Look, I knew he would never dare to hurt you and he only wanted the Matrix. Remember, I have been in business with these guys for a long time and know their routine.'

She turned away and caught a sight of herself in a mirror, one of many in this gilded reception room. What she saw made her leave the room and look for some place to clean up. Corvo shook his head and sighed. He sat among the debris in the hallway to contemplate his next move.

With the Matrix in his hands, he could extort whatever he wanted out of the Russian players in the Tontine. They could never survive if their oil and gas could be shut off at will. Was now the moment to use it?

CHAPTER 33

The sentry stepped out into the road and held up his hand. He was dressed in desert fatigues and wore a forage cap, not a helmet. The compound behind him had been fenced by a mesh cordon but without barbed wire or floodlights installed. Major Prokovief was surprised at first, but then realised this unit had been designed to bring about reconciliation not warfare, and this underlined it.

'Good morning, Major. Welcome to Camp Progress, we are expecting you.' It amused him that someone took the trouble to choose a name which sounded the same in English and Russian.

Nobody thought to name it Syrian Progress! he thought drily.

At the camp headquarters, he sat while a young lieutenant set out the plans of the area and a map of the remaining quarters of the city, where operations were forbidden.

'This area has been the last to hold out, and commando sections are flushing out snipers and pockets of survivors.'

'I was told the city had been taken! How is it that we are here where fighting units are still engaged? This is absurd. How can we try to reconcile our position when the Syrian population are still under threat?' His question was wasted on the young man, who just a few weeks before had arrived at his first posting.

'We've had no casualties yet, Major. We are kept up to date on developments as they occur.'

Serge Prokovief said nothing, but the young man did not miss the expression on the senior officer's face;

the narrow-eyed look and pursed mouth as he stared at him.

'Very well, show me to my quarters and then we will inspect the camp.'

The dusty huts laid out in rows of identical buildings were adopted by the troops in the way servings soldier do. That is to say, each hut had its own special character. One, painted white, boasted an aircon unit; the next was painted green and flew a Russian flag on a makeshift flagpole. Further down the path between the huts, the variations continued till they reached the officers' quarters and the guardroom. Here, immaculate white lines surrounded the buildings and the paintwork was standard military khaki.

After putting his kit away, Prokovief went to the station office to be briefed.

'When will the other staff from Moscow arrive? I am waiting for Ms Petrova to report for duty.'

'Yes, we have had contact and she will be arriving tomorrow.'

Much needed to be done, organising the base and instructing the staff in their new duties. Groups of officials, some military and some recruited from NGOs, needed briefing. Many members of the group had no idea of the practicalities of their new role.

Two teams in particular were new to Prokovief. The Red Crescent surgical unit and the CAR. The chief of the Red Crescent unit, a senior doctor from Syria, maintained his surgical unit as an independent section. The Conflict Arms Research (CAR) was set up to identify and prosecute the arms manufacturers who supplied the Intifada and ISIS rebels. The United Nations approved of their work and had drafted them into Prokovief's camp.

Ocksana arrived and was driven out to the camp. The harsh sunlight and windy conditions were no surprise. The bright sunlit streets and waterside of Istanbul were a far cry from this desert location. There was little protection from the searing blaze of the sun, and the glare of the sand as it threw back a reflection of the light stung the eyes. Prokovief came out to meet her.

'Welcome to the Shangri-La!' he drily remarked. 'A lodge is waiting for you in our summer oasis.'

One glance at the portable cabin allocated to her was enough to underline the joke.

'Yesterday I was in the Grand Hotel in Istanbul, and now I see I have the Sultan's palace!'

Despite the conditions, it thrilled her to be active once more and she set herself up as best she could.

The major held a briefing the following morning.

'While you are here, I must insist you log your personal details. My best information is that the remaining terrorists are still active in the few buildings in the Clock Tower district. We will get daily briefings from the military sources, but you must register with the office where you intend to go and what you are doing. Is that clear?'

The various groups mingled and swapped details, introducing themselves to other parties assembled in the camp. One of the men at the meeting introduced himself to Ocksana. He was an all-Spanish man, Julio Gonzales. 'I noticed you were new and wondered what task you volunteered for?' She explained her connection with the White Helmets.

'But they're disbanded!'

'I know, but Moscow sent me because of my contact with Syria. I suppose they think I could do some good here.'

Gonzales explained he was the only CAR operational member who they could spare for Northern Syria, and he felt isolated. He spoke English in nervous bursts of speech as if impatient to get the words out. He stooped so that his tall figure bent into a curve, maybe from spending too long in some laboratory examining microscopic samples.

'What is it that you do?' Ocksana was curious to find out what this bookish character was doing there.

'We collect and examine spent ammunition to identify the suppliers. This way we can bring pressure on the rogue states which are dodging the UN embargo.' His gaze became intense as he explained how their efforts in Iraq brought an end to the Chinese supply of arms to the Intifada. 'We feel sure we can do the same here in Syria.'

Serge Prokovief wandered over to introduce himself, and did the same for Ocksana.

'You will be doing us a great service if you can quickly expose the source of their weaponry. We believe most of it comes from China, but we cannot take action unless we find proof.' He laid a hand on Gonzales' sleeve to assure him of his support. Then he turned to Ocksana.

'Well, Miss Petrova, we must find something interesting for you.'

His smile reminded her again of James.

'Please call me Ocksana, now we are in civilian mode. It's six years since I wore uniform!' They discussed service life and she explained she had been a fighter pilot in those long-gone days. Julio Gonzales mentioned he served in the Spanish Navy before secondment to CAR.

Prokovief grinned. 'This is good news! I need people with experience in this job. Frankly, I am nervous of civilians with little combat background in these conditions. Let me know what you need, and we will speak later.' He nodded and moved on.

The day was filled with form-filling and requisitions of materials and equipment. Ocksana named James as her next of kin and gave the FCO in London as his contact address.

'Is there any restriction on taking leave locally?' she asked, knowing that James would want to be with her. There was no restriction, provided the location had been approved. All attempts to reach her old contacts in the White Helmets met with negative results. She raised this with Serge. 'Where can I find out what has happened? Surely they can't have disbanded without notice?' He shook his head, and looked down and away. 'I'm afraid the fact is they have been proscribed by the Syrian Government, and we can do nothing about it.'

'Why?'

'It's internal politics, Ocksana. They worked on their own and Baghdad would not allow it.' He had difficulty in meeting her gaze, knowing that it was less than the truth. He went on, 'We can't be seen to encourage an organisation at odds with Baghdad, I'm sorry.'

She could see it was useless to pursue the topic and obvious he could do nothing to rectify the situation. She said nothing for a moment. Then she asked, 'So what can I do here? My connection was with them, as you know. What else should I be doing?'

'Well, there's so much to be done!' He spread his arms in a wide gesture, embracing the dusty acres stretching beyond the camp. 'You have the skill to help us rebuild what we demolished in our efforts to destroy ISIS. We should make amends, don't you think?' He leant forward and held her attention with a long look.

There was no denying his sincerity and she felt moved by his words. Perhaps she had become too focused on her own importance to appreciate how she ought to respond to the human crisis facing this damaged country. Her military training might be useful.

'Tell me what I should do.'

He smiled and stroked his chin. 'Well, our Spanish technician seems a bit lost! He needs a hard-headed soldier to knock him into shape! He's lost outside a laboratory and yet he does a valuable job! Do you know anyone who can shape him up?' A grin spread across his face.

'Do you mean a *babushka*,' Ocksana joined in the joke, 'or a *starshina*?' – making a reference to a sergeant major in the forces.

'Maybe a bit of both. He is valuable because he can identify ammunition and arms coming illegally into terrorist hands.'

The project appealed to her. For too long she had conformed to the unscrupulous policy of Moscow in Chechnya and Kazakhstan. Now, this was a worthwhile task and a new enthusiasm surged through her system. She went immediately to find Julio Gonzales and see what she could do.

CHAPTER 34

Room 12b in the block known as 'The Back Office' was nothing more than a converted cloakroom. A desk, a computer terminal and two chairs made up the totality of the furnishing 'indented for'. This was James's new bureau – his 'station'– and the place he did his best to avoid. Lying unfinished on the desk was the report he had promised to produce after his return from Istanbul. The memory of that trip with Ocksana still lingered on, aided by the tiresome obligation to get down to office work. The sound of high heels clacking down the stone corridor outside distracted him easily and he sat up.

'Mister Ballantyne?' It was a voice he did not recognise, and when the girl put her head round the door, he wished he did. She was small and slim; her eyes were blue and her grin infectious.

'Can I come in?' She was already inside, but that was not a problem; there was no space between the door and the nearest chair.

'Well, yes! You see how you easy it is! Come on in.'

She sat on the edge of one of the steel-framed chairs as if frightened to put her weight on it. Then she swept her blond hair out of her eyes and looked at James as if she expected him to say something. He paused for a moment to reflect on what he was expected to do, then smiled and said, 'Do you have something for me? Or am I supposed to have something for you? The suspense is killing me!'

'Well, I'm Mary Fuller, hasn't central warned you?'

'Do I need a warning about you? Have you come to find out how I skive through the day? It's true!'

She burst out laughing, holding her hand over her mouth.

'No! Nothing like that! I've been assigned for training with you for the next three months.'

Ballantyne reached for the phone. 'Can you tell me what's going on? I've a Mary Fuller here who says you have put her on to me for training. What the hell is going on?'

The voice at the other end was inaudible to her, but the tone of the conversation was not difficult to detect. The level of sound increased with every minute and ended when Ballantyne slammed down the phone with an exasperated sigh.

'Well, you see how incompetent they are in this constipated organisation! They tell me it was published in "Orders" a week ago. How the hell was I to know when I've just got back from leave?'

Then he looked at her and her red cheeks, and realised she was upset. 'I'm sorry, but you must understand how awkward this is.'

She looked him in the eye. 'Well, no! I don't see problem. You're back here now, and here I am!'

James laughed out of sheer surprise; she obviously didn't take offence easily.

'But what can I teach you? Do you realise I am usually sent on undercover missions which no one else wants to do? They can hardly expect us to work in tandem!'

'Well, maybe you need someone back here to keep in touch with? Are there things like reports you have to file? Or permission you need to do something? I could help.'

The word 'report' rang like a bell in his mind. Supposing he could pass off that tiresome job onto someone else and be free of paperwork? It sounded brilliant.

'Look,' he gave her one of his sincere looks, as if he had a divine message to impart, 'could you look at this mess I'm making here and now? I can't type and think at the same time!'

She got up and stood beside him, leaning over him, and the scent she was wearing made him acutely aware of her. Her hair brushed his shoulder and he instinctively leant towards her as if drawn by the intimacy of their near contact.

'This isn't very good, is it?' she said. 'I can redo this if you want, and bring it back for approval.'

He grabbed the unfinished script and printed the page still on the screen quicker than a conjuror.

'Here! Do what you can! Your internship starts now!'

She laughed and scooped up the papers. 'Where shall I work? Is it okay if I use this PC?'

He nodded, and was out of the door before she sat down. It was like a gift from the gods and he meant to use it well! Without a word to a soul, he brought out the Yamaha 650 and got kitted out for a ride. Within the hour he was waiting at the main gate of the RHA barracks at Woolwich, presenting his ID to the guard room.

The orderly officer was called Tom Bering, and James introduced himself. He listened keenly to James's request and sat him down in the Mess to explain what he wanted.

'You see, I need to be brought up to speed with the latest weaponry and I'm told this is the place to be.' He gave him an outline of his work at the FCO to make sense of his enquiry.

Bering grinned. 'It's a lucky day for you! I've bugger all to do and have to mope around here till six o'clock, so let's see what's on offer. Do you mind if I check your ID with the FCO?'

James gave him the extension number for his own office and kept a straight face as the young officer checked his identity with the person at the other end of the line. How was he to know it was a girl called Mary Fuller who had just started work that very morning?

He nodded to James. 'Fine. I have just the man for you. Staff Sergeant Tanner is about somewhere. He's your man.'

They walked across to the armoury and Bering introduced him to Tanner. The oil-stained 'denims' worn by the artificer brought back memories of dusty tours in Iraq, with weapon cleaning as the essential chore of everyday life.

Within a minute, all three were deep in a discussion about the merits of the Uzi compared with an AK47 in combat situations. Then Ballantyne asked about latest kit and Tanner's eyes lit up.

'We've got some of those new IWI Masada automatics!' His voice took on an edge of excitement. 'The Israelis don't know we've got them and will be pissed off!'

He showed Ballantyne the new 9mm automatic nestling in its foam-packed box. James pulled it out and immediately registered its light weight. The barrel was short and set in a dull brown casing, not steel blue; the trigger guard was wide and the trigger had two elements to prevent misfiring,

'With a mag of seventeen rounds, this is the dog's bollocks.' Tanner felt at home in the company of two soldiers and he caressed the lethal weapon like a newborn baby.

Ballantyne looked at him and paused for a moment. Could he trust this soldier who he'd never seen before? But he needed some extra clout when dealing with Sala Abramovic and co. This gun would be it.

Bering left them for some minutes to carry out a routine check and James took a chance. He explained briefly what his task was and how he needed a first-rate weapon to defend himself.

'You know as well as I do, the standard issue Browning is too heavy and jams. I've used a Makurov but I need one of these.'

Tanner nodded that he understood and scratched his chin. 'The only way we could swing it is if you were allowed one for field trials. If we get the okay for that, then it's a runner.'

Ballantyne knew the answer was Melford. If he would play ball with the War Office, he could push the paperwork through. They parted with an understanding that someone up high would okay the deal.

'But bring it back!' Tanner looked sad at the prospect of parting with one of his favourites.

By the time he was back in Whitehall, James had worked out a plan. To persuade Melford to expedite the approval from the War Ministry, he would offer to go back to Abramovic and bring in the latest info on the Tontine. He took the immaculate report along with him to the office.

Melford read it and sat up. 'This is dynamite, James! Now things are really hotting up! But who has the Matrix now? The Spanish police report a firefight with casualties outside Madrid in the last few days. They believe it is Mafia related, but it seems to me it's a struggle between parties to the Tontine. We must find out and maybe warn the Russians.'

Ballantyne shook his head in disbelief. 'Am I hearing right? Tell the Russians? We've gone to all this trouble to stymie the Tontine and you suggest we give the Matrix to the opposition?'

Melford shrugged and looked out of the window, avoiding Ballantyne's stare. 'You may be surprised by what diplomacy requires, but it is none of your business to direct foreign policy. If we can get some advantage over the French or the new administration in the USA, then it may be worth it.'

Now James knew why he had his doubts about joining the service. Double-dealing and deception was the ethos of diplomacy. Nothing was as it seemed. The real task he performed was to give the FCO an advantage in international gamesmanship. They were not really concerned with the dynamics of the Tontine. The prospect of world monopoly in raw materials was being decided by the Great Powers, not by plutocrats. The fact that some individuals could steal national resources from the population of poorer nations was insignificant in their eyes. What mattered was 'balance' between states in an everlasting game. It took a little time to sink in and re-adjust to reality.

'So, who am I meant to target? Have I risked my life for some international game? Maybe you'll explain?' Ballantyne slammed his fist on the desk.

Melford leant back in his chair as if to retreat from the attack. 'You must understand I could not bring you into the picture while we were still gathering information,' his voice took on a soothing tone, 'the policy has changed as a result of the brilliant work you have done, James. We appreciate your work and it has been noted.'

'So, you're letting the American Tontine members off the hook? I can't believe it!'

James stood up and walked out without another word. His original plan to get permission to use the new automatic and offer to re-engage with Abramovic had completely vanished. He walked out into Birdcage Walk and across Horse Guards Parade without registering where he was going. Eventually, he sat in St James's Park and considered what he had to do.

First, he had to acknowledge he was now employed by the FCO. For months he had refused to accept that he had given up his independent status, but now it was too late. The future seemed greyer than before but then he thought about Ocksana and the promise of a life together. It offered a counter-balance to the bitter pill of submitting to the FCO regime.

He reminded himself, *In any case ,you prick, you've been in this mess since you first agreed to work for them!*

It was getting chilly and he decided to walk back. Fumbling for his cell phone, he realised he had left it in the little office he now called his own. When he got back he couldn't find the phone. The room was different; tidy and clean. The desk was clear and the computer seemed brighter, as if someone had wiped off the residue of months of use.

He rang the block administrator. 'Who's been I my room?' The reply was that his office was not on the room list for cleaning. It must have been Mary Fuller. Now he couldn't find his phones; his desk was in a different state and there were no pens or notepads where he left them. Thank God his automatic was locked away!

At that moment, she walked in. She had a smile on her face as if she expected grateful thanks for a job well done.

'What the hell have you been doing? Where are my phones? I can't find anything!'

Her face blanched and her smile faded. 'I thought it all needed tidying up!'

He frowned and looked around. 'There is no sign of my phones. I keep one for personal calls and the other is a "special" for operational purposes. Where are they?'

She blinked and bit her lip. 'I'm sorry; they are in the top drawer.'

He said nothing and pulled out the two phones.

'I charged them both.'

'Well, leave them next time.' He felt he had perhaps overreacted, and looked away as if looking for something else.

'Did Mister Melford accept your report?' She moved to wrong foot him by bringing up the work she had done with his report. He had to admit she had done a good job, and he nodded to admit it.

'Please don't touch the two phones in future. You can't know what they are used for; you could be putting me in danger.' He wanted to scare her, even though he was doubtful she could harm him. His remark brought a response he did not expect. Her eyes widened and she put a hand to her mouth.

'What's the matter? What happened?' He saw the confusion and fear written large on her face. She stood with her arms wrapped around her and said nothing.

Then she said, 'I didn't know. You never told me.'

'What didn't I tell you, for God's sake?'

She looked up at him, her eyes were wet. 'I answered the phone.'

'Which phone?' She pointed to the cell phone Abramovic had given him.

'What did you say?'

She dropped her head to avoid his gaze. 'He asked for Jim.'

'Yes, but what did you say?'

Her answer was almost inaudible. 'I said you were out but would ring back later.'

'Did he say anything else?'

She hesitated, then said, 'He asked me where I was and what I was doing on the line?'

Ballantyne shut his eyes. A nightmare was beginning. It was vital to get as much information as he could to combat the problem. He spoke calmly.

'So what did you say?' She was fighting back tears and could not speak for a few seconds. Eventually, she said, 'I told him I was your secretary and could take messages.' She faced him at last and looked into his eyes. 'I'm so sorry, James. I had no idea.'

The harm was done. Maybe he should have warned her to stay away from the phones? Was he in too great a hurry to get out that morning to give her a briefing?

He lied. 'It's okay. I'll fix it. I will probably be away for some time, so find another station to work with, will you?'

She nodded and turned to the door. She faced him once more and whispered something he didn't catch, then she was gone.

He had to move quickly. The first step was to inform Melford of the breach. The second was to think of a way out. He unlocked the drawer and took out his Browning, plus the box of twenty-five rounds he kept there. Then he walked round to Melford's office and told him what had happened.

'Maybe Abramovic is out of the country. If so, you are in no immediate danger.'

'But if he is here?' James said. 'I'll have to deal with him quickly or the whole surveillance is blown!'

'No. You are too much at risk. Lay low and take leave away from the danger area. I'll do what I can to cover you.' Melford pressed his lips together and looked out of the window as if finding the answer in the clear blue sky outside. 'You asked me for that test firing permit for the Israeli gun. I've okayed it and it is arriving today. Seems good timing!' It was as near a joke as he'd ever made.

He stood up and leant forward towards Ballantyne, as he stood at the desk. 'I suggest you get the weapon and I will authorise a field test for you at once.'

'Okay. I'll stay clear and lie low.' Then he added, 'It's not the girl's fault. Don't blame her. I should have been more careful.' Melford shrugged and said nothing.

For once, James almost felt affection for the old warrior, but cynical thoughts about being the cat's paw for other people stifled the thought. Instead he rang Woolwich, spoke to Tanner and arranged a meeting for that evening. The gun was in his hands by nightfall.

Later, Tanner arrived at the FCO and handed over the Masada 9mm.

'Do you have enough ammo?' Ballantyne nodded, and they spent a few minutes going through the servicing instructions for the gun.

'Remember, it fires level, don't compensate for recoil, it has none.' James nodded and thumbed ten shots into the magazine. It felt good.

What to do? He braced himself for the hard decision. He was not going to hide. A confrontation with Abramovic was unavoidable. He was a marked man if he tried to hide. He could never be safe unless he eliminated the risk.

He got on the bike, put the Masada in the side pocket of his leathers and rode north to the Haringey safe house.

CHAPTER 35

She found Gonzales in his workshop. It was a brick building with an air-conditioning unit humming in the window. A portable generator *put-putted* cheerfully as it powered the computer where he worked.

'I'm ready for my lecture!' She paused at the door and waited for him to look up.

On the screen she saw an image of a brass shell case. It was difficult at first to make sense of it, until she realised she was looking at the base of the casing. Figures and a few letters were stamped on the baseplate.

'This is what we are looking for,' he explained. 'The manufacturers have to stamp their markings on each shell to identify them. As a result, we have a means of finding out where they came from.'

'So what can we do about it?' The information seemed insignificant to her.

'Don't you see?' Julio's eyes glowed with enthusiasm behind the thick glasses. 'We can trace the consignment back to its source and prove who is supplying ISIS with ammunition!'

She feared that her questions were exasperating this gentle, serious man and she tried to soften her queries a little. 'Do you mean we can influence these suppliers in some way?'

He smiled with delight. 'Not us! We are just the cogs in the machine. No, it's the UN who can bring pressure on them, and they already have. These 50mm casings came from China and there are fewer in the haul than last month. It means the supply is drying up.' He pointed to a heap of dusty brass lying by the desk.

'What's the haul you speak of?'

'We go out to areas which have been cleared by the army and take samples of ammunition to identify, then we report to the UN officers and they take it up with the UN Council.'

Ocksana felt at last that she could do something to bring this terrible conflict to an end. It might be a small effort, but it would contribute to the resurgence of an injured nation.

'Tell me, what I should do? You realise I am no scientist, but I have a lot of experience in combat situations.'

Gonzales took off his glasses and grinned. She noticed how he rubbed his eyes and stretched; it reminded her of the peasants in the Steppes, easing their bent backs from years of toil.

'You won't need your combat skills here, I hope! We only move in when the all clear is given by the army. But we are short-handed at the moment, so there's plenty to do.'

She smiled and asked him when she should start.

'Better clear it with the director, but I need more material as soon as possible.'

The twilight came early in the town and the muezzin, at six-thirty, brought work to a close all over the liberated part of the city. For the Non-Government Officers (NGOs) and the Syrian staff, this meant time for relaxation and meals. Ocksana met Prokovief in the recreation area reserved for Europeans. He was out of uniform and sitting at the bar. 'Well! You look happy. Have you found something to do?' He smiled his special smile which reminded her so much of James. She took a stool beside him and ordered a vodka and tonic.

'Old habits die hard for us Cossacks!' He laughed and raised his glass to her.

'*Zdanovye*!' They clinked glasses and sat silent for a while.

After a while, he told her about the shortage of volunteers and how this hampered the tasks he wanted to do.

'I haven't enough military personnel to oversee the battle zone. We have to rely on the Syrians for the latest reports.'

'How often do you get updates?' she asked.

'Every evening, but the info varies with the person on duty. God forbid I should criticise our Arab friends, but some are better than others.'

The look he gave her had a lot of meaning. 'Anyhow, check with me tomorrow if you are going out and I'll let you know where it's safe.'

They joined with other NGOs for the evening meal and Ocksana felt very comfortable with the group, sharing their services for the benefit of the community. The mix of nationalities gave a cosmopolitan flavour to the occasion and she enjoyed herself. Her attempt to ring James that night didn't get through and she went to bed looking forward to the tasks ahead. She slept well.

The morning light filled the room; a muezzin on a loudspeaker echoed through the streets and she got up and showered in the basic little cubicle allotted to her. What was the most serviceable kit to wear in such dusty conditions? A big khaki shirt and tan denim trousers with plenty of pockets, and desert boots. After breakfast she reported to the guard room, where she knew the military information could be found. Prokovief was there, bending over a map of the city. He pointed to a thick blue line which zig-zagged across the plan.

'This is the latest report. Can you look at the area marked as safe? I've had it checked earlier today and it seems okay, no changes from last night. Are you fit to try your luck?'

She nodded and smiled, to show she was ready to work.

'Right, Lieutenant Hashid will escort you to the collection area that Gonzalez has indicated. Get Julio to brief you. Good luck, see you tonight.'

The young lieutenant dressed in Syrian army fatigues saluted smartly as he introduced himself.

'Welcome to Raqqa! If you will follow me I shall show you the way.' He set off in front of her, and they stopped at Gonzales' hut to collect a canvas bag and a camera.

Gonzalez explained: 'We need to collect 50mm cartridges today and to photograph their location. This helps to pinpoint where the last fighters were based. Are you okay to try this spot?' She nodded and smiled at him. It seemed like a task with few complications. Gathering up the kit she put on the khaki cap which he gave her for sun protection.

'Don't stay out in the sun for more than an hour, it takes some getting used to!'

Hashid weaved his way through a chaos of damaged buildings and left her at a broken-down wall surrounding an area of burnt, blackened rubble.

'This was a rebel position till yesterday. Look how they wasted ammo!'

He saluted and went back the way he'd come. Heaps of dusty cartridges and shell cases lay on the floor, and she took out the camera to begin the task of recording. After an hour, she had filled the canvas bag and made her way back to the compound. She felt hot and dirty. Julio Gonzalez sat at his desk and came to examine the finds.

'Very good! These are another batch, I reckon. Look at the markings on the casings! North Korean I think.' He held one bent casing under a microscope and pointed out the markings to her. It made her feel good to be useful. The conditions were harsh but she knew she had the strength to do the job. They went back to the rest area and took a break for a meal and some shade. The thermometer showed 41° and rising.

'Do you reckon you can go out again?' Gonzalez looked at her with some care.

'Yes, sure, when I've had a chance to shower and change.' She was eager to show how well she could cope with the extreme heat, and was confident she knew the way back to the site.

'Okay, see you in about an hour and let me know how you feel then.' He tapped her on the shoulder as a sign of approval and went back to his work.

The shower was tepid but did a miracle in restoring her mood. Changing into a clean brown shirt and putting her hair up felt good. She made her way back to the ruined house and the discarded casings. There was plenty to keep her busy.

*

Ahmed scrutinised the slim figure squatting among the debris, sifting through the heap of spent cartridges. The scavenger wore no uniform, just a khaki shirt and old trousers and a peak cap. There was a camera slung around his neck and from time to time the figure stopped to take photos of one of the casings.

It was a hot day even for Raqqa, and he wiped his face with his *shermagh*. Nothing else moved in his field of fire, so his gaze returned to the figure scrabbling among the ruins. Bored and impatient he trained his sniper rifle on the stooping figure. Two hours had passed and not a single shot had been fired. Was it worth taking a shot and revealing his position to any of the government troops surrounding his perch? For three weeks he had survived the onslaught by the Syrian army. Even Russian Special Forces had not penetrated into this last outpost in the city.

A sound made him turn sharply. He grabbed his 9mm automatic. A bearded face poked through a gap.

'Salaam!' It was Abbas, his loader, with a pack of ammunition. Crawling to the slit in the wall, he peeked out at the scene.

'What's the infidel doing? Is he a madman?'

Ahmed shrugged. 'Who knows, foreigners come here to show off.'

They watched together as the figure sifted through the dusty refuse, collecting a section of different calibre shells. A wisp of dark hair drifted out of the cap.

'Shoot him!'

Ahmed shook his head. 'No! One unarmed Kaffir and we get a shitload of fire down on our heads. It's not worth it!'

The moment passed and the figure disappeared.

Back among the remnants of a mosque, Commander Osmani rubbed his eyes and rested his weary back. It was the second day of an attack by government troops and he longed for a minute of quiet or rest. Surrounded and short of fighters, he sensed this was the last outpost for ISIS in the city.

'Well, what is he doing?' He stared at the sniper. 'Do I have to tell you to eliminate a Kaffir? Don't you understand what has to be done?'

'But listen, he's not carrying a gun and he's scavenging among the rubbish. I never saw this before.'

An explosion outside the walls brought them to the floor and for a few minutes a silence replaced the sound of gunfire. A wounded man screamed nearby and Osmani scrambled out of the building. He turned abruptly and dismissed Ahmed.

'If he comes back again, send for me.'

Ahmed nodded and crept back to the sniper hole. Nothing emerged within his field of fire so he sat back, resting his head against the brick wall. In the background intermittent gunfire chattered among the ruins, but it was simply everyday life and had lost its significance. He dreamed of his life in Yemen before the Caliphate called for volunteers; family life with his wife and children. Was it ever going to be the same? He pushed the thought away. If Allah (Peace be upon Him) wills it.

A sound jolted him to life. Down in the ruins someone was stepping quietly among the debris. He squinted through the spyhole. The same young European was picking up discards.

He kicked his loader to life, 'Get el Akbar!' and the man crept away wriggling through the dust to avoid making a sound. The commander arrived bareheaded and eyes heavy with fatigue.

'What is it now?' His voice sounded hoarse with impatience.

Ahmed pointed down to the slender figure stooping among the casings on the dusty floor.

'Is he armed?'

'No, just as before. He carries a sack and a camera.'

El Akbar ran his hands through his hair. One more decision among so many. The chance of escape was dwindling with every moment. There were fighters needing orders; plans to be made. What was the Will of the Caliphate? To surrender or fight on?

He let out an exasperated sigh. 'Kill him!'

The high-velocity bullet drove through her body, spinning her round like a marionette, flinging her arms in a wild gesture. For a moment, her eyes seemed to look upwards as if seeking the sunlight or some message from above. Then she stumbled and fell dead among the casings.

CHAPTER 36

It was dark. No lights showed from the house. Ballantyne parked a safe distance away and watched. Memories of the meetings he attended as 'Jim' came back to him. The wild parties, the savage fights over nothing and the suspicion he endured at the beginning. He wondered what had happened to Bilan, the gypsy hitman who disappeared some months ago. Did he join the Russians as he claimed?

After thirty minutes, he lost patience and moved to a side street to get to the passage which ran along the backs of the houses. Originally, these pathways were made to allow access for coal and other bulk items to be delivered to the terraced houses. Now, they were overgrown alleyways for foxes, cats and prowlers. He picked his way carefully through the rubbish and reached the back of the house. Still, there was no sign of life from the windows. The back-door lock took just an elbow punch to give access to the kitchen. He paused for a full minute before opening the door. Not a sound. The door opened easily on oiled hinges. Stepping over the broken glass, he crept along the hall to the room where Assurov used to give instructions. The house was empty.

The smell of smoke and cooking still hung in the air so he made a rapid check of the desk, shelves and drawers for a clue to the whereabouts of any of Abramovic's gang. He moved upstairs to the first bedroom when a sound stopped him dead; a key was turning in the lock of the front door. He pulled the Masada from his side pocket and cocked it, the slide moved silently. Slipping through a door, he found himself in an empty room with no curtains on the windows. Street light flooded in to make it bright as moonlight.

Voices speaking a foreign language echoed through the hall and he could hear them walking down to the kitchen. Two men. A silence fell. It was obvious they saw the state of the back door. Steps ran through the ground floor and then up the stairs. He braced himself behind the door, gun in hand. A figure burst into the room and halted within two feet of him, looking towards the window. As the man turned, Ballantyne saw the handgun held in a brace position coming round to aim at him. Dropping to his knees, Ballantyne fired and the man cannoned back against the wall then slid to the floor. The sound of the gun filled the room and bounced off the walls. He charged out into the corridor, holding the automatic in front of him.

As he emerged, a figure darted into the room at the far end of the corridor and slammed the door. He had no chance to take a shot and ran straight to a position to the right of that door. The sound of a window opening focused his mind. He paused a second and kicked the door open. The window stood wide open. He waited outside while he peered into the room; no one in sight. Turning to face the open door, he fired twice into the panels at waist height. It swung back towards the doorway and he caught sight of the second man as he crumpled to the floor. It was Abramovic. His eyes were open and he clutched his stomach with one hand. The other hand held a pistol and he raised it in James's direction. He was too weak to fire and after a second, it fell to the floor. He formed some words as if to speak but they were lost in the flow of blood which streamed from his mouth. Then he was dead.

Ballantyne ran back to the other room to the first man. He lay face up. It was not Assurov. The sound of the gunshots must have been heard in the street. He ran down to the kitchen and bolted through the backyard and down the alley to the side street. Lights appeared in several houses as he ran, but nobody came out into the streets. He reached the motorbike and got clear in a minute.

After half a mile, he pulled up and sat astride the bike. His fingers inside his gloves were trembling so that he could barely grip the levers. He hugged himself to stop the tremors and wondered at the strange effect. It was certainly not the first time he had been in a firefight or killed a man. In all the years of combat, he never experienced a reaction like this. What was different? Had his mind turned against violence? Slowly, the answer emerged as he contemplated the episode. He'd set out to kill. This was not an incident in a fight where he had to protect himself. He went there to eliminate Abramovic if he could find him, or whoever got in his way. It was the first time.

He rode on to his flat and took a long shower, very aware that things had changed. He took the Masada apart, cleaned it carefully and went to bed.

CHAPTER 37

It rang five times before James reached for the phone.

'Good morning, Mr Ballantyne. Mr Melford would like to see you today. Would midday suit you?' The genteel tones belied the meaning of the message. James knew such a call meant serious trouble or some unexpected crisis.

He fell back onto the bed and wondered what they wanted. Had Whitehall found out about last night? No. That was impossible. Could there be some new development in the strategy concerning the Tontine? Possibly. Whatever; he could not ignore it. He dressed slowly and made his breakfast; coffee and some stale-bread toast. It took him a long time to get the events of last night in perspective. The incident at Abramovic's house in Hackney altered in his mind. Last night he had felt the significance of the cold-blooded killing; now it appeared to be less momentous. He began to see it as a necessary step in self-defence; a pre-emptive strike against certain attack. He persuaded himself it was justified and, in a sense, legal. But at the back of his mind the accusation of cold-blooded murder, like a black dog, trod softly behind him.

He walked along Millbank and turned into Whitehall with a clearer head. He didn't need to tell Melford any of the details, except that a trap was set for him at Hackney. He had been forced to shoot Abramovic in self-defence. That was what 'they' wanted to hear; the elimination of another member of the Tontine. It never occurred to him that he deluded himself as well as lied to 'them'.

The time was only eleven-thirty, so he went back to his mini-office. To his surprise, Mary Fuller was sitting behind the desk. She stood up quickly, tilting the chair backwards; eyes astonished.

'What are you doing here?'

'I thought I should clear things away. I felt so bad and had nowhere to go.'

He thought back to the confrontation the day before and how her slip put him in danger. Now it had no significance; the danger had past.

'Well, it was serious but I'm sure you learnt how important it is to be cautious.'

She looked away and lowered her head. 'I'm so sorry, it was my fault. Maybe I should have joined some other section?'

He gave a half smile. 'Yes, let me help you to find the right person to work with and let's forget the past.' Relief flooded her face and she forced a faint smile.

'That would be great. Maybe I shall do some good somewhere!'

She gathered up some papers, and as she left he felt pleased that she would find a useful spot in the bureau. She was an attractive person and would do well. He began to wish she had remained, if only to type up the report he would be submitting about last night's incident. He sat down and tapped away a brief account of the event and printed it out for Melford.

At twelve-fifteen, he knocked on Melford's door. Everyone knew him as a stickler for punctuality, yet he rose to meet James without a word of complaint.

'Sit down James, I specially want to speak to you.' His face was expressionless but he seemed restless, moving about in the chair and avoiding James's eye.

'There's some bad news and I want you to hear it first from me.' Still he hesitated and fidgeted with a pencil he picked up from the desk. Had the Americans vetoed some plan? Had the Tontine exercise been abandoned? Why this solemn interview? James began to feel uneasy.

'I've just got a call from a man called Prokovief; he got our number from the UN in Baghdad. Do you know him?'

'No idea. What does he want?'

'He rang to give us bad news. It seems there has been an accident and Miss Petrova has been hurt badly. They knew you were her next of kin.' He broke off as if reluctant to go on. James stared at him and saw the look on his face; the averted eyes and grey pallor, so different to Melford's normal expression.

'What are you saying? Is Ocksana in hospital? What happened?' It was maddening to be told something in segments. Why didn't he come right out with it?

'I have to tell you James, she died. She was hit by a sniper bullet and died at once. I'm sorry. What can we do?' He stayed silent, unable to find words to console.

Ballantyne sat in his chair, gripping the arms tightly, his face set in stone. He could say nothing. The shock worked like a drug stupefying him; he had never contemplated such a possibility. Ocksana? Her vitality and capability were her unique gifts. How could she be dead?

Trivial things leapt into his mind. *But she was in Baghdad just days ago. I spoke to her!* Then, *She never went near the war zone. How could it be possible?*

An irrational anger was rising in his blood. Someone must be responsible! It was too unfair that the life of the one person he worshipped had been taken away. His life was ruined and the future blotted out at a stroke.

'Let me speak to this man. Who is he?'

'I've got the number here.' Melford passed a note across.

James got up without a word and walked quietly back to the little office. He shut the door and sat down, the piece of paper with the phone number on it crushed in his fist. The image of Ocksana lying dead in some dusty area formed in his mind, even though he'd learnt little of the circumstances. He pushed the image away.

The senseless anger gradually diminished as the full effect of the loss began to take hold of him. Instead, a wave of guilt washed over him. Why did he not stop her from going to such a dangerous place? He had taken no steps to check out what she was going to do. Who was this man Prokovief? Why did he know nothing about him? All these questions whirled round in his brain and he held his head in his hands to try to steady himself. Outside, the humdrum noises of ordinary office life went on as if the world had not changed. Nobody bothered him; no one knew or cared about him, the world was indifferent to him.

After a while, he felt the slip of paper in his fist and took it out, smoothing out the wrinkles. He read the number and reached for the phone. A strange dialling tone told him he connected to a distant exchange.

'*Draste*! Prokovief here.' The voice, so obviously Russian, sounded businesslike and brusque.

Ballantyne for a moment could not form the words he wanted to use, then he spoke in Russian. 'You can tell me about Ocksana?'

He could not bring himself say more.

'Is this James? I am so sorry. We checked the site before she went out, but you can never be sure they don't come back!'

James held the handset tightly, trying to control himself, when his mind wanted to scream out: '*You senseless bastards! You sent my love into danger!*'

He kept a level tone. 'What was she doing there?'

'She volunteered to collect shell casings for identification.' Then he added, 'It's vital work for the UN and she was eager to help. We shall miss her, I'm so sorry.'

James held the handset against his forehead; he did his best to conquer the rage inside. He was silent for so long, Prokovief asked, 'Are you still there?'

'Yes. What have you done with her body?' He heard himself talking as if it was someone else. 'Is she buried over there?'

'No. We are holding the body for your instructions.'

Again, a pause. James wanted to say: '*What I want is the vibrant living person – the girl I love.*' He hated the corpse; he wanted nothing to do with her lifeless remains.

'Bury her in Syria! You took her; now bury her!' He put the phone down and sat with his hands covering his face. For once, he was glad of the little private space they called 'his office'.

CHAPTER 38

The floor was littered with rubbish and scraps from two days of neglect. James stayed in bed. Nobody had contacted him. He wanted no condolences from people who hardly knew him; the kind who wrote 'Our thoughts are with you' and other worn clichés. Grief was like a gunshot; it took time to heal and then the scar remained.

He regretted his outburst when he told them to bury her in Syria. He had been selfish, consumed with the loss he suffered and not regarding others. Although Ocksana had no immediate family, he recalled the Russian general, her godfather, Grigor Vasilich, who rescued them in Omsk and she regarded with such affection. The least he should do would be to ensure he knew. He shaved, showered and got dressed. Going back to his desk, he sensed the subdued atmosphere. Eyes averted or shy smiles as he passed by, everybody too diffident to speak to him.

He dialled up Melford, preparing himself for a difficult conversation. He had no desire to be bombarded with contrived sympathy, but he wanted Melford's help for two purposes. First, to show he was ready for work; nothing hurt more than reliving time and again what might have been. Work was the antidote. Secondly, he wanted to find a link to Vasilich to tell him what had happened. He owed it to the man who rescued him.

To his relief, Melford seemed businesslike. 'James, glad to hear from you, what can I do?'

He explained why he wanted to contact the Russian general and the problem of getting through to him on a personal level.

'Leave that to me, I can find out through Communications. It should be a good test for them!'

James went back to his cubby-hole office and searched for the scrap of paper with the Syrian phone number. He felt compelled to try and put right what he said to the man who informed him of her death. The desk was clean; the shredder empty and no sign of any debris. He tried to recall the name but failed. He could do nothing, but it left a hollow feeling that he could never correct what he said in that moment of shock. It was still true he had no wish to have her buried in some English graveyard; she would live in his memory, not in some burial ground.

Melford rang an hour later. 'Pretty impressive! I've got a number for some military airfield in southern Russia. It's somewhere near Omsk. Do you think it's the one?'

The image of Grigor Vasilich in his full regalia, pulling rank on the Omsk police to get James and Ocksana released, sprang instantly to mind.

'Yes! That's the place! Great work! Give them five stars.'

'Okay. Will you come back to me for a word after you've spoken to him?'

'Of course.' Ballantyne thought no more about it as he scribbled down the number.

It was six o'clock Omsk time when the call went through. A woman answered the phone with the clipped tone and sharp voice of military personnel. When he asked to speak to General Vassilich, he was put on hold and expected a wait of many minutes as the formalities of Russian protocol were carried out.

A voice boomed out from the receiver. 'Who is this? Is it James?'

Ballantyne replied and before he could add anything, the voice brayed again.

'Where are you *Mal-chik* (boy)? What are you doing?'

It was difficult to stem the wave of greetings to allow a moment to tell Grigor about Ocksana., but he managed.

'What I have to tell you is hard, Tovarich, so be strong. It's about Ocksana. I must tell you she has been killed.'

There was a sound from the Russian end of the conversation. A gasp and a low cry. Then a blast of sound which blew the phone away as if an explosion detonated at the other end of the line.

James let it subside and listened for a reply.

'Where did it happen? Who did it?'

He told the facts as quickly and as simply as he could, and dealt with the inevitable questions about security and negligence which followed.

'My sweet little fighter is gone. How can this be? You must come to us and we will mourn together.'

'I will try someday soon, Grigor, but you keep her in your thoughts forever.' James used the expression so familiar in Russian.

Strangely, it felt good to share his grief with another. Something in him responded to the emotional outburst though he could not express the same surge of feeling.

He forgot the request Melford had made to speak to him, and it was a surprise when Mary Fuller put her head round the door to ask him to contact the director. Her blonde hair falling cross her face and her blue eyes were anxious.

'I'm sorry, I forgot to try to find a slot for you. You can understand, I'm sure,' he said.

She smiled and nodded. 'Of course! Don't worry about me.'

'Where did you move to?'

'Well,' she looked him in the eye. 'I joined Mister Melford's office and there's plenty to do.'

'That's good. There would have been little to do if you had stayed with me.'

She looked at him quickly and then smiled. 'Anyway, when you're ready he'd like to see you.' She lingered for a short while as if waiting for an answer, but then left hurriedly. James wondered if he had been too abrupt with her or done something wrong, but he followed after her and put the thought aside.

When he reached Melford's office he found his boss was not alone. The bulky figure of the American, Bob Harding, sat legs spread wide almost overwhelming a chair.

'Hi, James! We need you, fella! Come on in.' A hand like a catcher's mitt gripped him and propelled him into a chair alongside the desk. There was no word of condolence and James appreciated that this old warrior knew what was best in the world of combat trauma.

Melford shifted slightly in his seat and scratched his nose. 'I asked Colonel Bob to come here to explain what we would like to do, if you are okay.' He had trouble in looking directly at Ballantyne. James wondered what new scheme he was trying to sell; another ploy to help the Americans?

The American butted in. 'Now we know where the Matrix is, we have to get it or at least destroy it before harm is done.' He nodded to Ballantyne as if to engage him in the point of view. James said nothing.

'We have to neutralise these motherfuckers before they destabilise our economy.'

There was no doubt he meant the US economy. James was puzzled. 'If they cut off Russian oil or gas supplies, how does that harm you? You can make up the difference.'

Harding shook his head, 'No way! That would throw the ball straight into the Iranians' hands. We have fracking potential for our own supplies but that leaves the grease-balls with a huge advantage worldwide.'

Then he paused and looked James in the eye. 'It cannot happen.' There could be no doubt what was number one on their priority list.

'Well, what do you want from me?'

Melford joined in. 'You can see, James, how useful your connections with some of the Tontine will be. You've built up a link and we can use that to gain access to the Matrix. Do you feel this is a job you can do?'

He needed a moment to take stock. They already knew he had been exposed accidentally to one group of Tontine members and he had been forced to act 'with extreme prejudice'. They also knew he had knowledge of the rival faction. What was their 'angle' on this situation? It soon became clear.

James said nothing, waiting for the next gobbet of information to be revealed.

The big American shifted in his seat, leaning forward so that he nearly tipped out of the chair. 'You got the insider know-how James, you can get in with that bum Corvo and screw their system.'

The picture was emerging. They wanted him to risk his neck with a member of the Tontine who was one of the most dangerous men in Europe, just to back up the Russians and probably to put power into the hands of American plutocrats. A grim smile twisted Ballantyne's face.

'I can see you like the idea.' Melford thought he understood James's reaction.

'We hoped you would!' Harding grinned and nodded his agreement.

It was time to clear a few things up.

'Look, I understand what game you're playing, and it stinks! I was recruited to try to break an international conspiracy to control world resources. I put my life on the line to do that. Now you tell me that the real intention was to play politics with Russia and screw the Iranians. What sort of tame dog do you think I am?'

Melford sat stunned. His eyes blinked behind the thick-rimmed glasses and he sat upright. Faint pink spots appeared on his cheeks and he pressed his lips together, so they formed a thin straight line.

'Look, we are trying to deal with a menacing situation; a threat of disaster. It's not a meeting of some Hampstead snowflakes discussing peace; we have a job to do and though unpleasant, it's necessary. I thought you would understand that by now!'

The American got up and stood behind his chair, looming over Ballantyne like an elephant.

'We get what you're saying, James,' his tone was like honey, 'we salute you for what you've done. Honest to God, no one else could have done what you did. But this is the real situation. We need you. You're a stand-up sort of guy; you know what's to be done. Help us out here.'

James bit his lip. He was not going to swallow all this bullshit. He said nothing, and was about to get up and leave when Melford spoke again.

'Just remember, James, it was Corvo who supplied ISIS with weapons and ammo.'

He let the remark hang in the air like a primed hand grenade ready to explode.

In a split second, the image of Corvo's warehouse outside Madrid, packed with those distinctive camouflaged boxes, flashed into James's mind; the lorries being loaded. He shook his head as if to fling the image away, but it remained and morphed into a vision of a broken body among spent, discarded brass casings; a picture he had never seen in reality, but which haunted his imagination.

He got up and left the room.

Harding looked at Melford and shook his head, 'Cheap shot.'

Melford shrugged.

*

James fired up the Yamaha and rode south over Vauxhall Bridge. He had no destination in mind; the day was clear and the road dry. As he cleared the suburbs he felt the tension of the last days slipping away and a feeling of exhilaration coming back. He turned off the M25 on to the winding roads leading to the South Downs. The turns and twists demanded total concentration. Within the hour he reached the broad back of the hills above Brighton and took the A27 towards Arundel. The sun tinted the hills with deep shadows and gold highlights as it faded in the west. He stopped on a hill above Bury, where the view stretched down the valley towards the sea. It was quiet, and traffic had ceased. He felt better; the stress of the last days had passed. Somehow, the concentration of the ride released the tensions which had tormented him.

He sat watching the sunset creeping over the land and considered the future. It was no good acting on impulse. His life had panned out the way it had because he rejected conventional humdrum jobs – even despised them. He had chosen to follow the path which led him to risk his life. What was behind this instinct? Excitement? Challenge? Or was it a need to prove himself against the world?

With the sunset and the tranquil mood settling over him in the warm evening, he rode on slowly to a little pub he remembered set away from the world in Burpham on the Hill. He took a room; drank some beer; ate a good meal and went to bed.

CHAPTER 39

Corvo sat in a large leather chair waiting for the waiter to bring him a whisky. He preferred the best Japanese malt but here in his London club it was unavailable. The great windows looked out on Green Park, and a shaft of bright sunlight brought out the warm colours of the room; the Turkish carpets and the mahogany furnishings. A casual observer would see a rich man at his ease, but the truth was very different.

He had the Matrix under his control and now was the moment to see how far he could manipulate the Russians. What would they pay to get their hands on it? Or maybe better to sell it to the Americans? This meeting would answer that question. He sipped the drink and acknowledged a fellow member with a brief remark, but he was nervous and making an effort to seem calm. Who would be coming to the table? The answer came directly.

Two men were being ushered towards him by the porter. One was a thickset man of about fifty years of age; the other a much younger man with slim build and oiled black hair. They looked uncomfortable in these unfamiliar surroundings and one or two of the members viewed them with curiosity.

Corvo stood and extended his hand. 'Baron Julio Corvo, at your service.'

The older man took his hand and gripped it. 'We have come far to meet you and hope you are well.' He spoke good English, but Corvo recognised a Ukrainian accent.

'I am Mikhail Brezhnev, and my son Ilyavic is vice president of Uraloil.'

Corvo smiled warmly. 'If you will allow me to lead the way, I have reserved a room for us, so we can talk freely.'

Brezhnev frowned. 'We are happy here in your charming club, we do not wish to go elsewhere.'

'I'm afraid we cannot talk business in the club rooms – it is a rule, but we have a room upstairs where we can discuss matters in private.'

The two Russians exchanged looks but followed him up the stairs to small room, set with a table and four chairs. On a sideboard were dishes of cold food and a wine cooler with a long-necked bottle inside. Corvo indicated the food with a gesture and they sat down at the table.

'Please help yourselves if you would like refreshment.'

The Russian, Brezhnev, interrupted him. 'First, show us you have the Matrix.'

Corvo raised his eyebrows as if shocked by the remark, then he tapped sharply on the table and a man appeared carrying a briefcase. It was Garcia; he placed the case on the table and stood back against the wall.

'This has cost me many lives and much money. But I imagine it is more valuable to you than to me.'

Corvo leant forward and opened it; the Matrix gleamed softly, its black frame contrasting with the gleaming electrodes.

The bulky Russian stirred in his seat. He frowned and pointed a finger at the machine. 'Who designed this? How do we know it can do what you say?'

'My dear Mister Brezhnev; you would not be here if you doubted its value. Do you recall the 15th of

November, 2017? Let me remind you: a total blackout of all gas supplies through the Kazak supply lines lasted for twenty-four hours. It was never explained, was it?' There was a lilt to Corvo's voice as he reminded them of the incident. He knew the cards were all in his hands and he enjoyed it.

A shadow flickered across the face of the younger man, Ilyavic. 'Get down to business. Tell us what you want?'

'Let us say, two billion US dollars. It means nothing to you; but I need it to be available now. I am not prepared to wait and find myself manoeuvred by ingenious delays. The details of the payment I can give you later.'

Ilyavic spread his hands wide. 'Do you think we can authorise such a sum without government approval? It's impossible!'

'I can give you a week to come back with an answer, and,' he paused, 'the money, of course.'

Brezhnev exchanged a look with his son and nodded. 'We will consider this with our commission and come back within a week.' He got up and bowed curtly. 'Please show us the way out.'

Corvo stayed seated and motioned to Garcia. He led the men out.

When he returned, he sat at the table and helped himself to the food from the side table; Corvo took the bottle of Riesling and filled two glasses.

'We need to watch our backs here. They won't pay up if they can surprise us and take it. What do you suggest?'

Garcia grinned. 'Would you like some good news first? I've just heard. Abramovic is dead!'

'Did the Russians reach him? What happened?'

He outlined the story of the ambush in the house. 'But no one knows who did it, could be one of his own men.'

They discussed various theories but reached no conclusion.

'Let's wait and see. All we can know is that at least one competitor is out of the race. See if you can get hold of the Irish man who worked for him as a mercenary. He will know, and we can use him if we pay him right.'

Garcia nodded and raised his glass. '*Salud*!'

CHAPTER 40

Early morning traffic filled the road back to London. James reflected on the contrast with the previous day. How the bright, warm day eased his mind and now the everyday turmoil of traffic brought back reality. By the time he reached the western suburbs, his mind was clear. He faced life without Ocksana; he had to be occupied, no longer caring about the tasks he was asked to perform. His aversion to killing vanished when he shot Abramovic; he searched for him in order to kill him. Nothing could mask the reality that he had been offered a way out but chose to reject it. A second man lost his life, even though in self-defense. All this percolated down into his subconscious, and by the time he arrived at Whitehall, he felt focused, unemotional.

Talking to Melford would be difficult, and he put it off like a visit to the dentist. It needed to be done, but not yet. Then he had a bright idea: he could tell Melford indirectly. He rang the controller's office and Mary Fuller answered. Mary Fuller. The sound of her voice brought back the incident which changed his life, but it had something soothing about it which pleased him.

'Mary, it's James Ballantyne. Could you come up and have a word with me?'

She looked different, more serious, her hair pulled back from her face, held tightly in a shining coil on top of her head. She wore a black sweater and a slim grey skirt which enhanced her figure. She stayed cool and professional.

'What can I do, James?'

'I have to see your boss sometime today or tomorrow. I have decided to go ahead with his plans, but would you break the ice for me? We parted after a spat and maybe you could help?'

She tilted her head and gave him a quick look. 'Yes, I heard about that! He was fuming for about an hour after you left. Don't worry, I'll straighten it out.'

She smiled, and he felt sure things would pan out alright. Her eyes were deep blue; he wondered why he had not noticed this before.

'Thanks. I'll be back this evening, so maybe I'll face the dragon then.'

She nodded and went. He heard her heels tapping as she ran down the corridor.

He rang Woolwich and asked for Staff Sergeant Tanner. 'Can I come down for a chat? I need to know a bit more about things.' He avoided speaking of the automatic. Tanner agreed to meet him in the afternoon. He pocketed the Masada and rode directly to the barracks, and was waved through by the guardroom. Obviously they knew he was coming. When they were alone, he showed him the gun. 'I need to know a few things.'

'Such as?'

'It's not for sale, at least not in the UK, so is there any barrel marking or rifling which identifies it, as far as you know?'

Tanner paused and looked keenly at Ballantyne. 'You mean for ID from a spent bullet?'

Ballantyne nodded.

The soldier tilted his head and shuffled his feet. Then he looked at Ballantyne and said, 'Only the Israeli Special Ops use this gun, and the reason they do is because it's effective and the rounds are untraceable. Does that answer your question?' They said nothing more about the gun. Ballantyne asked if the firing range was open and Tanner led him to a Nissen hut with a warning sign – 'LIVE FIRING' – on the door. They practised targets at ten metres and twenty-five, using the full seventeen rounds on each. The gun made an unusual barking sound unlike the sharp percussion of a conventional 9mm. With fifteen hits grouped on the target shape, both were pleased.

'You see why this has an advantage? Low recoil and lightweight.'

Ballantyne smiled wryly. 'No wonder they try to keep it to themselves.'

He left Woolwich with a box of 9mm ammunition and a promise to keep Tanner up to date on its performance.

*

Melford was still in his office when James knocked at the door.

'Glad you can work with us on this,' he said, as if they had never clashed. 'I've done my best to find out where Corvo is and I feel sure that will be where the Matrix can be found. Immigration say a Julio Corvo entered the UK last week and stayed till yesterday, flying out to Geneva.'

'Did he travel with anyone else?'

'A woman called Rodriguez had the seat next to him. Maybe she was with him.'

'What help can I get if I'm stopped at the airport or in Geneva?'

Melford frowned. 'I can't give a permit for a weapon.'

'Maybe not, but I need some cover to get a weapon out of the UK. If I am stopped, I could pass as a sky marshal or suchlike.'

'All right, the best I can do is put you on an El Al flight to Geneva with a pass, but you will have to find a passport with a new name. We haven't time to make one for you. Can you do it?' James nodded, and gave him the name on the passport Assurov provided months ago.

'Very well, you'll be booked on a flight for tomorrow evening. You can collect the pass here tomorrow a.m. and the expenses. Is there anything else we need to clear up?'

'Yes.' Ballantyne looked him in the eye. 'Am I to seize the Matrix or destroy it? What about Corvo?' Like an electric discharge, the meaning flashed between them without a spoken word.

'Do whatever is necessary.' The controller looked down and began to shuffle the papers on his desk. 'I'll authorise a Section 7 permit from MI6.' (Section 7 of the Intelligence Service Act 1944.) 'That will cover you.'

'Very well.' Ballantyne got up and left. There was nothing more to be said.

Heathrow was jam-packed. A Friday evening with the weekend crowd eager to rush home. Ballantyne took his rucksack and made for the airside check-in. An Israeli policeman built like a cage fighter checked him and examined the Masada he laid on the table. He spoke in Hebrew; Ballantyne shook his head. Then in English, 'How did you get this?' pointing to the gun.

'From Special Forces.' He looked the security man in the eye and stared him out.

'How much ammo?'

'Just one box.'

The man's eyes flickered and he pushed the gun back across the table. 'OK, go with God.'

Ballantyne put it into the side pocket of his leather jacket and joined the queue slowly boarding the plane. He had been allocated an aisle seat in the back row. The crew welcomed him, pleased to see a guard on the flight.

They'll not be so keen when they see me bail out at Geneva!

Scanning the rows of passengers, it became obvious they were mainly traveling all the way to Tel Aviv. He asked the steward for the passenger list and ran his eye down the names and destinations. Only three were leaving the flight at Geneva. He tried to identify who the other two were, and the manifest indicated where they sat. Both were men. One was a dark, tall man dressed in grey suit; he had a carry-on case and a duty-free bottle of whisky. Ballantyne ignored him. The second wore dark glasses and a baseball cap pulled down tight on his head. He had no hand luggage and as he turned to leave, he glanced around as if checking the other passengers.

The look of surprise on the face of the chief steward was comical as James waved goodbye. He opened his mouth to protest but by the time he formed words, James had exited the rear door and was halfway down the steps to the ground. He kept the baseball cap in sight and joined the passport queue. Another flight had just arrived; blending in with the crowd was easy.

They passed through without a hitch and the man joined the hurly-burly around the carousel to collect their baggage. Ballantyne watched from a distance.

After a while, the man took off his cap and glasses, rubbing his eyes. This was the first time Ballantyne had had a chance to see his features properly. He was bald, his skin dark and eyes hooded under thick brows. It was an easy face to remember, but Ballantyne did not know him. The man waited for some package from the hold as James watched.

'Be careful!' a voice whispered over his shoulder. James jumped aside and twisted to face the face the speaker. A hand gripped his arm and a face he knew grinned at him.

'Bilan! You mad gypsy! What are you doing here?'

'Are you the only spy at work? I come here like you, to earn my wages!'

James was so distracted that he lost sight of his target for a moment. They grinned and Bilan pointed a finger. 'Look!'

The dark man found his luggage and was heaving it onto a trolley. There were two large suitcases. He trundled towards the exit and Bilan motioned James to follow. Outside, a Lexus 450 waited for him and he got in, throwing the suitcases in beside him.

'Quick!' Bilan dragged James to the taxi rank and pushed him into one. Not a word of explanation had been said, but James sensed the urgency. As the taxi moved off, Bilan sat back and grinned at James. They followed the Lexus.

'You working for who?' he said. 'Not Abramovic! You know he's dead?'

Ballantyne nodded; it wouldn't help to explain how Abramovic died, or who killed him.

'You told me you were going to work for the Russians. Is that right?'

The gypsy shrugged. 'Yes, I work with them, but it's a contract, you understand? They pay and I work.'

Ballantyne watched as the Lexus left the motorway and headed up a winding road towards the mountains.

'Why is this man important to you?'

Bilan looked keenly at James. 'You recall our trip to Rumania? I warned you about Corvo. Have you forgotten?'

Ballantyne shook his head. 'No, you said he was very dangerous. I believe you!'

Bilan shifted in his seat. 'The man we follow is Diego, he is Corvo's henchman. I want to find out where he is going and trace Corvo.'

James was mystified why Bilan showed an interest in Corvo. Was it the Matrix he was searching for? Or could there be some discrete activity involving Corvo and the Russians?

'Tell me why you're here? Is Diego your target?'

Dark eyes stared at James with curiosity. Ballantyne sensed this was not the time to reveal the Matrix secret. If the Russians knew, they would destroy it. His task was to seize it as ransom for diplomatic advantage.

Ballantyne decided to lie. 'We suspect Corvo of the elimination of Abramovic and other crimes. He is wanted in the UK for murder.'

Bilan sat back and was pondering. 'Murder, for sure,' he said, 'Corvo would kill his own child if it suited him. I have to find him and put an end to him.' He looked out of the window at the snow falling; they were climbing the twisting mountain road. He let out an exasperated sigh. 'Look at this!' He wiped the window impatiently. 'Tracks.' Ballantyne knew what he meant. Any movement around the target would be easily traced;

it curtailed freedom of action and made target security much easier.

The Lexus continued up the mountain for two miles then pulled into the drive of a large hotel, Die Kaiser Hof. Bilan told the driver to drive on. After the next turn in the road, they stopped and drove back to Geneva. 'Where you stay?'

James lied again. 'I have a friend here and don't know the address – I ring him when I get a new phone.' Bilan nodded; there was no need to explain why James needed a new phone. The gypsy scribbled down a number and handed it across.

'Just make contact when you have one, we can work together on this. Agreed?'

Ballantyne grinned. 'Like old times?'

The gypsy punched him lightly on the shoulder and got out of the car. 'Do it quick, there's no time to waste.' Then he was gone.

Finding a phone shop in Geneva was easy, and within half an hour James had a basic Nokia in his hand and made contact with Whitehall. He reminded himself to delete the number; memories of Mary Fuller and Abramovic swam before his eyes.

He found a hostel near the railway station in the Cornavin district and bought two plans: one of the city and an Ordnance Survey map showing the contour lines and main roads of the Canton. Next, he searched for a charity shop down near the station to buy old ski clothes. Nothing he had could withstand the bitter weather he expected up on the high slopes where he would have to operate. He found plenty of choice. The only problem was to find dark clothing. It seemed the Swiss favoured bright reds and blues for choice, and this limited his selection. Eventually, kitted out in drab well-worn anorak and ski trousers, he found a pair of snow boots and left the shop.

'Are you sorted?' Bilan sounded eager to get on with the job when he rang him.

'Where shall we meet?' James held his map in his hands. 'I've got kit and we need a rendezvous. Where do you suggest?'

The gypsy told him he had been on the lookout for Garcia for the last three days. Between flights, he used a cafe in town. He gave the address and James found it on the map.

'OK. In half an hour.' He went back to the hostel and changed into the ski jacket. It smelled of old sweat and ski wax, but fitted well enough. There was plenty of room for the automatic and even ammunition in the pockets. Ballantyne loaded the gun and left the rest of the ammunition hidden in his backpack at the hostel.

Snow was falling in the silent streets. It got dark and late. When he found the café, the lights threw a yellow glow on to the pavement outside. Sounds of music and raised voices filled the air. This was no sober Swiss cafe. He pushed the glass door and went inside.

CHAPTER 41

Bilan sat at the back of the cafe talking to a young man. With a nod, he broke off the conversation and made room for James on the bench beside him.

'That boy is Yuri's son, Grigor, my family. I sent him to check the hotel and how many men Corvo had.' He frowned. 'Is bad news. Bad situation.'

'What do you mean, "bad situation"?'

'Snow all around and deep. Many other people and Corvo has the top suite.'

'No chance of a sniper shot?'

Bilan shook his head.

'Top floor is above treeline, so no way to get a view of him. No. We must find a way of getting him out of there.'

Ballantyne brought out his OS map and they studied the height of the hotel compared with the surrounding hills. It confirmed the report.

'Did he find out how many guards are involved?'

Bilan shook his head. 'No, but we can spend a little time in observation and work it out.'

They agreed to go up the following morning and check it out.

James knew a big change had come over him. The recent past reminded him how he baulked at the sniper shot in Rumania; how Bilan had carried it out. Now he was unfazed as they talked about assassination. It surprised him that he cared nothing for the life of the man they meant to kill. Something had been cut away in his soul and he felt inert. He gained strength from the task he had set himself. It prevented pointless reflection on what might have been, and occupied his mind. A cold determination to eliminate the man who had caused the death of so many victims, including Ocksana, gave him an energy to act without remorse.

'Now, you got to meet my team!' The gypsy threw back his head and shouted to Grigor, pointing to the bar and gesturing. The young man nodded and brought beers to the table. Two other men followed him.

'This is Vashti.' A big, dark faced man with a beard took James's hand in a paw like a bear and spoke something by way of greeting.

'This is Lash.' He was a slim man in his twenties, dressed in black, with a crest of dyed blond hair. He nodded quickly and walked way to join a girl on the other side of the bar.

'Are they sound?' Ballantyne felt doubtful about them both. They seemed too wild to be reliable.

Bilan frowned. 'What you mean? They are my family!' The gypsy squinted at him. 'Jim, you know how I work and if I trust, you trust.'

It took a split second for the fake name to sink in, and then James remembered the initial meeting and his 'Irish' persona, when they worked for Assurov.

'Okay. What about weapons?'

Bilan smiled and his black eyes gleamed. 'We have AK47s and Vashti's specials.'

He waved to the big man and when he approached, put his arm round his neck in an affectionate hug. A short chat in Roma brought a laugh to the big bear's face. He fished into his bulky ski jacket and showed his fist. Inside nestled a hand grenade. James recognised it as a M75, known as a 'Kaski'. Vasti grinned and pushed it towards him. 'Serbia.' James shrugged. He had no need to say anything. Thousands of these grenades had passed through illegal hands since the Balkan war.

The younger man stayed at some distance and Ballantyne could see he regarded the older men with little respect, preferring to impress the girls in the bar rather than mingle with the others. He made a mental note to keep a watch on him.

They spent several hours together and agreed to meet at the railway station in the morning.

'Nine o'clock?'

Bilan shrugged. 'Whatever.'

James knew that meant between nine and noon, or thereabouts. It was Roma time. He found his way back to the hostel and dropped onto the bed.

Most of the others staying at the hostel were migrant workers, going to work in the early hours. He found it impossible to sleep beyond 7 a.m., so he got up and dressed in the old ski kit he bought yesterday. He cleaned the automatic with an old rag and checked the slide action. Then topped up the magazine to a full load and cursed himself for not getting a second one; reloading could waste a vital minute in combat. Seventeen rounds took some time.

The station was just a few hundred yards away, so he strolled to the cafe inside the concourse and had a coffee and croissant. The waiter asked if he was German and when he answered in English, began to practise his language skills on him. They kept up a broken conversation for a few minutes.

'Where can I get some camping kit?' The waiter pointed down the avenue and gave directions.

The shop was better than he expected. It bulged with ex-military clothing and surplus equipment, plus the usual basic camping gear. An elderly man sat on a stool at the back, reading a newspaper. He raised his head as Ballantyne came in but said nothing and remained seated. Steel spectacles rested on his nose and a cigarette drooped from his lips. He seemed indifferent and ignored James. Among the dusty shelves were uniforms and caps from several national units; army and police equipment discarded for newer kit or surplus stock. Ballantyne suspected there would be more interesting items in the back room.

He came to the counter. 'Have you any military equipment I can see?' The old man put down the paper and pushed the eyeglasses up his nose. He grumbled and got up. 'Maybe some stuff in the back, but you have to check for yourself.' He lifted the flap of the counter and James stepped through. Beyond a felt curtain, he saw a row of shelves stacked with gear. Belts, packs, water bottles of different types and sizes. There were racks of hard equipment such as picks, spades and reels of wire and rope. None of this could be any use, but then he caught sight of large wooden boxes stashed under the shelves. He recognised them as ammunition boxes and pulled one out. Inside lay a heap of discarded weapon parts. Rifle bolts, barrels and magazines. He rummaged through the jumble and selected a couple of magazines that looked familiar. He was alone, so he took the Masada out of his pocket and detached the mag. The first two were obviously useless, but a third he recognised as a Browning 9mm. He slipped it into the slot and clicked it home; it fitted with a little resistance, but the action worked. James thanked his lucky stars and came back into the shop.

'Okay, I'll take this. Can you sell me a pair of binos?'

The old man put out his cigarette very deliberately and gave him a long look. For the first time, he showed some interest in this new customer.

'You want binos and magazines?' He squinted at Ballantyne. 'But you don't want camping gear, do you?' He didn't expect a direct answer. James stared back at him without blinking. A drawer was pulled open and it revealed a selection of battered binoculars and sniper sights.

James went to the door to test a pair, then tried another. These were perfect.

'Okay, I'll take this pair and the mag. How much?' They bartered and agreed a price. As he prepared to leave, the old man approached him.

'Maybe you need something else?' He cocked his head to the side and licked his lips. Ballantyne said nothing, waiting to find out what was on offer. The man bent towards him.

'I can put you in touch with a friend. He was in the Serbian army. Do you understand?'

'Go on.'

'There are items which you won't see in my shop, but might suit someone like you. I can contact him.'

It was very clear. Weapons were obtainable if you paid well.

'Perhaps I'll come back to you.' It seemed foolhardy to show too much interest, but the prospect of a supply of more firepower was tempting. The old man nodded. 'I'm always here.'

Back at the station, he found Bilan and Vasti drinking at the café. It was ten o'clock in the morning, but they had glasses of vodka in front of them.

'You said you have AK47s and grenades. We must have something bigger to do the job properly. I have an idea.'

The gypsy frowned and stirred in his chair. 'What more do we need?'

'If we have to deal with vehicles or buildings, those are not enough!'

He threw his head back and pointed to his companion. 'You not seen Vasti work with his specials!' He nudged the hairy giant, who seemed bemused, then translated what James had told him. Vashti folded his arms and stared. His face grew red; he shuffled on his chair and spat on the floor. Ballantyne got the message.

'Look, if we could get rocket launchers or a bazooka, we'd avoid problems.'

'How we get such things?' Bilan teased him. 'We raid the Swiss Army?'

In two minutes, James explained what he'd discovered. The two gypsies talked together for a minute and agreed to see what was on offer. 'Maybe a trap,' warned Bilan, 'but we check it.'

When they appeared at the shop, the man took a look at them, then went to the door and locked it. He bit his lip and stood with his back to the door.

'You want something else?'

Bilan stood over him.

'You have friends in Serbia?' The question had a wealth of meaning.

He nodded and moved towards the counter. Vashti stepped in front of him and reached behind it. A quick glance underneath revealed a sawn-off shotgun, and Vashti grinned as he waved it in the air.

Ballantyne could see this was not going well. Gypsy diplomacy did not work.

'Just make the contact for us and we'll leave you alone.'

The old man fidgeted but picked up the phone and dialled a number. Within a second, he was speaking Serbo-Croat in a high-pitched voice. Bilan listened closely. He snatched the phone from the man's hand and spoke directly to the other person. After a minute or so, he gave the handset back to the shopkeeper and the call ended.

'We take a look tonight and he' – pointing to the trembling man – 'comes with us.'

Later, in a hired car, they watched the hotel for indications of the crew who would be protecting Corvo. The bright, reflected light from the snow threw a spotlight on the front and anyone coming or going showed in sharp focus. By five o'clock they were about to give up, when a car arrived and two men got out. Bilan stiffened and grabbed the binoculars.

'God's blood! It can't be!' He pointed to the men. 'That's Brezhnev!'

Ballantyne took the binos. The men looked around as they climbed the steps to the front door. He did not recognise them.

'Who are they?'

'Brezhnev is a Russian oilman. How can he be visiting Corvo?'

Bilan looked again but the two men had disappeared.

'But your contract is to eliminate Corvo for the Russians?'

Ballantyne had never seen Bilan in a state of confusion before. His face flushed; a vein throbbed in his neck and he swore under his breath.

'I do what I'm paid for. But this…' He broke off and shook his head. 'This is something else.'

There was silence as they both tried to make sense of the facts.

Ballantyne spoke first. 'Either this is a trap for you, or there's more than one faction at work in Russia.'

The gypsy nodded.

'Let's get back and work this out.' He started the car and they drove quickly back to the city.

Perversely, the appearance of the Russians increased Bilan's interest in obtaining serious weapons. As they discussed the meaning of Brezhnev's arrival, he became eager to meet the 'Serbian' and see what he could provide.

'We go mobhanded,' he said, 'and no problems.' This was accompanied by a broad smile and he turned to the other men and told them. It led to more vodka and noisy chatter.

This is a gypsy idea of a night out! thought James, as he forced down his third shot of cheap firewater.

They piled into two cars: the hired one and a battered Renault which Vashti drove. Nobody mentioned weapons, but Ballantyne had no doubt they were all armed.

They picked up the old man and bundled him into the car; he sat very still. Following instructions, they drove to the industrial outskirts of the city and pulled into the yard of a disused factory. Vashti parked his vehicle where they could see across a wide space in front of the battered building. Bilan took station nearer the entrance; they both waited, engines running.

'Get out and find him.' The shopkeeper clambered out and walked slowly towards the dark, brick-built structure and disappeared inside. Then a torch lit the entrance and two men stepped out into the yard. The headlights revealed the old man from the shop and a tall figure wearing a ski mask. The masked man beckoned to the car.

'Okay, I go,' said Bilan. 'Watch me and keep the headlights on.' He got out and walked casually to the hangar. The three men disappeared inside. Ballantyne got out and quietly followed them. It was insane of Bilan to go in alone. He stopped at the doorway and watched. A dark lorry was parked inside with its tail-board dropped. Bilan examined something on the floor. It was three feet long, with dull green paint and a white nosecone.

Ballantyne called from the doorway. 'You need me to check the weapon?'

The three men spun round at the sound of his voice; the masked man reached for a hidden gun but Bilan spoke sharply and the man relaxed.

'Come on, Irish. He has a couple of toys to show us. I can use your help.'

Ballantyne nodded and walked slowly towards them, keeping his hands in sight.

'I thought you would, these are not your sort of play-things!' The gypsy grinned and translated for the masked man. He said nothing.

Laid out for inspection was a rocket launcher James had seen once in the Balkans, a Malyuka, Slovakian-made and very battered.

He shook his head. 'No good. It looks bad and has to be wire-guided. We can't use it.' The gypsy looked at the man and he packed it back into its casing.

In the back of the truck Ballantyne saw a familiar shape. An RPG Soviet-made rocket known as a MKX. In Afghanistan, it had been every mujahidin's friend, hiding around every corner.

'That one,' he said. 'Cheap. How much? We need three rockets.'

Bilan took over the bargaining and eventually paid out in US dollars.

He went out and waved to Vashti to bring his car nearer. He drove to the mouth of the building and kept his headlights on. He stood at the side of the car with his pistol in view, as the others put the RPG and ammunition into the back of the vehicle. They left the casings and boxes behind. A few words to the man from the shop and the Serbian, then they moved off in convoy, making sure they were not followed.

Bilan's face reminded James of a schoolboy. His smile and bright eyes lit up his face with joy as if he had just scored a goal. He drove in a wild, boisterous way swerving from side to side and taking corners with verve.

'Now we finish the job good!' he shouted, and pummelled Ballantyne's arm with his fist. James looked over his shoulder at the RPGs rattling against each other at every swerve and shook his head in disbelief.

'Okay. Go easy! For fuck's sake!'

Eventually, the message got through and they arrived in the city at a moderate pace. It was the first time Ballantyne had been to where the gypsy clan stayed. It was a caravan park in the industrial area and several motorhomes filled the space, together with a jumble of old cars and brand-new pick-up trucks.

'Let's take some time to think through what we have seen,' said Ballantyne. 'Your target may not be the same as mine in the light of that.'

'I see no problem. I contract with Stasi to deal with Corvo. I will deal with him.'

'Yes, but these men… does this mean you have a different assignment?'

Bilan stood up. 'I am paid to do job and will do it. Not some other contract. But it is clear we must act quickly. If not, complications.'

Ballantyne did not share his view. Complications had already surfaced in the shape of Russian plutocrats involved with Corvo. Getting the Matrix was a different game now. They settled down to plan the attack. Both agreed there was no time to lose.

CHAPTER 42

She lay half asleep in the soft bliss of the silk sheets, her black hair spread out across the pillows. The sound of water from the wet-room next door brought her back to life, and the fact she had to join him for a business meeting. Corvo was never on vacation. She longed for a period of peace with no crises or travel, but it was never going to happen as long as she stayed with him.

They spent the morning skiing with their guide on the slopes above the hotel, but Corvo insisted they return in good time for a meeting later in the afternoon. He wanted sex and she lay wondering what had excited him this time; she felt hungry and tired, but she slept well after it was over.

'This may be the most profitable day of the year! We can't be late!' A tight-lipped smile creased his lips but he never explained what he meant. He wrapped himself in his robe and chivvied her into the shower. The water glistened over her body and he watched her with pleasure as she soaped herself slowly, deliberately cupping her breasts as he stared.

He pays for it, so he may as well enjoy it. She wondered if this meeting could bring enough into Corvo's pocket to stop the endless travel and secret assignations. It was time to move on if she could break away without danger.

By five o'clock they were in the large salon on the ground floor. In a corner, the sound of a piano underscored the light murmur of conversation. She made an entrance before Corvo, capturing the attention of the whole room. It pleased him, and he acknowledged every glance with a slight bow. They took up a position where he could scan the whole room. Itzak Brezhnev and his son Ilya arrived soon after. They moved with easy confidence across the room and waved their bodyguards away.

'My compliments, Madame.' The stocky older Russian made an attempted bow but only managed to nod his head. Corvo motioned them to chairs and called for champagne. He eyed them both, watching for some sign that they had agreed to his price.

It had been discussed in some detail before, but they had never met. The Russians were inscrutable.

'Tell me what you decided,' he smiled encouragingly. 'Do we have an agreement?'

It was the younger man, Ilya, who responded. He leant forward and grinned: he showed his teeth and reminded Corvo of the wolf in fairy tales. It did nothing to reassure him. 'We have managed to raise the amount, but of course, we need an account to transfer funds.'

'That is no problem. I have accounts in Swiss banks here and in Zurich. A simple phone call with the passwords will effect the deposit. How do you wish to make the exchange?'

Itzak Brezhnev said, 'We feel this is an occasion for a celebration.' His eyes glistened like flints. 'I reserved the mountain restaurant for us tomorrow night and would be honoured if you both would join us to conclude the deal. Once the transfer has gone through, we can take possession of this Matrix and be free to enjoy ourselves. Do you agree?'

Corvo sensed the risk this posed, but concealed his thoughts. 'With pleasure. Will we be alone?'

'Yes, I feel this is an occasion when the public need not intrude.' They laughed together at the joke and arranged to meet once the transfer had been set up. Later, Diego reported that he had given the codes to them and confirmed the handover for the following night.

*

Vashti raised the question of where to attack.

'How can we go into a hotel full of people and shoot the bastard?'

'Is it because you want to use your toys, Schav (boy)?' Bilan teased the big man and pointed to his pockets. 'You will have to wait and see!'

'Maybe up the mountain? They will ski and maybe we could get a shot on the piste?' Ballantyne put the idea forward reluctantly because it did not assist him in getting the Matrix. He kept his own agenda hidden from the others.

'Okay, let's go and see. Just you and me.'

He waved at Vashti. 'Not the mob. Gypsies on skis? Never!' They laughed.

'We can hire a Ski-Doo and look like rich tourists,' he said, and slapped his thigh with delight. 'Ha! We'll impress the girls and cross the mountains like Genghis!'

He raised his arms in triumph and roared with laughter. Ballantyne grinned and rang a hire shop to book for the following morning.

They spent the evening together in the gypsy enclave, cleaning their weapons and drinking with the crowd. James slipped away about midnight and got back to the hostel; it was as quiet as a nunnery by comparison. Next morning, they met and took the ski bus up the mountain. The weather was bright and the ski station full. James and Bilan in their dark, scruffy ski clothes looked a little out of place among the bright young people, but when James paid for half a day's hire, the mechanic grinned and waved them away. He expected they would be back, exhausted, before the first hour was up. Ballantyne pulled the starter cord and the two zoomed away, scattering a few slow skiers still fitting their skis.

It became obvious that a hit on the mountain tracks in daylight could not be done. They tracked each piste around the ski station and there was no point at which it was possible to set up a sniper site.

'Look at this!' Bilan was exasperated. 'Everywhere nothing but bodies! Is no good, we have to go back.' James agreed. As they scooted down the main piste, the Kaiser Hof chalet faced them with its crowd of skiers on the terrace taking a break or lying on sunloungers, catching the sun. It was irresistible. Bilan jumped off the machine before James had stopped and shouted for a waiter. Many of the clientele turned to frown at the man in the grubby anorak. Murmurs of 'Russians' and 'Roma' drifted on the crisp mountain air. The waiter bowed; he knew better. The best tips he got came from scruffy plutocrats who looked like this.

Ballantyne was the first to see the printed notice on the main door.

'What is happening tomorrow night?'

'The restaurant is closed, *mes excuses*. One of the hotel guests is giving a private dinner.'

'Who?'

'The Comte Corvo, I believe.'

The waiter enjoyed pronouncing the title with gusto in front of the whole terrace. It added tone to the quality of clients he served. He could not have anticipated the effect it had on his two scruffy customers. Bilan sat up slack-jawed and stared; James sat still and left his drink untouched. The waiter reflected how the day-trippers were easily impressed and turned away to serve another table.

Nothing was said. They settled back and for once were silent. The same ideas were running through their heads. Ballantyne looked up at the trees and mountains which formed a perfect bowl around the chalet restaurant. Bilan studied the slopes leading away towards the city. They got up, leaving no tip, fired up the noisy machine and left in a cloud of blue smoke.

CHAPTER 43

The ski shop manager stared wide-eyed as the two foreigners arrived in a cloud of snow and pushed into the shop. They wanted to rehire for the rest of the day. He quickly made up a figure and it was agreed without complaint.

These Englishers are like children. They have to play with a new toy!

They left the machine and took the bus back to the city. Bilan barged into the bar where Vashti and the others played cards.

'Get up! We are leaving now!' Three gypsies looked bemused.

'Vashti! Collect the gear and meet me at the car!' His voice rang with urgency, and without explaining further, he pushed him out into the street and back to the campsite.

Ballantyne went directly there and began putting ammunition into sports bags to prepare for a return to the slopes. On the way down, they worked out a plan. It was clear they needed to set up a position before the sun went down. There would be no chance to do so once the morning ski slopes were full, and impossible to work after nightfall. The time slot was now. James wished he'd had the chance to get more 9mm ammunition from his rucksack back at the hostel, but it was out of the question; he'd have to make do with the boxes in hand.

They were a team of three. Vashti found an old ski bag to hide the RPG and the rockets. Only he could lift it into the car. The AK47s were wrapped in plastic bags and ferried with the rest into Vashti's Renault. He set off before Bilan and Ballantyne could stop him.

'God's blood!' Bilan shook his fist at the car as it vanished. 'Give me patience! If he cocks this up, I'll shoot him myself.' He knew he couldn't stop the car, but it was imperative that they got going quickly and the two bundled the rest of the equipment into the hired car and set off in pursuit. They caught up as the Renault parked at the ski shop near the lift. It was three thirty and some of the ski crowd were coming down the mountain to finish the day. Ballantyne fired up the Ski-Doo and with Bilan on the back, loaded with bags, they rumbled up the piste, dodging skiers on the way. Ballantyne cursed the way things turned out. His military training rebelled at the shambolic way things were being done; a crew he didn't trust; no proper preparation; and the prospect of spending a night on the slopes without a decent bivvie.

They reached the plateau where the restaurant nestled in its sheltered corner. Bilan chose a spot above the building and they unloaded the bags and hid them among the trees.

'You stay here,' said Ballantyne, 'I'll get the rest, the light is fading and we mustn't be seen when the *pisteurs* pass through.' The gypsy nodded and blew on his fingers. 'Bring me a bottle, quick!' Ballantyne fired up the machine and set off among the tired skiers, swerving and spraying them as he passed. Shouts and swearing followed him down the trail. By the time he had returned, the sun dipped below the mountains and a chill crept up the valley. They unloaded and James put on the big coat Vashti lent him.

'Okay. Do you reckon you can drive this thing down to the ski base?'

He gave the gypsy a challenging stare. Black eyes glowered and with a clenched jaw, Bilan jumped astride the machine and roared away, carving a wide arc in the snow in a barely controlled dash down the piste. James shook his head in disbelief and faced up to a night in the mountains. He made a snow cave with the bags and plenty of snow, then covered it with branches. Inside, he was protected from the wind, wrapped in the coat which smelled of smoke and sweat. After an hour, he heard the *swish* of their skis as the *pisteurs* came down the mountain, checking for casualties or damage. They passed without stopping.

Alone, his mind went back to times when he had been isolated before: in Afghanistan, high in the Hindu Kush, waiting in ambush for the Mujahidin; hiding from ISIS in a cellar in Basra and waiting for rescue. But each of these had been with companions, sharing the heat or the cold together. This solitude among the dark pines and winds was something else.

In the bowl of the valley, the Kaiser Hof chalet radiated light and noise. The piste was illuminated from below, and from time to time Snowcats tracked their way up to bring clients to the luxury of the restaurant. Wrapped in furs, they stepped down from the cabins into the bright warmth of the building. Outside the circle of light, the snow took on a faint blue tinge as if to emphasise the chilly surroundings.

Ballantyne curled up inside the coat and dozed. After some time, the noise from below ceased and he was alone. Sleep wouldn't come and as he sat half asleep, the thought of Ocksana lying among the rubble of Syrian chaos kept slipping into his mind. He knew it was imagination; he'd never seen the location. Yet the image hovered, reproaching him in some way. He tried to turn his mind to something else. What did they need to do tomorrow? Was there enough ammunition? Yet it crept back like a malign shadow from some dark corner of the mind, to spoil his rest. He realised then that he was wrong to leave her body in the pitiless ruins of Syria, where humanity was basic and life cheap. Self-pity had consumed him and now he knew he must go there to right what he had failed to do. In that moment of clarity, he felt as if he made a compact with her and it eased his mind. He fell asleep.

CHAPTER 44

Six a.m., and the slopes were alive. Tracked machines were clearing the pistes for the new day. Ballantyne eased himself out of the corner of his den and groaned. His back ached and he had to beat his arms and legs back to life. Down in the valley, the chalet was dark and empty. He longed for a warm drink but there would be no sign of life in the restaurant till much later. He watched the movement on the slopes and paid attention to the chalet itself. It was a wide building with a glass frontage; shaped like an alpine house with a pointed gable. In front was a circular drive and a sun terrace which attracted skiers. He recalled it from the day before, when they had stopped there. Behind, the mountainside loomed and there was no open space. He noted this particularly because it meant there could be no escape that way.

Time hung on him. It was an age before he caught sight of Bilan emerging from the public Snowcat which brought the early skiers and the staff of the chalet onto the untouched snow.

'Here! Take this!' A bottle of grappa was thrust into his hands and he took a pull with gusto. The fire burnt his throat but by the time it reached his gut he felt good.

'Vashti will come up this afternoon, we don't want him mewling in the cold! We can get a good look by ourselves.' James agreed and took another swig; he would agree to anything if it meant he could get moving again.

They waited out of sight till the chalet opened.

'What's the story about the Russians who turned up yesterday?'

Bilan frowned and sniffed, ‘I checked with Moscow’ – he meant KGB – ‘Brehznev is a greedy man! No friend of the president! He has some interest of his own. He is no friend of Russia.’

‘So what do we do if he is there tonight?’

The gypsy looked into the distance and avoided James’s gaze. He said just one word. ‘*Ustranit.*’ James understood. ‘Eliminate.’ They said no more.

Mingling with the skiers, they went inside to the breakfast room and sat in a corner to eat. James ate well, and they took care to avoid the waiter they had spoken to on the previous occasion. The dining room was next door and had windows which looked out onto the side of the building.

‘We can’t get a good view from the front. We’ll need to approach from the side. It makes a get-out more difficult.’ Bilan nodded but remained untroubled.

‘No matter, we don’t expect surprises, do we?’ The Roma believed a ‘Duende’ protected them, but Ballantyne inwardly prepared himself to deal with any unexpected response.

A spot well above the building was chosen for observation and by mid-morning they were content with the sight-lines on each approach to the chalet. Ballantyne wrapped himself in the coat and bedded down behind the equipment. Bilan sat smoking at a spot someway up the hill but protected from the piste. By three o’clock, a whistle brought him to his feet and he climbed down to the area outside the chalet, where a dark figure lurked. It was Vashti. He looked like a refugee from some gulag in Siberia. He wore layers of dark clothing and a fur hat he must have pulled from some dustbin, his dark face lost in a scarf. Ballantyne could pick him out from a distance. He looked like a tramp on parade.

For Christ's sake, get him out of sight quickly!

His words seemed to fly directly to Bilan, who grabbed Vashti and pulled him away from the crowd adjusting their skis. The men trudged up the hill, grumbling and struggling in the thick snow. James never felt more uneasy about the task ahead and looked at Bilan with exasperation. He shrugged but said nothing.

By the time the sun was setting, they had cleaned their weapons and Ballantyne had agreed positions with Bilan. He felt a surprising sense of exhilaration. No twinge of conscience about the task to be performed crossed his mind. He felt a strong urge to destroy the man who had indirectly brought about the death of Ocksana. He chose a spot for himself where he could see straight into the dining room. He watched as the staff set up a table with care near the window.

'Just four people dining,' he said, and Bilan peered at the scene. There were candles being set up and flowers arranged on a square table. Screens had been placed behind the setting. It made a contrast to the brilliant table setting.

By five o'clock, the crowds had dispersed and the scene became calm. Vashti was placed in position at the back of the building with instructions to watch the fire door in case of an exit that way. Lights went out in the main part of the restaurant, leaving only the front of the chalet illuminated, and the part of the dining room prepared for the private dinner. The silence was like a film set awaiting the entrance of the actors. Ballantyne felt that kick of expectation before battle and stirred in his hideout.

CHAPTER 45

Ilya Brezhnev placed his laptop on the table and registered his password; within a few seconds, he was in communication with his bank in Zurich. He scanned his encrypted emails and sent replies where needed. All that had to be done was for the bank to carry out his instructions precisely. The plan was to delay the payment of Corvo's sum by transferring it through banks in the Caymans before payment. What could be better than to outwit Corvo and hold the Russian Federation to ransom at the same time?

'Are you sure this will work?' The older man looked over his shoulder as Ilya worked the computer. The screen was filled with figures and code words, but it was a puzzle to him.

'All you have to do is smile! I can explain everything to Corvo, and he will fall for it like a baby.'

'*Naglost!* (Chutzpa!) You need back up! I will sort it out.'

The young man shrugged and said nothing. The old guard never changed. They still thought in terms of nerve gas and elimination; there were new ways to skin a cat.

By seven in the evening, they were ready to leave. A Snowcat was standing by and Itzak arranged their own driver to look after them. The night was still. The snow lay like powder on the piste, only the laboured noise of the engine broke the silence as it climbed the slope. The front of the restaurant was flooded with light as they arrived. The driver stayed outside, armed with an Uzi automatic.

Ilya inspected the table and the menu.

'I prefer we should have more privacy. Why not bring the table away from the window and draw the curtains?'

The head waiter bowed, and within a minute the table disappeared from outside view. With a nod of approval, Ilya returned to his father in the bar.

The older man stood uneasily at the counter, fiddling with a glass. He dismissed the barman and looked keenly at his son.

'What protection did you bring? Your laptop won't help!'

Ilya smiled broadly and slipped his hand inside his jacket. He pulled out a Beretta revolver with a three-inch barrel, then put it away.

'I suppose you've brought a cigar or two?'

They laughed, and the old man showed him a silver pistol with an ivory grip.

'Old friends are best! I got this in New York, twenty years ago!'

They drank a toast to themselves and sat at a table near the door. Within a few minutes, the sound of a motor coming up the track caught their attention. They watched the main door. Corvo and his mistress, in furs, came in and gave their coats to the doorman with a smile.

La Diabla was spectacular. Her dark hair, dressed with pearls, shone in the bright lights of the foyer. She wore a red silk dress; her slim waist and the curve of her hips drew attention to the slit in her skirt, disclosing a long, slim leg. The neckline hinted at the shape of her breasts without revealing too much flesh. She smiled, confident in the impression she made.

'What a lovely surprise! Thank you for a wonderful idea!' She held out her hand to Ilya and smiled at Itzak at the same time. The young man kissed her hand in a formal way, and the older man clapped his hands in appreciation.

'This is not fair, my friend! How can we deal with such charm? How lovely!'

Corvo bowed, then he shook hands with each of them and they sat in the bar. A waiter brought in champagne. Corvo noticed at once it was Roederer Crystal in clear glass, not black.

'My compliments, Ilya, your taste is impeccable!'

It was Itzak who took the bottle and wrapped it in a white napkin.

'We have a tradition; we celebrate in Russian style.' He nodded at the waiter who handed him a sabre, its blade exposed. With a flick he slashed the bottle, and the neck was cut cleanly away. None of the liquid foamed out and he handed it to the man to fill their glasses. Diabla clapped and Corvo smiled thinly.

'Once a Cossack. Always!' Itzak bowed and presented the first glass to her.

They moved to the table. Ilya had been arranged it with Corvo on his right side and his father opposite. Diabla sat on his left. She looked up through her lashes at him and occasionally made eye contact. He wondered what it would be like to share a bed with her. Corvo brought his attention back to the business at hand.

'Let us begin. You have my coordinates? I checked today but no credit had been received. Is there a problem?' He watched Ilya.

'No problem!' The Russian smiled warmly and leant forward with mock sincerity. 'As you know, with such a large amount, our colleagues transfer money through several channels. They have confirmed the deal and I assure you the transfer is complete.'

The elder Brezhnev nodded in confirmation, but his hand slid to his pocket where his familiar gun lay.

Corvo sat back and took a bite of the Lobster Thermidor in front of him.. He ate it slowly, without reply. Then he turned to La Diabla.

'My darling, could you call Diego to bring the merchandise in?'

She left the table and Diego appeared in a second, with an aluminium case. He sat quietly on a chair at the back of the room and said nothing.

'We can enjoy ourselves while waiting for news of the transfers, can we not?' Corvo was the soul of affability, sitting back and tasting every dish brought to the table. They drank to each other and Diabla flirted with both Russians. Ilya then sent the waiters away with a wave of his hand.

He got up after a short time, and explained, 'I will call the banks and find out the latest news.'

'Please do so.' Corvo's smile disappeared. 'We expect good news. If not, then we must say goodbye. Do I make myself clear?' The young Russian nodded and shrugged his shoulders, got up and left the room.

Corvo turned towards the older Russian and put a hand on his shoulder.

'Please don't move. I must ask you to understand we are friends, yet I have to take precautions.' He glanced at Diego and the man moved quickly. He pulled Itzak's arms behind his back and pinioned him to his chair, his cries stifled. Corvo took the pistol from him, looked at it and tossed it away with a sneer. He pulled the Russian's face close and held him by the hair.

'You know the expression, "Wise guy"?'

The old man could not speak.

'I hate the expression, but it has its uses. How did you think you could fob me off with this tactic?' Wide-eyed, he squirmed in the chair, but Diego held him tight. 'Keep still!' A knife at his throat stopped his struggle.

Corvo gestured to his mistress and she stepped behind the curtains. Taking a position behind the Russian, he waited. It was a minute before Ilya reappeared. With him was the guard who had waited at the door. He had the machine pistol in his hands and pointed it in the direction of the group.

'Consider!' Corvo shouted. 'There is no need to be hasty! Just let my bankers talk to the consignees and all will be well. You realise I must take precautions.'

The young Russian stood still and the gunman hesitated, looking to Ilya for instructions.

'Everything will be settled by tomorrow, I give you my word!'

'That is not what you agreed.' Corvo stabbed his finger at him. 'I can see what this is, you mongrel!'

Without a sound, Diabla emerged from behind the curtain and fired two shots at the guard. She held the automatic in both hands and swivelled to cover Ilya as soon as the man fell.

Corvo gave a tight-lipped smile and moved to disarm him, but Ilya backed away and reached inside his jacket. He had the Berretta in his hand before her gun fired. Again, two shots in quick succession and he pivoted and fell.

La Diabla looked at Corvo and he nodded. She brushed a wayward lock of hair back in place, smoothed her dress and sat down. Diego released the old Russian from his grasp.

'You assassins!' Brehznev broke into a wild rant in Russian and went down on his knees beside his son. Blood from the wounds was seeping into the carpet and onto his hands as he tried to lift Ilya's head. Corvo took hold of him again. The knife was still in his hand. The older man grabbed Corvo's hand, but the knife slit his throat in one movement. The body fell alongside the body of his son, and his blood formed a pool around his head.

There was no sign of any of the staff. The building had been abandoned. Corvo stooped and collected the casings from Diabla's gun, then took her arm and they made their way to the Snowcat. It was time to go.

CHAPTER 46

Bilan nudged him as the sound of a Snowcat whined up the piste from below. Ballantyne stirred and saw it arrive at the chalet in a cloud of snow. They could make out the figures that jumped out; they were the Russians they had seen before. The driver stayed with the machine.

'Shall we move closer?' Bilan questioned their position, a hundred metres from the window they had targeted.

'Too far for you?' James nudged him and the gypsy punched him back. They watched the window as the men talked to the staff, and in a moment of disbelief saw curtains pulled across the view and the targets vanish.

'*Madre de Puta*!' Bilan sat, eyes wide.

Ballantyne could not help grinning. 'Here we are, freezing our balls off, and we've lost sight of the targets! Pretty professional! Come on, we need to rethink this. Look! We have to move. Let's cover the front entrance to shoot as they come out.'

Bilan pursed his lips. 'Maybe we have neutrals to cope with.' He meant the staff.

'Well, we can 't stay here, so we'll have to deal with it. Come on.'

They crawled out of the pit and climbed further up the hillside, opposite the chalet entrance. Ballantyne took one of the AK47s with him, and Bilan lugged the RPG and his AK47 to the spot. They had closed the distance to about fifty metres. It was at that moment the second party arrived. It was easy to make out the figure of Diabla as she was handed out of the Snowcat. Her crimson dress shone in the reflected the light from the snow, and the driver carried her across the sludge as far as the front door. Corvo followed, dressed in a black fur coat.

Like fucking Count Dracula, James thought.

He registered that Diego was in attendance, and reminded himself he had not warned Bilan how dangerous the man was. The Spaniard followed the pair in but sat in the hall. Waiters passed across the hallway within their sight from time to time.

'Wonder what the bastards are eating,' said Bilan, and he sat chafing his hands and blowing into them. James saw the champagne cross to the dining room and imagined the picture of these plutocrats competing with each other in opulent extravagance. How long would it take? Diego disappeared from view.

Suddenly, the driver from the first Snowcat jumped down and ran into the chalet. In their hide, Bilan and Ballantyne sat up. Nothing happened for a few minutes and they sat back. Then, from behind the curtain, muffled sounds reached them.

'Is that gunshots?' It was difficult to tell. But again, the same percussive sound pulsed in the air. This time they both knew it was the sound of a silencer from an automatic weapon.

Before they had time to think, a waiter and a man dressed in an apron rushed out of the front door. A moment later, others appeared from the back of the building, running hard away from the chalet.

'Hope Vashti stays in position.' Bilan looked doubtful.

'Christ, I hope he doesn't shoot the poor bastards!'

Then, there was silence.

As if by telepathy, at that moment Vashti plodded into sight round the corner of the building, obviously confused by the sudden exit of the staff. Before they could warn him, Corvo was moving out of the front of the building, making for the Snowcat parked outside. He turned, pulled a gun from his coat and fired before Vashti could move away. The shot took the big man in the stomach and he collapsed face down in the icy sludge.

'Quick!' Corvo shouted behind him and he looked up, to check for any sign of further danger. Diabla ran out of the entrance and into the vehicle in a split second. Ballantyne heard the sound of the engine and fired in that direction, not picking a target but simply to cover any further shots from the hotel. After two shots, the AK47 jammed and he dropped it. By the time he had the Masada in his hands, the tracked car was in motion and speeding away.

Bilan had run to Vashti and crouched by his side. 'He's gone,' he said, and bent over the body to close the eyes. 'The big man; he never had a chance.' The gypsy said no more, but kneeled beside the body with his head bent towards the fallen man.

Ballantyne left him there and moved cautiously towards the front of the hotel. He could see some of the hallway as he approached and hear noise coming from the direction of the dining room. He moved forward, gun in both hands.

Diego was dragging a body towards the front door. It was the older Russian he had seen arrive earlier.

'Stand still!'

Diego dropped the arm he was pulling and stood upright. He was unarmed. Ballantyne moved closer to check him, and watched as the Spaniard stepped back from the corpse. Before he could search him, a figure pushed him aside and flung himself at Diego. The force of the attack took Diego back against the wall; Bilan seized him and dragged him down. The sounds from his throat were not words; guttural noises deep within the gypsy's soul belched out in his rage. Ballantyne stepped away and left them. He saw the knife in Bilan's hand and heard the sound as the gypsy plunged it into the man's throat. The body writhed, feet rapping against the marble floor, then lay still. When he stepped away from the body, Ballantyne took Diego's gun and cell phone and put them in his pocket. Walking into the dining room, the body of the young man, Ilya, still sprawled across one of the chairs. He left him there and shook Bilan by the shoulder

'We can do no good here. Get hold of that gypsy boy and send him to find out where Corvo goes. He must go back to the Kaiser Hof hotel, and he must track him from there.'

Bilan stood up and wiped his hands. Then he nodded and reached for his cell phone.

The only word James understood was 'Grigor', and he recalled the young man with the flashy clothes he saw at the gypsy encampment. Bilan folded the cell phone and nodded to him. 'Okay.'

Outside was the second Snowcat. Leaving the two bodies to be found next morning, they struggled to move Vashti to the machine. It took all their combined strength to shift him. Bilan said nothing, but his bloodshot eyes betrayed the mournful loss he felt. There was nothing useful James could say. Vashti had lost his life in a moment of bewildering confusion and nothing they could have done in that instant would have saved him.

Driving down to the hotel, Ballantyne made an assessment of what they must do to put things right. He felt the humiliation of the setback keenly. His pride was hurt, and the knowledge that Corvo and his woman had outsmarted them stung like a whiplash. He realised now that it was Diabla who had fired the deadly shots, not Diego or Corvo. He had seriously misjudged her. He had never encountered a woman like this before. Her combination of allure and deadly skills eclipsed his knowledge of the female fighters he had met in Afghanistan or among the Kurds of Northern Turkey. He would make no concessions next time. They dumped the Snowcat at the back of the hotel and manhandled Vashti's body into the hired car still parked there.

'Wait while I see if we can get a fix on Corvo.' James ran to the concierge desk, but the night porter knew nothing about recent departures.

Bilan drove directly to the gypsy camp. A crowd formed round the vehicle, and within minutes the distinct sound of mourning rose from the women who formed a circle round the body lying on the floor of one of the huts. Searching the crowd, Ballantyne looked for Grigor, in the hope he could tell him where Corvo had gone, but there was no sign of him.

Perhaps that's a good sign – maybe he's still in contact!

The men looked grave and stayed silent. It was as if they locked in their feelings and kept their anger inside. Ballantyne stood on the edge of the crowd as Vasti's wife and daughters dressed the body in silk robes among the wailing mob. He knew the gypsy custom was to bury their dead within a day of death. There would be no possibility of Bilan or the tribe doing anything before that was over. It must be his responsibility to move quickly, if any trace of Corvo could be found. He scanned the crowd for any sign of the young man, Grigor, He was not there.

A file of men formed once the body had been prepared, passing the bench on which Vashti had been laid, and each man bent to kiss the face of the dead man. Ballantyne joined the line and paid the same tribute. Vashti had never smelt so sweet.

Bilan stood next to the widow, and it was difficult to speak to him. He caught James's eye and Ballantyne weaved through the crowd to join him.

'Don't wait,' said the gypsy. 'I will contact you when we get a lead on him. Do what you can in Geneva, in case he has not slipped away.' There was no need to identify who 'he' was. James nodded and slowly made his way through the crowd.

The chipped paint of the hostel brought Ballantyne back to the world of seedy living with a bang. At the desk, the same old man with the same cigarette hanging from his lip sat with a newspaper in front of him. It was as if he had never moved during the whole time he'd been away.

'You're overdue. I kept your spot, but I want cash in advance now.'

Ballantyne nodded and paid in Euros. The grubby man counted the cash and sniffed. 'Next time I need Swiss francs.' He passed over the room key and turned back to his paper. Inside the small room, James checked his holdall and the general layout of the fittings. Everything seemed in order, including the ammunition he had left in the bag.

It was time to reflect on the turn of events. He flung the dirty ski jacket on to the floor and kicked off the sodden boots. Stretched out on the bed, he placed the automatic on the floor beside him. Corvo would be far away by now. The mission was a disaster.

Sleep crept up on him like a thief, stealing his thoughts in a warm blanket of oblivion.

CHAPTER 47

The ferry to Gozo filled with weekenders, escaping the noise and bustle of Maltese traffic. Young people stood on the quayside and peered at the wealthy, who chose the calm lifestyle on the smaller island. The passengers ignored them and turned to the bar on board to enjoy themselves.

'Will you join us for lunch tomorrow? Perhaps a game of backgammon afterwards?' A small man dressed in a white suit stood talking to a tall, distinguished Italian. His plump wife nodded in unison and smiled warmly. 'Do come! We expect a decent crowd and I'm sure they would be delighted to meet you.'

The tall man bowed slightly. His card read '*Comte Corvo di Lampedusa*', and he enjoyed the status. His slight smile, full of condescension, was intended to convey limited approval of the invitation.

'Most kind. If I can rearrange my schedule, it would be a pleasure.'

He had left the Kaiser Hof as soon as they got down from the mountain, leaving a false forwarding address in Paris to distract any pursuit. A hired plane from Geneva had taken him to Gibraltar, where he met his shipping agent and arranged transport to Malta. This last leg to the smaller island needed no subterfuge. He felt confident he had covered his tracks. It seemed prudent to avoid attention for a short while. The villa on a hill had been a convenient hideout for many years. Its location gave him a sense of security, with its good sightlines and difficult approach. It needed just two men to keep watch and service their needs. Diabla liked it for the comforts and social life they created in this small exclusive social circle. Corvo knew very well how to keep her at his side. Her loyalty was as strong as the lifestyle he provided; he enjoyed the slight spark of uncertainty which she brought to his life, the edge of danger he sensed in her presence and the excitement of the way she made love.

Only one detail raised a query in his mind. Diego must have disposed of the bodies by now but had not made contact. Something must have happened, and he wanted to know. He rang the number on his cell phone. The call fizzed with noisy interference and conversation became impossible. He texted instructions to come back to La Grangja, and went for a swim. On a sunbed, Diabla watched as her lover dived into the pool. She wondered if he could avoid repercussions from the 'disposal' of the Russians after the failure to capitalise on the Matrix. That avenue of success was now closed, and no doubt the Brezhnevs had powerful friends. Her own future appeared a little more uncertain if she stayed with this man. She gave it much thought.

***

The sound of a cell phone woke Ballantyne from a muggy sleep. In among the pile of dirty discarded clothing, an unfamiliar tone puzzled, him until he recalled the phone he picked up at the chalet. The screen showed 'Jefe', obviously Corvo. He ran to the basin and turned on the tap. As Corvo began to speak, he held the phone near the running water. It was impossible to hold a conversation. In the broken contact, James said very few words but repeated 'texto' several times before putting the phone down. It was a stroke of luck, even if Corvo did not text. With the right help, it would be possible to hone in on the cell phone site within a mile or so.

A few hundred metres from the hostel, a phone shop offered international calls at premium rates. Few people bothered to use these shops, so the man greeted him with enthusiasm. He dialled the general number of the FO and endured the ordeal of automated questions till he heard, at last, a voice he recognised.

'Who is this?' The gentle voice of Mary Fuller reminded him of the moment when he berated her for the slip she made when she was his intern. He felt a sense of relief mixed with guilt, as he pictured her blue eyes filled with tears when she realised what she had done.

'Can you pull a job for me? I need some geek to trace a cell phone number off record, if you get me?'

'Is that you James?' He had forgotten to say his name in the urgency of the moment.

'Sure it's me, Mary. Look, I have a cell phone number of the man I'm chasing and need to locate him, pronto.'

At once, she was alert. He gave her the number and arranged to ring her back in an hour, and every hour after that.

'I can tell you now, the prefix is Malta. I have the code book right here.'

'Can they put a fix on the location?'

'I don't know, but let me get onto it; and James, look after yourself.'

A pleasant hint of concern crept into her voice; it was the first time she had called him 'James'. He reflected that he hardly knew her, but she already wanted to help him. It was good he could count on her; to put such a request through 'the channels' would take eternity.

Back at the hostel, he took time to clean his gun and decide whether to contact Bilan. He felt some concern about contacting the gypsy. They had very different goals and the prospect of a conflict of interests was very real. Clearly, Bilan would never give up the task of eliminating the man responsible for the death of his kinsman. What complicated the matter was the Matrix. If removing Corvo went wrong, or by accident the Matrix was destroyed, Ballantyne would fail in the one project he had promised himself to complete. The risk was too great, and he could not take the chance of relying on the gypsy and his gang to do what he wanted.

Maybe after I find out if this trace works. No point in deciding now.

Filling the wasted hour before he could check with Mary Fuller was not easy. An expectation of a lead on Corvo raised his spirits, and increased the tension. Money was another burden. He had used up all the money from his latest paycheck and blessed his luck in keeping back some of the cash from earlier work. The payout in Romania had been lodged in a French bank, Credit Agricole, and he kept the credit card for emergencies; that moment had arrived. He found a branch in the centre of the city and withdrew Euros, then returned to the hostel. The grubby man at the desk looked up from his paper.

'A man called to see you.'

'Well? Did he leave a message?'

'He's still here. Get him out. I don't have Roma in my place.' His lips protruded in a sneering pout and the cigarette almost fell from his lips. He looked away quickly, expecting abuse. Ballantyne ignored him and climbed the stairs. He needed to think up some excuse to keep Bilan at a distance till he had collected information about Corvo. The man in the room was Grigor. He lolled on the bed, his boots up on the blankets, and he moved casually to make room for James.

'Hi! Irish, Bilan sent me to make contact. He wants help in tracing that Italian after he escaped.'

Ballantyne looked steadily at him and then jerked his head.

'Get off my bed, you don't sleep here – I do!'

The young gypsy took a moment to decide what to do and, looking him in the eye, stood up slowly, brushing the bedclothes in a studied manner. A sly grin creased his face.

'Sure. This is such a good hotel, you should get room service to change the sheets!'

Ballantyne felt his temper rising. This was the young man who disputed Bilan's orders before they went to find Corvo at the mountain restaurant. Then he had been given the task of trying to follow him down to the hotel. What had he done?

'Tell me what you found out about Corvo. Did you track him?'

The young man shrugged his thin shoulders inside the cheap leather jacket.

'I found he had flown out from Geneva to a place in Spain, or somewhere down there. It was too late to catch him.'

'What was the flight number. We can check it.'

The gypsy looked back at him with heavy lidded eyes.

'What you mean? I tell you he got away. I came back and told Bilan. What more you expect?'

Ballantyne felt his fists forming as he listened to the arrogant reply. Maybe Grigor saw the effect his sullen defiance had on the man, since he backed towards the door and put his right hand behind his back. James had no doubt a knife would appear if he was not careful.

'Okay. Go back and tell Bilan I'll contact him when I have more info.'

'Sure, Maestro.' With that, the young man slipped through the doorway like a rat down a hole.

That solves my problem, James thought. *I'll leave the gypsies out of it for the present. Bilan may be in trouble with the others.*

He rang Mary back, and she sounded eager. 'Yes, I've got the markers on that phone. It's not in Malta; it's on Gozo, an island off Malta. It looks quite small and the location is somewhere in the area around Mgarr.'

James gripped the phone in excitement. 'You are a star! Thanks a bunch for that. I'll make it up to you when I get back. Tell Melford I reported in briefly, will you, but don't say where I am going yet. Okay?' He rang off before she had time to reply, too engrossed in this new information to catch the uplift in her voice.

It took just a few minutes to pack and get out of the hostel. The flight to Malta had to be through Milan, so the Masada pistol had to be left behind. Regretfully, he stashed it in a left luggage box at the airport and joined the embarkation queue. He felt bad to be without a weapon, but was confident he could find a source when he arrived. A text came through on Diego's phone as he was about to board. It read, '*Meet at La Grangja*'.

It was all he needed.

CHAPTER 48

Waiting for a through flight at Milan Linate was as frustrating as a traffic jam on a bank holiday. Hot faces and impatient passengers jostled with officials. The announcements by loudspeaker were, as usual, unintelligible. James sat in the VIP lounge and contemplated life. One or two problems demanded his attention. Firstly, the exact whereabouts of Corvo. This island, Gozo, seemed to be small and full of holiday homes, making enquiries more obvious and dangerous. Secondly, he had no weapons or backup, unless he signalled Bilan. His instinct was to keep Bilan out of the frame. The episode with the young gypsy, Grigor, had shown how unwise it would be to involve the clan in any delicate operation. Bilan himself was totally sound, if impulsive, but it was not going to be possible to segregate the leader from the pack. He could not control the younger members. So, he reckoned, it was better to act alone.

Weary from the second flight to Malta, he took a taxi into Valetta and booked in to a two-star hotel. He paid in advance. It was late afternoon and the heat of the sun had cooled among the narrow streets of the old town. A cold douche under a mean shower brought Ballantyne back to life. It reminded him of the prison in Omsk, where he had spent some days after entering Russia from Kazakhstan. Outside in the street, people gathered in the cafes and restaurants as the evening closed in. A Turkish cafe with tables outside caught his eye. He knew how often such places attracted both Turkish and Balkan people. Maybe it was the cuisine, or the hookah pipes squatting like statues beside each table. Or maybe the company of the ex-mercenaries and lowlifes he had met at other cafes of this type.

He took a table outside, but as far away from the door as possible. A waiter brought an elegant pipe to his table and prepared a smoke. Wafting the charcoal to life, he placed it above the fragrant tobacco and took a quick draw on the long pipe. The smoke formed a billow of cloud above their heads, then he added a small plastic mouthpiece to the pipe and handed it to Ballantyne. It was pleasant to sit and watch the world pass while drinking a coffee and drawing occasionally on the pipe. It was not long before he attracted some attention. He knew the sight of a northerner was unusual in this locale, and was not surprised when a small, thin man stopped in front of his table and smiled a greeting. The accent was Australian.

'See you like the *sheesha*,' he said. 'Never got the hang of it myself. Got a cigarette?' He looked at James with a smile.

'No joy, I'm afraid, but I can stand you a coffee if you want.'

The little man nodded and pulled out a chair. 'Good on you! Haven't seen a Pom for some days. They mostly stay uptown. Maclintock's the name.'

He held out a leathery hand and James shook it. It was like an old leather glove with bones inside.

They chatted in a guarded manner while the coffee sat untouched in front of the man. James guessed that in a few moments he would be propositioned about some scheme to make money fast, or to buy some special gifts which were not available to the general public. It was amusing, and he expected to learn a bit about the lowlife of Valetta.

'Ever been to Gozo?' Ballantyne took the chance of turning the chat in his direction.

'Gozo?' Maclintock sat back and scratched his nose. 'Maybe. I can get you there at a good price.'

'No, I just wondered what it's like. Maybe quieter than here.'

The Australian threw back his head and snorted. 'Too right! No fun there. Just poncey Russkies and their tarts, swanning about with their poxy bodyguards. You don't want to go there!'

'So what do you suggest? I've got a few days to kill.' Ballantyne waited for the pitch. It might be interesting.

Maclintock leant forward. 'I can get you into a good little game of cards – straight-up players – no wiseguys. Fancy a punt?' His ferrety eyes gleamed with anticipation.

'Not my bag,' said Ballantyne. 'Maybe a little trade in hardware would suit me.'

There was a small silence as the Aussie took in the meaning. He scratched his nose and shifted in his chair.

'Now that costs a lot of cash. What is it you want? This ain't Smith and Wesson.'

'Just a handgun and ammo. I have something I need to do and feel a bit vulnerable.'

It had its effect. Swivelling round, Maclintock cast a look round the street and at the other people in the cafe. 'Look, I don't know what you're up to, but you can't get me involved. Okay?' He went on, 'There's a lad I know who might be able to help you, but count me out, you understand? I never heard what you said.'

James nodded. 'What do you want for the intro?'

'Maybe a fifty would do. Sterling, of course.'

Ballantyne fished in his pocket and brought out three ten-Euro notes. 'This is what it's worth. Take it or leave it.'

The little man hesitated and looked hard at Ballantyne. Not a flicker crossed James's face.

'Okay, but I'm out of this. You know?'

Ballantyne nodded.

They left the cafe and walked up to an alley leading away from the main street. A single street lamp threw a pool of light on the mouth of the passage, but further down it was dark and shapes moved in the dim shadows.

'I'll wait here. You make contact and bring him here if he's interested.'

Maclintock bit his lip and paused, looking down the dark area.

'Okay, but come off the street for Christ's sake. You stand out like a fuckin' beacon!'

Ballantyne stepped into the alley and waited as the man scurried into the darkness. For a split second, a gleam of light showed where he had opened a door. Then, after a minute, the same brief light showed two shadows moving up the alley. The second man wore overalls like a mechanic. His head was covered with a hood and only his nose and chin were exposed.

'This is Marten,' said Maclintock, 'you can speak together, but I go now.' He turned away and was gone in an instant, without a sound.

The man, Marten, nodded to James, and indicated they should move further down the alley. He had a torch and held it close to his body so that little light escaped to the street.

'Is this what you want?' A battered Browning 9mm was in his hands. There were numerous scratch on the grip and the barrel had lost its original bluing. Ballantyne tried the action and was surprised to feel how smooth it was. The registration plate had been scratched away, and Ballantyne concluded it was a relic from some NATO operation, maybe Bosnia.

'Rounds?'

Marten pulled a handful out of his pocket and began to load the magazine.

'I'll do it,' said James, and took the magazine from his hands. It was important to test the action of the spring. It only took nine rounds.

'Okay. What's the price?'

They haggled for short while and Marten kept looking towards the street. The price was one hundred Euros, and James paid eighty. He pushed the gun down into his belt at the back and covered it with his jacket, the magazine went into his pocket. They said nothing and parted; Marten to the alley, and Ballantyne stepped out into the street and walked on. The weight of the gun gave him a sense of security which he'd missed ever since he left Geneva.

The last ferry for Gozo left at midnight and he made sure he embarked with a group of others to avoid attention. He never went back to the hotel. It was time to find Corvo and finish the job.

CHAPTER 49

The crossing took twenty-five minutes, and Mgarr Harbour gave the impression that no one sleeps on Gozo. The fishing boats, ferries and the bars were in endless activity. But beyond the town, the countryside lay in a warm, star-filled night. Ballantyne kept away from the streets and found a hut above the town where he could shelter. There was no wind and he managed to sleep on the hard earth floor. Dawn brought him back to life, and he wandered down to eat at a bar which had opened to serve the fisherman and the ferry staff on early turn.

There was yoghurt, bread and honey with a black bitter coffee on offer, and his appearance did not draw particular attention. Maybe migrants and students often spent the night on the beach or in the hills behind the harbour. Enquiries about the Villa Grasja met blank stares, but when he mentioned Corvo, looks were exchanged among the men.

'What you want with "The Baron"?' An old man with white hair sat in a corner leaning on a stick. 'You work for him?'

Ballantyne shook his head. 'No, I'm looking for work and someone told me there might be some on the estate.'

'You won't find a job!' The old man turned to the others in the room. He took off his cap and pointed to Ballantyne. 'He thinks he'll get work up at Grasja!'

It caused a ripple of laughter among the men.

Someone shouted out, 'Unless you are a Russkie!' This brought a general shout.

'Why?' James put on a puzzled look.

'Look, the grand count is rarely here and we get no crumbs from his table. He brings in his own men and we see nothing. He's a mystery man.'

He told himself to drop the enquiry. Too much interest in Corvo would be dangerous, and he had enough information to work with. Finishing his meal, James strolled out into the street and walked away. As a precaution, he stopped a few yards away to check in a window if anyone followed him. The road seemed clear.

The midday heat felt intense, and he could not climb the hill out of the town without drawing attention. Nobody stayed in the open; no cars drove past; the world slept. Ballantyne dropped out of sight behind a barn and waited till the streets came alive again.

'You want a lift up?' One of the men he'd seen in the bar leant out of a van and called to him, pointing up the hill. He got up and went to the window. The driver was a curly-haired man, about fifty, with a wide smile. He wore an old straw hat and ragged overalls.

'How far are you going?'

'Just up the hill to the farm beyond the villa. I can drop you if you want.'

It was too late to change the story. If he declined the lift, his reason for being there was exposed as a lie. In a small town, news of a stranger asking for Corvo would spread in a flash.

'Cheers! I'll try my luck. Thanks.'

As they rumbled up the hill, Ballantyne realised he had to deal with Corvo at once. If he did not strike now, he would have lost the initiative. By the next day, Corvo would be on notice and his chances of a clean getaway were gone. The automatic lodged in the small of his back seemed heavier all of a sudden and more uncomfortable, like a nagging pain he had to endure. He had to get moving.

The road twisted back and forth as the van climbed the hill. The noise of the engine made any conversation impossible, which suited Ballantyne. It stifled further questions. From time to time the roof of a large house emerged among the trees and disappeared again at the next corner. Eventually, the driver pulled over just before a pair of iron gates and pointed.

'If you find some work, you can buy me a drink tonight!' He laughed and with a wave drove away. A minute was all he needed to plan his approach. The stone walls around the estate were topped with barbed wire, but with care he managed to drop down inside the grounds. He waited to see if any alarm had been sprung or any dogs released. Nothing moved. Clearly, this place existed as a refuge which Corvo kept away from his contacts as a hideout, with no cadre of bodyguards and nothing to draw attention to it.

Pity he forgot the natives! You can't keep a secret from the locals!

He got to a position within a few hundred yards of the house and lay down to take stock. It was a large, mellow two-storey stone house with a verandah spanning the south side. The upper floor included a terrace with canvas shades. All the shutters were open and gave the impression of an innocent summer home. The lawns extended around the house and a curved swimming pool formed a blue crescent next to the verandah. Approach would be difficult, there was no cover near the building itself.

The quiet was shattered by an unexpected sound from above. Whirling noise and a pulsating vibration; a helicopter slowly dropped onto the lawn beside the house. A whirlwind of dust and greenery rose around the machine as it settled clumsily. Ballantyne crouched lower and read the name on the side of the machine. 'Malta Heli-Services.'

The pilot remained in the cockpit while another uniformed man ran to the house. Within a minute, Corvo, followed by two guards and the co-pilot, ran to the helicopter and the aircraft took off in another storm of debris. A minute later, by contrast, the silence returned and the cicadas in the bushes resumed their twittering.

From the terrace, a woman strolled out towards the swimming pool. She wore a silky blue shift and her hair loose: La Diabla. It was the first time James had seen her in casual clothing. Her long blue/black hair drifted round her like a veil, occasionally hiding her shoulders and profile. She stopped to take off her sandals, and slipped out of the sundress. For a moment she stood at the edge of the pool completely naked, then dived in without a splash. Ballantyne was mesmerised. This woman, so beautiful and yet so deadly, was the most dangerous creature he had ever known. He knew very well that she had killed the men in the chalet above Geneva. He recognised her two-shot technique as the mark of an assassin. But she radiated sexual power that was impossible to ignore. He made an effort to turn to the question of what to do.

Clearly, Corvo and his guards were out of range for the moment. How long that would be was unknown. He had taken care to check whether any bulky case had been put in the helicopter. Nothing of any size had been loaded, so it was likely the Matrix itself remained here. He had to make a decision: whether to abort the strike and wait for Corvo's return, or to find and seize the Matrix if it was in the house. He found it an easy one. Bilan and the gypsies had the vendetta, not him. The task James had set himself was to recover the Matrix. Chance had thrown this opportunity in his way and he must take it.

Crawling away from the house, he circled the courtyard to watch the back of the building. A maid or cook came out to hang clothes from the washing lines, but no one else appeared throughout the fifteen minutes he spent on observation. He ran to the shade of the building, gun in hand. Sheltering under a window, he waited for a second time to note the sound of movement within the house. All the noise came from the kitchen area and as he moved towards the front of the house, the stillness encouraged him.

An open window invited attention. One quick glance showed him the room inside was empty, and he slid over the sill and waited behind a sofa beneath the window. It was a bedroom, with a large elegant bed adorned with brass rails and canopy. He admired the luxury and imagined, for a split second, the image of Diabla lying across its silken cover. Then he moved to the bathroom door and checked it was clear. It was the last thing he saw. A blow caught him on the back of the head and he fell into the blackness of deep unconsciousness.

Slowly, he felt life returning with a pain thudding inside his head. He tried to open his eyes, but the image was blurred and it took a few moments to focus. All he could see was the outline of a figure sitting in front of him. His arms were pinioned against the bedrails with plastic ties and he struggled for a second to release them, but it was futile. He had been tied to the bed.

CHAPTER 50

Gradually the image cleared, and Diabla was sitting on the bed drying her hair with a towel.

'Who gave you the idea of creeping into my bedroom?' Her tone was casual, as if he was a house guest flirting with her. 'Didn't you realise there are two doors to this room? Besides, you should have realised I was barefoot and would make no noise.' All the while, she tended her hair in casual way, wrapping it up into a turban as she finished.

'I've seen you before, you were there when Assurov tried to get the Matrix, weren't you? Do you always pick the wrong side?' Her eyes looked straight into his and he had to turn away; her stare confused him and his head hurt. A mess of broken stone was scattered across the carpet. She followed his gaze.

'Yes, I loved that statue and you broke it. Perhaps you should pay for it?'

He tried to test the bonds which held his wrists. She put a finger to his mouth and said, 'Shush! You'll make it worse. Besides, you don't want to resist.'

In her hand a small knife gleamed. At first sight, James thought it was an ornamental decoration, but she held it against his chest. He felt the point cutting through his shirt, scratching his skin as it tore away the fabric. He tried again to pull against the bonds, but the white plastic held firm and the bed head creaked with the strain.

She laughed, throwing her head back, revealing the smooth surface of her throat as the thick black hair fell away over her shoulders. She was naked, and she tore the rags of his shirt away, stripping him to the waist. He kicked out with his legs but with a lunge, she jumped astride his body and looked down in his face. She pulled on his arms to bring herself within an inch of his face, her legs straddling him. He was transfixed.

'What do you think you can do, chico? Did you think I was at your disposal?'

Her breasts were above his chest, and he felt her nipples harden against him as she moved against his body with a sinuous motion. Her eyes seemed bigger and she smiled down at him as she drew the little knife down his chest, scratching a path along his body. Ballantyne tried to struggle against the quick arousal she brought to his body, but all sense of resistance was fading away as she brought her lips close to his skin and began to explore his body with small kisses. As she reached his waist, he could not fight the excitement she had created, and then she tore away his clothes. All he wanted was to enter her and surrender. She took his cock within her and sat upright with a thrust which made him moan. Her hands pressed against his chest and she looked down on him with a fixed stare. He pressed upwards against her and she jerked against the pulse of his body with an action of her own which brought a cry from his lips. He wanted to touch her breasts as they moved softly above him, but the bonds would not yield. In some strange way, it added an unexpected thrill to the coupling. She said not a word but her breath came in quick gasps as she moved quicker and more fiercely against him, leaning back at last to force her hips time and again into his sex with a ferocious strength. At last, with a shriek, she bent forwards and lay across his chest, her body glistening with sweat. He lay exhausted under her body and they stayed locked together for some time. Then she rolled away and fell back against the bedding.

After a while, she stretched and got off the bed. He watched her as she walked to the next room, her slim figure and long legs outlined against the light from the window. Then he heard the shower working and looked about him. The little dagger sat amongst the crumpled bedclothes, but his attempts to reach it were useless. His wrists were raw where he had twisted and chafed the skin and he gave up. He lay inert, spreadeagled on the bed.

When she came back, her hair was swept up on top of her head; she had dressed in a robe and carried a small silver handgun. Using the small knife, she cut him free and stood away.

'You can get up now and make yourself comfortable.'

He sat up, rubbing his wrists. 'Do you have to use a cosh to get laid?'

She smiled and nodded. 'Yes, it saves a lot of small talk. You'll find some clothes in the shower room.' She waved the gun in that direction and Ballantyne did what he was told. The chafing round his wrists stung as the hot spray cascaded down, but it revived him; he found a T-shirt and jeans in a cupboard and reappeared in the bedroom, rolling up the pants to fit him.

'Give my thanks to Corvo. Get him to shorten these trews for me.'

She smiled, looking at him in the oversized clothes.

'No need, he won't want them back! Come and have something to eat.'

She waved him ahead of her and they passed through to the verandah. James was confused by her manner. She behaved as if what had happened was a romantic interlude, yet she held him at gunpoint and knew he was there to kill her, or at least take the Matrix away. He stayed silent, to wait for some clue and any opportunity to take the initiative.

She sat across the table from him and put the pistol down beside her. There was coffee and orange juice already set out on a white tablecloth.

'Now listen,' she said, 'I have an idea. You want the magic box, don't you?'

He said nothing.

'I know Corvo is going down. His fight with the Russians is foolish, and now he has got some tribe of gypsies on his track. If you found us, then others can make their way here too. I won't be dragged down with him. I want to get out.'

James smiled. She was a peach. Loyalty meant nothing to her and she had worked out the odds.

'So what do you suggest?'

'I have the Matrix here with me. If I let you have it, you must protect me from them.'

'Why should I?'

She picked up the little shiny pistol and pointed it at his heart. 'You forget who you're dealing with. I can kill you or fuck you if I want!'

It was no time to play hardball. She had all the advantages, and Ballantyne knew it. Besides, he would get the Matrix handed to him on a plate.

'Okay. But how could I protect you? He will find out I took it and you are in deep shit.'

She leant forward and for a moment his eyes strayed to her cleavage, exposed as she moved. She knew what she was doing and made no effort to cover herself.

'When he gets back, I can fix it that you attacked me and grabbed the machine.'

'What about the maid? She will know the truth.'

'Don't worry about her I'll fix her.' He didn't want to ask how.

She went on, 'But you can tip off the hunters where he is, and the job will almost be complete.'

He arched an eyebrow. 'Almost?'

'They have to know I helped you and get an assurance I will be safe.'

He looked doubtful.

'Okay. I'll pay them to protect me! I can pay!'

'Show me the Matrix, let's see it.'

She stood up, still keeping the gun on him, and motioned him towards the salon. They crossed the floor and she pointed to an antique desk beside a window.

'Open the second drawer.'

He found the metal case and opened it. The machine lay snuggly in its foam bed.

'Smash the door. Make it look good.' She waved the gun to emphasise the idea.

He nodded and took a kick at the fine walnut door. It cracked and fell open.

'Now, make a call to the gypsies, I want to hear the whole thing.'

He retraced his steps to the bedroom, where his mangled clothes lay on the floor. The cell phone was still in his pocket and he dialled Bilan's number.

'Put it on speaker,' she said, and kept the gun on him.

Bilan answered, and for a few seconds there was a stream of curses aimed at James and his heritage, but it subsided and he explained briefly how he found Corvo and how to reach the Gozo.

He turned to her and held the phone towards her.

'How long is he away?'

'Till tomorrow evening.'

He explained how Diabla had to be left out of any reprisal. She had given the information to lead them to Corvo. It was not the truth, but it would do. Eventually, Bilan agreed and told James he would be on his way at once.

She smiled as he snapped the phone shut.

'Good, I can set him up and blame you. You'd better go while you can. Take the damn thing and get across before he gets here.'

Ballantyne grinned, and asked, 'I suppose I can't have my gun back?'

She laughed and blew him a kiss. 'That's all you're getting.'

He grabbed the Matrix and left the house without looking back. He wondered if he would ever meet such a woman again.

CHAPTER 51

The aluminium case was heavier than he expected. Carrying it down the drive, he realised it must be lodged somewhere; he could not operate with this cumbersome pack beside him. Leaving the island before Bilan and Corvo arrived was out of the question. He must oversee the action. His knowledge on the ground and about Diabla was essential.

Wrapping the case in some old sacking, he stuffed it into the hollow of a venerable olive tree on the opposite side of the road and waited. He guessed correctly; within half an hour, Diabla, in a blue open tourer, drove down the drive and turned away from the town, obviously intending to avoid meeting Ballantyne. Whatever she had in mind, he knew it meant trouble. Was she going to warn Corvo? Did she mean to escape now, before the attack happened? He took no bets with himself; the odds were too high.

The hours waiting in the shade stretched on and James fretted. He felt powerless, and his thoughts went back to the moment when he lost his automatic and fell unconscious in the bedroom. His head was still sore, and his pride dented, but the memory of her and the sex they shared brought a rueful smile to his face.

Not all bad, then.

It dawned on him that the villa was empty, or if not, only the maid remained inside. Maybe he could get his gun or some other weapon while Diabla was away.

He took the route he used before and found his way to the same spot outside her bedroom with no difficulty. The room had been cleaned and the bed made. The sound of activity came from the other side of the house. He slid over the sill and went directly to the bedside table; nothing. A desk stood against the wall by the door. He searched quietly, starting at the bottom drawer first. In the second drawer, wrapped in a silky shirt, he found his battered Browning. He pumped his fist in the air and blessed the gods of fortune, went to the window and started to climb out. Then a sound stopped him.

Coming up the drive was the tourer. Diabla had two men with her. James ducked down and ran to the door. Avoiding the kitchen area, he burst out into the yard and slammed through a doorway into a dark work-room. There was a small window. He heard instructions being given as the men followed Diabla into the yard.

'When they come, you need to cover the back of the house. Okay?'

There were grunts for reply and the sounds receded. One of the men passed the window and Ballantyne saw he was in uniform, with shoulder flashes that read 'Armour Shield'.

What had she done? These were not Corvo's hench-men. They were security guards, hired from some agency. What plan did she follow? Corvo would not want some hired hacks to work for him. He paid for dedicated troops who carried out his orders.

James slipped out of the building and made his way to the scrubland behind the house and hid, trying to work out what she had planned.

The cell phone buzzed. It was Bilan.

'Hi, Maestro! We're here. Where do we meet?'

Ballantyne cupped his hands over the phone to answer, and found out they were in Mgarr, at the ferry terminal.

'Stay where you are. I'll join you in an hour. Keep out of sight!'

He moved carefully around the boundary and got back to the road. Just then, the unmistakeable sound of a helicopter sent him diving for cover. Corvo was returning! Diabla had lied to him. Obviously, she had deliberately misled him. He waited as the sound faded and surged again as the machine took off. If the plan was to work, it had to be tonight, before Corvo could react to the loss of the Matrix.

The road to the town went downhill and Ballantyne got to the outskirts in fifteen minutes. A quick call to Bilan, and they joined up.

'What's the setup? How many are they?' The gypsy fidgeted, unable to sit still with eagerness. Ballantyne briefed him on the layout and the numbers at the villa and they worked together on a rough plan of attack.

'Okay, let's go! No time to waste, we can surprise them now.'

'Hang on! I need some food and rest. I've been out in the field for twenty-four hours.'

James did not feel he needed to mention his episode with Diabla. Fatigue sapped his ability to think clearly, and some food would revive him. Bilan nodded and turned to one of the gypsies.

'Get him a drink and some food, quick. Go to the bar and bring some brandy too!'

For the first time, James looked at the crew. Grigor and another young blood sat smoking, cupping their cigarettes in their hands like schoolboys. They looked at him with a hostile, wary look, as if they resented the trip they had been forced to make. His heart sank; they were toy soldiers, worse than useless. Lady Luck would have to be on their side.

Eating warm food brought some energy back into his body. In a few words, Bilan explained how they had reached Malta and made contact with the Zingari family on the island.

'We have family everywhere,' he boasted, and showed the weapons they had borrowed from the clan. Two Kalashnikovs and an elderly Sten gun, dating back to the Second World War. 'But this is Vashti's revenge.' He held up a box of grenades and James saw they were already primed. A careless impact might set them off and blow them to pieces. The gypsies didn't care, they handled them like toys, throwing them to each other and juggling two or three at a time. Ballantyne kept quiet, but did his best to keep a distance from the young pair.

He called them together and explained what he had learnt. The layout of the house, stables and the personnel they could expect. 'Remember,' said Bilan, 'we go for Corvo. Don't touch the lady, she is worth money.' It didn't seem helpful to express doubts about her reliability. He made it his special task to watch her and protect them against treachery.

It was twilight as they set off for the villa. Bilan had hired a van in Malta and drove them up the hill to the spot Ballantyne chose. There was enough light to see the house and grounds. He armed himself with the ancient Sten gun and kept his Browning tucked inside his belt.

By the time he reached the stables, short bursts of automatic fire were coming from the front of the house and the muffled explosion of grenades inside the building. Crouching behind some straw bales, he watched the back of the house. The sound of gunfire continued intermittently for some minutes, then a figure burst out of the back door and ran towards him. It was Diabla. She wore a black jumpsuit and her hair was tied back under a cap. Behind her, one of the security guards in uniform dragged a body with him. James could make out that it was the second guard he had seen before. They made for the storeroom he used that morning and slammed the door. He heard the groans of the wounded man and the frantic efforts of the other man to give him aid. There was no sound from Diabla.

Bilan had made it clear, he wanted to deal with Corvo himself. However, James could not stay inactive, knowing a firefight was going on. With Diabla protected in the stables, he ran round to the front of the house to assess the situation. Grigor lay headlong on the lawn in front of the house; a pool of blood saturated the ground near his head. Inside the house, shadows flickered against the walls as gunfire illuminated figures as if by lightning. It would be madness to go inside without knowing the layout, so he ran back to the yard. Anyone coming out into the yard would be in his sights.

At that moment, a figure staggered from the house and called out.

'Cara! The car! Get the car!'

The slim figure was unmistakeable. He held a hand to his left side and in his right fist he held an Uzi submachine gun. A faint moonlight revealed his face. Wide-eyed and grim, his tall figure hunched over like a crookback, it was a likeness of Corvo he had never seen before. Gone was the arrogant stare and elegant pose. He raised his voice again.

'Cara! Diabla! Help me quick!'

Before Ballantyne could move, she appeared from the shadows. Corvo staggered towards her and dropped the gun as he went. She stood still, and James watched as she raised the silver pistol and shot Corvo twice in quick succession. He crumpled onto the cobbles and lay still.

'Stand still!' He aimed two-handed at her and she turned towards him.

'You bungled it! I had to finish the job. What did you expect?' she said.

In the dim moonlight, he saw the thin smile she gave as she lowered her gun and approached him. She looked directly into his eyes, defying him to shoot her.

He kept the Sten gun aimed at her. 'Okay. Stop where you are!'

A shadowy figure emerged from the stables, aiming at him. Ballantyne crouched and fired from the hip; the ancient machine gun stuttered a few rounds before jamming. The body fell back into the doorway and lay still: it was the second guard Diabla had brought with her.

Where was she? A car started in one of the garages and accelerated away down the drive at speed. It was the Alfa Romeo she had used earlier. All he saw was the tail lights in a cloud of dust. She had gone.

Bilan emerged from the house and walked over to the body of Corvo. It lay face up, the arms flung out as if in surrender. He bent over to examine the body, and spoke some words in a language Ballantyne didn't understand. Then he turned to James.

'We must go now, pronto. We leave Corvo to the police and to God. Come, we need to take Grigor with us!'

They met the second gypsy boy at the front of the house and carried the body to the van. Ballantyne wiped the Sten gun clean of his fingerprints and threw it into the bushes.

'Make something of that bloody relic!'

It amused him to think of the puzzle the gun would create when forensics tried to make a match with an up-to-date computer file.

He pulled the Matrix from its hiding place and joined the others. They drove down to the harbour and dispersed. The gypsies left on the first ferry to arrive that evening, but Ballantyne hung back. He wanted to find out where Diabla had gone. In the harbour office, there was no Alfa Romeo logged on the manifest for the last two ferries. Gone without a trace.

He waited till a late ferry, when a crowd of young people were returning to the main island, and mingled with them. They talked excitedly about the explosions at the villa and how the local radio got the news before the local police. It was time to disappear.

CHAPTER 52

Spring came late that year. The trees in Green Park showed very little new growth by the end of April, and daffodils were the only sparks of colour in the city. Melford walked slowly through the park, wondering what he could tell the American official who had called the meeting. Months back, he had met Bob Harding of the State Department and they had planned the next stage of the campaign to undermine Russian interest in the oil industry. Since then, the allegations of hacking presidential campaigns and Russian support for the chemical attacks in Syria made the US eager to activate their plan. It would be a 'sticky' meeting.

'Good to see you!' The bulky American was waiting for him in an interview room. 'Tell me how things are going.'

Melford smiled and fidgeted with his pen. 'Well, we expect a report from the agent any day now, but it seems clear he has had to go static for a while.'

'Static?' The big man sat up, looking puzzled.

'Yes, I mean he has not been in contact for some time and we have to assume he is keeping quiet on purpose.'

'Didn't I meet him?'

Melford nodded brightly. 'Yes, that's correct. Very experienced man!'

Harding scratched his ear. 'Seemed to me he had some cockamamie ideas about the Matrix!'

'I assure you, our instructions have been explicit. He knows what to do.'

'Well, when can we expect some development? I have a whole string of monkeys on my back!'

Melford nodded as if in sympathy, and diverted attention by picking up the phone.

'Excuse me, I'll just get an update from the section.'

He dialled Mary Fuller, and after a few minutes she appeared, looking trim and carrying a file.

Harding stood and smiled at her. 'Good morning, young lady, I see you have some news for us!'

She blushed and grasped the file in front of her in an instinctive gesture. She had her patter ready as Melford had discussed, but instinctively hated the process.

'We have a full pattern of Ballantyne's behaviour and movements, and it's clear he will report in any day now.'

The American relaxed and sat back, admiring her bright eyes and amusing himself at her expense.

'Well. That's fine and dandy. I know you will keep me in the loop. This means a lot to the White House!' If he thought he would impress her, he had picked the wrong girl. She smiled and went to the door.

Harding called after her. 'Could you bring me a coffee, I like it black.' She paused, nodded and left.

He winked at Melford. 'They like to be appreciated!'

Minutes later, a tea lady in a pinafore knocked at the door. 'Someone want coffee?' She had a mug in her hand and held it out; her hand shook a little and Harding grabbed it before she spilt it. It was tepid and milky.

They exchanged views on several topics and promised to 'rain check' on points of mutual interest. At last, the meeting closed with Melford's assurance that targets would be met, and all plans were operational. He closed the door with a sigh and said a silent prayer to the gods of good fortune.

***

James sat in cafe in Republic Square and took his time preparing a robusto cigar for a smoke. They had no Cuban cigars, but a good quality Honduran one was acceptable. The first draw proved that it was going to be a good one. He had waited on the island for a few days to discover the reactions to the 'Terrible Shooting on Gozo'. The papers blamed warring drug gangs and began a campaign to force the police into more action against the evil Mafioso from Sicily infiltrating the islands.

He felt inertia after the momentum of the last few weeks. The final confrontation had achieved everything he set out to do. The FO would be pleased; he had only to draft a report to complete the work. They would overlook his failure to keep in touch when they could get their hands on the Matrix.

But what had he achieved in all this? The task had taken him away from Ocksana at a critical time and with terrible consequences; he had risked his life to achieve the recovery of the complex mechanism. He reminded himself of the discussion with Melford and the American, whose name he forgot, about the bargain they hoped to make with the Russians. The scheme was like a vortex spiralling down into a pit of deception.

He wanted no part of it. Had he risked his life for this? To hell with them!

He gave a tight-lipped smile and called the waiter.

'Where can I buy a good strong hammer?'

Lightning Source UK Ltd.
Milton Keynes UK
UKHW02f1002070618
323830UK00007B/512/P